For wea...
and p...

THE CONNELLYS: CHANCE, DOUG & JUSTIN

Three fantastic, page-turning, sensual
love stories presented by three of your
favourite authors

We're proud to present

MILLS & BOON®

SPOTLIGHT

*a chance to buy two bestselling novels
by favourite authors every month
– they're back by popular demand!*

THE CONNELLYS: CHANCE, DOUG & JUSTIN

The SEAL's Surrender
MAUREEN CHILD

Plain Jane & Doctor Dad
KATE LITTLE

And the Winner Gets...Married!
METSY HINGLE

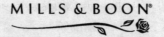
MILLS & BOON®

This collection is first published in Great Britain 2007
Harlequin Mills & Boon Limited,
Eton House, 18-24 Paradise Road, Richmond, Surrey TW9 1SR

THE CONNELLYS: CHANCE, DOUG & JUSTIN
© Harlequin Books S.A. 2007

The publisher acknowledges the copyright holders of the
individual works, which have already been published in the UK
in single, separate volumes, as follows:

The SEAL's Surrender © Harlequin Books S.A. 2002
Plain Jane & Doctor Dad © Harlequin Books S.A. 2002
And the Winner Gets...Married! © Harlequin Books S.A. 2002

Special thanks and acknowledgement are given to Maureen Child,
Kate Little and Metsy Hingle for their contributions to the
THE CONNELLYS series.

ISBN: 978 0 263 85676 7

064-0507

Printed and bound in Spain by Litografia Rosés S.A., Barcelona

The SEAL's Surrender

MAUREEN CHILD

MAUREEN CHILD

was born and raised in Southern California and is the only person she knows who longs for an occasional change of season.

An avid reader, Maureen looks forward to those rare rainy California days when she can curl up and sink into a good book. Or two. When she isn't busy writing, she and her husband of twenty-five years like to travel, leaving their two grown-up children in charge of the neurotic golden retriever who is the *real* head of the household. Maureen is also an award-winning historical writer under the names of Kathleen Kane and Ann Carberry.

To Sandra Paul, Barbara Benedict, Angie Ray
and Michelle Thorne:
Thank you for the ambush and for my tiara.
You guys are the best.

One

He hated parties.

Give Chance Barnett a machine gun, and he was a happy man. Tell him to mingle, and you got a mean dog on a short leash.

But, Chance told himself, sometimes a man just had to bite the proverbial bullet. And this was a big one, in his humble opinion. Hell, it was damn near a mortar round.

He clutched his bottle of imported beer in a tight fist and made his way around the periphery of the party. His gaze narrowed slightly as he silently assessed his new family. A hell of a way to meet the relatives, he told himself, yet couldn't think of a better way to handle it.

There probably wasn't a *good* way to introduce him and his twin, Douglas, to the rest of the Connellys. Though to give them their due, they'd all taken the news of the twins' existence a lot easier than they might have. After all, it wasn't every day you met thirty-six-year-old illegitimate twin relatives, was it?

Though he had to admit that none of the Connellys had treated him and his brother as though they were somehow not good enough to be part of the family. Hell, even Miss Lily and Tobias had come home early from Palm Springs just to meet him and Douglas. Chance's gaze shot to the older couple. Correction, he told himself silently, his *grandparents*. Weird. He smiled as he watched Tobias trying to slip past his much smaller wife, but Miss Lily, cane or no cane, was too fast for her husband and snatched that glass of whiskey from his hand.

Interestingly enough, the big man just gave her a smile and a peck on the cheek. What would it be like, Chance wondered, to spend your life with one person? To love that one person so much that some fifty-odd years later, the stamp of it was still clearly on your features?

Those two old people had somehow managed to raise a dynasty. Amazing really, if you stopped to think about it. Sure, the Connellys were practically

American royalty. But they actually were *real* royalty as well.

And Chance and Douglas Barnett were a part of it.

He shook his head and moved on, drifting through the crowd like a finger of fog. A strident female voice caught his attention, and he slowed his steps, listening.

His half sister, Alexandra, a tall woman with raven-black hair, a too-important manner and sharp green eyes was center stage, where she seemed most comfortable. "I'm *so* sorry you won't have a chance to meet my fiancé," she was saying, "but Robert was called away on business."

Everyone in her audience nodded sagely, but all Chance could think was, Lucky guy. At least the missing Robert had gotten out of attending this party. He moved on, turning a bit too fast and feeling the pull of the stitches in his side.

A reminder of the reason he was able to be here at this party. If he hadn't been wounded on his last mission, he'd have been happily out trooping through a jungle somewhere. And as soon as he was healed enough, that was just what he'd be doing. Hell, he kept his duffel bag packed and ready to go.

Man, was he ready to go. He needed to get back to his SEAL team. Needed to get back where he belonged. He scowled to himself. He caught a glimpse of Doug, chatting it up with a few of their new relatives, and almost wished that he was half as at ease with people as his brother. Hell, he'd even heard his twin talking to one of their new cousins about his ex-wife and how the reason they'd broken up was because she hadn't wanted the children Doug wanted so badly. Yeah. Chance's brother was sliding right into this and didn't seem to have any trouble at all stringing the name *Connelly* behind the Barnett they'd grown up with. But then, Doug always had been the reasonable twin. Which was probably why Chance had grown up to be a fighting man and Doug had become a doctor.

Okay, he thought, way too philosophical.

"Excuse me, sir." A low-pitched voice came from right behind him and Chance spun around to face a tuxedo-clad waiter. "May I get you something from the bar?"

Chance held his beer aloft. "No thanks," he said, shaking his head at the realization that these people probably dealt with in-house waiters and butlers all the time. "I'm covered."

Maybe it was the military training and maybe it was just his own innate need to be in control at all times, but Chance rarely had more than one beer at a party. Even one like this, where he felt more out of place than a pauper in a palace.

The waiter moved off soundlessly into the milling crowd and Chance shook his head again. How had he wound up here? he wondered. And just how soon could he make a polite exit? He moved off into a corner of the room, kept his back to the wall and let his gaze slide across the people filling the cavernous room.

A SEAL in a Lake Shore mansion? He chuckled inwardly at the absurdity of it. Hell, nobody would buy that. He stood out from the elegantly dressed crowd. His U.S. Navy whites were startling in a sea of bright colors and black tuxedos. But for the first time in his life, he was also in a room filled with people he was actually related to.

He and Douglas had grown up alone, raised by a single mom who'd done her best. But she hadn't been able to provide enough of her own presence to satisfy her boys—let alone provide relatives. So here he stood, a thirty-six-year-old man suddenly meeting cousins and half brothers and sisters for the first time.

Weird.

He took a sip of beer, swallowed it and silently admitted that family wasn't necessarily a bad thing. It was just going to take some getting used to. From across the room, Douglas caught his eye and gave him a "Do you believe this?" look and a half smile. Instantly, Chance felt more at ease. He and his twin had pulled each other through plenty of scrapes over the years. And as long as they could count on each other, then tacking the name *Connelly* on after the Barnett wouldn't change much.

Still, he could do with some air.

Instinctively, he moved toward the sliding glass doors that led onto a balcony. The muted noise of conversation and softly-played piano music followed him as he skirted the crowd. But as he neared the glass partition, his plan for solitude fell apart.

A woman stood on the balcony in the late-afternoon sun, her short, light-blond hair tousled by the wind. He knew her. Jennifer Anderson, Emma Connelly's social secretary. They'd met a couple of times in the last few days. She wasn't very tall, but every inch of her looked to be packed to perfection. She wore a deep-green dress with a flippy sort of hem that stopped just short of her knees, displaying to their best advantage what looked to be excellent legs. Her breasts were high and full and her waist was narrow enough that he figured given a chance, he could span that distance with both hands. Her back was straight as she stared out at Lake Michigan, but he frowned as he noticed she kept one hand clapped across her mouth and couldn't quite hide the droop in her shoulders.

Instantly, something inside him stirred to life. The protective instinct was strong and he felt it push him outside. He slid the glass door open, and the wind off the lake tried to shove him back into the party. But SEALs didn't give up that easily.

Chance ducked his head, stepped quietly onto the stone balcony and soundlessly closed the door behind him.

"Get a grip, Jen," the woman muttered to herself before he had a chance to announce his presence. "Crying's not going to help. It's only going to make you look like hell."

Well, he couldn't resist responding to that.

"Lady," he said softly, "all the tears in the world would have a hard time pulling that one off."

She turned quickly, her body language letting him know that she wasn't pleased at having been found giving in to tears. But she recognized him right away and the Keep Out sign in her eyes blinked off.

"You surprised me," she said, lifting one hand to swipe away the telltale track of tears on her cheeks.

"Sorry," he said, though he really wasn't. "Old habits. I'm used to moving quietly."

One blond eyebrow lifted into an arch. "This isn't exactly the jungle, Commander," she said. "Around here, most people knock."

"Ah," he said, walking closer, "but you knock when you want to come *in*. I was coming *out*."

"Great," she muttered thickly, turning her face back into the wind. "Semantics."

Jennifer stared out at the horizon, deliberately ignoring him in the hopes that he'd go away. She couldn't very well *order* him off. Not one of the long-lost sons for whom this party had been arranged. So either he left of his own accord, or she'd be forced to go back to the party and pretend everything was all right.

Please God, let him leave.

Apparently though, God wasn't listening.

Chance Barnett Connelly moved up right beside her and curled his hands over the wrought-iron balcony railing. She glanced down at those strong, tanned hands and noticed that his knuckles whitened with his grip. Obviously, he felt as tense as she did. But their reasons, at least, were very different.

"So," he said, keeping his gaze locked on the wall of clouds hanging just at the horizon, "what seems to be the problem?"

"Problem?" She straightened up. The last thing she wanted or needed was sympathy. Especially from a man she didn't even know. Besides, he was a Connelly. If she told him, then soon everyone would know and she'd like to put that off for as long as she could. At least until she'd had a chance to talk to Emma Connelly first.

Along with being her boss, Emma was as close to a mother figure as Jennifer could claim. Her own parents had died years ago, and but for her daughter, Sarah, Jennifer was alone in the world. Which had never really bothered her. Until yesterday.

"Yeah," Chance said, shifting her a glance, "when I see a beautiful woman alone and crying on a balcony while there's a party going on not five feet from her...well, I naturally figure there's a problem."

She inhaled sharply, taking the cold wind inside her, needing the bracing strength of it. Then, she forced a cheer she didn't feel into her voice. "Thanks for asking, but I'm fine. Really."

"Uh-huh."

"I mean it."

"Yeah, I can see that."

She looked at him from the corner of her eye. "But you don't believe me."

"Nope."

"Well," she said, pushing away from the balcony railing, "that's not my problem, is it?"

He reached out and grabbed her forearm. "Don't go."

His touch felt warm and strong and seemed to wrap itself not only around her arm, but around her bruised heart, too. Jennifer stopped short and lifted her gaze to look into amber eyes the exact color of fine, aged brandy. Her heartbeat stuttered slightly. His jaw looked as though it had been carved of granite. His nose had obviously been broken at least once sometime in the past. His brown hair was military-short, but even at that, there was a slight wave to it that made a woman want to stroke her fingers through it.

And good Lord, he was tall. With shoulders broad enough to balance the world. Today she could surely use a pair of shoulders broad enough to lean on. But Jennifer was too used to standing on her own two feet to take advantage of a near stranger in a weak moment.

As if he could read her mind though, he said, "I didn't mean to intrude, but now that I'm here, why not let me help if I can?"

Tempting, she thought. Oh, so tempting. But no. She shook her head. "I appreciate it, but—"

"I'm a stranger."

"Well," she said, "yes."

"Sometimes that's better." He kept his grip on her forearm as if he expected her to scurry for the door. Which she would have done, given half a chance. Then he smiled and her stomach flipped over. "Telling your troubles to a stranger is like talking to yourself. Only you don't have to answer your own questions and run the risk of being locked in a padded room."

A return smile tickled the corners of her mouth and she had to fight to keep it from blossoming. Which was a good thing actually, since she hadn't had a thing to smile about since talking to her daughter's doctors yesterday. And that stray thought was enough to wipe the beginnings of humor from her face.

A cold, empty well opened up inside her and she felt her heart slide into it.

"Hey," he said, letting his hand slide from her forearm up to her shoulder, where his fingers squeezed gently. "Come on. Talk to me. Maybe I can help." He dipped his head a bit and gave her another half smile. "I'm a SEAL. Trained to be a hero. So let me ride to the rescue here, okay?"

Jennifer glanced over her shoulder at the party just beyond the glass doors, then turned back to look at him again. What the heck, she thought. She *could* use a shoulder at the moment. And his were certainly broad enough to hold up under her assault.

"It's my daughter," she blurted before she could change her mind.

His gaze darkened slightly. "You have a daughter?"

"Yes." Just the thought of Sarah brought up her image in Jennifer's mind and she smiled to herself. Big brown eyes in a round little face that was usually smudged with dirt. Pigtails that were really no more than tiny wisps of light-brown hair caught up in barrettes at either side of her head. Small, pudgy hands and short, sturdy legs. Butterfly kisses and sticky-fingered hugs. Tickle bugs and belly laughs.

Doctors in white coats, long, dangerous-looking needles and Sarah's tears.

"Oh, God," Jennifer half moaned and clapped her hand to her mouth again, not sure if she was going to be sick or start screaming.

It was all just so damned unfair.

"Come here," Chance said, turning her as he spoke, shifting to hold her, wrap his arms around her.

And because she needed a hug so badly, she went.

Nestled against that wide chest, she hung on for a long moment, wrapping her arms around his waist and drawing on the strength he so casually offered. She felt him awkwardly patting her back and for some silly reason, it helped. Though she knew it didn't actually change anything, the physical act of being comforted soothed the frayed edges of her soul, and just for an instant, the world didn't seem as terrifying as it had only minutes ago.

"Tell me," he said, his voice a gruff whisper coming from somewhere above her head. "Tell me what's wrong."

"Sarah," she said, saying the words aloud for the first time since the doctor had so clinically outlined the trouble the day before, "my baby. She needs an operation. On her heart. There's a small hole in it."

"Aah…" A comforting sound, more of a deep breath released, maybe, but it too helped. She felt his sympathy in the gentle tightening of his grip on her. "How old is she?"

"Eighteen months," she whispered, looking past him to the lake, but really looking at her mind's-eye picture of Sarah. "She's so small. So tiny. This shouldn't be happening."

"No, it shouldn't," he said softly. "It sucks."

Jennifer nodded. "Yes," she said, grateful to hear someone else say what she'd been thinking, "it does."

Two

Chance wasn't a family kind of man by any means. But he felt Jennifer's fear as if it were his own. It rattled through her small body with the force of a freight train and shook him to his bones.

His every instinct told him to rush in and defend. Protect. But none of his training would do a damn sight of good here. And that realization was a bitter pill to choke down.

Hell, he couldn't even think of something helpful to say. It sucks? Real eloquent, Chance.

He continued to hold her though, hoping his silent support helped in some way. Strange, a few days ago, he hadn't known or cared that any of these people existed. Now he was standing on the balcony of a *mansion,* for Pete's sake, holding a weeping woman.

"What am I doing?" Jennifer muttered as she pulled back out of his arms and took another step away from him just for good measure. "I'm going to rain mascara all over your white uniform."

No she wouldn't, he thought, looking into those forest-green eyes of hers. They were big and wet and sad, but there was no smudge of dark makeup around them. Just the remnants of tears she was fighting to control. Damned if he didn't admire her for that, too.

She could be wallowing in the fear that was close to strangling her, but she wasn't. Instead, she was holding herself together through the force of her will. Hell, she didn't even want sympathy. So what exactly was it he could do for her?

"Do you want to go back inside?" he asked.

"God no," she said, shaking her head and moving back to the railing. Keeping her face averted from both him and the sliding glass doors behind them, she said, "I don't want them to know I've been crying. I just couldn't take the questions right now."

Privacy. Something else he could understand. Well, if he couldn't escort her through the maze of party-goers, he could at least make her eventual trip inside a little easier. "Okay. Just wait here, then. I'll be back."

Before she could say anything, he opened the sliding glass doors and stepped back into the party. Noise assaulted him and he instantly missed the relative peace and quiet of the balcony.

Focused, Chance paid no attention to the people around him. He moved through the crowd as if he were on a mission. He kept his goal in mind and went about accomplishing it as quickly as he could. Which wasn't as easy as he'd expected. There were just too many people.

He cast one quick, nearly wistful glance at the front door, then forgot about leaving and went on with his quest.

When he walked into the kitchen, the folks in there looked as surprised as they would have if lightning had struck the butcher-block work island in the center of the massive room.

"Can I help you, Mr. Chance?"

Grateful, he looked to the woman on his right. Mentally, he scrambled for her name and came up with it an instant later.

"Ruby, right?" he asked.

"That's me," the housekeeper said, giving him a nod sharp enough to shake loose a graying red curl from her topknot to lie askew in the middle of her forehead.

In the few days he'd been in town, Chance had

seen this woman running the Connelly household—
and family, for that matter—with an iron fist. Grant
and Emma might think they were in charge, but the
truth was, Ruby was the brass around here.

The short, slightly rounded woman with kind
blue eyes had the ability to get things done, and
Chance appreciated that. Even while keeping under
radar, staying unnoticed himself. He'd seen how his
half brothers and sisters scampered when Ruby
gave an order. Hell, even his father, Grant, didn't
argue when she laid down the law.

Clearly, she'd been in charge so long, she never
even considered the possibility that people wouldn't
obey her without question. In the military, she
might have made it to the Joint Chiefs of Staff.
Here, she ran the Connelly household like a well-
oiled machine and wouldn't accept anything less.

"Now, how can I help you?" she asked, snatching his attention as she would have the hand of a
child inclined to wander off.

Chance glanced around at the others clustered
within hearing distance, reluctant to speak up with
so many eager ears nearby. The housekeeper noticed and clapped her hands sharply. "What are you
bunch staring at? Get about your business. Don't
you have drinks and canapés you could be serving?"

They scattered like windblown leaves, and, in

seconds, he was alone in the room with Ruby. "I'm impressed," he said.

"For running them off? Don't be. I am sorry about them, though," the woman said, with a shake of her head. "They're day help for the party and their mamas apparently forgot to teach them any manners."

He smiled. "I have a feeling you'll take care of that."

She straightened up and puffed out her chest. "I'll do my best in the short time I have them," she assured him. "So what is it you need, Mr. Chance?"

He winced a little at the implied title. Now, people calling him "Commander," he'd earned. He could even live with "Hey, sailor," but "Mr. Chance"? No way. That was just way too highfalutin. "Just, Chance, all right?"

One corner of her mouth twitched, but she only nodded. "Chance it is, then." She studied him for a long minute, then said, "You know, you've the look of your father around the eyes. More so than your brother does."

Chance shifted uncomfortably. He didn't necessarily want to be reminded that he looked like the man who'd managed to ignore both him and his brother their whole lives. What was he supposed to say to that, anyway? Thank you didn't seem appropriate somehow. So he ignored the comment entirely.

After all, it wasn't as if he'd come here looking to find family. He already had his family. Douglas. With the death of their mother, all they had left was each other. And that had always been enough before.

The only reason he was here at all was as a favor to Doug. And if he hadn't been shot by that sneaky little terrorist on his last mission, he wouldn't have had to put up with any of the pomp and circumstance surrounding the Connellys. But then, he wouldn't have been here to ride to Jennifer's rescue, either, would he?

And that thought returned him to why he'd come to the kitchen in the first place.

"Any chance I could get a glass of water and a box of tissues?" he asked.

Ruby narrowed her eyes thoughtfully as she looked at him. "Feel a crying jag coming on, do you?"

Chance played along. "Yes, ma'am. I'm feeling real emotional."

She snorted. "Yeah, I can see that." But without another word, she bustled around the room and came back with just what he'd asked for. As he turned to leave the room, though, her voice stopped him. "You tell Jennifer for me that everything's going to be all right."

He looked at her. Shouldn't be surprised, he thought. He'd already discovered that nothing much went on around here that Ruby didn't know about. "What?"

"I've been with the Connellys for more years than I care to admit. Not much gets past me. I know there's something wrong."

Nodding, he told her, "You would have made a good admiral."

"Phooey," she said, waving one hand to dismiss him. "Admirals are small stuff. I'd have made a good president."

"You know something?" he said, giving her a wink, "I believe you." Then he slipped from the room before she could give him any orders he'd be too afraid not to follow.

"Oh, this is good," Jennifer told herself aloud as she clutched the balcony railing and stared out at Lake Michigan. "Way to ensure your employment, Jen." Shaking her head, she blinked back tears that still threatened and solemnly vowed they wouldn't fall. She'd already screwed up big-time.

What had she been thinking? Crying on the shoulder of the guest of honor at her employer's party. The one time she indulged in a good old-fashioned pity party, she had to be caught by Mr. Tall, Dark and Dangerous.

"For goodness' sake," she grumbled, tightening

her grip on the cold iron railing. She lifted her face into the wind sweeping in off the lake and told herself that if she was very lucky, the newest addition to the Connelly family would keep her embarrassing behavior to himself.

Although, for all she knew he was inside now, trying to get Emma to come out and comfort her, readily handing off the crazed secretary to someone else. She could almost imagine him, stalking through the party, heading for the front door as fast as he could. And she couldn't really blame him, either.

What man wanted to be a human tissue for a weeping woman? Especially one he hardly knew.

Behind her, the glass door slid open, allowing a brief pulse of conversation and piano music onto the balcony, and in an instant, the door closed again, sealing off the intrusion.

She didn't turn around. She didn't have to. She knew who it was. She *felt* his presence almost as an electrical charge. Her nerve endings hummed and the hairs at the back of her neck stood straight up.

Probably not a good sign.

"Sorry I took so long," he said and darned if his voice didn't scrape along those already tense nerves.

Get a grip, Jen. He's your boss's stepson. He's a stranger. He doesn't give a damn about your problems and there's nothing between you but an embarrassing crying jag.

So why was her stomach suddenly in knots and her breath coming fast and hard?

Because you're an idiot, she told herself just before turning to look at him.

Well, that didn't help any. He was just too darned good-looking, that was the problem. He looked like a poster boy for navy recruiting. Or like one of those navy lawyers on that television show. His uniform shone a bright white against the backdrop of the blue lake and shimmering April sky. The ribbons decorating his chest drew her eye as did the SEAL pin he wore proudly. Then she looked farther up, into his eyes, and saw...concern. And that nearly did her in on the spot.

Darn it.

"You okay?" he asked.

"Oh, dandy," she told him and sniffed.

He held out the box of tissues and she gratefully snatched one free of the dispenser. She wiped her eyes, blew her nose and still didn't feel better.

"Here, drink this." He offered the tall, pale-blue glass he carried.

"What is it?" she asked as she reached for it. "Hemlock?"

"Nothing so deadly," he said with a half laugh. "Just water."

She took a drink, letting the liquid soothe her

tight throat before trying to talk again. Lifting her gaze to his, she said, "Thank you. For the tissue and the water."

"Here to serve, ma'am," he said.

"But I bet you didn't expect to have to go above and beyond the call at a party."

He shrugged. "Hey, a party, a terrorist situation—the SEALS can handle it all."

"Good to know," she muttered, then, still clutching her glass of water, turned around again to stare out at the lake. She couldn't keep looking at him. That just wasn't good for her equilibrium. Way better on her nerves to stare out at a lake the size of an ocean, its choppy waves slapping toward Lake Shore Drive.

"Tell me about your daughter," he said quietly and Jennifer's eyes closed briefly on a twinge of something as painful as it was tender.

But she supposed she owed him this, for crying all over him.

"Sarah's so smart," she said, and though her voice started out thin and trembling, talking about her pride and joy strengthened it. Shaking her head, she continued, "She started talking before she was a year old and now she's already arguing with me." Jennifer chuckled, and the sound grated against her throat. "When she's a teenager—" *when* not *if,* she told herself silently "—we'll probably lock horns all the time."

"Probably," he said agreeably. "God knows Doug and I drove our poor mother nuts when we were teenagers. Of course your Sarah most likely won't be into drag racing, so that's one worry you won't have."

She flicked him a glance, not at all surprised by his little admission. He was a SEAL, after all. And clearly he loved his job. So it naturally followed that as a kid, he would have sought out dangerous pastimes.

Just like Mike, she thought with an inward acknowledgment of old pain. The two of them would have gotten along great together, no doubt. Then, as if he'd sensed what she was thinking, the man beside her spoke up again.

"Your husband must be just as proud of her as you are," Chance said.

"My husband's dead," she said, tasting the words it had taken her so long to get used to saying.

"Oh. I'm sorry," he said.

"You didn't know," she said softly. "No reason to be sorry. He's been gone almost two years now." She sighed heavily. "He never even knew Sarah."

A long uncomfortable minute passed before he said, "I was raised by a single mother," he said. "I know how hard it is."

She looked up at him, into those whiskey-colored eyes and read understanding there. And darn it, she appreciated it. Though Emma was beyond kind and a good friend as well as an employer, she couldn't really appreciate what it was like to be the sole person responsible for raising a child. Not when she had Grant, as much in love with her today as he had been years ago.

Then he said, "If you don't mind my asking, how did your husband die?"

"Mike was a police officer," she said, lifting her chin just a bit. "He was killed in the line of duty. I was still pregnant with Sarah when he died. He never even *saw* her."

"Maybe he did," Chance said and she looked at him. "Maybe he sees her every day."

"I'd like to think so."

"I've seen enough things over the years to convince me that anything's possible." He paused for a long minute, then said, "I never knew my father, either." Then he stopped and laughed shortly. "At least, not until a few days ago."

She shook her head in sympathy, though she was glad to turn the subject away from Mike. "I can't even imagine what that must be like," she said, choosing her words carefully now. "Finding your blood father after so many years..."

He nodded, lifting his face into the cold, sharp wind. "I know what you mean. I'm not real sure how I feel about it, either. But," he said, giving a quick look over his shoulder, "it meant something to Doug, so here I am."

"You only came here for your brother's sake?"

"Why else?"

"To get to know your family?"

"Nah. My mother's gone now, so my family is Doug. The rest…" He shook his head again as if he didn't know quite what else to say.

"The Connellys are nice people," Jennifer said, wanting him to know that this new family of his was ready and willing to welcome him.

"Seem to be."

"They've been wonderful to me and Sarah."

He gave her a slow smile. "If your daughter's anything like you, I can't see that that would be a hardship."

Oh, that smile was just as dangerous as the man, she told herself, taking a mental step backward. She didn't need this kind of complication right now. Her world was Sarah. Her attentions had to be devoted to making her little girl well again. And to help her keep her attentions focused, she knew the best thing to do was to keep her distance from this man.

"I, uh—" She glanced at the sliding glass doors with real regret. Though she knew she had to leave the balcony, she wasn't looking forward to making small talk while her heart was aching. Still, this party was a big deal for Grant and Emma. Hadn't Jennifer and her employer been planning it for weeks? No, heartache or not, she had to do her job.

"I'd better get back inside," she said and even she heard the reluctance in her voice.

Chance straightened away from the railing and looked from the doors to her. She wasn't ready to go back in there and face the chattering mob. He could see it in her eyes. The vulnerability was still there, etched deep.

It was none of his business, of course, but still, he felt a kinship of sorts with her. She was a single mother, as his own mom had been. Her husband had served the public, his country, as Chance did, only *he* had paid the ultimate price. A rising wave of protectiveness filled him and before he could think more of it, he said, "I think the party can get along without either of us. So why don't you let me take you home instead?"

She thought about it for a long minute, and he could see in her eyes just how much she wanted to get out of here. The question was, would she?

"As much as I'd like to," she said, "I don't think I should—"

"With that crowd in there, no one will even miss us."

"Emma would."

He acknowledged that with a brief nod. "Okay, then, we'll stop and tell her we're leaving. I should say thanks, anyway."

Now that her objections were taken care of, all that was stopping her from taking him up on his offer was the fact that he was a virtual stranger—long-lost relative of her employer or not. "You can trust me," he said softly.

Her lips twitched slightly. "It's not that," she said.

"Then what? I'm just offering you a ride home, not a weekend trip to Jamaica." Why was he trying so hard to convince her? He wasn't sure. All he knew was that suddenly he needed to be the one to see her safely to her door.

She looked beyond the glass doors again to the party, and he saw her shudder. She really didn't want to go back in there. And damned if he could blame her. He had no interest in rejoining the mob, either.

And playing on that feeling, he said, "You'd be doing me a favor."

"What?"

He smiled. "You'd be rescuing me from mingling."

Her lips twitched. "A fate worse than death?"

"Oh, definitely."

She nodded, and he knew this battle was won. "Well," she said, her decision made, "I suppose I shouldn't turn down my one chance to be a hero."

Three

─────

A thick wall of noise welcomed them back inside the Connelly mansion, and for one brief moment, Jennifer thought about turning tail and disappearing again onto the balcony. But it wouldn't do any good. She had to make it through the minefield of the party to make good her escape at some point anyway. Better to do it now, when she had a tall, imposing man striding beside her, subtly clearing a path.

Faces flashed past as Chance steered her through the crowd with one strong hand at the small of her back. His touch felt warm, comforting, somehow. Strange, but she hadn't experienced that little nicety since Mike's death and she hadn't realized how much she had missed it. But then, she'd realized over the last couple of years that it was the small things that, once they were gone, left the biggest holes.

Now there was no one to hold her chair out for her at a nice restaurant. No one who knew how to whistle for a cab loudly enough to gather up a regular cluster of them. No one to kill a spider in the bathroom in the middle of the night. No one to warm her feet on, or to whisper to in the movies. No one to care for, to cook for, to worry about.

A wistful smile crossed her face. Of course, any self-respecting women's libber would have a heart attack if she could read Jennifer's mind. But she didn't care. She had always considered herself pretty liberated, but when it came right down to it, she'd *liked* being married. She'd *liked* being half of a team. And sometimes she missed that feeling so much, a slow, deep ache wrapped itself around her heart.

But then all it would take was one sweet smile from Sarah and everything was all right again. Silently, she reminded herself that she would never be alone again, not really. Not as long as she and Sarah had each other.

And that thought made her think of the heart operation her baby needed, and tears welled up in her eyes. It didn't seem to make a difference that the doctors all assured her that it would be a simple thing, as operations went. That though any procedure carried risks, Sarah had an excellent chance at a full and complete recovery.

Because no matter the kind words and assurances, Sarah was her baby. Her family. And the thought of losing her was simply too much to contemplate. She couldn't even imagine a world without her little girl in it—so she didn't. Jennifer blinked frantically, slammed a mental door on the dark, worrisome thoughts and hurried her steps. All she wanted now was to get out of here before she could be bombarded with concerned questions.

"There they are," Chance muttered, bending his head close to her ear.

Her gaze shifted to the right and she saw Grant and Emma Connelly, having what looked to be a very involved discussion with Seth. None of them looked very happy.

Jennifer slowed down instinctively, not wanting to intrude on what was obviously a strained moment. Shaking her head, she shot a glance up at the man beside her. "It looks like they're busy. Maybe we shouldn't interrupt."

He took her upper arm in a firm, but gentle grip and gave her a smile. "We won't interrupt them for long. Then they can go back to whatever it is that's got them all frowning so."

As they approached the threesome, Jennifer overheard Seth saying, "I just have to go and see her. I don't want to hurt you, Mom," he said to Emma, "but Angie Donahue is my birth mother. And I have to know why she suddenly wants to see me." He reached for Emma's hand and gave it a squeeze. "I'll be fine. I promise. And I'll be back."

Through teary eyes, Emma glanced at Grant, who kept his gaze focused on the young man in front of him, as though, if he studied him hard enough, he'd be able to pull the thoughts from Seth's mind. Finally, though, the elder Connelly said gruffly, "You do what you have to do, son. We're behind you all the way. Just like always. And we'll be here waiting for you when you come home."

Whatever the boy might have said in response was lost when Emma noticed Chance and Jennifer approaching. She smiled in welcome and made shooing gestures at Seth with both hands.

"And what are you two up to?" she asked as they came closer.

"I just wanted to say thank you, ma'am, for your hospitality," Chance said, then added, "and to say goodbye."

"Goodbye?" Grant asked abruptly. "Already?"

Jennifer's gaze flicked from father to son and though she knew Chance probably wouldn't be happy to hear it, she privately acknowledged just how much he looked like his biological father. But it wasn't just their features they shared. Both of the men had an air of self-confidence about them that people naturally gravitated toward.

It was part of the reason Grant had done so well in the business world—and why Chance would inevitably continue his rise through the ranks. No doubt one day he'd be an admiral. Men like the Connellys were born conquerors. All that differed were the prizes they sought.

"Jennifer's not feeling well," Chance was saying, "so I offered to take her home."

"Aah…" Grant nodded thoughtfully as his gaze flicked from his son to Jennifer and back again.

Jennifer felt her cheeks warm up at the knowing gleam in Grant's eyes, so she spoke up quickly. "I, uh—" think fast, Jen "—have a headache," she finished. Well, that was brilliant. But she didn't want to go into Sarah's medical problems now. Not at the party. "Commander Barnett was kind enough to offer me a ride."

"Barnett?" Grant stared at the man who was his son.

A touchy subject, Jennifer knew. Chance quite naturally wanted to keep the name he knew. The name his mother had given him. Grant, just as naturally, wanted his sons to use his name.

It would be interesting to see who eventually won this little tug-of-war.

"Sir," Chance said, holding his right hand out to his father, "thank you. It was a nice party."

Grant harrumphed. "You hated it."

"Pretty much," Chance acknowledged.

"Knew you would. Too much like me."

Chance nodded shortly. "Maybe."

Grant dropped one arm around his wife's shoulders. "Emma's the party-giver around here. Loves the hustle and bustle. She just tells me when to show up."

Emma gave his broad chest a playful slap, before looking at Chance. "It's true, you know. He'd much rather be out taking over small companies or sailing, or...well, just about anything."

Jennifer watched as a small smile curved Chance's lips, and to her surprise, a curl of something delightful spiraled through her in response. Oh, that probably wasn't a good sign.

"Then maybe we are more alike than I'd thought," Chance allowed as Grant took his outstretched hand and gave it a firm shake.

His father smiled. "I'll settle for a maybe. For now."

"Seems fair," Chance told him.

"All right, then," Emma spoke up. "Jennifer, I hope you're feeling better tomorrow. Why don't you take the day off?"

"Oh, that won't be—"

"A day off's not going to bring the world to an end," her employer told her firmly. Then she shifted a look at Chance. "You drive carefully.

Without Jennifer, I'd never get a thing done around here.''

"Yes, ma'am," Chance said, and in seconds he had Jennifer turned around and headed for the front door. They skirted the edges of the party and avoided being stopped again. Their steps clicked on the cold marble of the main staircase, then echoed as they moved into the grand entry hall on the main floor. Here, the marble gleamed and shone in the spill of late-afternoon sunshine slashing through the wide front windows. Chance left her just long enough to grab their coats, and once she was bundled up, he ushered her outside into the bite of the cold Chicago wind.

"I'm parked just up the street," he said. "Why don't you wait here and I'll go get the car?"

"Thanks, I'd rather walk."

"Suit yourself," he said smiling, then offered her his arm.

Arms linked, they took the short flight of steps to the sidewalk below, crossed the narrow strip of lawn and turned onto Michigan Avenue.

"I can't believe you found a place to park around here."

He grinned at her and Jennifer sucked in a breath. That really was a devastating weapon he had tucked away. Thankfully, her defenses had been strengthened over the last two years.

"I'm a SEAL, remember? We excel at the impossible."

"I'll keep that in mind."

While they walked, he talked, as if somehow sensing that she wasn't in the mood to discuss her problems anymore tonight. She listened to stories of his and Doug's childhood, heard the pride in his voice when he talked about his mother and what she'd managed to accomplish all on her own. She hoped that one day Sarah would be as kind when talking about her.

God knows, she tried to be both mom and dad. But it wasn't easy. Despite having a great job with the most understanding employer in the free world, Jennifer was pushed every day, wondering how to get everything done. She had no idea at all how women with less going for them managed to survive.

"It must have been so hard for her," she finally said, looking up at him. The wind blew strands of blond hair across her face and she plucked them out of her way so she could see him clearly.

He stared off into the distance as if looking into years past and nodded. "Yeah, it was," he said, "but we didn't know that at the time. She made it look so easy. Mom wasn't the kind to sit around and whine about finding herself. Or wishing that things were different. She used to say that the only thing you could change in life was yourself. So do the best you can.''

''Smart woman.''

''Oh, yeah.'' He turned his head to look down at her and gave her yet another of those great smiles. ''She would have liked you.''

''Really? Why's that?''

''Because your daughter's so important to you.''

Something clutched at her heart, but Jennifer only said, ''She's everything to me.''

''I can see that.''

''That easy to read, huh?''

''Does the phrase *an open book* mean anything to you?''

Jennifer laughed in spite of herself. She'd never had much of a poker face. ''Mike used to say the reason I was so honest was because I just couldn't pull off a lie.''

''Good a reason as any,'' he said and stopped alongside a cherry-red SUV.

''This is yours?'' she asked and wondered why she was even surprised. If this wasn't a guy's car, she'd eat it.

''Rental,'' he said and opened her door. Holding it for her as she got in, he added, ''I'm just in town for a while.''

She automatically reached for the shoulder harness. ''Where do you go when you leave here?''

''Back to my SEAL team.''

"And then?"

"Won't know until just before I go."

He slammed the door, walked around the front of the car, then opened the driver's-side door. Sliding onto the front seat, he latched his seat belt, stuck the key in the ignition and turned it. The engine leapt into life with a muffled rumble of sound.

Shifting slightly in his seat, he winced and Jennifer asked, "Are you okay?"

"Yeah," he said. "I just keep forgetting to move slow. Think I pulled a few stitches is all."

Stitches? The question must have been written on her face, because he gave her a shrug and an it's-no-big-deal look before saying, "Took a hit on my last mission."

"A *hit?*" she asked, her gaze dropping to his side as if she could see right through his uniform. "You mean you were shot?"

"It's nothing major," he said. "Just cut through the meat."

"Ah," she muttered, with a sage nod. "A *minor* gunshot wound. And did you actually call it a flesh wound at the time, in the finest John Wayne tradition?"

His brows drew together as he watched her. "What's the problem here?"

"Oh, not a thing," she said and gripped her hands together in her lap as she turned her head to stare out the windshield. Just like Mike, she thought. They were cut from the same cloth. Dangerous jobs. Dismissive of hazards. No big deal. How could any sane person think it was no big deal to face the possibility of death as a matter of course? What was it that drove men—and some women—to take jobs that threatened their lives?

"Jennifer," he said, over the low roar of the engine, "you want to tell me what's got you so tense all of a sudden?"

She swiveled her head to look at him. The planes and hollows of his face stood out in stark relief. He looked hard and dangerous—but for the gentleness she could still read in his eyes.

"I don't get it," she finally blurted. "What is it about you guys?"

"Us guys?" he repeated, a half smile on his face. "Care to be more specific?"

"Men like you. And Mike."

"Your husband."

"My *late* husband," she corrected, then muttered, "I don't know why that phrase is used. It's not like he's going to be on time somewhere. He isn't late, for heaven's sake. He's dead."

"Jennifer—"

"No, I want to know," she said, meeting his gaze and holding it. "What is it that makes you deliberately seek out the kind of profession that endangers your lives? Is it for the thrills? The rush of constant peril?"

His mouth tightened briefly. "I've spent years in training to do my job, and I'm guessing your husband did, too. You don't put in that kind of effort just for the thrill of it."

"Then why?" she asked, knowing he was right. Mike had worked hard at being a police officer. He'd loved it. Had lived, breathed and eventually *died* for it. She couldn't ask him why now, so she wanted an answer from this man who lived his life the same way.

"To serve," he said softly, simply. "To help. To fight for my country. Sounds corny, huh? But that's the plain truth of it."

His words seemed to echo in the enclosed space as he went on.

"Military or cop, we do what has to be done. It's not for some rush," he said and added, "and I think you know that. It's not an easy life, but it's the only one I know. Or want. And I'm guessing it was the same for your husband."

Jennifer drew one long, shuddering breath and released it. Watching him, listening to him, she knew he was right. Felt it. And a part of her even agreed with him. But admitting that brave men were necessary and actually living with one were two different things. She'd put in her time in the trenches. She'd worried every time Mike left the house. And it hadn't kept him alive.

She wasn't interested in living with that kind of fear again.

No. There was only one person in her life now. Her daughter. And thoughts of Sarah were all she had time for. Anything else would just be a distraction right now. A distraction she didn't need.

Even if it was six feet two inches of solidly packed muscle encased in a snow-white naval uniform.

Four

"**T**urn right here," she said and watched the familiar neighborhood pass as Chance steered the SUV down her street. Oak Park, Illinois, came by its name honestly, she thought, not for the first time.

Ancient oaks lined nearly every street, stretching long, leafy arms across the avenues to form what in summer, were cool green tunnels that blunted the steamy heat. Now the first of the new leaves were just beginning to sprout, and the skeletal trees rattled their limbs together in the wind as if clamoring for their new spring outfits.

Jennifer smiled to herself as she noted the sidewalks that rolled up and down like cement waves.

Unlike other big cities, where the slightest bump in a sidewalk meant death to the offending tree, here city workers just slapped fresh cement atop the protruding roots. They protected their trees and the city was the better for it.

"It's a nice street," Chance said and she gave him a quick glance.

"Yes, it is," she agreed, and inwardly cringed. Well, one sure way to discourage him was to bore him to tears. But in her own defense, with thoughts of Sarah constantly simmering in her mind, it was hard to try to make conversation.

So instead of even trying, she looked at the houses as they passed. Some were like hers, old, with wide front porches supported by stone pillars. Others were brand-new, boasting lots of glass and sharp angles. Not too long ago the neighborhood had been dying, but in recent years young professionals had discovered the beauty of Oak Park and had infused it with new life. It was practically trendy now, and if Mike hadn't inherited their house from his late aunt, they never would have been able to afford to live there. "Frank Lloyd Wright's house is just around the corner."

"The architect?"

"Uh-huh," she said. "It's a lovely place even if it is a little on the modern side for me."

He slanted her a long glance. "Just an old-fashioned girl, are you?"

She shifted in her seat and folded her hands in her lap. "About some things, I guess," she admitted. "Like these old bungalow-type homes. They're just cozier...warmer somehow. They've got character."

"I think I know what you mean," he said, and she turned to look at him. He gave her a half smile. "The older places have weathered the storms. They've earned the right to be here."

An interesting way to put it, she thought. But so true. "I guess that's it," she said. "Some of these places have been here more than fifty years. Sheltering families, withstanding tornadoes—and all they need is a little care. A part of me even feels sorry for the poor houses that are torn down to make way for some spanking new glass-and-chrome disaster."

He laughed then. "A romantic. Who would have thought it?"

Romantic? Nope. Not her. Maybe once, she thought, remembering how young and naive she'd been when she'd married Mike. She'd looked at the world through rose-colored glasses. When they'd moved into his late aunt's cozy bungalow on this street, she'd assumed that they'd still be sitting on the front porch together when they were eighty.

But that plan had been buried with Mike, and now she considered herself more of a realist than a romantic. No more believing in happily ever after for *this* girl. Her fairy tale had ended. But there was no point in explaining all of that to Chance Barnett. He wouldn't be around long enough to care. He'd made no secret of the fact that he was itching to be gone. A couple more weeks and he'd be off living his dangerous life—which was just as well, she thought. Because she—she would still be here, trying to walk a minefield while carrying precious cargo.

And just the thought of Sarah was enough to bring her right back to the terrifying reality that was now her life.

"The house on the left is mine," she said abruptly, lifting one hand to point. "The blue one, with the wagon in front of the steps."

Her heart seized briefly as she realized that there was a very real chance that Sarah and her wagons and toys—the same ones Jennifer complained about being left all over—might not be a part of her life much longer. But no. She wouldn't even entertain the possibility. Hadn't the doctor told her this was a relatively simple operation? Hadn't he assured her that though there were always risks involved in surgery, this one was practically a cookie-cutter job?

Cookie-cutter.

How could anything requiring her daughter's tiny chest to be opened be considered cookie-cutter?

Tears leapt into her eyes and she blinked them back as Chance pulled into the driveway. Parked directly in front of them was her own car, still listing to one side on its flat rear tire. She'd come outside that morning to find it like that, which explained why she'd been at the Connelly mansion with no ride home.

And why she was now sitting here beside a man whose very presence was a distraction she so didn't need at the moment.

He put the car into Park and turned off the motor. Instantly, a rush of silence filled the car and the only sounds came from a group of kids two doors down playing basketball against a garage. The steady thump of the bouncing ball felt almost like a heartbeat, and the minute that thought raced into her brain, Jennifer pushed it out again.

"Looks like your car had an adventure," he said quietly.

At his words, she smiled in spite of herself. "When I was little, I used to think that when their owners were asleep, cars would take off on their own. You know, go for drives along the beach, meet up with other cars at the garage to share a quart of oil."

He chuckled.

"Apparently," she said on a sigh, "*my* car took a bad bump somewhere along the road."

"So why didn't you fix it?"

"Gee," she said, giving her forehead a light slap, "why didn't I think of that?"

"Dumb question, huh?"

"No," she said, "not really." After all, since Mike's death, she'd had to take care of lots of things on her own. Like stopped-up sinks or blown fuses. "I should be able to do it, but I just haven't taken my tire-changing class yet."

"How about I do it for you?"

She flicked him a quick glance. A part of her longed to say, That'd be great. But the smarter side of her knew that she didn't need to be indebted any further to Chance Barnett Connelly. Actually, the more distance she kept between herself and a man who could start her blood simmering with a look, the better. "No, that's okay. Thanks, but you really don't have to."

"I know I don't have to," he said, snatching the keys from the ignition and palming them. "But it's no big deal."

"Right," she said, grabbing for the door latch, "and black grease would look great on those dress whites of yours."

A moment ticked by before he gave her a wide, sheepish grin.

Something inside her turned over with a loud thud and slapped hard against her heart. Good grief.

He shrugged and said, "Oh, yeah. Forgot about that. Guess I'm really not in my best mechanic's outfit."

No, she thought, but his heartbreaker outfit looked just fine. Too fine.

And on that thought, she spoke up. "Well," she said, unhooking her shoulder strap and reaching for her purse on the floor, "thanks for the ride."

He opened his car door and got out, then walked around to her side of the car. She watched him come with an inward sigh. Apparently he wasn't going to just drop her off and race away. And she wasn't entirely sure how she felt about that.

He wasn't good for her equilibrium. Oh, he seemed nice enough, but for heaven's sake, she hardly knew him. Yet in the last few hours she'd wept all over his uniform—and Jennifer *never* cried—plus, she'd felt...*stirrings* deep within her and darn it, she wasn't interested in stirring anything but a pot of soup.

So, it was time to tell the navy man to go for a long sail to...somewhere. All she wanted now was to get inside, alone, check on Sarah and make a cup of tea.

Chance opened her door for her and extended one hand to help her down. Jennifer looked at his open palm for a long minute, trying to decide if she should take it or struggle out of the oversize car on her own. Instantly, an image of herself, skirt riding high on her thighs as she slid inelegantly from the too-high car, shot through her mind and just like that, her decision was made.

"Thanks," she said and slipped her hand into his. Warmth skittered up the length of her arm and splintered inside her chest, sending shafts of heat dancing throughout her body. His fingers curled around hers and she felt his grip right down to her bones.

"My pleasure," he murmured, his gaze meeting and holding hers.

Uh-oh.

The minute her feet hit the driveway, she pulled her hand free, but it didn't help. She felt his touch anyway, as surely as if he was still holding on to her. Curling her fingers into her palm, she deliberately ignored the sensation and gave him her best, brightest, phoniest smile.

"Well," she said, then paused to swallow hard and lower her voice just a notch or two, "I guess I'd better go inside now."

"I'll walk you to your door."

"That's not necessary," she began but saw the determination in his eyes, and knew that she wouldn't be getting rid of him that easily. Nodding, she headed for the front door, listening to the sounds of his footsteps right behind her. And she couldn't help wondering if the *S* in SEAL stood for Stubborn.

Or maybe Sexy.

Oh, good grief.

She pulled the screen door open and walked quickly across the wide front porch.

Chance watched her. Hell, he couldn't *stop* watching her. The sway of her hips, the brush of her hair against the collar of her dress, the trim line of calf and ankle. And then there was the vulnerable shine in her green eyes. Damn, the woman was enough to bring the strongest man to his knees.

And he wasn't exactly in peak condition at the moment.

When she stopped at the closed front door, he took just a moment to look around the cozy little screened-in porch. Rag rugs dotted the cement floor that had been painted a glossy barn-red. Dolls had been plunked down at a tiny table set for an imaginary tea party, and he felt a tug of tenderness for the sick little girl he'd yet to meet.

Chance shifted his gaze back to the woman in front of him and admiration for her crowded inside him. He knew exactly how hard her life was. His own mother had worked herself to an early death taking care of him and Douglas. He remembered how tight money had always been and how tired his mother usually was. But he also recalled clearly what it felt like to be loved unconditionally.

Recalling the look in Jennifer's green eyes when she'd told him about her daughter's problems, Chance knew that whatever Sarah's medical situation was, she at least could count on her mother's love.

But on the heels of that thought came other memories. Memories of the men his mother had dated and the way Chance had felt about them as they filed through their lives with numbing regularity. He couldn't blame his mother for wanting to find love. But he did blame those men for pretending to care about him and Doug and then disappearing without a backward glance when the relationship ended.

He'd long ago made a vow to steer clear of single mothers himself. He wasn't going to be one of those guys who blasted through a kid's life leaving behind nothing but a memory and a string of broken promises. And until today he'd kept that vow.

So what in the hell was he doing here?

Jennifer opened the door and stepped inside. Before he could ask himself too many more uncomfortable questions, Chance followed.

The first thing he noticed were the toys. Dolls and coloring books and stuffed animals littered the floor. The front door opened directly into the living room and from where he stood, he could see everything. Well-worn, overstuffed furniture crowded the small space and somehow managed to look inviting, rather than cramped. Doilies graced the tops of the highly-polished tables and a small, tidy fire burned in the hearth across the room. The walls

were a soft peach color and dotted with framed
family pictures. A doorway off to the right led into
what looked like the kitchen and to the left was a
darkened hallway that probably branched off into
the bedrooms.

"Mrs. Sorenson?" Jennifer called out as she
walked into the living room and tossed her purse
onto the closest table. "I'm home."

"In here." An older, female voice answered and
Jennifer headed straight for it, moving toward the
hallway on the left. She seemed to have forgotten
all about Chance and he knew damn well he should
leave. But he didn't. Instead, he walked along behind her, despite knowing that he had no business
pushing into her life any further than he had already.

Somehow, for some reason, he just wasn't ready
to leave yet. And he didn't really want to think
about why.

Four doorways opened off the short hall, but Jennifer made right for the last one on the right. Looking over her head, Chance could see the pale-yellow
paint on the wall and what looked like a mural of
daisies. Then he was in the doorway, and there he
stopped while Jennifer headed straight for the crib
on the far wall.

"How is she?" she asked.

A short, round woman with gray-streaked red
hair and deeply-etched laugh lines gave her a smile.

"She's fine now. Wanted to play, then tuckered herself out, poor sweetie."

Jennifer reached into the crib and smoothed one hand across her daughter's dirty forehead.

"Should have cleaned her up, I know," Mrs. Sorenson was saying, "but she was just so tired, I thought, why bother?"

"It's fine," Jennifer said. "I'll clean her up later."

"Well," the woman said, picking up her paperback book from the table beside the rocking chair she'd been occupying up until a moment ago, "if you need anything, you give a shout. Although," she added thoughtfully, "it looks as though you have all the help you'll need for a while."

Jennifer glanced at her and saw the speculative gleam in her neighbor's eyes as the woman gave Chance a slow once-over. Inwardly she sighed, knowing that sooner or later, her babysitter was going to want details about the tall, gorgeous hunk of sailor standing on the threshold. But not now.

"Eva Sorenson," Jennifer said, "Commander Chance Barnett Connelly."

The older woman gave him a quick grin. "I love a man with three names."

His grin matched hers. "Then I'll keep all three of them, for sure."

"Hmm," Eva mused, "cute and quick, too." She tossed a sidelong look at Jennifer. "Watch out for this one, honey. He's probably got a half dozen girls in every port.''

''Only half a dozen?'' Chance asked, his voice teasing.

''Quality, not quantity,'' Eva retorted.

''I'll remember that.''

Briefly, she inclined her head toward Jennifer, then warned not too subtly, ''See that you do.'' Then she inhaled sharply and said to no one in particular, ''Jim'll be wanting his dinner soon, so I'd better go. You know how that man is when he isn't fed on time.''

''Cheerful?'' Jennifer asked, since she couldn't ever remember seeing anything but a smile on Jim Sorenson's broad features.

Chuckling, Eva said, ''Hey, living with a perpetual optimist isn't all a picnic, you know.''

And then she was gone, slipping out the door and leaving Chance and Jennifer alone with the sleeping child. If he had any sense at all, Chance told himself, he'd be hot on the babysitter's heels, headed for his car and then his hotel.

But apparently his brain was on vacation, because he walked farther into the room and didn't stop until he was standing beside Jennifer staring down at the little girl lying beneath a flowered quilt.

He threw a quick glance at the woman beside him and noted the worry staining her eyes despite the soft smile curving her lips. She looked up at him briefly and said, "Chance, meet Sarah."

Love filled her voice and Chance couldn't help being moved by it. Then he shifted his gaze to the child with the dirty face and lopsided pigtails that weren't much bigger than the barrettes holding them in place. Her tiny, rosebud mouth was parted in sleep and as he watched, she lifted one grubby little fist and rubbed her eyes before rolling onto her side. Then she blindly groped around for a battered stuffed bear that was lying just out of her reach.

Chance moved the scruffy beast with one missing ear in closer and the little girl grabbed for it, latching on to his hand instead. Her tiny fingers clutched at him and held on tight.

A long deep breath rushed from his lungs.

And just like that, he fell in love.

Five

As that thought shot through his brain, Chance jerked back as if he'd been hit by a stray bullet. Absently, he watched the tiny girl's now-empty hand reach for and grab her stuffed animal. She pulled it close, buried her nose in its ratty fur and sighed in satisfaction.

Chance shoved his hands into his pockets and tried not to notice that he could still feel the toddler's surprisingly strong grip around his fingers.

"Are you okay?" Jennifer whispered, and he threw her a quick, wary glance.

"Yeah," he said, moving another uneasy step back from the crib. "Yeah, I'm fine."

Good job, Barnett, he told himself. Hell, he'd been in dozens of tight situations. Stared down the barrels of way too many guns. Slipped into and out of hostile nations without turning a hair.

And one soft stirring for a sick little girl had him ready to bolt for cover. He pulled one hand free of his pocket and scrubbed it across his face. This he hadn't counted on.

A pretty woman. A jolt of desire. Okay. But he hadn't planned on tenderness and wasn't at all sure what to do about it now that it had entered the picture.

"You don't look okay," Jennifer said and led the way quietly from the room.

Not surprising. A man suddenly slapped with feelings he'd never encountered before was liable to look as though he'd been hit in the head with a two-by-four. It was just that the girl was so tiny. So helpless. And damn it, a kid that small just shouldn't have to be sick. Scowling, he pushed those thoughts aside and concentrated on the woman in front of him.

He was only a step or two behind her and even with his thoughts churning, he managed to lower his gaze long enough to admire the sway of her hips and the shapeliness of her calves. Damn, but high heels did amazing things for a woman's legs.

And as dangerous as it was to be thinking about

Jennifer's legs, it was safer than dwelling on other, even more dangerous thoughts.

As soon as she walked into the living room, she stepped out of those heels and instantly became softer, more vulnerable somehow. And just as quickly, Chance's internal radar sent out a warning ping. Admiration for a single mother was all well and good. But did he really want another complication in his life? Wasn't dealing with a newly-inherited family enough at the moment?

"Hello?" she asked, prodding gently. "I asked if you were okay, remember?"

"I'm fine," he said firmly, silently congratulating himself on the fascinating conversation. Hell, what had happened to the glibness he was noted for with women? "Just tired, I guess. Not completely back up to speed yet."

Her features paled a bit, but she recovered quickly, he gave her that.

"How badly were you wounded?"

"Like you said before—just a flesh wound."

Jennifer folded her arms across her middle, dipped her head briefly then looked up at him again. "I'm sorry about that."

"Don't be."

"No, I shouldn't have said it."

"I'll live," he assured her and took a step closer. He couldn't seem to help himself. Everything about her drew him in. She touched something inside him and though he knew he should be fighting it, he surrendered to the feeling instead.

Her scent drifted to him. Her eyes looked wide, troubled, and for some damn reason, Chance wanted to do something—*anything*—to help. As he came closer, she shook her head in warning.

"Chance," she said, then corrected herself, "Commander Barnett—Connelly— Blast it."

A flicker of a smile danced across his face and was gone again, but in that instant, Jennifer knew she was in trouble. This man was pure, undiluted, top-grade sex appeal.

"Chance will do," he said and the amusement in his tone told her that he knew exactly what she was up to. Trying to put distance between them.

His amber eyes focused on her and it was like looking up into twin topazes. Her breath hitched and she wanted to back up, but there was simply nowhere to go. For the first time, she resented the fact that her living room was so darn tiny. A little maneuvering room was needed here and she was flat out of luck.

"Look, I appreciate you giving me a ride home, but—"

"But you'd rather I left now."

"Exactly," she said. "No offense, it's just—" Why couldn't she talk? Or think? He was too close, that was it. That broad chest. The startling white of his uniform against the deep tan of his skin. The cluster of medals and ribbons pinned above his heart.

Medals.

For bravery? For being shot?

For living the kind of dangerous life that had already robbed her of a husband?

Instantly, her heartbeat evened out, her breathing came just a bit easier and she felt control again. That's all she'd have to do. Remind herself continually of the fact that Chance Barnett Connelly was a man to whom life equaled danger.

And she'd had enough danger in her life already, thanks very much.

She lifted both hands, palms out, to stop his ever-increasing advance. It worked.

"What?" he asked, and he was so close, she felt the brush of his breath dust across her forehead.

A whisper of goose bumps raced along her spine, but Jennifer ignored them. She *had* to.

"This isn't a good idea at all," she said, "and I think you know it, too."

"Maybe," he said and his gaze moved over her features as surely as a caress.

She shivered, but shook her head. Steeling herself, she said, "I'm not interested in joining your group of 'girls in every port.'"

He actually looked offended. "Hey, I didn't say that. Your baby-sitter did."

"Yeah, but she was right," Jennifer muttered,

knowing it had to be true. No unmarried man who looked like Chance was hurting for company.

He took a half step back and she breathed a little easier.

"No, she wasn't," he said.

Jennifer looked up into his eyes and caught a glint of anger shining in those golden depths. Well, better anger than the desire that had been there a moment before. Much easier to deal with.

"It really doesn't matter, does it?"

"Yeah, it does," he said, his gaze locking onto hers. "There's something between us, Jennifer. Call it chemistry. Hell, call it lust."

"I'd rather not call it anything," she said.

"Ignoring it won't make it go away."

"Worth a shot," she quipped nervously and a moment later cringed to realize that by saying that, she'd actually admitted that there was something to ignore.

He nodded slowly and moved away. "I'm gonna go now."

Thank heaven.

"But I'll be back."

And as he walked toward the front door, Jennifer couldn't help wondering if that last statement had been a warning or a promise.

It turned out to be both.

The clatter of two small feet on the linoleum announced Sarah just a moment before that little voice shouted, "Chanz here!"

Expectation, excitement and dread all coiled together to form a knot in her throat that Jennifer dutifully swallowed back. Wrist-deep in soapy water, she looked back over her shoulder and smiled at her daughter.

"Tell Chance mommy's coming, all right?"

"'kay," the child said and spun around to run back the way she'd come.

"*Walk,* Sarah," Jennifer called out and was pleased to see the girl instantly slow down. Now shuffling her feet in obvious disgust, she left the room.

Chanz. Her daughter was nuts about Chance Barnett, and the feeling appeared to be mutual. He'd spent so much time here in the last three days that Jennifer now automatically set an extra plate on the table for him. Somehow, he'd managed to invade her life, captivate her daughter and send her own hormones on a white-water raft ride—all with very little effort.

Shaking soapsuds off her fingers, Jennifer grabbed a dish towel, dried her hands, then reached up to smooth her hair. Silly. She didn't *want* to look good for Chance Barnett, so what did she care if her hair was a mess?

Just a female reaction, that was all. It didn't mean anything. It didn't mean—

"Well, hi there, Chuckles!"

Chance's voice floated through the living room and into the kitchen where it raced up the length of Jennifer's spine and tickled the base of her neck. She hardly heard Sarah's delighted laughter over the roaring in her own ears. Her stomach took a nosedive and her breath came fast and hard.

For heaven's sake, she was acting like some teenager waiting for her prom date to pick her up. This wasn't a date, she reminded herself. And she sure as heck wasn't a teenager. So why couldn't she stop these ridiculous flutters of excitement that rippled through her whenever he was close?

Shaking her head, she muttered, "Quit stalling and get out there. Otherwise he'll think you're hiding from him."

She was, of course, but he didn't have to know that.

Chance sat on the couch, Sarah on his lap. The little girl held a book open and was stabbing at the pictures with one index finger.

"Tuttle."

"Turtle," he corrected gently and smoothed one hand over the back of the child's head.

"Yes," Sarah agreed, nodding sharply. "Tuttle."

Chance grinned and, as if sensing her presence, looked up directly into Jennifer's gaze. She felt the power of that stare right down to the soles of her feet. The man really packed a wallop.

"We're reading," he said.

"So I see." And darned if they didn't look like father and daughter. So cozy. So comfortable with each other. So— Don't go there, she warned herself even as she started walking toward the twosome.

"Momma come sit, too," Sarah announced, then shifted her gaze back to the book. "Doggie."

"Sure is," Chance agreed.

The little girl reached for his cheek and turned his face to hers. "Me wanna doggie."

"We talked about this, baby," Jennifer said, drawing Sarah off Chance's lap to sit with her. "You can have a doggie when you're all better."

"Me better," the girl insisted.

"Not yet," Jennifer said, past the aching knot in her throat, "but soon."

"Now. Better now."

She wished that were true, but looking into her little girl's face, Jennifer could see the dark violet shadows beneath her big brown eyes. Her skin was as pale as fine porcelain and just as fragile. Her little body might look sturdy, but it held a damaged heart, and until that was fixed, Jennifer would take no chances with her baby.

Her family.

"Wanna doggie," Sarah pleaded, leaning in and

tipping her head to one side for that extra special emphasis all children seemed to know instinctively.

"I'm sorry, honey, the answer is no."

Her bottom lip shot out and she folded her chubby arms across her chest. Then with as much dignity as an eighteen-month-old could manage, she stomped out of the room.

"No dog?"

Jennifer slanted the man beside her a look. "Not until she's well enough to play with one."

"It might help her to—"

"I know you mean well," Jennifer said, interrupting him before he could side with Sarah against her, "but she's my daughter and I have to do what I think is best for her."

"I'm not arguing," he said, lifting both hands in mock surrender.

"You were going to."

He looked like he might argue that, then gave it up and admitted sheepishly, "Yeah, I was."

"It's not easy saying no to her," Jennifer said on a sigh as she slumped back against the cushions.

"I noticed," he said with a chuckle. "I think she had my number from day one. All she has to do is look up at me with those big brown eyes and I'm her sucker."

Yes, Jennifer had seen that. He'd developed a special relationship with Sarah, and, though it worried her a little, she was also pleased. Sarah didn't have enough family in her life, and no close male relatives. It was good, wasn't it, to have Chance here, even for a little while? Or was she making a mistake in letting the two become friends? After all, when Chance left, as he would eventually, Sarah would miss him desperately.

And not, she thought with an inward twinge, just Sarah.

A crash from the other room shattered that train of thought.

"Sarah?"

Jennifer shot up from the love seat and raced across the room, her heart pounding in time with her hurried steps. "Sarah honey?" she called, "Are you all right?"

Dashing through the hallway, she rounded the corner and came to a sudden stop. Sarah stood in the center of the room, staring at the toppled dollhouse, lying on its side on the floor. She must have collided with the little table it sat on when she ran into the room. But it didn't matter. All that mattered was that she was safe. Relief coursed through Jennifer's body with the strength and overwhelming power of a river bursting its banks.

Huge tears formed in the little girl's eyes as she looked up at her mother. Jennifer dropped to her knees, gathered the girl up close and held her tightly. "Are you all right, baby? Are you hurt? You have to be careful, sweetheart. You shouldn't run. Just walk, all right? It's okay, don't cry. Don't cry…''

Her soothing words flowed into a steady stream of comforting sounds and hums, and Chance stood in the doorway, watching. Morning sunlight poured through the gleaming windowpanes to fall like a golden spotlight on Jennifer and her child as the two of them clung together like the only survivors of a tragedy.

He felt distanced from them, left out of this tender moment, and it surprised him to note just how much that bothered him. Inhaling deeply, he leaned one shoulder against the doorjamb and kept his gaze locked on the two females who had somehow become too important to him. His own heart rate was just slowing down. Amazing how the sound of a crash could scare you when a kid was involved. Hell, he'd come through firefights with less of a reaction. Yet as the seconds ticked past into minutes and still Jennifer hadn't released the girl, he began to wonder.

He wondered if Jennifer had always been this protective of the child, or if it was as a direct result of the heart problem that she was so terrified.

Six

"**W**hat is he up to?" Jennifer stared across Emma's office at the soft, soothing Monet hanging on the wall opposite her. But neither the violin music drifting out of the stereo nor the filmy greens and blues of Monet's gardens were going to be enough to calm the nerves jangling throughout her body.

"Why does he have to be 'up to' anything?" Emma answered the question with one of her own.

Sliding a glance at her employer, Jennifer gave her a rueful smile and said, "You would have made a good psychiatrist. Get the patient to answer her own questions."

"Oh, honey," Emma said, leaning forward to place her hand atop Jennifer's, "you're not a patient and you sure as heck don't need a shrink."

"I'm not so sure," Jennifer muttered with a shake of her head. Then she took hold of Emma's hand and gave it a hard squeeze before releasing it to lean back in her chair. "Lately I feel like I'm losing my mind."

"Of course you do," the older woman said. "You're worried sick over your baby."

True, Jennifer thought, as Sarah's sweet little face appeared in her mind. Every waking moment and most of her dreams were filled with half-frenzied, panic-filled thoughts of a nebulous, dangerous future. But to be honest, if only with herself, Chance was taking up a lot of time in her thoughts, too.

Blast it.

Heck, blast *him*.

She hadn't asked for this. Hadn't wanted any more complications in her life than already existed. She didn't need this right now. He was a distraction. Oh, a gorgeous one, granted, but still a distraction.

And she couldn't afford to have her concentration scattered right now. It didn't have anything to do with him personally, of course. It was just a bad time for her to try to have a relationship.

Jennifer groaned inwardly. Heck, even *she* didn't believe that.

There wasn't another man alive who could distract her from her worries right now. It was only Chance. Him. That smile. Those eyes. The way his voice rippled across her skin and made her think of hot summer nights. The gentleness he always showed Sarah.

"Oh, for pity's sake," she muttered and clapped one hand over her eyes.

Emma chuckled softly and took a seat beside her on the small floral damask sofa. "He's getting to you, isn't he?"

Jennifer parted her fingers wide enough to be able to peer at her employer. "Do I have to answer that?"

"Ah, honey," the woman crowed, "you just did!"

Emma Connelly was more than Jennifer's boss, she was a friend—and the closest thing to a mother Jennifer had. Which was why the woman felt completely at ease offering her opinions, whether they were asked for or not. But to be fair, it wasn't nosiness prompting her. It was concern. Emma'd been nothing but kindness itself ever since Jennifer had started working for her. And Jennifer thanked heaven every day that she had a good job with excellent insurance benefits.

But that didn't mean she was going to bare her

soul and start confessing the legion of confusing feelings she had for Emma's stepson.

Apparently, though, she didn't have to.

"Face it, child," the woman was saying with a grin, "you never stood a chance. That man's got his daddy's charm, and add that to how good he looks in his uniform, and, well—" Emma shrugged good-naturedly. "He just plain outgunned you."

"Maybe," Jennifer admitted as a mental image of Chance filled her mind and caused her heartbeat to stagger drunkenly. It took every ounce of her will to combat that feeling, but she managed. "But, Emma, I just can't deal with him now. There's Sarah to worry about and—"

"Darlin'," Emma interrupted, "I won't tell you not to worry, you'll do that anyway. Any mother would. But we've got the best doctor there is to perform the operation. Her hospital bills are taken care of."

Jennifer opened her mouth, but Emma cut her off.

"And no arguments, either. I don't want you worried about meeting deductibles or filling out paperwork." She sat up straight, picked up Jennifer's hand and patted it gently. "As for Chance, I'm not saying you should throw caution to the wind here. But on the other hand, where's the harm in enjoying the company of a handsome man? Where's the harm in having a bit of something for yourself in the middle of a trying time?''

''Emma...'' She didn't mean any harm, Jennifer knew. But Emma didn't understand that even if Jennifer was interested in a man right now, it wouldn't be Chance. All fire and danger, he wasn't exactly the home-and-hearth type. ''Don't go building fantasies, okay? He's only here temporarily and—''

''Honey, I'm not booking the church,'' Emma said softly. ''All I'm saying is that you should try to relax a little. If Chance wants to offer you a strong shoulder to lean on during a hard time, why not take him up on it?''

Jennifer shook her head and smiled. ''You know, women's libbers around the country would howl if they could hear you.''

''Twaddle,'' Emma blurted with a wave of one hand, effectively dismissing hordes of irate feminists. ''There's a difference between being a strong woman and a hard one.'' Standing up, she ran the flat of her hands down the front of her meadow-green Chanel suit while she continued. ''Men and women weren't meant to stand alone, sugar. We complement each other's strengths and weaknesses. That's the whole point.''

''Sure, in a perfect world,'' Jennifer said on a sigh.

''Nothing's perfect, Jennifer,'' Emma said, ''but

it doesn't have to be as complicated as you make it, either.''

"Maybe," Jennifer conceded, more to end the conversation than for any other reason. She knew Emma meant well, but she also knew that her employer, despite her logical mind and keen business sense, was a romantic at heart. And there was nothing Emma would like better than for Chance and Jennifer to strike enough sparks off each other to ignite an eternal flame.

But that wasn't possible. First off, there was no such thing as eternal. No happily ever afters outside of fairy tales. The world just didn't work that way. Yet Jennifer was pretty sure she'd never be able to convince Emma of that. So what was the point of trying?

"Now," the other woman was saying, "it's late. Why don't you go on home to that baby of yours?"

Automatically Jennifer checked her wristwatch and then, frowning, looked up and said, "It's only three, Emma. I work until five."

"You work until I say you're finished for the day," her employer corrected gently. "Now get yourself home."

A little stab of guilt flashed within her briefly as Jennifer thought of the mountains of letters she still had to get signed and mailed. But in the next instant, she decided that if her boss wasn't worried about them, why should she be? Besides, it'd be

fun to get home early and spend some time with
Sarah. Nothing strenuous, of course, she couldn't
risk that. But they could sit on a blanket in the sun
and watch the clouds.

Just thinking about it made her smile, so she
stood up and walked to her desk before she could
change her mind. "All right, I will."

"Good. And don't you come back until after that
baby's well and home again."

Swinging her purse strap over her shoulder, Jennifer turned and stared at her boss. "I can't do that.
The surgery's not for a few days and then—" She
shook her head as if to clear the mental picture of
her daughter's ordeal. "There's too much to do.
The correspondence alone—"

"Poo."

"I beg your pardon?"

"Poo on the letters," Emma said sternly, walking across the room to stand directly in front of her.
Cupping Jennifer's cheeks in her hands, she said,
"I can take care of myself for a while. You spend
time with your baby—*with* pay. And I'll take no
arguments here, honey."

Jennifer had seen that steely look in Emma's
eyes before and knew it signaled the fact that her
mind was made up and already set in concrete.
Slowly, she nodded. "All right, then," she said and
was rewarded with a smile. "Just don't discover
that you can get along without me, okay?"

"Not a chance, honey. Your job'll be here waiting for you."

"Thanks, Emma," she said. "Thanks for everything."

"You're welcome. Now get going."

Jennifer did as she was told and headed for the door. Before she could leave the room, though, Emma's voice stopped her briefly.

"Say hello to Chance for me."

Jennifer glanced back over her shoulder. "He's staying here at the mansion. You'll see him before I will." She hoped.

"Uh-huh," Emma said.

"You're hopeless."

"Hope*ful,* honey. There's a difference."

Shaking her head, Jennifer headed down the hall and toward the staircase. At least with the time off she'd been given, she wouldn't be running into Chance at the mansion anymore. And that would be for the best.

So why wasn't she happier about that?

He'd had no idea it would be this much fun.

Someone should have told him what it was like to spend time around kids.

But, Chance admitted silently, if they had, he wouldn't have believed them anyway. Besides, maybe all kids weren't as terrific as this one.

He looked down into Sarah's big brown eyes and

felt himself go all soft inside. Like her mother, she had the ability to touch something within him that he hadn't even been aware of.

In the last week or so he'd spent so much time with Jennifer and Sarah that he almost couldn't imagine living any other way. How had he gotten along without fierce hugs from tiny arms? How had he managed to get through his whole life without seeing Jennifer's lips curve in a smile? Without seeing her eyes light up with pleasure or the way her hair seemed to damn near sparkle in the sunlight?

"Cha-anz," Sarah wheedled, somehow managing to make his name two syllables. "Sving, Chanz," she said, grabbing a tiny fistful of his pant-leg and shaking it.

"Sving?" he repeated with a laugh. "What are you, Swedish?"

"Sving." Sarah's bottom lip jutted out and Chance laughed. Hard not to. But dutifully, he picked her up, set her onto the swing and locked her into the baby seat. Then moving behind her, he gave her a small push and listened to the musical sound of her laughter.

She was magic. Pure and simple. And some day this kid was going to have the boys lined up outside her door. But as soon as that thought hit, he realized that he wouldn't be around then. He wouldn't know about her first skinned knee, her first bike ride, her first crush, her first date. He wouldn't be there to threaten those hormone-charged teenaged boys. He wouldn't know if she was happy or sad or lonely or laughing.

Hell, she wouldn't even remember him.

And with his next breath, he wondered if Jennifer would remember him—or want to remember him. Strange, for so many years, he'd done his best to be forgettable. He'd never had a relationship that had lasted for more than a week or two. But that had been the plan. He hadn't wanted a woman waiting at home for him. Hadn't wanted to have to worry about anyone but himself.

Well, it had worked like a charm.

There was no one who gave a damn if he lived or died. Except for his brother, of course, and that was completely different. That fact had never bothered him before. But it did now.

Ever since he'd looked into a pair of eyes greener than the sea. Ever since he'd stood alongside a short, curvy woman whose scent was enough to open up every closed door inside him. His back teeth ground together and his mind filled with images of him and Jennifer locked in a full body embrace. Want coursed through him and he knew a desire he'd never known before. This woman had reached him as no one else ever had.

The way she moved, the way she talked, the way she loved her daughter—everything about her made him hunger for what he'd never wanted before. And he knew damn well she wasn't interested. Jennifer and Sarah were a unit. The two of them were a solid wall, shutting out everyone else—including him.

Something cold and empty opened up inside him and to avoid thinking about it, he slowed the swing, unhooked Sarah's belt and picked her up, cradling her against his chest. For one long moment, he enjoyed the sturdy weight of her in his arms and the feel of her soft cheek pressed to his. How was it possible to love so much, so quickly?

And how would he ever leave her and her mother?

Sunshine poured down from a clear April sky and spattered the backyard with dappled shade from the surrounding trees. It was a picture-perfect scene. All that was missing was Jennifer.

Easing back from the baby a bit, he looked her dead in the eye and asked, "So, you think Mommy's going to be mad about the swing set?"

"Mommy?" Sarah's smile widened.

"Yeah, she has that effect on me, too," he admitted. Then, walking around the edge of the newly-installed play gym, he held Sarah at the top of the slide, one arm wrapped firmly around her middle. "You ready?" he asked.

She nodded fiercely, sending her tiny pigtails fluttering in the soft breeze.

"No, don't!"

Startled at the unexpected voice, Chance tightened his hold on the baby and looked across the yard to the back door. Jennifer stood on the threshold and even from a distance, he read the anger in her eyes.

Well, hell. Not exactly the reaction he'd been hoping for.

"What are you doing?" she demanded as she marched across the patio and then the grass. She stopped alongside the slide, reached up and plucked Sarah from his grasp. Tucking her carefully against her body, Jennifer then did a quick check, making sure her daughter was all right.

Chance bit back his irritation. Did she really think he couldn't be trusted to take care of a child?

The baby, picking up on her mother's tension, instantly began to sniffle and cry. Jennifer soothed her with a rocking motion and a few pats on her back—all the while shooting daggers at Chance.

"You're home early," he said, hoping to defuse a situation he didn't entirely understand.

"Just in time, apparently."

"What's that supposed to mean?"

"Where's Mrs. Sorenson?" she asked, looking around the yard as if expecting the older woman to leap up from behind a shrub.

Chance shrugged. "I told her she could go home early and I'd watch the baby."

"*You* told her?" she repeated, swinging her gaze back to his.

"Well, yeah," Chance said, shoving his hands into his pockets and stalling a bit. This wasn't at all how he'd imagined her reaction. Hell, he'd worked his butt off, deciphering instructions that read like Greek and putting this playground together in a matter of hours. He'd expected a delighted coo of appreciation for his efforts and maybe even an enthusiastic kiss. Good thing he wasn't a man to disappoint easily. "I was here and there was no point in both of us watching one little girl, so…"

"You're unbelievable," she muttered, shaking her head and staring at him as though he had three eyes, all of them blind.

At the sound of her mother's upset tone, the baby started crying in earnest. Now she was beginning to hit notes only dogs would hear.

Chance winced in sympathy and tried to figure out where he'd gone wrong. Things had been fine a minute ago. But then, Pearl Harbor on December 6, 1941, had been a pretty quiet place, too.

Jennifer started in on him again and he figured the only sure way to keep from getting killed was to pay attention.

"Mrs. Sorenson is *my* baby-sitter. You don't tell her when to stay or leave."

"But I was here and—" Why was he defending himself? She was being totally unreasonable. Couldn't she see that? Hell, he'd spent all day putting together a child's fantasy of a swing set, complete with slide and sandbox. He glanced over his shoulder at the bright blue-and-green monstrosity and his earlier pride in his handiwork shot right down the tubes.

"Why?"

"Why what?"

"Why *any* of this?" she demanded. "Start with why are you here?"

He shoved one hand along the side of his head and just for a minute, wished that the military would allow longer hair. It would have given him something to grab hold of and yank.

"I had to put the swing set together, for one," he said and before he could elaborate, she cut him off.

"Speaking of that, who told you to buy that in the first place?" Her gaze quickly scraped over his prize before settling back on him again. "I can't afford a swing set."

Okay now. Enough was enough. He hadn't asked her for a dime and she damn well knew it. "I bought it. As a gift. For Sarah."

Jennifer's eyes flashed and he knew this was going to get worse before it got better. Damn it, what was the woman's problem, anyway? Couldn't a man do something nice without being thrown on the barbecue and roasted?

"What?" she asked, sarcasm dripping from the

words. "The store was all out of stuffed animals, so you had to buy a swing set?"

"Sving," Sarah cried, burying her head in the curve of her mother's neck.

"Hah!" Chance shouted in victory and pointed at the crying baby. "*She* likes it!"

"*She* likes ice cream for dinner," Jennifer pointed out. "That doesn't mean it's good for her!"

Sarah let out a wail that tore at Chance's heart.

"Wanna sving…"

"Not now, honey," Jennifer murmured. "You could get hurt. Besides, you have to rest."

"She won't get hurt," Chance said and couldn't quite hide the impatience in his voice.

Her gaze should have sizzled him on the spot. "You can guarantee that, I suppose?"

"No," he said, folding his arms across his chest in a defensive position he felt he needed. Actually, he wouldn't have minded a flak jacket, either. Still, he tried to be the voice of reason. Hell, somebody had to. "But, Jen, kids get hurt all the time. It's a normal part of childhood."

She drew her head back and glared at him through narrowed eyes. Twin spots of red stained her cheeks and her breath came so fast and furious, it was a wonder she didn't hyperventilate. "Sarah's not a normal kid, though, is she? She has a heart condition. She shouldn't be running around or swinging or sliding or whatever else thing you have set up here.''

''I wouldn't have let her get too tired,'' he said, offended that she would think he wouldn't be careful of the child.

''And are you a doctor? You know how much tired is good and how much is bad?''

''No, but—''

''She's *my* daughter, Chance,'' Jennifer said. ''I have to do what I think is best for her.''

''And that's what?'' he asked. ''Basically just sitting in her room?''

''If that's what it takes to keep her healthy, yes,'' Jennifer snapped.

''What kind of life is that?'' he asked, remembering how only minutes ago, Sarah had been laughing and enjoying herself, and wondering how it had all ended so abruptly. And why was he fighting with Jennifer when all he really wanted to do was grab her to him and take her mouth in a slow, deep kiss?

''A safe one,'' she said.

''Jennifer,'' he said gently, moving in closer, laying one hand on her shoulder, ''you have to let her be a kid, too.''

The anger in her eyes flickered out, like a match in a windstorm, and just as quickly a sheen of tears rose up and she blinked frantically, trying to keep them at bay.

"I want to," she said, shaking her head as she looked up at him. "But I can't. I have to keep her safe. She's all I have." Her arms came around her baby and held her tightly. "She's sick. She has to be careful. I have to be careful for her. She depends on me. And I don't know what I'd do if I lost her…"

An invisible fist grabbed Chance's heart and squeezed it, hard. Reaching out, he gathered Jennifer and the baby and drew them into the circle of his arms. Cradling the two females who'd so captured his heart, he stood in the dappled shade and silently made a vow to do everything he could to protect both of them.

"You won't lose her," he whispered as he rested his chin atop Jennifer's head.

She snuggled in closer to him, wrapping her free arm around his middle. "Is that a promise?"

"You're damn right it is," he said and held her tighter, as if the strength of his arms alone could keep the three of them safe from any dangers the world had to offer.

Seven

The next few days flew by in a blur of worry and fear. Jennifer tried to hide her concerns from Sarah, but the baby was just too perceptive. Picking up on her mother's tension, the little girl was whiny and pretty much miserable. If it hadn't been for Chance, the two of them would have driven each other nuts, she was sure.

But Chance *had* been there—nearly every minute. He arrived right after breakfast and wouldn't leave until well after dinner. Since Sarah's medical problems had been discovered, there were any number of people in Jennifer's life who insisted she call them if she needed anything. And undoubtedly, they meant it. But Chance was different. He didn't wait to be asked—he was just there, doing whatever he could to help, even if it was just listening to Jennifer talk, or reading a story to Sarah.

He'd become a part of their lives and she wasn't even sure how it had happened. The cold, logical, reasonable part of her brain kept screaming at her to use caution. To keep a safe distance between them. And she knew darn well she should be listening to such solid advice.

But on the other hand…she looked across the room at the man sitting on her sofa, holding her sleeping daughter, and her heart lurched in her chest. Not easy to stand firm against a man who not only sent sparks of awareness skittering through your bloodstream, but also managed to show such tenderness toward your child.

It had been too long, she told herself firmly, as Chance stood up and smiled at her.

"I think she's down for the count," he whispered, and walked closer to her.

She's not the only one, Jennifer thought, thankful that the one thing Commander Wonderful couldn't do was read minds. "I'll take her," she said and scooped her arms beneath Chance's as he eased the baby into her care. Skin brushed over skin, heat shimmered, breath quickened. Jennifer pulled in a gulp of air and told herself she was being an idiot. She wouldn't make more out of this than there was.

"She's gonna be a heartbreaker one day," he whispered, and she wished he would quit doing that. When his voice was just a hush of sound, the word *sexy* didn't even come close to describing it. Then he added, "Like her mother," and Jennifer felt that odd rushing sensation coursing through her veins. It was as if every ounce of her blood was racing south of the border to pool in one achy spot that throbbed with every beat of her heart.

She swallowed hard, told herself *again* to get a grip and said, "One day's a long way off. Right now I'm just concerned with getting her through the surgery tomorrow and getting her well."

"She will be," Chance said and reached out to skim a lock of her hair behind Jennifer's ear. His fingertips brushed her skin, then slid down the length of her neck before falling away, and Jennifer shivered slightly in response. Heck, she couldn't help it.

A woman would have to be *dead* to not respond to this man.

"I'll be back in a minute," she muttered and escaped into the hallway, carrying her precious bundle. She walked into Sarah's darkened room, giving a quick glance at the butterfly night-light on the wall. Soft, muted colors strained through the butterfly's wings to lay patches of red and yellow and blue across the floor.

Sarah pulled in a breath and Jennifer's heart

caught. She was just so tiny. So helpless. And she was counting on her mother for so much. To keep her safe. And well. And happy. Jennifer was doing her best. Now she could only hope it would be enough.

She laid the baby down in her bed and pulled the blanket up to cover her. Smoothing one hand over her silky, fine hair, Jennifer hummed a series of low-pitched notes that didn't add up to a song and lost herself for a moment in the wonder of watching her baby sleep.

Which probably helped to explain why she didn't hear Chance enter the room until he was standing right beside her at the crib.

"You move too quietly," she said in a barely heard whisper.

"The government pays me to be sneaky," he said just as softly.

She turned her head to look up at him and caught the full effect of the smile he had aimed at her. Something inside her flip-flopped dangerously. Dozens of thoughts spilled through her mind, each of them scrambling to make themselves heard.

Jennifer knew darn well that the best way to a single mother's heart was through her child. How many men, she wondered, had gotten close to a kid in order to win over her mom? Certainly more than a few had tried with her. But she wasn't that easily fooled. Or charmed. Just as she'd seen through them, she was able to see that this man wasn't playing that game.

He genuinely cared about Sarah. It was in his every touch. His every smile. And her daughter was crazy about him in return.

Which only made this situation even more risky. Sarah loved him. That meant that he was already an accepted part of the little girl's life. And that, in turn, meant that he would be missed when he left. And he *would* leave.

Jennifer's heart did that weird little hip-hop again and she wished she could just for a moment reach in and still it. Didn't that flighty organ realize that caring about Chance Barnett Connelly was only asking for trouble?

"What are you thinking?" he asked, and she blinked, drawing herself out of the jumble of thoughts to face the predicament staring right at her.

She took a long, deep breath hoping to steady her voice, then said, "I'm thinking we should get out of this room before we wake her up." Giving Sarah one last glance, Jennifer turned and led the way out of the baby's room and didn't stop walking until she was in the center of the living room. Here, at least, there were bright lights and the radio crackling with the sounds of sixties' rock and roll. There were no patches of soft light, no need for whispers, no need to stand close together in the darkness.

Running her hands up and down her forearms,

she told herself that was a good thing. Too bad her body wasn't listening.

Chance walked directly to her and stopped just an inch or so short of actually touching her. Everything in her ached for him to reach out, grab hold of her and pull her into his arms—so to be sure that didn't happen, she backed up just a step.

"Are you all right?" he asked.

Concern rang true in his voice and she wanted to say, Heck no, I'm not all right. I'm scared. And lonely. And hungry for you. But she didn't. She couldn't.

"I'm fine," she finally managed to squeeze past the knot in her throat. "Just tired. That's all."

"And worried."

She sighed. "That, too."

"What time tomorrow does Sarah have to be at the hospital?"

Oh, God. Desire withered in the space of a heartbeat and was completely swallowed by fear.

"Ten."

"I'll be here at nine."

Her gaze shot to his. She read his determination in his whiskey-colored eyes and knew even before she started arguing with him that she would lose. "You don't have to do that."

"I didn't say I *had* to," he said softly. "I said I'd be here."

And she knew he would be. If there was one

thing she'd learned in the last week and a half, it was that when Chance gave his word, he didn't break it.

"I should try to talk you out of this," she heard herself say. "But I'm not going to."

"Good," he said and flashed his grin at her. "You'd lose."

"There is that," she admitted, since he was a pretty formidable foe. After all, she still had that swing set in her backyard, didn't she? "But that's not the only reason."

"Yeah?"

"Yeah." Okay, so she wasn't ready to admit that she wanted him as badly as a teenager feeling her first blast of hormones. But she could at least be partially honest. "I don't think I could stand taking her in by myself. I mean, I *could* take her, but then I'd be alone while they were getting her ready for—" Suddenly she didn't even want to use the word *operation.* Didn't even want to think about a team of doctors and nurses hovering over her baby's inert body.

Jennifer's eyes squeezed shut, blocking out the mental images that were always too near lately. And when she felt Chance's arms come around her, she simply leaned into his strength, giving quiet thanks that he was there.

"You don't have to be alone," he told her, and

she felt the brush of his breath across the top of her head.

His heartbeat hammered beneath her ear and she clung to the steady, sure beat of it. "I know. Thank you."

He pulled back a bit and when she looked up at him, she saw the slight frown tugging at his lips. "You don't need to thank me for being here for you, Jennifer."

"But—"

"I'm not here as a favor."

"I know that," she said, and swallowed hard. Staring up into his eyes, she watched desire, hunger and compassion flit across their surface and her insides twisted. "I really do know that."

He nodded slowly, keeping his gaze locked with hers. "Good. Because the only reason I'm here with you is because here is where I want to be."

"I'm glad," she said, needing to let him know just what his presence meant to her. She hadn't expected to care about him. Hadn't wanted to care about him. But those feelings were there. She could keep them a secret from him, but there was absolutely no point in trying to pretend to herself.

One corner of his mouth twitched up into a mere shadow of the full glory that was his high-voltage grin—and even that was enough to set off fireworks inside her.

He gave her a hard, tight hug, then let her go

before she could do something stupid like ask him to keep holding her. Good heavens what was happening to her?

For days she'd struggled successfully against these feelings, and now she was suddenly just a passenger on a hormone-driven train running out of control.

Reaching out, he trailed his fingertips down the side of her cheek, then let his hand fall to his side. "Try to get some sleep tonight, okay?"

She nodded.

"I'll see you in the morning."

She nodded again, her throat way too tight for words to slip past. So, in silence, she watched him walk across the room, open the front door and step out, closing it behind him.

Sleep? No way. There wouldn't be any sleep tonight. And it wasn't just fear for Sarah that would keep her wide-awake for hours. It was the desire pumping through her system and the knowledge that tomorrow she'd be with him again. Things were only going to get worse.

"Please try to relax, Mrs. Anderson," the doctor said in his most practiced, kind-to-the-family tone. "I have every expectation that the operation will go smoothly."

Smoothly.

Jennifer wrapped her arms around her middle and

tried to ease the chills that snaked through her bloodstream. But nothing helped. Knowing that her baby would, in just a few hours, be lying on an operating table was enough to give her bone-deep shakes.

"Can I see her again?" she asked and hated that her voice sounded so small and tinny.

The gray-haired doctor with the gentle eyes glanced from her to Chance and back again before he said, "I don't think that's a good idea." When Jennifer would have argued, he interrupted her neatly. "Sarah's being prepped for surgery and it's best if you just leave her with us until after it's over."

Over. An ugly, final word, Jennifer thought, shifting her gaze to the mint-green walls. Why mint green? she wondered absently. She'd always hated the color, and had come to loathe it during the time she'd spent in this hospital as Mike lay dying.

Oh God, *dying.*

She shivered and gulped in a breath.

"How long?" she blurted. "How long will the operation take?"

"Hard to say," Dr. Miller said. "Anywhere from two to six hours, usually."

Usually.

Another doctor's words swam to the surface of her memory and rattled around in her brain. *Just a cookie-cutter operation.* But there was nothing "usual" about this. Her baby was going into an operating room.

Jennifer's stomach pitched suddenly and she clenched her teeth together.

"Thank you, Doctor," Chance said into the silence and stepped up beside Jennifer, dropping one arm around her shoulder and pulling her up tight against him.

Grateful for his support, she leaned into him, and instead of worrying about her knees folding, forced herself to breathe and concentrate on the doctor's words.

"Just try to relax," Dr. Miller said, then winced as if he knew just how ridiculous that advice sounded. "I'll be out to see you as soon as we're finished."

"We'll be here," Chance assured him as the doctor turned and headed for a set of double doors behind which lay Sarah and operating rooms and too many other hazards to think about.

Chance kept one arm around Jennifer and guided her down a short hallway that smelled of antiseptic and fear and into a small waiting room.

A TV perched black and silent on a shelf in the corner of the room. Vinyl couches in appalling shades of orange and green dotted the linoleum floor. Scarred but clean tables held a scattering of magazines and newspapers and a coffee-and-tea-vending machine stood guard near the door. On the far wall, windows and a glass door looked out onto a small plant-filled patio.

He sat her down on the couch nearest the patio and took a seat beside her. They'd already spent hours here at the hospital. His gaze shot to the clock on the wall. One-fifteen. And there were still hours left to go.

Suddenly antsy, he stood up and shoved his hands into his jeans' pockets, looking for change. "Would you like some coffee? Tea?"

She looked up at him, and a cold, hard fist closed around his heart. Her eyes looked battered, terrified. And everything inside him wanted to help...*somehow*. Damn it. There had to be something he could do. At least when he was out on a mission, there were weapons to check and stow, battle plans to be made. Here, he was as useless as the outdated magazines.

"No," she said softly, her gaze sliding toward the doorway that led back to those double doors. "I don't think I could swallow anything."

"I know what you mean," he said and took a seat beside her again. "But we've got a long wait ahead of us."

She sat up straighter and stared directly into his eyes. "Oh, I'm sorry. You've already been here so long. You don't have to stay."

Chance sighed and ran one hand across the top of his head. "That's not what I meant. And I'm not going anywhere. Not till I know that you and Sarah are both fine.''

She folded her hands together and twisted her fingers back and forth nervously until he laid his hand atop hers. ''Good,'' she said, letting her gaze dip briefly before meeting his again. ''I'm glad you're staying. I really don't want to be alone right now.''

''You won't be,'' he said simply, sitting back and pulling her up close. Her arms slid around his middle, her head rested on his chest and it felt…right. Resting his head on the back of the couch, he closed his eyes and thought about the last time they'd seen Sarah. An IV dripping into her arm, her little eyes swollen from crying, she had looked entirely too small to be in that big bed.

But more than the misery of seeing Sarah lying there so helpless was the pain of having to watch Jennifer's terror for her child. He'd wanted nothing more than to ease that pain. To be the one she turned to. To be the one man who could hold her and help her through the worst moment in her life.

And that feeling had completely rocked him.

Opening his eyes, Chance stared up at the acoustical ceiling tiles. He'd never before wanted to be that important to anyone. He'd always prided himself on getting in and getting out. For years he'd kept his relationships shallow enough to make a puddle look deep. He'd figured it was safest that way. He wasn't like Douglas. He'd never wanted an ordinary existence.

He'd never wanted to matter.

To anyone.

And now that felt like the most important thing in the world.

Eight

An hour later, they sat opposite each other in the crowded cafeteria. Jennifer didn't feel like eating, but to placate Chance, she'd agreed to come downstairs and stare at a plate of very unappetizing food.

"You can't eat it through osmosis," he replied. "You'll actually have to put the food in your mouth and chew it."

Sighing, Jennifer dutifully picked up her fork and pushed a series of straight lines through her scoop of mashed potatoes. Then she quit trying altogether and laid the fork down again. Shaking her head, she looked at him and said, "I just can't. I'm sorry."

He nodded and gave her a long, understanding

look. "It's okay. Maybe later." Then he reached across the small table and moved the cup of hot tea closer to her right hand. "But at least drink this."

As a compromise, she took a long swallow, but knew she couldn't drink any more. Her stomach was tied up in knots. There was just no way to put anything in there and not have it turn into an acid bath.

Sitting back in her chair, Jennifer let her gaze drift around the crowded eating area. Doctors, nurses and other hospital personnel sat apart from everyone else. At a long row of tables, they laughed and talked and, in general, looked to be having a great time. To them, this place was just a job. Where they reported daily to work. Where they treated patients and handed out medications and still were able to remain distanced from the lives of the people they touched.

Quite a difference from the rest of the people clustered around the tables. Conversations were muted, strained whispers scraped the air and were interrupted occasionally by a choked-off sob or quiet weeping. Jennifer looked at her fellow prisoners and, noting the desperation in some of their eyes, realized she too looked haunted. By old fears? By new ones?

"What are you thinking?"

She shifted her gaze back to Chance with relief.

"I was…remembering the last time I was in this room."

"Tell me," he said simply.

Maybe he was just trying to get her to talk. To ease the slow passage of time. But whatever the reason, she went along.

"It was almost two years ago," she said and in her mind's eye saw it all again—only this time, she was an observer. "An officer had come by the house to tell me Mike had been shot. They brought me here, sat me down, gave me coffee and told me everything was being done." She could still feel the sympathetic glances thrown her way from the dozens of police officers lining the hallways as they waited for news about Mike's condition.

The police department really was a community. Not unlike the military, she supposed. When one of their number was hurt, the rest of them circled the wagons and did what had to be done.

She fiddled with the handle of her teacup and fixed her gaze on her fingers as she continued. "It was nearly an hour before one of the doctors came in." The memory took a hard jab at her heart and she winced with the remembered pain. "I knew even before he said anything." Her gaze lifted to Chance's again. "It was in his eyes. Grief, pity. He said he was sorry, but that there was simply nothing anyone could do."

Chance reached across the table to take her hand.

She held on to him tightly as if readying to take the big dip on a major roller coaster.

"They took me to him then," she said. "He was lying on a bed, still hooked up to a few machines that beeped along with his heart rate." She paused, then said, "He looked so tired. I even remember thinking that maybe all he needed was some rest."

Chance squeezed her hand.

She laughed shortly, but there was no matching spark of humor in her eyes. "I sat with him and stared at the green walls and counted the beeps and held his hand and told him that I would tell his baby about him." Still holding on to his hand, she sucked in a deep gulp of air and said, "There were two hundred and twenty-six beeps and then he died."

"I'm sorry."

"You have no reason to be sorry," she said, shaking her head gently. "It wasn't your fault."

"I know."

"It was Mike's fault."

"What?"

She saw surprise flicker in his eyes. Pulling her hand free of his, she folded her arms across her chest in an instinctively defensive posture. "Mike loved his job. He loved the rush of danger," she said, and couldn't completely hide the bitter tinge to her voice. "He wouldn't—or *couldn't*—give it up. Not even when I became pregnant and I asked him to. I never understood that about him. I still don't."

"I do," Chance said softly. "When the stakes are high, you're living life to the fullest." Shaking his head, he went on in a whisper meant only for her ears. "You can't appreciate living until you've brushed up against death."

She sucked in a breath, leaned in toward him and said simply, "Bull." And before he could open his mouth to counter that, she went on in a rush of words fueled by her own panic. "You and Mike are so much alike, you could have been twins. And neither of you makes any sense at all." Her voice dropped a notch as she pointed out, "Sarah is upstairs in an operating room right now, 'brushing up against death' as you called it. Think she's appreciating life?"

"That's different and you know it," he said hotly. "She's a helpless child. I'm talking about men. Men who need to test themselves and stand up to a job that needs to be done. If I could change places with Sarah, I'd do it in a heartbeat." His hands curled into useless fists on the tabletop as he went on. "What I do—and what Mike did—they're necessary jobs. Jobs that mean something to thousands of people. Mike kept others safe at a risk to his own safety."

"And died for it."

"True," he said, "and you know damn well he didn't *plan* on that."

"Plan or not," she countered, "it happened. And he left me alone and pregnant." Old pain reared up and with it came an anger at Mike she had thought long dead. Her gaze lifted to the ceiling and the floors above, where her baby lay on an operating table. "And now I'm alone, waiting to hear if my daughter will live or die."

He reached across the table to touch her arm, still tightly folded over her chest. "You're not alone now, Jennifer."

Her gaze locked with his. A tendril of awareness scuttled through her and she fought it down. He was here, with her, true. But not for long. And she'd better remember that.

Jennifer pulled in a long, shaky breath and released it again before saying, "I appreciate you being here, don't get me wrong…"

"But…?" He prodded her to finish that statement.

"But," she said, "you'll be leaving soon."

His mouth tightened into a grim, straight line.

"You're not really a part of this," she added, not unkindly and still felt a stab of guilt when she watched regret flash across his eyes. "You'll be gone soon and I'll be alone again. The reality is, you're just like Mike. You're anxious to be off chasing risks—and in the end, life will go on as it has. Sarah and me against the world. Alone.''

With that, she jumped up, nearly overturning her chair as it scraped loudly over the scratched linoleum. She grabbed her purse and rushed for the doorway, never looking back. If she had, she would have seen Chance hot on her heels.

He caught up with her in the hallway, grabbing her upper arm and pulling her around to face him. A sheen of tears blurred her vision, but even with that, she had no trouble making out the fury on his features. Her heart hammered in her chest until she wouldn't have been surprised if it flew right through her ribcage.

His grip gentled, but was firm enough to tell her that he wasn't letting her go. ''Don't lump me in with your husband, Jen. I'm not him.''

''I know,'' she said, feeling her stomach jitter nervously. Oh, she knew darn well he wasn't Mike. Being this close to him, feeling his strength pouring into her, signaled a sweep of emotion that she'd never known before.

Jennifer had loved her husband. But it had been a comfortable, warm love. A straight road of affection and tenderness, with no highs or lows to interrupt the sameness.

When Chance touched her, fireworks went off in her bloodstream. Her emotions went on a swift, sure climb—but could plummet again at a moment's notice. Haze enveloped her brain and a pounding, throbbing need settled down low in her body, making her want and need things she knew she shouldn't.

No, he wasn't Mike.

He was far more dangerous.

"Just let me go," she said, though even she heard the unsure tone in her voice.

"Not yet," he told her and started for the elevator that would take them back to the third floor and the waiting room. Four other people joined them in the tiny cubicle, so neither of them spoke. Silence reigned until they'd reached their destination. Then Chance led her across the room and out onto the small patio. Only there did he finally release her.

Jennifer rubbed her arm, but could still feel the imprint of his fingers on her flesh. She looked up at him and watched a dizzying array of emotions chase each other across his face, until she wasn't sure what he was thinking, feeling.

Finally, though, he inhaled sharply and blurted, "I'm sorry. I didn't mean to upset you. Didn't want to give you more grief than you're already going through here today."

"I know."

"But, Jen," he went on as if she hadn't spoken, "don't confuse me with your late husband. We're two different men."

"Different," she said, "but so much alike."

"At least in one thing," he admitted, closing the space between them with a single, long step. "We both care for you."

Trouble, her mind screamed, but her body just plain wasn't listening.

He cupped her face in the palms of his hands and bent his head to hers. She stared up at him, like a deer caught in the headlights, and tried to brace herself. But she had no way of knowing what the impact of his mouth on hers would be like, so there was no way she could have prepared for the onslaught of sensations that slapped at her.

A simple, brief, almost tender kiss. Just a brush of his lips across hers.

And the ground rocked beneath her feet.

When he pulled his head back and looked at her, she saw the same dumbfounded expression on his face that she knew was on her own.

"Wow," he said on an exhale of breath.

"Yeah," she agreed and leaned into his strength, grateful for the arms that came around her and held her steady. There would be time enough later to worry about that kiss and what it signified.

For right now, it was enough to know she wasn't alone.

"What's taking so long?" she demanded on her five-hundredth trip around the waiting room. "It's four o'clock. Shouldn't they be finished by now?''

Jennifer had nearly worn a path in the linoleum. She was making Chance tired just watching her. He understood the nervous energy, but he didn't like the wild look in her eyes. Or the pallor of her skin.

Standing up, he crossed to her and ignored the older couple sitting on one of the other couches. They'd been here for less than an hour and hadn't started getting impatient yet. Their time would come, he knew.

But for now he took hold of Jennifer's arm and steered her toward the glass door and the patio beyond. "Come on," he said. "Let's get some fresh air."

She threw a glance at the doorway behind them. "But if the doctor comes in—"

"He'll see us through the glass."

"Okay," she muttered, swiping one hand through her hair.

He opened the door and instantly a blast of cold, fresh wind slapped at them. Jennifer tipped her face into it, closing her eyes and inhaling deeply. Chance simply stared at her, captured by the picture she made. Blond hair tossed and tousled by the wind, her arms folded across her breasts, her chin tilted defiantly up, as if she was somehow challenging the gods themselves.

And he knew he would always remember this

moment and just how beautiful she looked despite the fear crowding her.

"God," she said softly enough that the wind nearly devoured her words, "I needed to get out of that room."

She turned her head to look at him. "Thank you."

"My pleasure," he said and meant it. Damn, it was good just looking at her. Her navy-blue sweater hugged her curves and her faded, worn jeans clung to her legs like a lover's hands. And even now, in this tense situation, she made his body hard and hot and ready for action.

Of course, remembering that too brief kiss they'd shared a few hours ago only fed the fires within.

"I've been thanking you a lot lately, haven't I?" she asked.

"I don't know. Are you keeping score?"

"Maybe I should," she said, and moved toward a bench in the corner of the patio. Studying him, she continued, "You've been great, Chance. Really. But what I'm trying to figure out is why?"

"Why what?"

"Why are you here?" she asked, pushing her windblown hair back from her face with a careless stroke of her hand. "Why are you spending an entire day sitting in a hospital, keeping me company?"

"I already told you that. I'm here because I want

to be here.'' And in fact, he added silently, couldn't imagine being anywhere else.

She shook her head gently and said, ''That's not telling me why, though, is it?''

''Does there have to be a reason?''

''Yeah,'' she said slowly, ''I think there does.''

He reached up and scraped one hand across the back of his neck. Uncomfortable thinking about— let alone *talking* about—his reasons, he managed to shift her attention just a bit. ''Emma stopped by earlier. Grant was here, too. Why's it so unusual to you that *I'm* here?''

She stood up and walked to stand in front of him. Tipping her head back, she caught his gaze with hers and didn't let it go. Chance momentarily lost himself in the green of her eyes and thought that in another time, another place, he just might try to drown in the depths of those amazing eyes of hers.

''What's unusual is,'' she said, ''I've known those people for a couple of years. And I know they care about me and Sarah. But still, they came, they visited and they left. You, though…I've known you less than two weeks and you've been right here beside me through most of this.''

Because he hadn't wanted to leave her. Would have done anything he could to stay with her. But on the other hand, if she'd rather he were gone…if it would make this easier on her, then he'd leave. It'd kill him to go, but he would.

"If you don't want me here," Chance said softly, watching her eyes, looking for a sign, "just say so."

Jennifer laughed shortly. "That is *so* not what I'm saying."

"What exactly *are* you saying, then?" he asked, torn between irritation and frustration.

"I guess I'm saying thanks. Again."

"Well, stop," he told her, his gaze moving over her features with a hungry touch, "I don't want to be thanked. I just want to be here."

Jennifer nodded and gave him a long, thoughtful look. Something flickered in her eyes, but he wasn't sure just what it was. And before he could find out, her gaze shifted slightly to look behind him and her face paled. "The doctor," she said on a tight gasp and headed for the door.

The doctor grinned and Chance felt the weight of the world slide off his shoulders. He dropped one hand onto Jennifer's shoulder in support and listened.

"Everything went fine," Dr. Miller said, looking directly at Jennifer, willing her to relax, believe. "Sarah came through like a trouper."

"Really?" Jennifer asked breathlessly. "She's all right? We can see her?"

The doctor then glanced at Chance before shaking his head slightly. "Not yet. She'll be in recovery for a couple of hours, but once we get her settled into ICU, you can both visit for a few minutes.''

"But she's fine," Jennifer repeated.

"She's fine," Dr. Miller said and reached out to give Jennifer's hand an understanding pat. "She'll be as good as new before you know it."

"Oh God," she whispered brokenly and lifted one hand to cover her mouth. "Oh, thank you, Doctor," she said and gave the man a fierce, hard hug that clearly surprised the hell out of him.

He patted her back awkwardly, sent Chance a sheepish smile then stepped back. "You're welcome. Now why don't you two go have some dinner and relax. I'll come get you when it's time to visit Sarah."

Then he left and Jennifer turned around to look up at Chance. "She's okay."

"She's okay," he repeated, knowing she needed to hear the words again and again.

"Good as new."

"Better," he told her firmly.

"My baby's all right," she whispered and threw herself at Chance, flinging her arms around his neck and holding on tight enough to cut off his air. But he didn't mind in the slightest.

"My baby's all right," she whispered, pulling her head back to look at him through teary eyes. "She really is. And it's over."

"It's over, Jen, and you made it," he said, lifting one hand to stroke his fingertips down her cheek.

"*We* made it," she corrected, then slanted her mouth across his in the kind of kiss he'd been dreaming about for days.

Nine

Lips, tongue, teeth, breath mingling, bodies touching; she gave him everything she had, everything she'd been holding back, everything she'd wanted to give since nearly the first minute she'd laid eyes on him. His hands moved up and down her back, scrubbing over her thick, cable-knit sweater until she swore she could feel the hard strength of his palms against her skin.

He devoured her, taking what she offered and returning it tenfold. He tasted of pulse-pounding excitement and dreams and soft whispers in the night. Her heartbeat thundered in her ears. Her stomach pitched and rolled. Her knees liquefied. She clung to him tightly, kneading her fingers into his shoulders, feeling the warm, solid strength of him surrounding her.

And when she finally broke the kiss and pulled her head back, she was struggling for air. She stared up into those whiskey eyes of his as her lungs heaved in breath after breath. Still dangling from his neck like an oversize pendant, Jennifer grinned up at him and said, "Now *that* was a wow."

"Honey," he murmured, "you ain't seen nothin' yet."

Something hot and rich and delicious coursed through her and she swallowed hard. Now that she'd kissed him, let him know just how badly she wanted him, there would be no going back. She knew that. She was counting on that.

Because now that she knew for sure that Sarah was going to be all right, Jennifer planned to take Emma's advice. She was going to grab a little something for herself in the middle of all of this. And if it hurt more when he left because of it, at least she would have the memory of being in his arms to hold on to.

"You're a man of your word, right?" she asked, letting go of his neck and dropping to her feet.

His eyes went dark and hungry. "Count on it."

"Oh, I am, Commander," she said. "I am."

Then she snaked her arm through his and leaned

into him. "But to make sure I'm at my best, I think I'd better eat something. Keep my strength up."

A slow, wicked smile curved his incredible mouth as he said, "Need strength, huh? Jen, I'm going to buy you the biggest steak in Chicago."

Two hours later, they were back from dinner standing in front of a familiar set of double doors.

ICU.

Jennifer took a deep breath, steadied her nerves and held on tightly to Chance's hand. How odd, she thought absently, that two weeks ago she hadn't known he existed. And now she was hanging on to his hand for dear life. She couldn't even imagine having to go into that room alone.

For two years now, she'd dealt with everything life had thrown at her. She'd been strong for Sarah and had tried to be both mother and father to her baby. It hadn't been easy. In fact, she'd been so lonely at times, she'd have given anything just to hear the sound of another adult voice in the house.

Now, having Chance standing beside her, lending her his strength, giving his quiet support—well, it meant more than she could have said.

"Ready?" he asked quietly, giving her hand a squeeze.

Not quite trusting her voice, Jennifer nodded and moved forward when he opened the door and held it wide for her.

The first thing she noticed were the sounds. A respirator whooshed noisily. And a steady series of beeps shot straight to her soul, reminding her all too clearly of that last night with Mike. But this was different, she reminded herself as she forced her feet to walk to the side of Sarah's bed. These beeps measured the strong, sure beating of Sarah's healed heart.

Jennifer looked down at her baby and a choked-off sob caught in her throat. Lifting one hand, she reached across the metal bars separating her from her child and gently, carefully stroked Sarah's hair. She was sleeping. Sedated, the doctor had said, until she didn't need the respirator breathing for her anymore. There was a tube in her airway, feeding to the respirator, and two IV lines hooked to her small arm for feeding and medication and several other tubes and lines that Jennifer didn't even want to think about.

"Oh, baby," she whispered around a knot of tears filling her throat.

"It looks bad, I know," Chance said quietly, placing his hands on her shoulders. "But she's going to be fine. The surgery's over and now all she has to do is heal."

"She's so tiny. So very tiny," Jennifer said.

"But tough," he reminded her. "Like her mother."

Jennifer reached up and covered one of his hands

with hers. While they stood there in silence, a gray-haired nurse with sharp, kind eyes came in, smiled and busily checked the tubes and machines, read the chart, then said, "Just another minute or two, Mr. and Mrs. Anderson."

"Oh," Jennifer said, startled by the nurse's assumption, "we're not—"

"I know," the nurse said, "you're not ready to leave your daughter yet. But she's going to be sleeping for the next couple of days. She won't know you're here and you could both probably use some sleep."

"Thank you," Chance said, and Jennifer shot him a quick glance.

"I promise," the nurse assured them, "I'll take very good care of your little girl."

"I—we— Can we come back in the morning?"

"You can come back and see her whenever you want to, Mrs. Anderson," the nurse said, before leaving them alone in the room. "You're allowed ten minutes with her every hour."

When the other woman was gone, Chance smiled down at Jennifer. "Didn't want to correct her and start up a conversation," he said, explaining why he hadn't told the nurse who he was.

Jennifer nodded and turned back to Sarah. For the first time since coming into the room, she tried not to notice the tubes and machines and instead, concentrated on Sarah's face. There was a flush of pink color in her cheeks and the ever-present shadows beneath her eyes were almost gone.

She *was* healing. Relief rushed through Jennifer, making her almost light-headed with the force of it. She'd lived with the fear of Sarah's heart problem and now her baby was on the road to real health. A future. She would grow up and get married and have babies of her own.

And Jennifer's own heart swelled with gratitude and joy. Leaning over the bars, she planted a kiss on top of Sarah's head and whispered, "I love you, baby. Sleep tight."

"Champagne was an excellent idea, Commander," Jennifer said as she held her glass out for another refill.

"We're celebrating, aren't we?" he asked and set the bottle down after topping off his own glass.

"Oh God, yes, we are," she said, taking a sip and laughing as the bubbly froth slid down her throat. "I swear, I feel light as a feather. I mean, I know she still has to recover, but she's *going* to recover."

"Damn right she is," Chance agreed and felt the rich, full swell of pleasure fill him. The baby would be fine. Jennifer was happy. And, he thought with a smile, well on her way to being just a little tipsy. But hell, didn't she deserve to be? She'd lived with a suffocating fear for too long and now the worst was over.

Moonlight streamed in through the lace curtains hung at the windows. Music drifted from the stereo on the wall and soft pools of lamplight dotted the floor. Jennifer lounged back against the sofa cushions, watching him with a soft, secretive smile on her face.

"What is it?" he finally asked.

"Just thinking," she said as she stood up and set her glass of champagne down on the coffee table.

"Well, this could be dangerous, then," he muttered, only half kidding. "Usually when a woman says she's been thinking, a man ends up in trouble."

She shook her head and her blond hair fell in gentle waves about her face. "Not this time."

"Really?" he asked, standing perfectly still as she approached him. "And why's that?"

"Because," she said, staring up into his eyes, letting him see the full force of her desire, "I'm thinking about that date we made earlier tonight."

"Is that right?" Everything inside him went hot and still. He wanted her more than he'd ever wanted anything or anyone in his life. And yet…Chance sighed and said what he had to say if he was going to be able to look himself in the mirror. "Jen," he started, "you've had a lot of champagne and—"

"Not that much," she argued, smiling up at him.

"Enough that it might make a difference in any decisions you make in the next couple of minutes." Damn it.

"You're the real deal, aren't you?" she asked and took yet another step closer until all that was separating them was the slender cord of desire vibrating between them. "An officer and a gentleman. Just like the movie."

Uncomfortable with that comparison, he shrugged it off. "I just don't want to take advantage of you when you're in a vulnerable frame of mind."

Jennifer laughed, a low, deep, throaty sound that rippled through the air and danced along every one of his nerve endings.

"What's so funny?" he asked.

"You," she said, taking his left hand in her right and putting her left hand on his shoulder. "For heaven's sake Chance, *I'm* the one making advances here."

"Yeah," he said, through clenched teeth. "I noticed that."

"Good. I was afraid you weren't paying attention."

"Oh, you've got my attention, honey."

"And I intend to keep it."

"No problem," he assured her.

"Dance with me," she whispered, tipping her head back and smiling up at him.

He arched one eyebrow. This he hadn't expected. "You want to dance?"

"Yes, I want to dance. With you. Now."

"Yes, ma'am," he said and pulled her closer. He was all in favor of anything that would keep her in his arms. Holding her tightly to him, he felt the press of her breasts against his chest and the warm grip of her hand in his. Her breath puffed across the base of his neck, starting a small fire that erupted in his bloodstream and quickly spread, sending heat to parts of his body that didn't really need the encouragement.

"You feel so good," she whispered a moment later.

"Not half as good as you do, Jen."

"I like that."

"What?"

"When you call me Jen," she admitted. "No one else ever has."

Something shifted inside him. Maybe it was the old loneliness sliding out of its familiar spot. Maybe it was the wall he'd built around his heart beginning to crumble. All he could be sure of was that he'd never been happier than he was at this moment, dancing in the soft light with Jen. He released her hand long enough to tuck his fingers beneath her chin and tilt her face up to his. Meeting her sea-green eyes, he said, "I'm glad I'm the first."

Then, still keeping their gazes locked, as if looking away might mean his life, Chance lowered his head and slanted his mouth across hers. The kiss began slowly, tenuously, as they rediscovered the magic they'd found only hours ago.

Electricity sizzled between them.

Heat exploded.

Hearts pounded.

And in seconds the gentleness was gone, replaced by a driving need that eclipsed everything else.

He couldn't get enough of her. That one thought slammed into Chance's brain over and over again. He needed her as badly as he needed his next fevered gulp of air. No, more. He needed her more. Breathing would mean nothing if he didn't have her.

His hands swept down her back to the hem of her sweater and then beneath it and up, up along the column of her spine, his fingertips tracing patterns on her silky flesh. She shivered in his arms and that tender response pushed him further, higher. With one quick, practiced flick of his fingers, her bra came undone and his hands shifted to take advantage. He cupped her breasts in his palms, never taking his lips from hers, never ceasing the greedy plunder of her warm, sensuous mouth. He tasted her and while his tongue danced with hers, his thumbs circled her rigid nipples, drawing a moan from the back of her throat that instantly set his soul on fire.

Chance groaned, too, knowing that she was drawing everything from him. Feelings, desires, things he'd banked carefully for years were scuttling to the surface and there was nothing he could have done to stop them, even if he'd wanted to.

One corner of his mind still shouted at him to throw up his defenses. To batten down the hatches and prepare to be assaulted. But it was too late. The years he'd spent alone were forgotten in the rush of desire.

He pulled his head back and, gulping in air, looked down at her. Her eyes were closed, and her mouth opened on a sigh as his fingers tweaked her nipples, tugging gently at the sensitive flesh.

''Chance,'' she whispered, her fingers digging into his upper arms for support. ''Chance, that feels so good. So...wonderful.''

His throat tightened. Just watching the play of emotions dart across her features was enough to swamp him. He felt stronger, braver, more sure than he ever had been before. And at the same time, his knees were weak and everything inside him was humbled, just to be given the gift of touching her.

''There's more,'' he promised, his voice low and deep, scraping against his throat. ''So much more.''

''Yes,'' she said, her eyes fluttering open to look up at him. ''Give me more. I want it all. Everything there is.''

"Everything," he promised and dropped to his knees in front of her.

Caught by surprise, Jennifer swayed into him slightly and he shifted his hands to her waist, holding her until she found her footing again. When her hands came up to his shoulders, he let his fingers glide along the waistband of her jeans, dipping just beneath the worn denim to dust across her flesh. "So soft," he murmured, "so smooth."

Her quick intake of breath was the only response, but it was enough.

Chance unbuttoned her jeans, then slowly pulled the zipper down, revealing a tiny scrap of blueberry-colored silk panties. Blood rushed to his groin and a fog rose up in his brain. The haze dropped over his vision but he blinked it back, determined to see her.

She swayed again and he gripped her upper thighs before tipping his head back to look up at her.

"Chance?" she asked, a world of questions wrapped in only his name.

"I promised you everything," he reminded her. "And this is just the first step."

Her hips rocked as she moved unconsciously into his touch. "But I want to feel you inside me."

Heat.

Pure, hot as the sun, molten lava, heat poured

through him. He tightened his hold on her thighs. "Oh, you will, honey. We *both* will. Trust me."

She nodded and gave him a half smile that reached down inside him and quickly turned him inside out. "I do, you know," she whispered. "Trust you."

Chance groaned again, tore his gaze from hers and turned his attention back to that scrap of silk. He needed it off her. Needed to see beneath it. To the treasures beyond. To the very heart of her.

He gave one strong tug and her jeans slid down her legs, leaving her standing before him with nothing between him and heaven itself but that small triangle of blue silk.

She gasped and his hands slid up her thighs again, along the backs of her legs until he was cupping her bottom in his palms.

Jennifer held her breath as his incredibly strong hands squeezed her behind with tender firmness. She was caught. Imprisoned in his grip. And she loved it.

The feel of his hands on her. The whisper of his breath as his mouth neared her body. The tension in the room. The pounding of her own heart that nearly choked the last breath from her.

She tightened her hold on his shoulders and looked down, wanting to watch him take her. Needing to see this man touch her in the most intimate way imaginable. And she wanted to remember it all. Everything about this moment was now chiseled deep in her mind. Every time she entered this room she would recall this moment. She would be able to see him, kneeling in front of her. His mouth nearing her body. She would feel his hands on her backside. She would experience the nearly paralyzing sense of anticipation.

And she would want to feel it all again.

But tomorrow would take care of itself, she well knew. And all of the tomorrows after it were yet to be faced. For now, there was him. His touch. His scent. His—

She sucked in a deep breath as his mouth covered her. He hadn't bothered to pull her panties down, but was taking her right through the silk fabric. She felt his hot breath. Felt the gentle scrape of his teeth as he explored her body. Felt the strength of his fingertips as he held her tightly and pulled her even closer to him.

His tongue scraped across the silk, creating a sensation unlike anything she'd ever known before. Wet heat surrounded her, tempting her, toying with her. She rocked in his hands, moving closer, but he continued his teasing. Again and again, he licked the damn silk that kept her from feeling him completely.

"Chance..." she whispered, her fingers clutching at his shoulders. "Please..."

He pulled away from her long enough to say, "Please what?"

Jennifer tossed her hair back out of her eyes, looked down at him and read the silent command in his amber gaze. He wanted her to say it. Wanted to hear her say how much she wanted it. How much she wanted *him*.

Body on fire, mind whirling, she gave him the absolute truth. "I want you to taste me."

Flames danced in his eyes, and, in the next heartbeat, he yanked her panties down and took her.

She gasped aloud and forced herself to keep her eyes open. She watched him take her. Watched his mouth claim her in a way that no one ever had before. His lips and tongue and teeth tortured her gently. He pushed her so high, she thought she would never be able to breathe again and she didn't care. All Jennifer wanted, all she could think about was his next intimate kiss. The next swipe of his tongue.

Her knees wobbled and she locked them, refusing to give in to any weakness that might deprive her of the rippling sensations already beginning to build within. His breath, hot and wild, brushed against her most sensitive flesh. He tasted and suckled and teased, and her world spun while fireworks exploded inside her, shattering what was left of her control, sending splinters of brilliant color flashing across her mind.

He shifted his grip on her and slipped one finger into her depths.

''Chance!'' His name shot from her throat on a choked-off gasp.

He didn't answer. He only redoubled his efforts, using his tongue to send her higher, faster, further than she'd ever been before. He caressed her body from the inside as he tortured her on the outside and Jennifer wanted him never to stop.

If she could have found a way to spend the rest of her life like this, she would have signed up for it. But even as she thought it, she felt her muscles tighten, tingle, and knew her climax was near.

She rocked her hips, moving in closer. She shifted one hand to cup the back of his head, holding him to her, as if afraid he would stop and leave her unfulfilled.

When the first shattering wave of completion took her, she surrendered to it, gloried in it and knew she was safe in the circle of his arms.

Ten

Chance stood up, caught her as she leaned into him and swung her up into his arms. One-handed, he swept her jeans and panties off her legs and let them fall to the floor.

"Okay," she said on a sigh as she looked up at him, "was that SEAL training or just a natural gift? Because I'm here to tell you, I'm impressed."

He grinned, despite the fever raging in his bloodstream. Her eyes were glazed, her cheeks flushed and even in his arms, her body still trembled with the force of her release. And it wasn't nearly enough. Not even close.

"You think *that* was impressive?" he asked,

shaking his head. "I keep telling you, Jen, you ain't seen nothin' yet."

She reached up, entwined her arms around his neck and whispered, "Wa-hoo!"

"That's the spirit," he muttered and tightened his grip on her as he headed across the living room toward the hallway. He'd waited as long as he possibly could. He had to have her. Here. Now. Before he lost what was left of his mind.

"Uh-oh."

His steps faltered and he glanced down at her. "Uh-oh? Not exactly what a man wants to hear about now, Jen."

"I know," she said, tossing her hair back out of her face, "but better now than in a few minutes."

"Okay, you have my attention," he said, stepping into her bedroom and walking directly to her bed. His fingers stroked the soft skin of her thigh while he waited for whatever news was important enough to interrupt this.

And he hoped to hell she wasn't going to say something like she'd changed her mind. That piece of news might be just enough to kill him.

One of her hands slipped from his neck, and she trailed her fingertips down his shirtfront, and Chance swore he could feel her touch right through the fabric of his shirt. Oh yeah. If she'd changed her mind, he was a dead man.

"I don't have any, um..." She stopped, shifted

her gaze to one side and muttered thickly, "this is nuts. I can have sex and I can't say *condoms?*"

He threw his head back and let loose a short, sharp bark of relieved laughter. "That's it?" he asked. "That's the 'uh-oh'?"

"Isn't it enough?"

"You remember when we stopped on the way here to pick up the champagne?"

"Yeah..."

He shrugged. "I picked up a little something else, too."

"Really?" Her eyes widened.

"Oh yeah." Chance laid her down onto the bed, dug in his pocket for a small package and tossed it onto the nightstand, then stretched out alongside her.

"My hero." She turned her head to smile at him. "You're really something, aren't you?"

"I try."

"I didn't realize that 'Be prepared' was a SEAL motto."

"Hey," he said, pulling her closer, "I started out a Boy Scout."

Her hands skimmed down, to his waistband, then she grabbed his shirt and pulled it free of his pants. "Boy Scout, huh?" she said, sliding her hands up beneath the fabric to caress his skin, "then I guess that means you also know how to start fires?"

His smile widened as he gave in to the need pulsing within. With one hand, Chance caressed the length of her thigh, watched her shiver, then murmured, "And I won't even need two sticks."

She arched into him, lifting her leg to place it atop his. "No," she whispered, "you sure won't."

He took her mouth, plundering her, tasting her, their tongues mating in a tangled dance that tortured as well as pleased. Chance's hands scooped up the bottom of her sweater until he had to tear his mouth from hers long enough to rip it and her bra from her body.

Then finally, finally, she was naked to his gaze and he feasted on her. The lush curves and valleys, the smooth silkiness of her skin. His fingers moved to encircle her nipples and when her head tipped back into the mattress, he muffled a groan. So responsive. So eager for his touch. He dipped his head to claim first one rigid nipple and then the other. Back and forth, he divided his attentions, driving her higher and higher. He heard her soft, whispered gasps, felt her body tremble, delighted in the way she moved into him, silently offering more of herself. And he wanted it all. He wanted to bury himself within her, he wanted to feel her body welcome him, surround him and hold him captive for the next fifty years or so. He wanted—no, *needed* to be a part of her. To be linked so intimately that she would never be whole without him again.

As these thoughts and more raced through his

brain, Chance tried both to make sense of them and to ignore them. He'd never felt this before. This...connection. It was as if he could feel her pleasure as well as his own. She moved and it touched him. She whispered and his heart responded. She sighed and his soul went up in flames.

Too much, one corner of his mind shouted. Not enough came the answer.

It would never be enough. He knew it even as he pulled back from her, stood up and yanked his clothes off. He felt it in her hot gaze. Knew it in the rush of blood to his groin. Recognized it in his pounding heart. Eternity with this woman would never be enough. He felt as though he'd been waiting for this moment, this night, most of his life.

And now that it was here, he told himself as he covered her body with his own, he wasn't going to ruin it by thinking so damn much!

Her thighs parted as he came over her and he relished the welcome. He knelt between her legs, smoothing his hands up and down her body, exploring every inch of her, reveling in the soft, exquisite beauty of her skin.

She held up her arms toward him and breathlessly said, ''Be inside me, Chance. Be deep inside me.''

''That's just where I want to be, Jen,'' he told her and reached for the condoms. Tearing one free, he opened the foil envelope, rolled it on and then turned his attention back to her. His hands scooped down her body to the small triangle at the juncture of her thighs. Delicately, deliberately, he stroked her center and smiled when her hips lifted off the bed.

"Chance!"

"Let it come again, honey," he urged her.

"No," she said, tossing her head from side to side on the mattress. Breathlessly, she continued, "Not without you. This time it has to be with you."

He slipped one finger, then two, into her depths. The warm, damp heat of her nearly pushed him over the edge, but somehow he managed to hang on to his tattered and unraveling control. He wanted her in a frenzy. Wanted her desperate for completion. Wanted her to want him as badly as he did her.

Only then would he allow himself entry to her body.

Again and again he stroked her, caressed her, his thumb rubbing across the most sensitive spot on her body until she whimpered. She planted her feet. Her hips rocked into his touch. Her hands fisted in the coverlet. She bit down hard on her bottom lip and groaned as he quickened his gentle assault.

And when the first tremor began shaking through her, Chance pushed his body into hers. He felt her muscles clamp down around him, felt the contractions, felt her release quickening within her. And it almost undid him.

He moved, creating a rhythm that Jennifer instantly matched. Her fingers clawed at his back. Her heels ground into his waist. She cried out as the last of her climax crested, and a heartbeat later he followed after her, groaning her name as he found a peace he'd never known before.

An hour or two—or five, who was counting?— passed before Jennifer staggered from the bedroom. Every muscle in her body felt weak and soft and, she thought, extremely limber.

A smile curved her lips as she slapped one hand on the wall for support and kept walking toward the kitchen. In the living room, the lights were glowing softly and music still drifted from the stereo that had been set to repeat.

"Should turn those off," she muttered and thought about the few extra steps it would take to accomplish the task. "Nope," she decided, preferring to use what was left of her strength to get to the kitchen where she could find something to eat.

Chance was still sleeping, but who could blame him? After the third time they'd made love, he'd simply collapsed. Of course, so had she. It was only her growling stomach that had wakened her. And once it was fed, she'd stumble back into bed and cuddle up next to her incredibly talented lover.

"Lover?" she said the word out loud, trying it on for size, so to speak. But then, what else could she call him? He wasn't her boyfriend. Nor a fiancé. And he certainly wasn't a one-night stand. So, she told herself, *lover* was definitely the right word.

But how strange. She'd never thought of herself as the type of woman to take a lover. She'd always been the good girl. The obedient daughter. The loving wife. The dedicated mother. The brave widow.

Frowning at that thought, Jennifer hit the light switch over the oven, preferring its tiny bulb to a blast of overhead lighting that just might blind her at the moment. Brave. Hah. She hadn't been brave. It wasn't as if she'd had a choice. She'd simply done what she'd had to do.

Just as she had tonight.

Oh, she'd needed this night with Chance desperately. She knew darn well it wasn't going anywhere, but that didn't seem to matter. Tonight would be enough. She would make it be enough. And if her heart ached for him after he'd gone, then she'd salve it with the memories of this one incredible night.

She pulled the refrigerator door open, bent down and looked inside, as if waiting for an invisible hand to offer her something. Frigid air wafted across her naked body and she laughed to herself.

"Naked in the kitchen."

"Sounds good," Chance said from the doorway. "I'll have one of those."

She gasped and straightened up. "You scared me. I thought you were sleeping."

One dark eyebrow lifted. "I was resting my eyes."

She laughed. "Then you should have them checked, because your eyes snore."

He gave her a rueful half smile and reached up to shove one hand along the side of his head. Jennifer's gaze locked on to the play of muscles beneath his bare skin and something inside her went hot and achy.

Good heavens, she thought, surprised at herself. *Again?*

He must have seen the flash of desire in her eyes, because he walked toward her, leaned across the half door of the refrigerator and gently tweaked one of her nipples.

Her knees wobbled.

"I woke up and you were gone," he said, scraping the pad of his thumb across the tip of her nipple.

She swallowed hard, pulled in a shaky breath and managed to choke out a few words. "I was hungry."

"So'm I," he said, cupping her breast in the palm of one hand.

"Oh my," Jennifer whispered on a long exhale of breath.

He eased his way past the open refrigerator door and backed her up against the wall. His hands cupped her breasts, his fingers tugged and pulled at the tips of her nipples until Jennifer ached all over and felt as if her body was burning up from the inside out.

She flattened her palms against the wall behind her, instinctively looking for something to hold on to. Cold air sighed from the refrigerator and pooled around them, locking their heated bodies in a chilly grip.

"I want you again," Chance said, burying his face in the curve of her neck. His teeth nibbled at her flesh and goose bumps raced down her spine.

"I want you, too," Jennifer admitted as he straightened up to look down into her eyes. "What's happening to me? To us?"

"Who cares?" he asked, letting one hand slide down the length of her body to cup her hot center.

"Oooh, not me," she said. "Not at the moment, anyhow."

"That's my girl," he whispered and lifted her off her feet. Turning around, he sat her down onto the butcher-block cooking island in the middle of the room.

The cool, smooth wood felt weird against her behind, but Jennifer was beyond caring. All she knew was that she had to have him again. Had to feel him inside her. Needed to experience the wild rush of his body dancing within hers.

"Now, Chance," she whispered, grabbing his head and pulling him close enough to kiss. "Be a part of me now."

"Oh yeah," he muttered and kissed her, taking her mouth in a kiss that electrified her.

Parting her thighs, she took him inside her and wrapped her legs around his middle, holding him in place. He rocked against her and she arched forward, meeting his every thrust and countering it with one of her own. She'd never known such hunger before. Never known the need he instilled in her.

Heck, she'd never walked around naked in her own house before him. Now she couldn't imagine ever wearing clothes again—not if it would keep him from her.

Her arms went around his neck and she caressed his tongue with hers, gave him her breath, her soul, her heart. His rhythm set and familiar now, she moved with him as easily as though they'd been doing this for years. And when he clutched at her and spilled his body into hers, she held on tightly and rode the wave of pleasure that only Chance could create.

But a moment later, that mood was shattered by two little words.

"Uh-oh."

''That's my line,'' she whispered, leaning her forehead against his chin.

Chance lifted her chin with the tips of his fingers until she was staring up at him. ''Where are we?'' he asked gently.

She cleared her throat, blinked and gave a quick look around. ''The kitchen?''

''Yeah. And where are the condoms?''

She thought about that for a long minute, then, ''Uh-oh.''

''Exactly.'' Chance disentangled himself from her and took a step back. Perfect Barnett, he told himself. Now that it's too late, keep your distance.

She scooted off the edge of the butcher-block island and reached out to close the refrigerator. ''Well,'' she said in what he thought was a perfectly reasonable tone, considering the situation, ''there's nothing to be done about it now, is there?''

''That's it?'' he asked. Hell, any other woman he'd ever known would be either screaming at him or throwing something at his head. Something heavy and preferably sharp.

''What do you want me to do?'' she asked, giving him a shrug. ''Throw myself into a lake? Besides, you don't have to worry anyway. I started taking the pill six months ago to regulate my cycle. So, I'm safe.'' She looked at him, a silent question in her eyes. ''As long as you're healthy.''

"I am," he said quickly, at least wanting to ease her mind on that score.

She nodded. "Then there's no problem."

"But—" He shook his head. No way. No way did he deserve to be let off this easy. "Damn it, this was my fault. I should have kept my head. Should have been careful."

"We were careful," she told him, then gave him a brief, wry smile. "Well, mostly."

"I didn't say 'we,'" Chance said softly, "I said 'me.' I'm the one who should have been careful. I lost control. For the first time in memory, I lost control."

Jennifer inhaled sharply, let it out again and grabbed one of his hands. "You know, Commander, I think that may be one of the nicest things anyone's ever said to me."

"Most women would be yelling about now, you realize that, right?"

She shrugged bare shoulders. "I'm not most women."

"You got that right."

"And I'm just having too good a night to ruin it now."

She turned around then and walked to the counter. Lifting the top of the cookie jar, she reached inside, pulled out a chocolate-chip cookie and took a bite. After she chewed and swallowed, she said, "But since I'm safe and you're healthy, why stress about something that's over and done?"

"You're amazing," he said simply.

"Thanks," she said and took another bite. "Right now I feel pretty amazing."

He watched as her tongue swept crumbs off her bottom lip, and an instant ache of need splintered through him. Then she walked across the room again, opened the fridge and got out the milk.

Handing it to him, she dived back inside. "So? Are you hungry?" she asked. "Want to split a sandwich?"

"Sure," he muttered thickly, his gaze locked on the curve of her bare behind. Food was the furthest thing from his mind. Right now his brain was filled with jumbled images and thoughts.

He'd just dodged a bullet and he knew it. Thanks to birth control pills, he wasn't in imminent danger of becoming a father—so he should be happy.

The problem was, he wasn't. Well, not entirely. At any other time, with any other woman, he'd be doing a mental happy dance about now. But this was Jen. And a part of him he hadn't known existed before tonight was damned sorry he hadn't made her pregnant.

Eleven

The next week passed in a blur.

Jennifer had never been more grateful for an understanding employer. If she had worked for anyone besides Emma Connelly, she wouldn't have been able to spend nearly every waking minute at the hospital.

Of course, she told herself as she walked into the waiting room with two steaming cups of coffee, her gratitude wasn't limited to Emma. Her gaze went straight to Chance, sitting on one of the vinyl couches. Smiling, she silently admitted that no one had ever looked more out of place. His long, denim-clad legs stretched out in front of him and crossed at the ankles, he had his brawny arms folded across his chest and a thoughtful expression on his face as he stared out the glass doors opposite him. He looked too...powerful, too lean, mean and strong to be locked up in this room. He had an air about him that sang of danger and wild places.

A whirlpool opened up in her stomach, spinning, churning, as she realized the truth in that thought. He *was* danger. Somehow, over the last couple of weeks, she'd been able to put that little slice of reality out of her mind. But the truth was, Chance was a temporary situation. Any day now he'd be taking off, headed for God knew where—into heaven knew what kind of risk.

Her fingers tightened around the paper cups until she wouldn't have been surprised to find them plunging right through the flimsy barrier into the hot coffee. What had she been thinking? What had she allowed to happen here?

And how would she ever be able to stand his leaving?

He looked up, as if sensing the turmoil in her mind, and his amber gaze locked with hers. Even from a distance, she felt the slap of the heat simmering in those golden depths.

"Something wrong?" he asked, pushing himself to his feet. "Is it Sarah?"

"No," she said quickly, wanting to assure him that the baby was fine. They'd looked in on her only a few minutes ago and she'd been sleeping in her hospital-issue crib.

"Good," he said, giving her the slow smile she'd come to know so well over the last couple of weeks. "I was worried that maybe they'd taken her back to ICU."

"Nope," she replied, forcing a light tone she didn't feel into her voice. "Doctor's orders still stand. She can go home tomorrow."

"Then why the long face?" he asked, taking the cup she offered him.

"Nothing." It was a lie. And a bad one, apparently. She saw it in his eyes. He didn't believe her.

He reached out and stroked her hair back from her face. He flicked a quick glance at the couple on the other side of the room, but they were fascinated with the news program playing on the television. Still, he kept his voice low when he spoke, so they wouldn't hear.

"There's something bothering you, Jen. Tell me."

She sucked in a long, shaky breath and blew it out again. Then shifting her gaze, she studied the oil slick on the surface of her coffee rather than look into his eyes. He was just too good at this. He'd worm it out of her and she wasn't ready to say what she was thinking. Might never be ready.

Heck, she'd just figured it out for herself: Somehow, she'd let Chance into her heart and now she had to find a way to get him out of it again.

"I'm just thinking about Sarah and how long it will take her to recover," she said softly. "That's all." And instantly guilt pooled inside her. What kind of rotten mother was she, to use her sick little girl as an excuse to her lover?

Oh, good grief, this has gotten way out of control.

"Hell, honey," he said, accepting this lie and pulling her up close to him, "the docs say that a few days' rest and she'll be better than new."

Jennifer latched on to that and clung to it as if it were a bobbing life preserver tossed into a raging sea. "It'll take longer than a few days," she said, more to herself than to him. She'd done plenty of thinking about this. She had to be careful with Sarah. Make sure the little girl didn't do too much, run too fast or play too hard. She didn't want Sarah taxing her new strength. Better to take it slow. Easy. Shaking her head, she said aloud, "She'll have to be careful."

"Well, sure," he replied, then paused for a sip of coffee. "No playing football for at least ten years."

She heard the amusement in his voice and bristled. "I mean it. This was a serious operation. She'll need time to recover. To heal."

He frowned down at her, concern sparkling in

those amazing eyes of his. "Honey, she's been healed by this operation."

"The problem's been *fixed*," she said. "But she hasn't healed. Not yet."

Chance watched Jennifer and wished he knew what she was thinking. In the last week they'd grown closer. At least, he'd felt that they had. Every day they spent together at the hospital, and every night they were together in her bed. He'd found something with Jennifer that he'd never thought to find. A connection. A sense of belonging that he hadn't known since he was a child.

For so long now, his only family had been Douglas. His one tie to the world. And it had always been enough. Until recently. Now, though, he knew he wanted more. He wanted to matter. To count for something beyond his job. He wanted to be an integral part of Jennifer's and Sarah's lives.

And as that thought struck home, he knew he needed them to want him, too.

Jennifer gave him a smile that looked too distracted to be real. There was something going on here that she wasn't talking about. Something beyond worries over Sarah.

And it bugged the hell out of him that she obviously didn't want to tell him about it.

"Jennifer?" A soft, female voice cut into his thoughts and he looked up as Tara Connelly Paige walked across the floor toward them.

"Tara," Jennifer said, holding out one hand toward the woman, "it's so nice of you to come by."

"Well," Tara said, nodding hello to Chance before returning her gaze to Jennifer, "I just wanted to bring a little gift for Sarah." She held out a small teddy bear in a ballerina tutu.

"She'll love it," Jennifer said. "Thank you."

"You're welcome. Hey, we single moms have to stick together, don't we?"

"You bet," Jennifer said, casting a glance at Chance.

Tara checked the elegant gold watch on her wrist and rolled her eyes as she said, "I can't stay. But I did want you to know we're all thinking of you. Especially me. I know just how hard it is to take care of your baby alone. To do all the worrying yourself."

"I know you do." Jennifer gave the woman's hand a squeeze. "And I appreciate it."

"Kiss Sarah for me, will you? Chance, good to see you again." Tara turned for the door, her high heels clicking against the linoleum. Glancing back over her shoulder, she promised, "I'll come to see you both at home in a couple of weeks."

"That'd be great." Jennifer watched the woman walk out the door and disappear around a corner.

"That was nice," Chance said and his deep rumble of a voice set her insides to shaking.

"Yes, it was."

"Are you sure you're all right?" he asked.

"Fine," she murmured, staring down at the ballerina bear in her hand. But she wasn't fine. There were too many thoughts racing around in her mind for that.

Single mom. Those two words had struck a chord that was still echoing deep inside her. She hadn't realized it until just now, but the truth of the matter was that she hadn't been truly on her own since Chance had blown into town—and into her life. For the past three weeks he'd always been there. For Jennifer *and* for Sarah.

Heck, her baby daughter prattled constantly about "Chanz," even referring to him occasionally as Daddy. An ache settled around Jennifer's heart as she silently admitted just how important Chance had become in their lives. And how big a hole he was going to leave behind when he left. As he would, any day now. His wound was almost healed. Pretty soon, he'd be heading out to put himself in the line of fire again.

Darn it, she hadn't asked for this. She didn't want to care for him. She didn't need this kind of pain again. She needed someone safe. Someone boring. Someone who would be home every evening at 5:15. She absolutely *didn't* need another warrior.

Her fingers curled into the bear's soft stuffed body. It was a shame, then, wasn't it, that it was the warrior she loved?

* * *

Two days later, Chance pulled into Jennifer's driveway and thought to himself how much it felt like coming home. A strange sensation for a man who hadn't known a real home since he was a kid.

Strange…but nice.

He threw the gearshift into Park, turned off the engine and set the parking brake. Then he just sat there. Staring at the house. Picturing Jennifer and Sarah inside. And imagining himself, thousands of miles away.

Scowling, he grabbed the steering wheel with both hands and squeezed until he wouldn't have been at all surprised to see the damn thing snap in two. It didn't help.

He was leaving. He had his orders. Just that morning he'd spoken to his commanding officer. In just a few short days, he'd be gone, headed back out into the unknown—and Jennifer and Sarah would continue their lives without him. In time he'd be nothing more than a pleasant memory. And not even that to Sarah. She was too young. She'd never remember him. Pain sliced at him. Chance tried to ignore it, but this ache went far deeper than a simple bullet wound.

This pain would follow him for the rest of his life. He knew it. And damned if he was going to allow that to happen. He wanted Jennifer. Needed her. And he knew damn well that she felt the same way.

Opening the car door, he stepped out, slammed it, then headed for the house like a man on a mission. Mentally, he started going over all of the arguments she might make and coming up with counterpoints for each one. This was the most important battle he would ever engage in and he was determined to win.

He knocked on the front door as a matter of courtesy, but didn't wait for an answer. Opening it, he stepped into the house that held so many of his hopes and dreams. Sunlight streamed through the curtain to lie in lacy patches on the floor. Warmth reached out for him and dragged him close. Closer than he'd ever been to such coziness.

''Daddy!''

Instantly, Chance's heart swelled. His gaze shot to the fresh-faced toddler already pushing herself up from the floor to run to him. He went down on his haunches, held out both arms toward her and grinned as she ran toward him eagerly.

''Sarah, no!'' Jennifer's voice sliced into the happy moment and shut it down.

The little girl stopped in her tracks and, frowning, looked from Chance to her mother, standing in the hall doorway. Her tiny bottom lip poked out into a full-fledged pout. ''Chanz here.''

"I see that," Jennifer said quietly, "but you mustn't run, baby. Walk. Slowly."

Impatiently, Chance sucked in a breath and stood up. Walking to Sarah, he scooped her up in his arms and gave her a kiss on the cheek that stopped her pout from becoming tears.

But it didn't solve the problem. His gaze followed Jennifer as she moved closer, coming to take her daughter from him. Once in her arms, she ran her hands up and down Sarah's body as if assuring herself the child was uninjured. And a flash of worried irritation swept through him.

"Jen, you've got to stop this."

"What?" she asked, not even bothering to tear her gaze from Sarah's flushed face.

"The doctor says Sarah's fine, but you're acting as though she's at death's door."

Sea-green eyes flashed up at him. "She's just out of the hospital," she reminded him hotly.

"Yeah," he said, agreeing to a point. "And I know she's still recovering. But," he added, reaching out to stroke the tip of his finger along Sarah's chubby cheek, "she's feeling pretty good now. Yet every time she tries to show her independence a little, you stop her and wrap her up in cotton."

Jennifer's head snapped back and she stared at him open-mouthed.

While she was speechless, he pressed his advantage. "If you coddle her too much," he said, keeping his voice soft, understanding, "Sarah will never get to enjoy the freedom and health the operation was supposed to give back to her."

"You don't understand," Jennifer said, shaking her head and tightening her hold on the baby in her arms.

"Yeah, I do," he said and meant it. He knew exactly what she was so terrified of. He'd seen it in her eyes since the moment they'd met. The thought of losing the daughter she loved so much had her frozen in fear. Yet now, the danger was over. Sarah could grow up healthy. Strong.

But Jennifer wasn't seeing that. She saw only the danger, not the gift.

"You couldn't possibly understand," she said, and he focused on her instead of his rampaging thoughts. "You weren't here for those months when walking across the room made her so tired she was gasping for breath."

"No, but—"

"And I didn't see you sitting up beside her crib at night, watching her little chest. Waiting for the next breath." Her voice broke and it ripped a hole in his own heart. "Hoping it would come."

"Jen," he interrupted, prodded by the pain in her eyes.

"No. No, I listened to you, now it's your turn." Keeping her arms wrapped around her daughter, Jennifer said, "You can't know how I feel, Chance.

You don't know what it's been like, living with this. Sarah is *not* your child.'' She paused, lifted her chin and inhaled sharply. ''You don't get a vote in this.''

The baby hiccuped and gave a little half cry and Jennifer instantly started bouncing her up and down in a doomed attempt to calm her.

Stung to the core, Chance just looked at her. ''No, you're right,'' he said softly, pushing the words past the knot in his throat. ''She's not my daughter. But we—the three of us—have been through a lot together in the last few weeks.'' His back teeth ground together briefly. ''And I thought we'd— Doesn't matter,'' he said after a second or two. She'd effectively pushed him out of their tight little circle, and that hurt more than he cared to admit, even to himself.

For damn sure he wasn't going to admit anything like that out loud to Jennifer. Still, there was more at stake here than his wounded feelings. There was Sarah's future to think about. And no matter what Jennifer thought, he loved that little girl, so he had to say something.

''Fine,'' he snapped, letting the pain inside flavor his words with a bite. ''I'm not her father. But I love her as though she were mine. And I'm not going to stand by and watch you smother her without speaking up.''

''*Smother* her?''

He heard the outrage in her voice, but he went right on. This was important and someone had to say it. "You can't protect Sarah forever, Jen. She has to run and fall. She has to scrape her knee and heal."

"Why?" she shot back, fury goading her words. "Why is it that you men think pain belongs in life? Why shouldn't I try to protect her from being hurt? Try to keep her safe?"

Frustrated, he argued, "If you wrap her up in velvet and tuck her away in a drawer somewhere, then she's not living. She's just existing. Is that all you want for her?"

Sarah's cries came in earnest now, but the two adults just talked right over them while Jennifer tried to soothe her.

"Living doesn't have to require taking chances," she said, shaking her head as she narrowed her gaze on him.

"Of course it does," he said, reaching out and grabbing hold of her shoulders. "Life *is* taking chances. Every morning when we wake up, we run the risk that this is it. This is the last day we get."

She blanched, but he plunged on. "That's life." Chance threw both hands high and let them slap back down against his thighs. "That's why it's so important how we spend each damn day. Bruises come with the territory. Everyone dies, Jen. It's how you live that counts."

Jennifer shook her head. She wouldn't listen. He could see it in her eyes. Frustration bubbled inside him. Hell, he hadn't come here to fight with her. He didn't want them squaring off against each other. Not when he had so little time left to be with her. Soon, he'd be back out in the field, and this cozy haven would be nothing but a memory.

And a sinking feeling in his guts told him that it was already sliding out of his reach.

"I want Sarah safe," Jennifer said tightly. "She's already run enough risks for a lifetime. She shouldn't have to know any more pain. Shouldn't have to grow up and be disappointed or hurt or left alone or…" Her voice trailed off into nothingness.

There it was, he thought. This was the real enemy he had to face. It wasn't worry for Sarah driving her. It was Jen trying to protect her heart. "This isn't just about the baby, is it?" he demanded, wanting the truth out where it could be faced—and conquered. "Who is it you're really trying to protect here? Sarah? Or yourself?"

Twelve

A deep, throbbing ache settled around her heart and pounded out a rhythm that ran in counterpoint to her heartbeat. It slammed home with the precision of a surgeon's scalpel and it was all Jennifer could do not to weep with the pain.

It didn't help to know that he was right about this, as he was about the rest of it. Logically, she knew she shouldn't treat Sarah as if she were made of glass. But she'd come too close to losing her. And now it was pure instinct to protect. Defend.

But it wasn't only Sarah she was bent on protecting. It was her own heart. If she allowed herself to love Chance and he were taken from her, it would destroy her. She'd lost Mike and survived, true. But what she felt for this man was so much more, it terrified her. And if she had to avoid crushing pain later by enduring slightly lesser pain now, then that was what she would do.

With that thought firmly in mind, she steeled herself and said, "You should go. Now."

"What?"

He looked incredulous, and she couldn't really blame him. This was coming out of nowhere, she knew. But it was better this way. For all of them.

She swallowed hard. "I mean it. Leave, Chance. Just go."

A harsh, humorless laugh shot from his throat. "You're kidding, right?"

"No," she said, shaking her head and holding on more tightly to the crying baby in her arms. "I'm not. I want you to leave."

"No way." He crossed both arms over his broad chest and planted his feet as if he was taking root.

"Damn it, don't you see that this is the only thing to do?"

"What I see is that you're using the excuse of an argument to chase me off."

She winced but didn't admit to a thing. "Why are you making this harder than it has to be?"

"*I'm* not doing this, you are," he snapped.

Sarah's cries notched higher in volume and Jennifer swayed, trying unsuccessfully to soothe the baby even while her own heart was breaking. She looked up at Chance, knowing this could be the last time she would ever stare up into those whiskey-colored eyes. Her soul cringed away from that truth, like a child hiding from the encroaching darkness. But she didn't have a choice. These things had to be said. Better now than later.

"Look," she began, pitching her voice to carry over Sarah's cries, "we both knew this was coming. You don't belong here, Chance."

"*We,*" he said in a furious mutter, "belong *together.*"

Oh, God. Before she could do something really stupid like throw herself into his arms and beg him never to let go, Jennifer shook her head, tears and flying hair blinding her. "No, we don't. You're action-adventure man and I'm the home-and-hearth type. It would never work. This...thing we've shared was temporary. We both knew that."

Hurt flashed in his eyes and regret pooled in her stomach.

"Is that right? Funny, it didn't feel temporary to me," he said, and reached for her again, but she stepped back, determined to keep him at a distance. When he spoke again, anger colored his words. "Damn it, Jen, you're just ending it? Like this?"

Hot tears rolled down her cheeks as she whispered, "This is the only way it *could* end. Don't you understand?"

"No," he said tightly, shaking his head, "I don't. I don't get how one of the strongest women I've ever known can turn her back on something fantastic just because she's too afraid to take another chance on life."

She flinched as if he'd struck her.

"Don't do this, Jen."

"I have to," she said. "For all of our sakes."

"I *love* you, damn it."

He looked as surprised by the admission as she was. Her resolve wobbled along with her knees. She was loved. By a man she loved desperately.

And it changed nothing.

"Goodbye, Chance," she whispered.

His features closed up and for the first time since she'd known him, she saw him for the professional warrior he was. Hard and cold, even his amber eyes flashed out a warning. Hurt radiated from him and simmered in the anger rippling off him in waves.

He lifted one hand and gently stroked the back of Sarah's head before turning around as stiffly as if he were on a parade deck. Jennifer watched him march across the room. She watched the front door open, watched him step out and watched the door quietly close again behind him.

Then all she heard was the sound of her own tears and her daughter's tiny voice, calling for daddy.

* * *

Three days later, the silence in the house drove Jennifer back to the Connelly mansion. Back to work. She needed distraction. She needed to keep busy. She needed somehow to fill the empty hours that kept crawling past.

She felt as though she'd been through a wringer. Jennifer had cried until there were just no more tears inside her. And it hadn't helped. There was still an aching, open wound inside her heart and she knew without a doubt it would never heal. All she could hope for now was a return to normalcy. A return to what her life had been like before Chance had entered it.

Even though a world without Chance in it held absolutely no appeal.

She sighed, hitched Sarah a bit higher on her hip and told herself to be thankful for small favors. Like Emma telling her to bring Sarah to work with her, so she wouldn't worry. "We'll be fine, sweetie. You'll see."

"Chanz here?" Sarah turned her head back and forth, looking all over the empty hallway of the Connelly mansion.

Jennifer's gaze swept the place, too, even though she suspected Chance had left a few days ago. After the argument they'd had, she was sure he'd been more than eager to get the heck out of Dodge.

"No, baby." Jennifer shook her head and forced a smile she didn't feel. "Chance is gone."

Those three little words somehow sucked all the air out of the room, so Jennifer continued on, headed for Emma's office and her old, welcome routine.

Seth Connelly planted a kiss on Emma's forehead, then took a step back. He threw a quick glance and smile at Jennifer before turning back to the woman he considered his mother. "I'll call after I meet Angie."

"All right," Emma said, reaching up to put one hand on his cheek. "You be careful."

"I will," he said, adding uselessly, "don't worry."

With that, he turned and headed for the door, pausing only long enough to grin at Sarah. Then he stopped in the doorway, threw another smile at his mother and was gone.

Emma's own smile only drooped a little as she looked at Jennifer. "So," she said, "how's our Sarah?"

"Doing very well."

"Chanz gone?" Sarah asked, her mouth screwing up into a pout.

"Yes," Jennifer said.

"No," Emma corrected.

"He's not?" Stupid, stupid, she told herself as a white-hot flash of excitement streaked across her heart.

"Not yet," Emma told her, taking Sarah into her arms. "He leaves day after tomorrow."

The older woman watched her, and Jennifer wondered absently if Emma could actually see her heart break. He was still here. But he was going to leave. And he'd leave never knowing that she loved him.

A cold chill crawled up her spine and Jennifer wrapped her empty arms around her middle. Without even Sarah to hold on to, she felt completely alone. And the cold seeped into her bones where she knew instinctively it was going to stay.

"Oh, God," she whispered, and wished she knew what the right thing to do was.

"Jennifer," Emma said softly, "love is a rare and glorious thing. Trust me. I know." She smiled sadly and shook her head as she cradled Sarah close. "I've seen how Chance looks at you—and how you look at him."

"Emma—"

"Honey," the other woman interrupted her, "if you let this love that's between you get away, you will always regret it."

Regret. The word echoed inside her over and over again until it took on the rhythm of her own beating heart. She already had regrets. She regretted that she'd never told Chance that she loved him. She regretted that she'd been on the stupid birth control pills and hadn't conceived during that first magical night with him. She regretted that she'd sent him off to a dangerous job letting him think she didn't care.

And it would only get worse, she knew. Even as her breath strangled her, her mind filled with images of his face, his smile, his touch, his kiss. Each of these and more would haunt her for the rest of her life. And every time she dreamed about him, she would have to acknowledge that *she* was the one who'd ended it. That *she* was the one who hadn't had enough strength, courage, to grab what she wanted and hold on tight.

The coming years stretched out in front of her and all she could see was an empty black void. No laughter. No kisses. No shared secrets. No more babies. No arms holding her in the night.

"Oh my God," she said past the knot of emotion clogging her throat. "I'm so stupid."

"Not entirely, I'm happy to see," Emma said.

"Where is he?"

"He went to Navy Pier."

Jennifer grinned, leaned forward and smacked a kiss onto Sarah's cheek. "Watch her for me?"

"Sure," Emma called out as her secretary ran for the door. "But after you accept his proposal, you've got some calls to make about Daniel's coronation!" But Jennifer was already gone. Shaking her head, Emma looked down at the baby in her arms and said, "Would you like a cookie?"

* * *

At Navy Pier, Jennifer threw money at the cab-driver, yelled "Keep the change," and leaped from the taxi. The weekday crowds weren't too bad as she sprinted down the long boardwalk. It was still too early in the year for the legions of tourists that would soon be streaming up and down the prome-nade.

Her gaze constantly scanning the faces she ran past, Jennifer knew only that she had to find Chance. Had to convince him that she was sorry. That she'd been wrong. Had to tell him that she loved him.

A fierce wind raced across the surface of Lake Michigan and pushed at her, almost as if trying to slow her down. She shoved her hair out of her eyes and raked the crowd again, looking for that chiseled jaw, that short, brown hair and quick smile. Those amber eyes.

Music blasted down at her from overhead speak-ers and a clutch of school kids on a field trip headed toward the tours being given aboard a navy ship at the end of the pier. Kiosk salesmen hawked cotton candy, sodas and hot dogs and she ignored them all in her single-minded search.

And finally, she saw him. Stepping out of one of the shops, he turned his face up into the sunlight and Jennifer's heart soared.

"Chance!" She called his name and started run-ning for him even before he turned, surprise etched on his features. She didn't give him time to think. She'd come this far, she wouldn't be stopped. Not when she'd finally figured it all out.

Throwing herself at him, she wrapped her arms around his neck and trusted him to hold on to her. He did. His arms snaked around her tightly and lifted her off the ground as she pressed her lips to his in a kiss designed to tell him what her fears had kept her from saying before.

Absently, Jennifer noted the smattering of applause her performance was drawing from the interested group of bystanders. But she didn't care. All that mattered was Chance. And being in his arms. Where she belonged.

At last, though, she broke the kiss and looked up into those eyes that held a promise of a future. And before he could ask the questions she knew were coming, she started talking, words jumbling over each other in her haste to be heard.

"I understand, Chance," she said, breathless, "I know what you were talking about the other day. Life. It's not worth living if you're not willing to risk everything."

"Jen—"

"No," she said quickly, shifting her grip on him so that she could cup his cheek, tenderly drawing the pad of her thumb across his skin. "No, let me say it. I *have* to say it."

He nodded.

"I love you, Chance Barnett Connelly." And once the words were out, she laughed, throwing her head back briefly and enjoying the pure pleasure sweeping through her. "I'm not afraid to say it anymore. I'm only afraid to live my life without you in it."

Around them, the crowd slowly grew as more and more people were drawn to the real-life drama playing out on Navy Pier.

"I finally get it," she said, willing him to believe, willing him to read the truth in her eyes. "Love. That's all that really matters. And if you're lucky enough to find it, you shouldn't be dumb enough to turn your back on it."

His arms tightened, but that was the only sign that he'd heard her. Seconds ticked past and Jennifer worried that she'd waited too long. That she'd missed the opportunity life had handed her because she'd been too afraid to grab it and hang on.

An ache settled in the pit of her stomach as Chance gingerly set her down onto her feet. When he let her go, she felt cold. And empty. But then he smiled and reached into his pants' pocket, pulling out a small emerald-green velvet box.

Jennifer's breath caught as she looked into his eyes and saw love shining back at her.

Chance felt as though someone had just lifted a three-ton weight off his back. "These last few days without you have been about the worst I can ever remember," he said and watched as a sheen of tears glistened in her eyes. He'd never been so glad to see anyone in his life. Hearing her call his name had sounded like the answer to a lonely man's prayer. "I'm not used to needing...well, *anyone*," he said and paused before adding, "but I need you, Jen. You and Sarah. And you should know that I was leaving here to go hunt you down."

"You were?" she asked and swiped away a single tear that rolled along her cheek.

"Damn right," he grumbled, remembering his plan for a siege of her heart. If he'd had to, he would have requested extra leave time, just so he could stay in Chicago long enough to convince her that she loved him. "I wasn't about to let you or *our* daughter get away from me."

She smiled and his heartbeat staggered. God, how had he ever lived this long without her?

"I want to be a part of your lives," he went on quickly, saying all the words he'd been rehearsing most of the morning. "I want to belong somewhere and I need that place to be with you."

"Oh, Chance, we do belong together. I was just too scared to admit that before." She lifted her chin and gave him a watery smile. "Well, I'm still scared. But I'd rather be scared *with* you, than *without* you."

He inhaled sharply, deeply and nodded. "Good.

Good. Jen, I can't promise to live forever—no one can—but I do promise I will *love* you forever.''

''I'll hold you to it,'' she warned.

''You do that.''

''Oh, and there's one more thing,'' she said, oblivious to the now substantial group of people watching them.

''What's that?'' he asked warily.

''More babies,'' she said. ''I want more babies.''

''Me, too, honey,'' he told her and gave her a quick, hard kiss that was powerful enough to curl her toes. ''The more the merrier.'' Hell, he got hard just thinking about her belly round with his child. But first things first. Opening the small green box, he said, ''There's just one more thing.''

Jennifer stared down at the huge solitaire diamond winking at her and gasped. Taking advantage of her surprise, he dropped to one knee, took her left hand in his and said in a loud, proud voice, ''Jennifer Anderson, I love you more than I ever thought it possible to love anyone. And if you'll marry me, I'll spend the rest of my life proving it to you.''

''And I,'' Jennifer said, pulling him to his feet, ''will spend the rest of my life thanking my lucky stars for sending you to me.''

''So that's a yes?'' he asked, one corner of his mouth twitching into a grin.

''Oh, you bet it's a yes,'' she said.

Chance slipped the ring on to her finger before she could change her mind and sealed its place with a kiss. Then he grabbed her tightly around the waist and swung her high into the air.

She grinned down at him, the cheers of the crowd ringing in her ears, and for the first time in far too long, Jennifer felt truly, magically, alive.

*   *   *   *   *

Plain Jane &
Doctor Dad

KATE LITTLE

KATE LITTLE

claims to have lots of experience with romance – "the *fictional* kind, that is," she is quick to clarify. She has been both an author and an editor of romantic fiction for over fifteen years. She believes that a good romance will make the reader experience all the tension, thrills and agony of falling madly, deeply and wildly in love. She enjoys watching the characters in her books go crazy for each other, but hates to see the blissful couple disappear when it's time for them to live happily ever after. In addition to writing romance novels, Kate also writes fiction and non-fiction for young adults. She lives on Long Island, New York, with her husband and daughter.

One

As Nurse Maura Chambers left Scott's office, she knew she'd never see him again. But he didn't say "Good luck" or even "Good-bye." He merely shuffled papers around on his desk as she slipped through the doorway, ignoring her, as if she had already vanished from his sight.

She stepped from the quiet chamber into the busy hospital corridor, resisting the urge to give his door one last, resounding slam. What good would that do her now? It would only give the major-league gossips on staff more to talk about. Hadn't they already gotten enough mileage out of her failed romance? Anyway, in a matter of days Scott would be gone for good, starting a new job and a new life hundreds of miles away. And she'd be free of him. Almost.

Maura took a deep breath and started down the

crowded hallway, willing herself to look as busy as everyone around her. She kept her gaze downcast, avoiding eye contact with anyone who might stop her to ask why she looked so upset. She didn't feel like talking about her problems now. Not to anyone.

As much as she'd dreaded facing Scott Walker again, she'd been obligated to disclose her secret. After all, he bore his fair share of responsibility. But it only took a moment for Maura to realize Scott didn't see the matter that way. Not at all. His reaction had been more than disappointing. More than cold or unsympathetic. His attitude and succinct advice had made her sick to her stomach.

Well, what did you *really* expect? she asked herself. Haven't you known for weeks now what kind of man he is? It had been clear to her ever since the night Scott had announced, out of the blue, that he was leaving Chicago General. Leaving the city entirely for a new job as a hospital administrator in Minneapolis. Why would he be any different now?

Looking back, she felt angry all over again to see his calculated tactics so clearly. How he had chosen a fancy restaurant for their talk, a place so exclusive and formal he could almost be assured she wouldn't make a scene. As the maître d' had led them to their secluded, candle-lit table, Maura had thought Scott might even be planning to propose.

He had a little speech planned for her, all right, but it wasn't about marriage. Quite the opposite. Getting to know her the past six months had been great. Really fun, he'd said in a sympathetic tone. But the problem was, he'd be moving to Minnesota in a few weeks. He'd found a great job. Just what he'd been hoping for. She wouldn't want to hold him back, would she? Besides, they both knew this was a casual relationship. No strings. No expectations.

Then, ignoring her stunned expression, he'd patted her hand. Long-distance things never seemed to work out, he'd added, so it was best for both of them to end it now. To make a clean break. In a few weeks, he was sure, she'd thank him for making it so easy. She'd be happy she was free to meet someone new.

He hadn't waited for her answer. She was far too shocked at the time to make any reply at all.

It was right at that moment that she suddenly saw Scott differently, saw his true nature clearly. How had she been so blind? Was he that adept at misleading people? While she thought they were involved in a serious relationship—one that could lead to marriage—he'd merely been using her.

Maura felt a bitter taste at the memory. She touched her fingers to her eyes. She was crying. It seemed impossible that she had any tears left after the way she'd cried that night. She stopped walking and leaned against the wall of the corridor. Shaking her head to clear her thoughts, she reached into her pocket for a tissue.

"Maura?" She felt a touch on her shoulder and turned to see Doug Connelly's tall, commanding form beside her. "Are you all right?" he asked kindly.

"Uh...sure. I've just got something in my eye. A bit of dust or something," Maura mumbled. She pressed the tissue to her eye. "It will go away in a second."

"Here, let me see," Doug offered.

"No, really...it's okay," Maura murmured. But

before she could resist, he took her chin in his gentle grasp and turned her face up to the light.

His touch was firm but light, as she expected. He was a pediatric cardiologist, adept at putting his small patients at ease. His questioning gaze considered her troubled expression and she was sure he could see now that she'd lied to him. She was upset and crying, pure and simple.

"It looks as if it might be gone," he said quietly. His hand dropped away, but he continued to gaze down at her, his warm, amber eyes filled with concern.

They stood in a section of the hallway that was mostly glass, offering a courtyard view filled with trees, flowers and benches. Visitors and patients used it mainly, but some of the staff were outside, too, stealing a few minutes from their demanding jobs.

"What a day," Doug said. "Sometimes in this city, you feel like winter will never end. Then all of a sudden—bam. You look up and it's spring."

"Yes, spring did come suddenly this year." Maura looked out at the trees and flowers in full bloom. She'd been so depressed and distracted the past few weeks, she'd hardly noticed the changes.

"Let's get some fresh air. You look like you could use it." Doug took her arm without waiting for her reply.

"Thanks, but I really have to get back to the floor." Maura glanced at her watch, trying to excuse herself.

But Doug wouldn't let her leave his side so easily. "You can take a break for a few minutes, Maura. We'll cut across the courtyard and you can catch the elevators on the other side. That's closer to your station, anyway.''

Before Maura knew it, they were outside, walking down a tree-lined path. She felt the sunshine on her skin and inhaled the soft spring air. Doug had been right: she felt better almost instantly.

She glanced at his rugged profile and tall, lean form. He walked with his hands tucked into the pockets of his blue lab coat, his ever-present stethoscope slung around his neck, clearly enjoying a break in his hectic schedule. She had worked with many keenly intelligent doctors and many dedicated ones, as well, but she'd rarely met a physician who possessed both qualities in such abundance. Doug was more than dedicated. He was known as a bit of a workaholic, but he was an excellent physician. Maura was sure she knew none better. His powers of concentration and focus seemed evident even now, in his thoughtful expression and the firm set of his handsome features.

They strolled along in silence, side by side, but it was a comfortable silence for Maura. She had first come to know Doug as a colleague, when she'd been caring for one of his patients. After that, they'd quickly become friends. Especially after learning that Doug and Scott had gone to college together and had once been good friends. They'd been out of touch for years and had met again recently, when Scott came to work at Chicago General.

She often wondered how much Doug knew about her relationship with Scott and how close the two men were now. Scott always claimed he liked Doug, but often made cutting remarks about him. Maura could see Scott was simply jealous. He had once hoped to be a doctor, too, but had dropped out of medical school his first year. The same school from which Doug had graduated with honors.

While she wouldn't consider Doug a close friend, she had always felt a subtle but very strong connection to him. From the start they'd been able to talk to each other in an open, honest way. Which was quite unusual for Maura. She had always been shy with men, especially one so good-looking. But she rarely felt awkward with him. Something about him just put her at ease.

"Sit a minute," Doug suggested as they came to an empty bench.

"Sure." Maura shrugged and sat down. The bench was in the shade, facing a small fountain surrounded by flowers. The sound of the rippling water soothed her frazzled nerves, as did Doug's quiet, solid presence.

"Maura, what is it? What's troubling you?" Doug asked finally.

She turned to look at him. "What do you mean?"

"I know you were crying back there. And you look pale as a sheet."

Maura felt suddenly self-conscious under his scrutiny. She pushed a strand of wavy hair away from her face.

"I'm fine…I mean, I feel a little under the weather today. Just tired, I guess."

"Yes, you do look tired. You work too hard."

"Probably." She knew it was more like crying too hard—and sleeping too little.

Doug was quiet again for a moment. Then he said,

"Is this about Scott? Are you upset because he's leaving on Friday?"

"No. Not at all." She shook her head.

That was what everyone must think, she realized. That she was still yearning after a man who had treated her so badly. "Relieved is more like it," she added. "I wish he was already gone."

"He didn't deserve you." Doug's tone was firm and deep.

"That's nice of you to say," Maura replied quietly.

"I wasn't saying it to be nice. It's the truth." He paused, as if uncertain whether to continue. Then he said, "I know it feels awful, right now. But give it time. Before you know it, you'll forget all about him." He leaned toward her. "Maybe you should take some time off, get away for a while," he suggested.

"Yes, maybe I should," she replied vaguely. Last night she had thought about visiting her sister on the West Coast, the only real family she had left. But she knew very well that no matter how fast or how far she ran, she could never escape this problem.

She turned and looked at him and could see he was sincerely worried about her. The look in his eye, the sheer kindness and consideration, was her undoing. She had been on an emotional roller coaster the past twenty-four hours, and having Doug, of all people, look at her that way made her feel as if she was about to burst into tears again.

She felt the moisture well up in her eyes and dropped her face into her hands. Then she felt Doug's strong arm circle her shoulders as hot tears streamed down her cheeks. Doug pulled her closer, his grip strong and warm around her, his chest firm under her cheek. She was crying hard, sobbing uncontrollably, unable to stop herself.

"It's okay," she heard him murmur against her hair.

She tried to speak and felt a giant lump in her throat again. No, it's not okay, she wanted to say. It's anything but.

"Just cry if you need to," Doug whispered.

"Oh, Doug…I'm sorry. I just don't know what to do…."

Her voice trailed off in another wave of tears and she pressed her face against his hard chest.

She felt Doug's strong hand stroking her hair. She felt the warmth of his body and breathed in the scent of his skin. With her eyes closed and her cheek nestled in the crook of his shoulder, she felt safe and protected. For the briefest moment, Maura allowed herself the lovely fantasy that she could stay this way forever. How much easier everything would be.

But that was impossible. She had to pull herself together. There was no one to help her out of this mess. Doug might offer his strong shoulder to cry on, but he didn't have a white charger standing by for a quick getaway. He was only trying to be a good friend.

She took a deep breath and forced herself to move away from his embrace.

"I'm sorry. I didn't mean to upset you by talking about Scott," Doug apologized.

"It wasn't that." She wiped her eyes and took a shaky breath. She felt him watching her, waiting for her to speak.

Finally, she said, "It's just that I have this problem...." She paused again and staring straight ahead, she admitted, "I'm pregnant."

She wasn't sure why she'd told him. The words spoken aloud sounded so final. So overwhelming. Doug looked shocked for an instant. Then he quickly hid his reaction, she noticed. He was silent for a long moment, and she watched as his pensive expression grew harsher. Angrier.

"With Scott's child," he said.

Though it wasn't a question, she nodded and looked away again.

He leaned forward and pushed his hand through his thick hair. "Does he know?"

"I told him a few minutes ago. In his office. That's why I looked upset in the hall," she admitted.

"He didn't take the news very well, I guess," Doug replied sternly.

"No. He didn't."

The ugly scene replayed in her mind, and suddenly she couldn't bear talking about it anymore.

"Listen, thanks for talking to me," she said as she stood to go. "But I'd better get back to work. I've already been gone way too long."

"I understand." He nodded and came to his feet. "Maybe I'll see you later, when I do rounds."

"Sure. And I'm sorry for crying all over you." He must see her as some kind of flailing, helpless female, she thought, when in fact, she was just the opposite.

"Don't even think about it, Maura." His tone was soft and sincere. Maura met his gaze briefly, then turned on her way.

She hurried across the courtyard, then entered the

hospital. To avoid the long wait for the elevator, she walked up three flights to the pediatrics department. Her supervisor, Gloria Jones, greeted her with a questioning look but didn't ask why she was so late returning from her break. There was plenty of work waiting, and Maura dug in, eager to focus on her patients instead of her problems.

As the afternoon passed, her thoughts returned to her disturbing confrontation with Scott—and her conversation with Dr. Connelly. She'd never had such a personal conversation with Doug before. But now she was thankful that, purely by chance, he'd been there for her at such an awful moment. Crying on his shoulder hadn't solved anything, but it had made her feel worlds better, lending her the boost she needed to carry on.

Some of the staff disliked the handsome pediatrician. They found him aloof and distant. But Maura had never felt that way. He was sometimes distracted by his work, and even brooding. But a more dedicated doctor would be hard to find.

She had never imagined he would also be such a dedicated friend, the kind you could really count on when things went haywire. But whether you liked Doug Connelly or not, he was clearly a man of strong character, and Maura knew without question that her secret was safe.

Her workday wore on, thankfully free of pressing emergencies, as she had a pounding headache that wasn't assuaged by the pills she'd taken earlier. Luckily, a night-shift nurse came in early, allowing Maura to go home.

She lived in a comfortable family neighborhood a

short distance from the hospital. She'd been lucky to find a reasonably priced two-bedroom apartment in a renovated brownstone. Her living room even had a working fireplace, which she really appreciated during the long Chicago winters.

The apartment was the first she'd lived in without a roommate, and Maura had loved decorating it to her own taste. She liked antiques, but since she could only afford a few small pieces, she used her knack for finding interesting items that weren't genuine antiques but still quaint and unique. The honey-tone wood floors were covered by area rugs, and the walls were warm shades of apricot and creamy white. Her home was her haven, her retreat from her hectic, demanding job. It was a private place where she could rest and recharge. Where she could hide away and sort out her thoughts when life tossed her some seemingly impossible crisis. Which was just the way she felt tonight as she slipped her key into the front door and went inside.

She dropped her mail on a table in the foyer without even glancing at it, then went straight to the bedroom and took a long, hot shower. Even though it was still early, she put on her nightgown and robe, then lay down on her bed, hoping to sleep. But worries immediately crowded her mind.

For some reason, instead of thinking about Scott, she thought about Doug, recalling the first time they'd met, months ago. She had recently started at the hospital and had been working the night shift. She was assigned to one of his patients, a four-year-old girl brought in with advanced pneumonia and serious heart complications. Purely by chance in the small hours of the night she'd discovered that the child was in serious trouble, in danger of heart failure.

When Doug found her with the patient minutes later, she was giving CPR as she waited for the crash cart and respiratory equipment to be hooked up. As Doug took charge, he barely said a personal word to her, but the respectful, grateful look in his eyes said it all.

That night she'd hardly been aware of his compelling good looks, or the smothering shyness that typically fell over her. Working through the crisis with him, she felt totally in synch, and the event somehow forged a mysterious but deep bond between them. She had never felt quite that way about anyone—not a coworker or even a romantic partner. But she had felt it that night with Doug, and forever after.

They had worked together for several hours to pull the little girl through. Even after Maura's regular shift was done, she stayed on, unwilling to leave until she was sure the child was going to survive. She knew that some people thought it unwise to get so involved with each patient's recovery. They advised compassion tempered by a cooler, more distant attitude to avoid the burnout that was so common among overworked nurses.

But Maura wasn't made that way. She hadn't become a pediatric nurse in order to be distant and detached from the children who needed her. She knew from the first that Doug was the same. Perhaps even more intensely involved with his young patients than she.

She later learned that the little girl's family didn't have much insurance and Doug had not even sent them a bill. While it was highly uncommon for a specialist of Doug's caliber to forego payment, she soon learned that it wasn't uncommon at all for him to work that way.

When morning came and the crisis had passed, she and Doug sat together outside on a bench in the same courtyard where they had talked today. They celebrated their victory, joking and laughing over cups of steaming coffee and sticky donuts. It was late January and the weather was frigid, yet she could still recall feeling elated by the cold air and early-morning light and the shared success in saving a child's life.

It was then Doug learned she was dating Scott Walker, and Maura learned Doug was Scott's old pal from college. There was something in Doug's reaction to the news that made Maura think he was disappointed to hear she was seeing someone. But the moment passed and later she decided she'd imagined the brief flicker of interest.

On her side Maura would never deny that she found Doug very attractive. But at that time she had felt so committed to Scott, she'd never once thought of Doug in a romantic way.

Besides, Maura reflected, even if she had been free, Doug was not her type at all. For one thing, she was looking for a man who would have time in his life for a wife and family. Doug was far too focused on his work to make family life, or even a romantic relationship, a priority.

And he could be temperamental at times. She had to acknowledge that his smiles and bright moods were rare. He seemed most often to be shadowed by some deep, mysterious unhappiness, and too often she found a dark, brooding look in his eyes when he thought no one was watching him.

What brought on that somber mood of his? Was it the pressures of his work? Maura had always suspected it was something more. Some deep hurt in his past, some painful loss. Doug had never spoken to her about his past, but she did know from Scott that he'd gone through a difficult divorce a few years back.

As the months passed, she and Doug always had so much to say to each other whenever they met. She'd run into him on her floor while he did rounds, in the hallways, in the cafeteria. He would ask her advice about his cases, and she enjoyed helping him figure out some knotty problem in a diagnosis or discuss a curious turn in a patient's condition.

It was unusual for a doctor of his standing to take a nurse into his confidence in that way, and she was secretly pleased, even proud, of the way he seemed to value her observations. But they didn't only talk about patients. They talked about all kinds of things, movies, books, traveling to exotic places, which they both planned on doing someday when they weren't working so hard.

But Maura had to acknowledge that, for all their interesting conversations, she still knew very little about him. The staff at Chicago General was always brimming with gossip, and while she avoided discussing other people's lives, she had overheard a few basic facts about Doug. He had been at the hospital since his residency and at one time had been married. He was divorced for almost two years, but no one seemed to know what had gone wrong. His ex-wife was now married to a prominent plastic surgeon, and some said she'd hurt Doug badly with an affair.

Even though she didn't have romantic designs on him herself, Maura wondered why he wasn't in a new relationship, or even married again, by now. But her knowledgeable co-workers answered that question, too. Many hopeful women had pursued the handsome doctor, but the relationship had always ended unhappily. Despite his giving, caring nature as a physician, it was reported that Dr. Douglas Connelly was distant and even difficult as a romantic partner. An emotional Mount Everest with wickedly icy heights to scale.

Maura suspected his single-minded focus on his work had been the real problem. She knew it would be one for her. Some people didn't need a home life and family. Maybe Doug was that type, she concluded. But a home and family was something Maura had always longed for, because she'd known so little security growing up.

When she'd met Scott, back in November, she'd believed at last she'd found a man who shared her values and outlook and wanted the same kind of life that she did.

Her thoughts drifted as sleep overcame her weary mind. How devastating it had been to discover that Scott had only pretended to be that kind of man, saying just what she'd wanted to hear in order to get what he'd wanted from her.

And by the time she saw him clearly, it was too late.

Two

Maura woke to the sound of sharp knocking on her front door. Her bedroom was dark, and the clock on the night table showed it was nearly eight. She sat up and pushed her hair back with her hand as she walked toward the foyer.

She wondered who it could be. Maybe her friend Liza, who lived downstairs. Liza often stopped by at night just to chat, mostly about her problems with boyfriends.

But Maura wasn't in the mood to see Liza. She walked toward the door and tightened the sash on her robe, wondering what excuse she could make.

Just as the knock sounded again, Maura turned the lock. "Just a second," she said.

She pulled the door open a space. Then felt herself jolted to the core by the sight of Doug's tall, imposing form.

"Doug. What are you doing here?"

She was rarely so blunt, but he was that last person she'd expected. He'd only been to her apartment once, when her car wouldn't start and he'd given her a lift home from the hospital. She didn't even realize he remembered where she lived.

"I was on my way home and thought I'd stop by. I went to your station after my rounds, but they said you'd left early," he added. "I hope you're all right."

He smiled at her, yet his gaze looked serious, questioning, as if he wasn't sure he'd done the right thing by surprising her like this.

"Another nurse came in early, so I was able to leave before the shift ended," she explained. "I was just taking a nap."

"Have you had dinner yet? We could get something at the café around the corner if you like."

"Thanks, but I think I'd rather stay in tonight. I mean, I appreciate you stopping over—"

"That's all right. But I did want to talk to you some more. You seemed so upset today. I'm not sure it's good for you to be alone."

"I-I'm okay," she insisted. "Really." But she wasn't okay and they both knew it.

"Maura?" Doug moved up to the opening in the door, his tone firm but concerned. "Please, let me in. I'll only stay a minute."

She took a deep breath. Then, without saying anything more, she stepped back and let him in. He was probably right. It wasn't good for her to be alone right now. She might feel better if she talked to him for a while. He knew Scott and he seemed so understand-

ing about her problem. Maybe he could help her sort
things out.

She closed the door and they stood facing each
other. A small lamp on a side table cast the foyer in
soft, golden light. Shadows emphasized his strong
features, his wide, firm mouth and amber eyes.

She suddenly felt self-conscious dressed in just her
bathrobe, but there was no help for it. She knew she
looked a mess, her hair hanging in wild waves down
past her shoulders and her eyes circled with shadows.
She met his steady gaze, then looked away, tucking
a strand of hair behind her ear.

"I know you're tired. I won't stay long," he promised.

"It's okay. I'm glad you're here." It was true, she
realized. She met his gaze, then looked away. "Let's
go into the living room."

She led the way and sat on the couch. Doug stood
a short distance away, his brows drawn together in a
frown. She suddenly wondered about the thoughts
causing that dark look. Did he think badly of her, that
she was not very particular or careful about her romantic partners? The irony was, if anything, it was
her naiveté and lack of experience with men that had
gotten her into this fix. But of course Doug wouldn't
know that, and she felt foolish trying to explain it to
him, certain he'd think she was making excuses for
herself.

Doug turned and sat down in the armchair across
from her. "You never really told me what Scott said
to you about the baby. Only that he reacted badly."

She sighed and gripped her hands in her lap. "We
didn't part on the best terms. I basically haven't

spoken to him since he broke up with me and announced he was leaving for Minnesota. When I went to see him today, to tell him about the baby, he offered to pay for an abortion...but that was all.''

"That bastard.'' Doug's eyes glinted with anger. "Is that all he said to you? He didn't say he'd help you through the pregnancy or support his own child?''

Maura had wanted to avoid relating the uglier details of the conversation, but now she decided to tell Doug all.

"No, just the opposite, actually. He said that if I had the child, it would be my responsibility and I'd have to take him to court before he'd share in any financial support. He also said he hoped I wouldn't make a big deal out of this. It would be bad for my career and for his, and he hoped that I'd...I'd be smart and do the right thing.''

"He said that?'' Doug rose to his feet, his fists balled as if he wanted to strike something or someone. "I'd like to do the right thing to him...that smug, self-righteous son of a—''

Maura had never seen Doug this angry. His powerful emotions frightened her. Was it due to some long-standing enmity or rivalry between him and Scott? A tension Scott had sometimes hinted about. Or was he simply angry on her behalf?

"Doug, please. I really don't care if Scott's involved. I did believe I was in love with him at one time,'' she admitted, "but now I can see I was in some fantasyland. I never really knew him.''

Doug turned to her again, and she thought her words had taken some of the edge off his anger.

"I was shocked at first by his reaction," she continued. "But maybe it's a good thing that he wants no connection to me or the baby. With any luck I'll never have anything to do with him again."

He paced across the room, then suddenly turned to face her.

"Yes, I guess you're right. You're certainly better off without him," he admitted in a calmer tone. "And my confronting him wouldn't help matters, would it?"

"Not at all," she assured him.

"Except to make me feel a hell of a lot better," he added, more to himself than to Maura. He took a deep breath and she could see him willing himself to cool off.

"Sorry, Maura. This doesn't help you any." He shook his head then glanced down at her. "Have you decided what you're going to do?"

He'd asked the question quietly, almost casually. Yet she sensed him focusing on her reply with laser-like intensity. Not just the way a friend would be interested, but as if the matter somehow affected him directly, as well.

"I want to keep my baby," she said firmly. "I have to."

"I knew you would say that." Doug's expression softened, and a warm light glowed in his eyes as he gazed at her. "But raising a child on your own will be hard. Harder than you think," he said knowingly. "My mother was a single parent. She didn't even have family to help her. She really did it all on her own. With twin boys, no less," he added. "Until I was an adult, I never even understood or appreciated how much she had to deal with. Sometimes I know I can never fully appreciate it, either.''

Maura had not known that Doug had been raised only by his mother. It couldn't have been easy for him growing up. The accomplishment of completing medical school seemed even more impressive now. He was right. It wouldn't be an easy road for her or her child.

''I know what you're saying. I've thought about this—the problems I'll face. But I can't see it any other way. I just can't put the child up for adoption,'' she added. It was hard to continue, but she forced herself. Now it was her turn to reveal some hidden part of her history. ''I know what it's like to be part of a family...but not really part of it. It's a terrible, lonely feeling. Like you're always on the outside looking in,'' she added quietly, remembering unhappier times.

''I'd rather raise my child alone and give it all the love one parent can give than sit and wonder, every day, if my baby is happy and cared for.''

''You were adopted?'' he asked.

She shook her head. ''A foster child, from the time I was about twelve years old. Both my parents died in a car accident. My sister and I had no close relatives to raise us. We were split up and sent to different foster homes. Some of the people were nice to me. They wanted to help and tried to make me feel a part of their family. But there were always problems. I never stayed anywhere for very long,'' she confided wistfully. ''Then I managed to get a scholarship to college and started living on my own.''

''How sad to lose both your parents so young,'' he

said gravely. "At least I always had my mother and brother. You never mentioned your family before. I had no idea."

"Yes, well, you never mentioned yours either," she said. "We've never talked much about personal things like this before, have we?"

"No, we haven't. But maybe it's long past time that we did."

He glanced at her briefly as he sat down on the other end of the couch, crossing one long leg over the other and stretching out his arm along the back of the sofa. Despite his size, he moved gracefully, Maura noticed, with a powerful masculine grace that was distracting to her.

"Considering all you've been through, Maura, I'd think you would have turned out differently somehow."

"Differently? How do you mean?"

"I'm not sure exactly. Not nearly as optimistic for one thing. And you're such a caring, giving person."

His thoughtful words lifted her spirits and, more than that, made her remember who she was and what she was capable of.

"I had a good start, I guess. I had two parents who loved their children and loved each other. We lived in a small town in Wisconsin, just outside of Madison. It was really an ideal childhood, you might say." She looked down for a moment and gathered her thoughts. "Sometimes when I think about my family life back then, I think it might be unfair to the baby to raise it on my own. I know that there are decent, good people out there who would give an adopted child lots of love and a wonderful home. And sometimes I do feel scared to do this on my own.''

She felt her throat tighten with emotion, making it hard to continue. She didn't want to start crying again but felt the tears well up in her eyes. "I don't know...I just feel so confused, so overwhelmed," she admitted in a shaky voice.

Doug touched her shoulder. He seemed about to speak, then stopped himself. She could see he was giving her a moment to calm herself and collect her thoughts again.

It was still hard for Maura to believe she was pregnant.

How could she begin to explain it to Doug, when she herself hardly understood how this happened? To her, of all people? She'd always felt that physical intimacy between a man and a woman was a serious step, part of a relationship that included love and commitment. Even so, she had little experience that way and had always been so careful.

But Scott had had a way of sweeping aside her doubts and Maura had believed that she loved him. She had thought herself so lucky that a successful, good-looking man like Scott had wanted her. She couldn't understand what had attracted him to a mousy little thing like her. She couldn't help it, but that was how she thought of herself. She knew she wasn't attractive and sexy like some of the women around the hospital. She was quite the opposite, the type people used to call a plain Jane, feeling most comfortable when she blended into the woodwork. Sometimes friends like Liza insisted that she had what it took to turn heads, if she would only play up her looks a bit. But Maura always thought they were just trying to be nice. She could never quite believe it.

Maybe she felt safer downplaying her looks. As a teenager, just starting to blossom, she'd had some bad experiences attracting the wrong kind of male attention—the clumsy and crass advances of boys and even adult men in her foster families. She had learned to put as little emphasis as possible on her appearance. In her heart she hoped that the right man would be attracted to what was inside, not to some pretty packaging.

That was part of the reason she thought Scott might be the right man for her. Plain Jane or not, Scott pursued her and wooed her, and she was very flattered by his attentions. While he sometimes acted thoughtlessly in a way that was hurtful to her, he always managed to win her back again. It was hard to stay mad at him when he turned on the charm.

She knew he had his faults. But didn't everybody? Maura didn't expect the man she married to be perfect. She had so little experience when it came to romance that she hardly knew what to expect. No wonder she now found herself in this situation.

She shook her head as if to clear her muddled thoughts, then glanced over at Doug. Their eyes met, his golden gaze full of concern for her. For her future and her baby's, she thought.

She unconsciously touched her hand to her stomach, which was still perfectly flat. Yet she imagined the new life growing there, minute by minute, hour by hour.

"I've been thinking I might leave Chicago. It's hard to raise a child here."

"Leave Chicago?" Doug's expression darkened. "Where would you go?"

"Maybe to Portland, to be near my sister, Ellen. Or maybe to Santa Fe. I have a good friend from school there. I might be better off someplace new, making a fresh start."

"I don't think that's a good idea at all, Maura," Doug said sternly. He abruptly got up off the couch and paced across the room again, looking almost as disturbed as he'd been hearing about her talk with Scott.

"It'll be difficult and stressful to start a new job and get settled in a new city," he pointed out. "What if the pregnancy doesn't go well? You'd be all alone, with no one to help you."

But she was all alone now, here in Chicago, Maura wanted to say. But she didn't want Doug to think she felt sorry for herself. She really didn't.

"I'm confused, I guess. What do you think I should do?" she asked, her eyes wide and questioning.

He stared at her a long time, making Maura feel suddenly very aware of being alone with him. She thought he was about to say something, then saw the firm set of his mouth as he mentally backtracked.

"I think there's a lot to sort out. But it sounds like you've made the most important decision of all. To keep the baby," he said. He sat down on the couch again next to her, their bodies close but not touching. "I'm not sure you can figure out much more tonight."

He was right. She was exhausted and it was hard to think clearly.

"I guess you're right. I can't figure out my entire

future in five minutes.'' She sighed and glanced over at him. ''But thanks again for listening. It's really helped me,'' she said sincerely.

''I want to help you any way I can, Maura. I mean it,'' he promised her.

The emotion in his voice surprised her, and before she could answer, he shifted over on the couch, closing the small space between them. He put his arm around her shoulder and held her close.

His nearness was a soothing balm to her soul. They didn't talk for a few moments, and Maura allowed herself to simply relax and soak up the strength and comfort he offered.

After a time she said, ''What really made you come here tonight?''

''Just what I said when I came in, I was worried about you and thought you could use some company.''

She honestly hadn't realized that Doug thought about her as much as he apparently did. Maybe he didn't think of her in a romantic way, but their relationship did seem to matter to him, she reflected.

Then he shifted and glanced down at her and she knew intuitively there was something more. Something he was reluctant to say.

''Look, I know this sounds crazy, but I feel like this is partly my fault. This problem of yours, I mean.'' She felt his broad chest expand as he took a deep breath. ''I've known Scott a very long time. I know how he treats women. I wasn't surprised at all when I heard about the way he broke up with you,'' he admitted. ''Months ago, when I first met you and learned you were seeing him, I thought about saying something to you. To warn you in some way about him. But I didn't want to interfere. I could see you really cared for him and he seemed to care for you. You seemed happy together,'' he added, sounding almost angry to admit it, Maura noticed. Though she couldn't understand why.

"Was I happy? Yes, at first I guess I was,'' she agreed. "Until I really got to know him.''

"I'd hoped that maybe you would figure him out sooner than most, and get through it without any serious damage. But it didn't turn out that way, I guess,'' Doug said. "Does it bother you to hear these things about him?'' he added.

Maura shook her head. "No, not at all. In a strange way it makes me feel better. When Scott broke up with me, I felt it was all my fault. As if there was some reason I couldn't make him love me and want to stay with me. Now I can see that it wasn't me at all.''

"No, not you at all, Maura. Scott would have been lucky beyond deserving if he'd made a commitment to you,'' Doug assured her. "Still, I feel responsible for how things ended up. If I had told you about Scott, about his past, maybe this would never have happened.''

Maura was stunned by his line of reasoning. She pulled back and stared up at him. "Don't be ridiculous. I'd never make that connection in a million years.''

"I know you don't see it that way. But I do,'' he argued. "I knew you were too good for him. I knew how he'd end things with you. Just like all the others. I should have warned you.''

"Even if you had, I wouldn't have believed you or taken your advice to heart," Maura replied honestly. "I really thought we were in love and that Scott wanted to marry me someday."

"Maybe you wouldn't have listened to me. Not at first. But it might have helped you see his true colors sooner," he added somberly.

Maura met his gaze. Perhaps that was true. But what good did it do to wonder about that now? She had to deal with the present and figure out some plan for the future.

"It doesn't matter. Let's not argue about it," she urged him. "The point is, I'm the only one responsible for dating Scott...and for everything that happened after."

She rose abruptly, then instantly felt her head spin. Doug was beside her in a split second, his arm wrapped tightly around her waist.

"Maura, are you dizzy?"

"Just a little. I haven't eaten much today," she realized. "That must be it."

He piled up some couch pillows so she could lie back comfortably. "Here, rest a minute. I'll fix you something."

"You don't have to do that," she said. "I can manage."

"I said rest," he ordered in a stern tone. "I'm the doctor, remember?"

When she looked up at him in surprise, he flashed a sexy, stubborn grin.

"Okay, okay. You win." She sat back with a sigh and a small smile. "I didn't know you could cook, Dr. Connelly," she added curiously.

"Me? I'm great in the kitchen—if you like scrambled eggs and toast."

Maura laughed for the first time in days.

"Eggs on the dry side, please. Just a little jelly on the toast," she replied as her head sunk back into the pillows.

"You got it." He leaned over and covered her with a throw, then strolled off to the kitchen.

Maura felt her eyes close, her scattered thoughts lulled by the sounds and tempting smells of Doug's cooking and the powerful, calming force of his presence. For the first time in days she felt some tranquillity and some hope about the future.

Her hands floated protectively to her stomach and she thought about her baby. During all her shock and worry, the single most important element in all this had been obscured, she realized. She was honestly thrilled to be expecting a child, no matter what the circumstances.

When Doug had asked about her intentions, she hadn't revealed half of her true feelings about the baby. The truth was she wanted this child more than anything. Becoming pregnant made her see that she was very much alone in the world. Maybe she had always wanted a child, to love and be loved by the one person in her life who would always belong to her. She had a good relationship with her sister, but Ellen lived in Portland and had a family of her own. Maura had no one truly close.

Since her parents' tragic accident and the trauma of watching her family fall to pieces, Maura had been on a private journey, longing to return to that special place of warmth, love and security she had known as a child. She had imagined creating that kind of stable, loving home life as part of a traditional marriage. But it hadn't happened that way. Now she had to play the cards she'd been dealt. Despite her worries and fears, in her heart she was grateful for the new life growing inside of her.

She loved her baby already and knew that she would do her utmost to give her child a good life, to give him or her all the love, security and happiness that a child deserves.

Even if she had to do it all on her own. It would work out somehow, she told herself. It would.

Eggs, milk and butter. A bowl, a frying pan and toaster. Doug easily found what he needed and set to work on Maura's dinner. Their conversation had left him all stirred up, as emotionally scrambled as the bowl of beaten eggs in his hand, and he was glad to focus on some practical task, like cooking. He poured the eggs in the pan, then glanced out into the living room. Maura lay with her eyes closed, and he wondered if she'd fallen asleep. Just as well, he thought. She needed a break. And so did he, to sort out his thoughts about all this.

He felt bad for her, even partly responsible for the fix she was in. He truly wanted to help her, to do what he could. Doug knew that everything he'd just told Maura was true. But he also knew that there was one reaction to her news he had not disclosed. A gut response even stronger than all the rest.

He wanted a baby. He'd wanted one for a very long time. It was the real reason his marriage had fallen apart, and after that disaster his chances of being a father seemed even farther out of reach.

After his divorce, he just couldn't seem to let any woman close enough for a serious relationship. He'd had that once, and once was enough. Romance was for movies and books, as far as he could see. People only fooled themselves into thinking those earth-shaking hormonal rushes were true love. After the tornado died down, there was only disappointment and pain.

So how would he ever be a father? Unless he got some woman pregnant by "accident," as Scott had done to Maura. But that would never be Doug's style.

He put two slices of bread into the toaster, then jammed it down with a bit more force than necessary. The news of Maura's pregnancy and Scott's reaction had felt like salt poured into an open wound. He cursed Scott for the way he'd treated her, and felt an even deeper bitterness for the way the man had turned his back on his child. Doug felt his jaw grow rigid as the anger swelled in him all over again. If a woman like Maura had come to him with news like that, it would have been the happiest day of his life. Why was life so unfair sometimes?

Doug scooped the cooked eggs onto a plate, then spread some jelly on the toast. He grabbed a fork and napkin, then headed out to the living room. But even before he reached the couch he could see that Maura was fast asleep. She looked so peaceful, as if she didn't have a care in the world. He didn't have the heart to wake her. Watching her sleep, he felt another wave of sympathy for her. She was such a good per-son. A wonderful person, truly. He really couldn't remember knowing a woman he liked or respected more. She didn't deserve Scott's mistreatment. She didn't deserve to face such an overwhelming problem all alone. But what could he do to help her? Stand by her as her friend? Give her money maybe, if she'd let him? There didn't seem much he could do. And what if she moved away? What then? They would lose touch and he'd never see her again. Or her baby.

The possibility upset him. He almost had the urge to wake her and get her to talk some more about her plans. Instead he set the dish of eggs on the coffee table, then sat down to wait.

Maura's eyes opened slowly. Doug's face, very close to her own, filled her field of vision. His golden eyes glittered in the shadowy light, rugged features tempered by a slight smile. She stared up at him, studying the strong lines of his brow and chin, his amber eyes, square jaw and wide, soft mouth.

Then he lifted his hand and softly pushed a lock of her hair off her cheek…and she knew she wasn't dreaming. This was real. Too real for her peace of mind.

"I'm sorry. I didn't mean to fall asleep again," she murmured.

"Better get used to it. Pregnant women fall asleep at the drop of a hat," he reported with a slight smile. "Your scrambled eggs got cold. But you looked so peaceful, I didn't have the heart to wake you."

He was seated on the edge of the couch near her hip and leaning over her. His gaze met hers, and she couldn't look away, feeling only vaguely aware of the movement of his hand, as it came to rest on the curve of her waist. Maura thought to sit up and move away, but she felt frozen in place. She felt as if everything was suddenly moving at a superslow pace. Even her words seemed delayed as she tried to speak.

"It must be late," she said finally.

Doug made no move to check his watch, and she wondered if he had even heard her. His gaze moved slowly over her face, studying her, feature by feature, as if seeing her for the very first time.

"You probably ought to go," she whispered.

"Probably," he replied in a low, husky tone. His hand moved from her hair to cup her cheek, and before Maura could utter a single word, his mouth met hers in a deep, hungry kiss.

The touch of his lips to hers started out as a sensual savoring. Maura's senses reeled with pleasure. All logical thought was totally short-circuited as Doug's supple lips teased and tasted, coaxing her full response. Her hands automatically rose up to his strong shoulders, and the feel of his firm muscles and warm skin under fingertips instantly melted her last resistance.

She made a small moan in the back of her throat, a sound of half pleasure, half surrender.

She felt his response as his arms moved tightly around her, his kiss growing deeper. Their passion accelerated instantly, from zero to one hundred in a millisecond. It was as if a mysterious switch, hidden somewhere deep inside, had been flipped. Her mouth opened easily under his probing tongue, and her arms wound around his powerful shoulders. She felt him move next to her on the couch and she shifted over, so that he stretched out next to her, their legs and arms and tongues entwined.

The kiss that had begun so tenderly grew bolder. Hungry and intense. A knockout sensual punch that sent Maura's senses spinning.

His embrace tightened as his tongue plunged into her mouth, sliding seductively against her own. His large, strong hands glided down her satin-covered back, sweeping over her waist and hips, then down to cup her bottom, pulling her close to his heat.

Then his warm lips left her mouth and wandered in a scintillating path down the column of her throat. His hand glided up over her soft curves and gently cupped her throbbing breast.

What was happening here? she wondered vaguely as she kissed him back. For all the months and all the intimacy she'd shared with Scott, he had never once kissed her like this.

No one had ever kissed her like this.

And never once had she felt this way in any man's arms. So vibrantly alive, so sensual, so uninhibited.

Then suddenly, as if remembering himself, Doug lifted his head. "Maura…" he murmured in surprise. He dropped his head against her shoulder and took a deep breath. "I shouldn't have done that," he admitted in a harsh whisper.

Then, with some effort, he pulled away and pulled her robe up to cover her shoulders. "I came here to help you, not cause more problems."

"I know that," Maura said. She believed it, too.

Still, she felt shaken. Shaken to the core. His merest touch had sent her up in flames. She suddenly realized with a shock the strong attraction they shared.

An attraction that she had so far been basically unaware of.

He sat up and took another long breath, then glanced at her with an awestruck expression. Then he got up and walked across the room as if he truly needed to put some space between them. He stood with his back to her, his hands on his hips.

Maura sat up, too, and fumbled with her robe. She wondered what he was thinking. Probably he was just plain confused. She felt confused, as well. One minute Doug was her pal, her surrogate big brother, and the next minute...

Well, to be perfectly honest, she always knew there was a spark on her side, but she'd been committed to Scott and never even dared explore those feelings. Besides, she only once had the slightest hint that Doug felt drawn to her that way. Did he have feelings for her that he'd never revealed because she was not free?

Then again, they had never been alone like this before, in such an intimate situation. An emotional tinderbox. That was it right there, she decided. Things like this can happen to people in a crisis. He'd just been swept away by the circumstances. He was feeling sorry for her, maybe even protective.

All these emotions had gotten confused in his mind. In her mind, too. It didn't mean anything. She couldn't allow herself to think that one kiss—one mind-blowing kiss, she had to admit—signaled something more.

Finally he turned to her, his handsome features calm and composed. She willed herself to act the same.

He looked about to speak, but she cut in before he could say a word. "That's okay. Don't even say it."

His thick brows drew together in a frown. "How do you know what I was going to say?"

"I just know," she replied. "You're sorry you kissed me. You didn't really mean it. These things happen. And you hope that it doesn't change our friendship. Right?"

He stared at her with a narrowed gaze. "Wrong," he said firmly. "I'm not the least bit sorry I kissed you. Surprised, maybe, and hoping you don't think I was trying to take advantage of you. But definitely not sorry."

"You're not?"

"Heaven knows, I didn't mean for it to happen like that, but it's probably just as well. It makes the next thing I want to say easier."

She was confused again. Had she missed something? "The next thing? Which is...?"

"Which is," he said slowly, drawing the word out in his deep, low voice, "that I've figured out what you should do."

He walked slowly toward her, and Maura felt her heartbeat quicken at the strange, unsettling light in his eye. Inner warning bells sounded. She couldn't put her finger on it, but she felt something was about to happen to her.

Something momentous and totally unexpected.

He was standing right in front of her now, his muscular arms crossed over his broad chest. She had to tilt her head back to look up at him. Her mouth felt dry as she started to speak.

"And what do you think that is?" she asked in a halting tone.

"Simple." His low, commanding tone gave her chills. "Marry me."

"Marry you?" Maura wasn't sure she'd heard him correctly. She couldn't believe he was proposing to her.

"That's what I said. I'm asking you to marry me," he repeated patiently, holding her wide-eyed gaze.

"But how can I marry you?" She knew the question sounded silly as soon as she spoke the words, but she was too stunned to edit her reaction. "I mean, our relationship…we're just friends. I can't just marry you."

She saw him blink, yet his expression showed no other reaction. She unconsciously bit her lip and looked away.

"A husband and wife *should* be friends," he replied smoothly. "Don't you think?"

"Of course I do. It's just that there has to be something more to it."

"Like love, you mean?" His deep voice held an uncharacteristically cynical note. "Let me tell you something, Maura. People get married every day thinking they're totally, wildly, unbelievably in love. And more than half of them end up having rotten marriages."

"Yes," she said quietly. She tucked a strand of hair behind her ear. "I'm sure that's true."

He was referring to his own failed marriage, no doubt, and she was curious to hear more. Yet she could tell it was still a painful topic and she didn't think it was the time to ask him about it.

"I know you think this sounds crazy," he continued. "I thought the same, too, when I first had the idea. But I've had some time to think it through while you were dozing," he gently teased her. "I know this could work. I feel it in my gut. I respect you. I care for you. We share the same values and understand the demands of the kind of work we both do. We both love children. And you even laugh at my bad jokes," he added with a smile.

"Only because I don't want to hurt your feelings. I know how thin-skinned doctors can be," she returned with a grin.

He laughed, and she met his warm gaze.

He really was so handsome. Even more so than usual right now, with that persuasive, hopeful expression on his face. And she knew that he was a decent man. Kind, even noble. Intelligent and successful, as well.

Any woman in her right mind would want to marry him, a little voice inside urged. But could she possibly go through with such a thing? They barely knew each other. They certainly weren't in love. Although after that kiss, there could be little question about physical compatibility…

No, she didn't dare think that far. Besides, even if they went through with it, he'd said nothing about it being a *real* marriage.

Still, as she glanced at him again, she felt her resistance melting away second by second. If he persisted in this amazing proposal, where would she ever find the strength to refuse him?

"I understand what you're saying, Doug. I feel the same about you…and I appreciate your offering to help me. Honestly,'' she added, meeting his gaze for an instant. ''But how can I marry you? I really can't.''

''Of course you can,'' he insisted in a quiet but firm tone. ''You absolutely can.''

''But it's not fair to you. You may regret it. I'm almost sure you will.''

''I won't regret it, Maura. I swear to you.'' His tone was utterly solemn and final, and his gaze held hers steadily.

She didn't answer. She just couldn't. She looked away, clenching her hands in her lap. ''I...I just don't know what to say.''

He walked over to where she sat, crouched down beside her and took hold of both of her hands, enfolding them gently in his own. ''Maura, I understand your doubts, I really do. But, believe me, I really want to marry you. I want to make a home with you and be a father to your baby. At least let's try. Look, let's make a deal. What if we agree to stay married until the baby comes. If you're not happy after that, we'll figure out what to do.''

Maura couldn't speak for a moment. She couldn't take her eyes away from his. She took a deep breath and prayed to heaven that she would do the right thing.

''For the baby. Maybe you're right,'' she finally said.

Doug smiled into her eyes. ''Does that mean you're saying yes?''

Maura stared straight ahead. Her heart was pounding so hard she was sure he could hear it. Could this really be happening to her?

She turned to him and touched her hand to his lean

cheek. "Yes, I'd be honored to marry you," she said quietly, the words just about sticking in her throat. "And I agree to your deal. If either of us wants out of the marriage after the baby comes, there'll be no questions asked."

"Good," he said simply, his voice so low and deep it made her shudder.

What in heaven's name was she doing, taking advantage of him this way, she wondered with a horrified shock. She was nearly about to take back her consent. Then he slowly smiled and leaned toward her, and every doubt scattered like leaves chased by a wild wind.

His face came closer and her eyes closed as his mouth met hers in a swift but possessive kiss. A kiss that set a seal upon her heart, affirming the promise they had made.

No, this wasn't a marriage based on love, Maura reflected. But despite her doubts, she'd go through with it. To set her life back on course. But more than that, for the sake of her child.

Three

Maura woke up at daybreak on Friday, well before the alarm. She had coffee, showered and carefully dressed in a brand-new pale-pink suit. The straight, knee-length skirt with a back slit made her slim legs look even longer, and the jacket's peplum style accentuated her small waist.

She removed from a small velvet box pearl earrings and a pearl choker, remembrances of her mother, and carefully put them on. It was times like this that Maura suddenly missed her family, especially her mother. She hadn't told anyone in Chicago about her decision to marry Doug, not even her sister or close friend, Liza.

She had always imagined a real church wedding, surrounded by friends and family, with a long, white gown and all the trimmings. But here she was, hurrying off to city hall to get married in secret—to a man she barely knew.

It had been just two days since Doug's impulsive proposal—and her impulsive acceptance. The time had passed in a dreamy haze as she and Doug had made their private plans. She had walked around the hospital, knowing she appeared perfectly normal on the outside, while inside she'd felt strangely unreal. She had agreed with Doug that a no-frills ceremony would be best, and through his step-brother, Seth Connelly, he'd found a judge who would marry them in his private chambers.

Doug had wanted to tell everyone right away about their plans to marry, but Maura had persuaded him to wait until it was a done deal. Maura had secretly worried that Doug might have had second thoughts—not that she would have blamed him. Or that maybe *she* would back out of the agreement. She'd known she wouldn't have been able to stand the embarrassment if she'd told people ahead of time and it hadn't worked out. She also hadn't wanted her co-workers asking a million questions or even giving her the usual, staff bridal shower. She'd felt like a bit of a fraud, knowing she wouldn't have been able to stand up to such close scrutiny.

Their hasty plans had given Doug only two days to clear his busy calendar and had given Maura little time to make room for Doug's belongings. She'd never seen his apartment, but had imagined the sparsely furnished studio, which reportedly didn't even have a real kitchen. Especially with the baby coming, her two-bedroom apartment was the logical choice as their new home.

Maura had distracted herself from her doubts by vigorously cleaning out her closets and the small second bedroom she used as a guest room and study. As she'd vacuumed and dusted, her gaze had kept returning to the blue sofa bed.

Would Doug be sleeping there at night...or sharing her bed? In the last two days they had talked over many practical matters regarding their marriage and quickly found agreement on every issue. But each time she'd considered bringing up sleeping arrangements, she'd shied away from the question. She'd felt so confused about it.

She was undeniably attracted to him.

If that kiss he'd given her prior to his proposal was any indication, he was attracted to her, as well. He had kissed her a few times since, in full view of their colleagues, too. When she'd asked him about it, he explained that he'd thought it was best to spark some gossip, so news of their marriage wouldn't come as a complete surprise. Then he'd jokingly added that they'd soon be married and she ought to get used it.

Maura knew she would have a part to play when they were out in public. They had agreed to act as if their marriage was a true love match, deciding it would make things so much easier at work and with both of their families, especially Doug's. Still, did that mean he expected their union to be a real one in every sense? Maura knew in her heart that if he wanted to make love to her, she wouldn't have the will to resist. But was that the best course for her to follow?

Their marriage still seemed so improbable at times, she often feared it would all dissolve in the blink of an eye, like a lovely but strange dream. Doug kept promising her everything would work out. But what if didn't?

But Maura tried to focus on the very immediate and positive present. She was running late, and Doug would be worried. She slipped a lipstick in her small handbag, then stepped into the impossibly high heels an eager salesgirl had talked her into. They matched the suit perfectly but were no match for Maura, who typically wore sturdy rubber-soled walking shoes for work every day. She wobbled more than a little in the heels, crossing the room to reach her dressing table. But as she approached the full-length mirror, she had to admit she looked...well, pretty darned good.

She placed the small matching hat on her head, secured it with pins and then pulled the pale-pink veil down over her face. It was just the feminine, glamorous touch she'd wanted. Maura felt as elegant and stylish as she'd ever been in her life.

She'd never been one to fuss over her appearance. But today was not only important because it was her wedding day, but because she finally had a chance to impress Doug. The only time he'd seen her dressed in anything but her baggy polyester uniform was the other night, when she'd been wearing her bathrobe and no makeup.

Maybe it was childish, but she knew he'd proposed mainly out of sympathy and because he was so noble. But when they met this morning she wanted to look so great that he wouldn't even recognize her. When they stood together and said their vows, she wanted him to feel anything but sympathy. She wanted him to be proud of her and feel he had no regrets in carrying through on his promise.

* * *

Doug paced anxiously in the old courthouse's cool marble lobby. He checked his watch for what seemed like the hundredth time, then pushed through a heavy door to stand outside. He took a deep breath of fresh air. It was a perfect morning in May, cloudless and mild, especially fair for Chicago. A perfect morning to get married. Friday appeared to be a big day in the matrimony department. A long line of couples had already assembled in the office on the fifth floor.

But his bride-to-be was late. Very late.

It wasn't like Maura. She was always so organized and punctual. He'd called her apartment twice, but there had been no answer. He knew that meant she must have left and was probably stuck in traffic. But it could also mean she was standing him up, he thought worriedly.

How many times in the past few days had she questioned their decision to marry? How many times had he needed to reassure her? But he knew it was right. Not logical perhaps. But simply and totally the right thing to do. For her and for him, as well.

He felt it in his bones, in his blood. He'd never felt so sure of anything before in his life. It was going to be easy to pretend that he and Maura were marrying for love because he felt so settled and sure about his decision. More settled even than the first time, when he had married Karen North, believing that he had made a lifelong commitment.

Karen was a golden girl, a tall, slim, gorgeous blonde. Every guy on campus wanted to get close to her. That was how Karen liked it, too. When they'd met, he'd never imagined she could go for a guy like him. For one thing, he was too serious, a real bore compared to Karen, either working one of his part-time jobs or in the library, trying to keep up his grades for the scholarship putting him through undergraduate studies and the one he wanted for med school. Besides, he was pathetically poor compared to her family.

But maybe that was what attracted Karen to him in the first place. He was certainly different from the people she'd known her entire life, growing up in her affluent Lake Forest cocoon. She'd admired him at first, found him so dedicated and with such strong values. But her admiration soon grew thin, Doug reflected. Once they were married, during his first year of medical school, Karen realized that unlike many young doctors, he was not dedicated to the idea of making money.

This came as a great shock to his young wife. She was sure that sooner or later, if she cajoled, teased and pressured him enough, Doug would come around. But her tactics pushed them even further apart. To the breaking point. By the time she announced that she'd found someone else—a plastic surgeon who shared her values, not surprisingly—there was nothing much left of their marriage to mourn, Doug reflected. Only the fact that they'd never had children.

Well, best not to dwell on the past. Not this morning, of all days. He hardly thought of Karen anymore. It still hurt if he allowed his thoughts to drift there. The betrayal. The humiliation. He had found it hard to allow anyone close again. All his relationships since that time had either totally bored him or had gone down in flames. He just couldn't seem to connect or give a woman what she wanted emotionally.

But Maura was different. He'd felt so from the first. She was sweet and openhearted, totally sincere. They shared the same values, the same outlook, the same dedication to their work. At times Doug felt so attuned to her, it was simply uncanny. Maura was the complete opposite of his ex-wife, that was for sure.

But did he love her? He respected her, admired her, felt protective of her and certainly had deep feelings for her. Feelings that even he hadn't been aware of until the other night. He knew now he'd been secretly jealous of her relationship with Scott Walker. He'd felt pleased when he'd heard that they'd broken up, although he hadn't admitted that.

But did he love her? Ultimately, the answer was no, he did not.

But Doug was equally certain he would never fall in love with any woman again. Not the way he had fallen so head over heels with Karen, as if she owned him, heart and soul. He never wanted to feel that way again about anybody.

He did want a child. And in the past few days he wondered if it was dishonest of him to offer Maura marriage but never explain that part of his reason. But each time he had the urge to tell her, some intuition warned him to hold back until they were married. He just had the feeling she wouldn't understand and might even back out of their plan.

And he didn't want that. He wanted to help her and help himself.

Some might consider what he felt for Maura a slim foundation for a step as weighty as marriage, but he knew it was solid and real. A bedrock to build a life on. Not some airy-fairy romantic fantasy or sexual chemistry that ignites in a flash, then burns out just as swiftly.

They would have an equal partnership. They would make a life together and raise Maura's child.

While he loved taking care of other people's children, healing them and making them strong and happy again, his professional satisfaction would never take the place of raising children of his own. It was an issue he and Karen had talked about often—argued about often, too.

But by the time they were financially ready to start a family, the relationship was already on the ropes. Karen knew how much he wanted a baby and had used that to blackmail him, refusing to get pregnant or even to make love, unless he gave in to her demands.

She wanted him to stop taking on poor patients who couldn't pay, she wanted him to leave Chicago General and start a practice in an upper-class community where he'd have regular hours and make more money. That was the price he had to pay to have a baby with her. She believed she held the winning hand. But her tactics pushed him even further away. As much as he'd wanted a child, he wouldn't "pay" for one by denying his true values and motivation for becoming a doctor. Besides, his speciality in pediatric cardiology made regular hours impossible. But Karen didn't seem to understand that. Or didn't want to. She kept insisting he would give up that part of his practice and just work as a general pediatrician. But Doug felt that request, too, was extremely unfair of her.

More important, he knew it was wrong to bring a child into their troubled relationship.

Now fate had brought him both a wife and a child. Doug sometimes wondered at his own impulsive decision to show up at Maura's door and propose marriage. But now it seemed as if he'd been handed a chance to make things right for Maura. And for himself. He pushed aside his doubts and grasped that chance with both hands. Now if only his reluctant bride would appear and they could get the nerve-wracking part of this entire business over with. He knew everything after that would work out just fine.

Doug spotted a taxi pull over to the curb and a woman start to emerge. God, what a woman, he thought as he watched her stand upright and smooth out her skirt before taking on the long flight of granite steps.

Was it Maura, he wondered. He thought he recognized her fine profile, her tall, slim build, but he couldn't see her hair, pinned up under a provocative little hat. And he couldn't see her face, with her chin dipped down as she climbed the steps and much of her face covered by a veil.

He suddenly realized he'd never seen Maura dressed up. Never seen her in anything but her uniform, actually. The woman approaching him could be Maura. He allowed himself to take a longer, more appraising look, then couldn't quite draw his gaze away. She was simply gorgeous. A total knockout. From her softly veiled features to her sexy high heels.

He felt disloyal watching this way if she didn't turn out to be his intended. But Doug couldn't quite take his eyes off this alluring vision, her perfect figure artfully displayed in a stylish, tailored suit, a petal-pink confection. All you could see of her face was a pouting pink mouth, her lips tempting to be tasted, explored, savored.

As she walked purposefully up the steps, straight toward him, his mouth grew dry. He still wasn't sure if it was Maura, his bride-to-be, and felt a mixture of lustful excitement and guilt watching the mystery woman's lean shapely legs carry her the remaining steps to where he stood.

No crime in looking, he wryly reflected. Married or not, I'm only a man. And this woman makes me glad of it, he laughed to himself.

Then she stood before him, inches away, her back to the early-morning sun, her face still shadowed by the veil.

"Waiting for me?" she asked in a breathless voice.

"Well, I...I—" Doug stammered and for the life of him, he couldn't tell for absolute sure it was Maura.

Then she laughed and lifted her chin so he could see her face. Maura's face, familiar, yet somehow exciting, unknown territory. Her smile lit up her lovely features, making her beautiful green eyes shine with emotion. He'd never noticed that before and he knew he'd be a lucky man to look up each morning and find that smile shining just for him.

Doug glanced down, suddenly remembering the bouquet of flowers in his hand, cream-colored roses, pink phlox and miniature orchids. The colors matched her outfit perfectly, as if it had been planned.

"These are for you," he said.

"What beautiful flowers. Thank you."

"You're very welcome." He knew he was still staring, but couldn't help himself. Her expression of delight and the fresh flowers in her grasp emphasized her natural beauty even more.

"Sorry I was late. My taxi was caught in traffic."

"I thought as much," he replied smoothly, though he'd actually considered the worst.

"You didn't recognize me at first, did you?" Her eyes sparkled with a teasing light.

He shrugged. "Of course I did."

"Oh? Why didn't you say something? You were staring at me as if I was a total stranger."

Doug paused for just a heartbeat. Then he leaned closer, slipping his arm around her waist in a tight, possessive gesture that made Maura's stomach drop to her toes.

"I was staring at you because you look so beautiful you take my breath away," he admitted in a harsh whisper. He dropped a hard kiss on her mouth, then quickly pulled his head away.

"Now let's get married, Maura. I think you've kept me waiting long enough."

When he pulled back a bit, Maura stared up at him, too astounded by his words and gesture to speak. Maura took the arm he offered, and with a deep breath, walked into city hall at his side.

The ceremony was brief and to the point, as Maura had expected. As the judge read the official script from a small black book, Maura could hardly concentrate on the words. She suddenly noticed how wonderful Doug looked, how tall and fit he appeared in his dark-blue suit, stark white shirt and burgundy silk tie. His brown hair was combed back and looked newly cut, his lean cheeks smoothly shaved. She could hardly recall seeing a man more handsome, and it was hard to believe he would very soon and very officially be her husband.

The clerk asked for the rings, and Doug produced two gold bands. Her ring was inlaid with three small rubies and engraved with a vine-like design. Doug's was quite plain and masculine looking, she noticed as she slipped it on his finger. She had forgotten all about rings and stared down at hers in surprise as the clerk finished the ceremony.

Once pronounced husband and wife, Doug's kiss to seal their vows was tantalizingly brief. Immediately after, in the split second they moved apart, she glimpsed a questioning look in his eyes and something more, a look that was pure male desire and sent a chill down to her toes.

Then, just as quickly, that look vanished, his expression showing little emotion at all. The clerk asked them to sign some papers. As Maura smiled and stood beside her handsome groom, the reality of what she'd done began to sink in.

She felt practically light-headed as they left the dark building and stepped out into the sunshine. But Doug seemed unfazed and clearly had plans. He took her hand as they walked down the stone steps—either as a gesture of affection or merely because he noticed her wobbling on her perilously high heels.

They started walking toward his car, and Doug kept firm hold of her hand. People were glancing at them, some smiled and said, "Good luck." Maura remembered her bouquet and realized it was a dead give-away—everyone knew they were newly married.

"I've made reservations for lunch at Bistro 53, but we don't have to go there if you'd rather not," Doug said, mentioning the city's latest epicurean sensation. "Have you tried it yet?"

"No problem," Maura laughed. "I really don't keep up with the hot spots much."

"I thought maybe Scott had taken you there. He liked to try all the latest places."

"We went out often enough, I guess. But after a while, mostly I cooked in. It was so much...cozier."

She didn't mean to mar their fine morning with bitterness, but she could hardly help herself when she talked about Scott.

Doug glanced at her, his mouth turned down in a frown. He abruptly stopped in his tracks, and she had to grip his arm to keep from stumbling. He didn't seem to notice.

"Listen, let's make a pact. From now on, unless absolutely necessary, no mention of Scott. We're starting off here with a clean slate. Agreed?"

"Agreed." Maura nodded and smiled. Doug was right. And so perceptive. Memories of Scott only brought her down. Her relationship with Doug was going to be difficult enough without lugging along that heavy baggage.

"On to Bistro 53," she said brightly. "What a nice surprise."

"It's our wedding day, Maura. We need to celebrate," Doug replied with an indulgent smile.

They reached his car and Doug opened the door for her. She'd been in the black sports car once before, but didn't recall that it was quite so small and so low. Her narrow skirt made it hard to wriggle into her seat.

She sensed Doug looking hungrily at a length of leg, revealed by the skirt's slit, then quickly glancing away. Well, they were married. The man was entitled to check out what he'd gotten for his trouble, she thought wryly.

Doug maneuvered the sports car easily through the city's heavy traffic, and they were soon driving on picturesque Lake Shore Drive, headed for the city's most fashionable neighborhood. At the restaurant a valet parked the car and the maître d' led them to a secluded table by the window, the magnificent lake in full view.

Perhaps it was their newlywed status, or maybe Doug had surreptitiously tipped the entire staff. Maura was not sure of the reason, but couldn't help notice that they were treated royally. Even better than one would expect in such an elegant restaurant. The decor was gorgeous, the food sublime. Maura's wedding day jitters soon dissolved, and she once again felt her familiar, warm rapport with Doug.

"What treatment," Maura finally remarked when their waiter brought them yet another special dish, compliments of the chef—an hors d'oeuvre portion of lobster Napoleon, with a delicate sherry sauce.

"You must come here often to rate such attention," she finally said.

Doug took a moment to swallow a small bite of his lobster, savoring the flavor. "Hmm, that was good. But no, they don't really know me. I've only come here once before, for lunch with my father. But I suppose the Connelly name goes far in this city. And it's your name now, too, Maura,'' he added with a small smile.

''The Connelly name. Oh, of course,'' she replied, feeling foolish for overlooking the fact that Doug was part of that eminent Chicago family.

The name brought to mind privilege, power, celebrity and of course fabulous wealth. None of which she associated with Doug. But shortly after they'd met, she'd heard bits and pieces of how he'd recently discovered he was a member of the prestigious clan. She had never asked Doug directly about the story but had always been curious.

She suddenly worried that perhaps Doug suspected her motives for agreeing to their marriage. Maybe he thought she'd only married him for his newfound wealth and connections. But then she swept the thought aside. Doug knew very well she would never resort to such a tactic. Not even to protect her child. During the past few days he'd had plenty of time to present her with a prenuptial agreement, to protect his interests should they divorce, and had never once even mentioned it. It made her feel good to realize how much he truly trusted her.

''Tell me, Doug. How did you first find out that you were a Connelly?'' Maura asked. ''When we first met, your last name was Barnett, right?''

''Yes, that's right. It was important to Grant Connelly, my father, that my brother and I change our names to his, once we discovered our true relationship. My brother was more resistant to it than I. But I'm getting ahead of myself,'' he added. He paused and sat back in his chair. ''Well, let's see… I've already told you that I was raised by my mother, Hannah. It was just me and my twin brother, Chance.''

Maura already knew that Doug had a twin brother and had a close relationship with him. Chance was a Navy SEAL and had recently gotten engaged to be married, she recalled.

''Naturally, as we got older we were curious about our father and asked my mom a lot of questions,'' Doug continued. ''But she would never tell us anything. Just that she was quite young when she'd known him and had loved him. But they couldn't be together and they were never in touch. I guess I got the idea that she didn't even know how to find this mystery man even if she wanted to,'' Doug added, shaking his head. ''Little did I realize his picture was in the financial section or the society pages of the newspaper almost every day.

''She'd never say anything negative about our father, either,'' Doug continued. ''In fact, she gave us the impression he was a good man. A decent person. But as I got older, I just couldn't buy it anymore. In a way, I guess I came to hate my father without even knowing him,'' Doug confessed, ''this faceless, heartless guy who had abandoned my poor mother when she needed him most. He didn't seem very nice or decent to me,'' Doug said bitterly. ''Still, my mother protected him. Her loyalty was limitless. And absolutely undeserved by my father, I thought.''

''It must have been very hard for you, dealing with all those feelings growing up.''

''Yes, it was.'' He met her gaze directly and for a moment she saw what he must have been like as a small boy, brooding over questions about his father and feelings of love and protection for his mother. He glanced out at the lake and took a sip of his coffee.

"When my mother died, one of her last words was my father's name. My brother and I knew instinctively that she had finally told us the identity of our father. But by then we weren't nearly so intent on finding him and confronting him. And we also wondered if it was true. My mother was heavily medicated in her final days. We wondered if she had been rational."

"Yes, I see," Maura replied, considering Doug's story.

"But as I went through her belongings, I found her diary. I'll never be sure if that was her intention all along, or if in her illness she'd merely neglected to destroy it. She'd recorded the entire story, her attraction and romance to an older man when she was just a student and working as a waitress in a diner near the campus. The man was young, ambitious and clearly headed for great things. She'd been his lover, confidante and everything in between. My mother believed in him totally. She was not only beautiful and intelligent, but a very loving person. So how could he resist her? According to her diary, he had claimed to love her, too. Though he must have seen that their age difference and different situations in life made any long-lasting ties unlikely." Doug looked out at the lake for a moment, and she could tell from his expression that it was hard for him to tell this story.

"Then, while her lover was traveling abroad, he met another woman. A woman more suited to his ambitions and plans. My mother read about their romance in the society column. This woman was a world figure—a princess, in fact, of marriageable age, so if she so much as smiled at a man it made all the celebrity gossip columns.''

Emma Connelly had been a princess of some small country, Maura recalled. The place was called Altaria, wasn't it? And Emma had given up her royal life to marry Grant Connelly, who was then just an up-and-coming American businessman.

''My mother, a waitress and part-time student, knew she could never compete with this rival,'' Doug continued. ''She also believed that my father would be far happier with his new love. So she made a truly self-sacrificing choice and simply disappeared from his life, without him ever knowing why. Or ever knowing that she was pregnant with his sons. He never knew what had happened to her or why she'd gone.''

''What a story,'' Maura said, awestruck. ''She must have loved him very much.''

Doug glanced at her, a look of surprise in his amber eyes.

''Yes, she did. Enough to put her own needs aside, even the needs of her children, in order to spare him the dilemma of making him choose. But it took me a while to realize that. While it only took you about five seconds,'' he added with a small smile.

Maura smiled and looked at the lake. ''Women usually have a better understanding of these things than men.''

''Men are a bit dense,'' Doug offered. ''Anyway, the truth was, my father never knew about my brother and me. This faceless mystery man I had hated all my life wasn't the heartless monster I'd imagined at all.''

"And he turned out to be Grant Connelly," Maura said quietly.

"Yes, the famous Grant Connelly. I couldn't believe it at first. But all the facts added up—the times, the dates, the places. My brother and I couldn't decide if we wanted to confront our father. Or how to do it. We thought maybe he'd deny our claim and think we were fortune hunters.''

"I never thought of that, but I suppose wealthy families like the Connellys have that problem all the time, people claiming they're related and due some piece of the family wealth," Maura said.

"Exactly," Doug replied. "But at the same time I was discovering these secrets, an investigative reporter working on a story about my father had dug up the information and told him he'd had two sons by Hannah Barnett. So we ended up meeting soon after that. When I finally confronted my father, he verified everything. I do believe he loved my mother and was terribly sorry she'd never asked him for help. That alone meant a lot to me," Doug said in a tone edged with emotion. "It went a long way toward changing my feelings about him and changing my anger to forgiveness.''

Maura didn't know what to say. The story was remarkable and a deeply personal confession. She felt so much for Doug, so much for the troubles he'd endured. She could see that, as much as he'd wanted to tell her about this important moment in his life, telling had been hard for him.

She reached across the table and took hold of his hand. "It was good of you to forgive him," she said.

"It wasn't nearly as hard as I'd imagined it would be," Doug reflected with a thoughtful expression. "My father is a remarkable man. He's done everything in his power to show us how much he regrets not having been there while we were growing up. The entire family has been wonderful to me and Chance. I have eight new stepsiblings and have met all of them so far, except for the oldest, Daniel, who is in Altaria and will soon be crowned king."

Wow was the only word that came to Maura's mind.

"I can hardly wait for you to meet Grant and Emma," he added.

"I'm looking forward to it," Maura replied diplomatically.

"I know you pretty well now, Maura. You look as if I'd just invited you to go bungee jumping off the Sears Tower." Doug's laugh was quiet and deep. "Don't worry. It will be fine." He twined his long lean fingers together with hers. "They'll love you, I'm sure of it. Don't be surprised if they throw us a big party."

The idea of being the center of attraction at a celebration hosted by the famous Grant and Emma Connelly was even more intimidating. Maura struggled to hide her alarm.

"You won't tell them that I'm pregnant, will you?" she asked suddenly.

He met her gaze, still holding her hand. "Not if you don't want me to."

"I don't. I mean, they'll find out fairly soon, no

matter what. As will everyone at the hospital,'' she added. ''But for now I'd prefer if we kept it to ourselves. Everyone is going to think you made me pregnant and then had to marry me,'' she added. Then another thought occurred to her, which was even more upsetting. ''They'll also think I was seeing you and Scott at the same time.''

''Who cares what anyone thinks?'' Doug said, his expression serious and intense. He gently squeezed her hand. ''I know we've done the right thing. This is going to work out for us. Let's just take it one day at a time, okay?'' His gaze implored her, and Maura couldn't help but smile.

''Yes, you're right. This is my life and I shouldn't give a fig what anyone thinks.''

''That's my girl.'' His smile grew wider, his reply giving Maura a slight jolt. She was indeed his girl now. More than that, she was his wife. She looked down at their hands clasped together on the table and noticed her shiny new wedding band.

''I never thanked you for the ring,'' she said. ''It's really beautiful.''

He turned her hand to see the stone better. Maura looked at it, too. The jewel sparkled in its golden setting, looking even lovelier than when he'd slipped it on her finger.

''Since we bypassed the engagement stage I wanted to get you something more than a plain gold band. Are you sure you like it? You don't have to say so just to be polite.''

Maura was touched—and even surprised—by his desire to please her. ''It's exactly what I would have chosen. It's perfect, Doug. Really.''

"Good. I'm glad." His gaze met hers again. His smile grew wider—even white teeth against tanned skin. Deep dimples appeared in his lean cheeks, tiny lines fanned out at the corners of his eyes. He was really so attractive. It just about took her breath away. Maura couldn't hold his gaze any longer and glanced away.

Doug paid the check, and they left their table. As they stood at the restaurant door, waiting for the valet to bring Doug's car, his cell phone rang. "My office," he said to Maura as he answered it.

Maura nodded. She knew Doug had arranged for another doctor to cover his patients today, and his office wouldn't be calling unless it was an emergency. At least she had a true understanding of his job. Marrying a doctor was not her ideal, but she knew the demands of his job would never be an issue for her. The grueling hours and priority of patients over family had destroyed many marriages. Maybe that was what had happened in Doug's first marriage, Maura thought.

Doug clicked off the phone and turned to Maura, his expression a mixture of regret and urgency. "I'm needed at the hospital. The Harris boy is in trouble. The doctor covering for me has another emergency and the attending is swamped."

"Don't worry, I understand," Maura assured him. "Good, here's the car," she added as the valet delivered Doug's sports car. "You'd better go. I'll get a cab."

"Are you sure? I could drop you off. It's not that far out of the way."

"I'll be fine. Why waste all that time?"

Doug started to go, then paused and stared deeply into her eyes. "I'm so sorry. I hate to run off on you like this. Especially today."

The tender look in his eyes touched her. She smiled at him and then, without thinking, touched his cheek with her hand.

"Don't be silly. I understand."

Besides, it's not like it's a real wedding day. Or a real marriage, she thought to add. Yet, something stopped her. At that brief moment she felt truly married to him.

She was quickly distracted by the stunning look of gratitude and relief on his handsome face. He swiftly bent toward her and dropped a quick, hard kiss on her mouth.

"I'll make it up to you later. Promise," he added as he got into his car. "And don't worry about unpacking my stuff. I'll take care of it."

"Don't worry," Maura said as she stepped back on the curb.

Maura watched the car quickly pull away. The hospital was not very far. He'd be there soon, she was sure. As for herself, she'd change into comfortable clothes and start unpacking Doug's things, no matter what he said. What else did she have to do on her wedding day?

Grant Connelly entered the spacious family room and settled on a large sofa across from his wife. She looked up from her book and briefly smiled at him. Their schedules were both so busy they rarely had time to have dinner together or spend an evening like this, simply relaxing in each other's company.

Grant was relishing the downtime. He casually studied the financial news of the day as Emma focused on her thick historical novel. Emma loved history. She had so many interests and still, after all these years, had so much intellectual curiosity and a drive to learn new things. That was something Grant had always admired about her.

Emma put her book aside and looked over at him.

"I'm worried about Seth," she said. "What if it doesn't go well?"

Grant met his wife's concerned gaze. After twenty years their son Seth was meeting with his birth mother, Angie Donahue. If all had gone according to plans, at this very moment, they would be sitting down to dinner and getting to know each other again.

Seth had not seen Angie since he was twelve years old, and Angie had basically given up on him. Seth had arrived at the Connelly home angry, sad and confused—doing poorly at school and a party to some minor brushes with the law. If not for our understanding and love, who knows what would have happened to him, Grant reflected.

But he was fine. More than fine, he was happy, successful, and productive. A man Grant was proud to call his son.

"I understand why you're worried, Emma. Really, I do," Grant assured his wife. "But it's only natural that Seth would be curious about his mother. You have to remember he's a grown man. She can't hurt him anymore."

"I worry for no reason, I guess," Emma conceded. "But I can't help remembering the way Seth was when he came to us, so angry and confused. So…damaged by her.''

"I remember," Grant agreed. "But that was long ago.''

Grant sighed, recalling Seth's first days in the Connelly household. Seth was mad at the world and wanted to punish every adult in it—particularly Grant—for his confusion and unhappiness. But day by day, with patience and understanding on the part of his new family, he gradually came to trust, respect and even love Grant, Emma and his stepsiblings. Military school helped, as well, to discipline Seth's strong spirit, strengthen his character and sharpen his fine mind.

"It was a difficult time for all of us, but we got through it.''

"Yes, we did," Emma met his gaze and smiled, communicating volumes in a single look, as only long-married couples can do.

It had been a dark moment in their marriage when Grant admitted that Angie Donahue had given birth to his son and that he'd been secretly supporting his former secretary and the boy for over twelve years.

Emma had been crushed by the betrayal, and they had even separated for a time. But when they'd finally reconciled, his wife, with her gloriously generous heart, had even agreed to take Seth and raise him as one of her own.

Grant had the sudden urge to thank his wife again for pulling them through, for being so forgiving toward him, so accepting of his mistakes and flaws. But words could never communicate the depth of those feelings. He simply tried to show her every day how grateful he was to still be married to her.

"He'll be all right, Emma. You'll see. He's always had questions about Angie and that part of his life. Questions we couldn't answer for him," Grant reflected. "Maybe filling in the pieces will help him sort out some issues in his own life."

"Yes, I think you're right. He's done so well for himself," she said proudly. "But I know he still has to work out some issues about his childhood. And about Angie. Maybe that's what's been holding him back from meeting some nice girl and getting married," she added.

Grant laughed. "Seth is never lacking for female companionship, as far as I can see."

His son's striking good looks, success as an attorney and powerful personality made him a magnet for feminine attention. Seth's problem was quite the opposite, Grant thought, more a case of having too many choices.

"I'm not talking about running around," Emma said. "I'm talking about falling in love. Settling down. These girls he brings home are gorgeous. But none of them seems to keep his interest for very long. I just want to see him happy, with someone he can really love. That's all."

"That's what we want for all our children, isn't it?" Grant asked his wife. "If they could each find half the happiness and love I've found with you, dear, they'd be very lucky indeed."

Emma stared at him a moment, a loving look in her sparkling eyes. "I feel the same about you, too. You know that," she said quietly. Then, in a different tone, "But enough. You'll make me get all weepy and I'm trying to finish this book."

Emma opened her book again with determination, though he could tell she wasn't really reading it.

"If you say so," Grant replied with a laugh.

He still loved her so much he felt his heart swell. It didn't seem possible that a man could live with a woman for so long and still have these feelings. He'd honestly meant what he'd said about their children. He truly wished that each of their sons and daughters could find the kind of marriage he and Emma shared. No amount of worldly fame or even material success could match that priceless treasure.

Coincidentally, Grant was still pondering these thoughts when the housekeeper announced a call from his son Doug. Grant picked up the call immediately.

"Doug, how good to hear from you. What's new?"

Emma put down her book. "Tell him I said hello," she whispered.

Then she was silenced by the amazed expression on Grant's face.

"You're kidding," Grant exclaimed. "That's fantastic news. Hold on. I have to tell Emma. She won't believe it."

"What's happened? Is he okay?" Emma asked in a rush.

"Doug got married today to a nurse he works with at the hospital. Her name is Maura."

"Married?" Emma clutched her chest. She felt breathless. "I can't believe it. Here, let me talk," she insisted, holding her hand out for the phone.

Grant sat back as his wife ecstatically offered her congratulations and then proceeded to interrogate

Doug about his new wife. Well, he deserved a little of that for eloping on them, Grant thought. Not that Emma would let him get off without some type of family celebration. He could already hear her firming up plans for Doug to bring his new wife over for brunch on Sunday.

She handed the phone back to Grant, and he added a few more congratulatory words to his son. Then Doug had to run. He was calling from the hospital and was needed again on the floor.

When Grant turned to Emma, she literally clapped her hands together. "I'd never imagined Doug to be the type to elope. It's so romantic. I can't wait to meet his wife. She must be terrific."

"Well, at least we got one son married off tonight, dear," Grant said dryly. "Not bad work for one evening."

Emma ignored his remark. "We'll have to give them a party, of course. Something informal but nice. Where she can meet the whole family."

Grant recognized that look in his wife's eye. She was off and running, as he had predicted. There was no stopping her now.

"I'd like to have something outdoors. Maybe at the lake house," Emma continued, mentioning their sprawling country retreat on Lake Geneva.

"Sounds perfect to me, but we'd better wait to ask Doug and his new bride what they think, before you call up the caterers and send out invitations," he teased her.

"They're coming for brunch next weekend," Emma said. "I can't wait to meet her. I didn't even know he was seeing anyone."

''Sounds like a whirlwind romance. Doug strikes me as the type who makes up his mind about something and does it.''

''Well, that's the way it is sometimes. You meet someone and you just know,'' Emma replied.

''Yes, that's very true.'' Grant remembered the first time he set eyes on Emma. Everyone else in the world seemed to just disappear. Within moments of saying hello, he knew she was the one. The complications of her life—and his—didn't matter. He knew he had to have her.

''Here, give me the phone,'' Emma said urgently. ''This is big news. I have a lot of calls to make.''

Grant laughed and handed his wife the phone. The secret was out. By the time Doug woke up tomorrow, the entire Connelly clan would know he was married.

Four

Maura heard the key scraping in the lock and then the sound of the door opening and closing again as Doug let himself in. The glowing numbers on the bed-side table clock read 2:32 a.m. He'd been called back to the hospital on an emergency hours ago, just as Maura was coming in after her work shift. They'd barely had the chance to exchange two words with each other before Doug had disappeared again.

That was the way their lives had been for the past week, like two people chasing each other in a revolving door. When friends at work asked how she was enjoying married life, she honestly couldn't say. She hardly felt married at all. Except for the scant evidence of her husband's existence—a shirt slung over the back of a chair, the lingering scent of aftershave in the bathroom—she hardly felt as if anyone at all was sharing her apartment.

He was trying to be quiet and considerate, but she had always been a light sleeper. The hot, muggy weather tonight made sleep even harder. She didn't have any air-conditioning, and the small window fan didn't help much.

She could picture Doug's face as clearly as if he were standing right next to her, his tired expression and five-o'clock shadow. He would be in the mood to talk over his case, especially if there had been some difficult treatment decisions to make. Ironically, they had talked much more in the hospital when they were merely friends than they had so far as husband and wife.

Should she get up and go to him? See how his emergency turned out? Then she rejected the idea, just as she had so many other nights. What would he think, seeing her at his bedroom door in the middle of the night? He would assume she wanted something more than conversation, that was for sure.

What did she want?

Maura honestly didn't know.

When he had moved his things into her apartment, just before their wedding day, Maura had put most of his belongings in her spare bedroom. It seemed the logical place to store the many boxes until they had time to sort things out. She had not purposely intended to send Doug a message that she expected him to sleep there. But she had been asleep by the time he'd gotten home their wedding night, and the next morning, she found him there.

The next day, and all the days since, she never had the courage to talk about it. After all, he didn't seem to mind sleeping alone. He seemed to assume that

would be the arrangement. If he'd expected something different, wouldn't he have made it clear by
now?

Maybe, despite the tantalizing way he'd kissed her
now and again, he wasn't all that attracted to her, she
thought. Though she had to admit, at least to herself,
that she felt different about him. Much different.

So that was why she felt awkward going to him
now, dressed in her nightgown. That was why she felt
their relationship tense and strained during those rare
moments they'd been alone together here since they
married.

If this was the kind of tension she had to face for
the rest of her life, Maura didn't think she could stand
it.

When she was sure he had gone into his room and
closed the door, Maura got up and headed for the
kitchen. She couldn't sleep without a cold drink. She
really wanted ice tea…but milk would be better for
the baby. Cookies and milk, maybe. No, just the milk,
she revised as she stared into the fridge. She didn't
want to gain too much weight. But one cookie
couldn't hurt. Would it?

Lost in her calorie quandary, Maura didn't notice
Doug's tall, powerful form in the doorway.

"If it isn't my phantom wife," he greeted her.

"Doug." Startled, she turned to him. "I thought
you were asleep."

"I thought the same about you."

His words were simple, but in his gruff, low tone
she heard something more. She met his heavy-lidded
gaze, then pulled out the milk carton, making a con-

scious effort to keep it from slipping right through her shaky hands.

He was bare-chested and barefoot, wearing just a pair of faded jeans that hung low on his lean hips. She'd never seen him with so little clothes on, and Maura could barely keep her eyes off his body.

The flash of pure hunger in his gaze made her suddenly self-conscious. She was wearing only a short nightgown, the sheerest one she owned, due to the steamy weather. She quickly sat down at the kitchen table, thankful that there was only a small circle of light cast by the fixture over the sink.

"Sorry if I made too much noise when I came in. I was trying to be quiet."

"It wasn't you. I couldn't sleep that well. It's so hot tonight." She busied herself pouring the milk, carefully avoiding his smoldering gaze.

"Yes, it is," he agreed. "Too hot for May."

And getting hotter by the second in here, she nearly replied.

"I heard we're in for some rain. Maybe that will cool things off," he said.

"Maybe," she agreed.

Here they were alone in the dark, both of them barely dressed, and all he could do was talk about the weather. Now, if that didn't prove he didn't mind sleeping alone in the spare room, Maura asked herself, what did?

He leaned back against the counter, watching her. She felt her mouth grow dry as he crossed his arms over his chest, his wide shoulders and upper arms bunching up into impressive knots of muscle. Thick swirls of soft brown hair emphasized his muscular chest. Her fingers itched to test its texture. Her gaze moved lower, to the flat stretch of abdomen above the edge of his jeans and a thin line of dark hair that disappeared into his waistband. She forced herself to look away and think of something else. Something other than Doug's amazing body...

"How's your patient?" she asked suddenly.

"A very good prognosis. She'll probably leave the hospital by the end of the week."

"That's great," Maura replied, her thought distracted by his alluring image, her fingertips imagining the smoothness of his tanned skin, or the rough stubble on his chin.

"Maura...I'm afraid I haven't been a very good husband to you." Doug's deep, halting tone cut into her wandering fantasies.

"Don't be silly. We haven't seen nearly enough of each other the past few days to tell what kind of husband you are," she replied in a joking tone. "Or for that matter, what kind of wife I'll be."

"You're a great cook," he pointed out. "I've been meaning to tell you. But you're never around when I'm eating the food you've left for me. Leaving a note seemed...silly," he admitted.

"I never find any leftovers. I figured you'd either politely hidden the stuff in the trash or you like my cooking. Or maybe you're hungry enough to eat anything."

"I like your cooking. Especially the beef stew. That was good." He smiled, a flash of even white teeth against bronzed skin, his expression sending even more heat shooting through her body than usual, it seemed. "It was good of you to fix me anything at all."

"It was nothing." She liked to do things for him. He'd been so kind to her, so generous. Yet she couldn't find the right words to explain her feelings. "What are wives for?" she joked.

"I'm sure you're beat at the end of the day. Especially being pregnant."

"I like to do it, honestly. It helps me unwind." Her voice lifted on a shaky note as he closed the small space between them and stood beside her chair.

"From work, you mean? Or are you worried about something else?"

She gazed up at him. He looked so big and powerful, looming over her in the shadowy light, his rugged features fixed in an intense expression. A look of concern, for sure. But beyond that, one of pure, masculine desire that made her pulse race. She turned and looked forward again, feeling frozen in place.

How could she begin to explain that it was him. Sharing this apartment with him, being married, but not quite knowing where they stood. Or how he felt about her.

And wanting him like crazy. Like right now, for instance.

"It's nothing in particular," she said softly.

"Go ahead, you can tell me," he urged her quietly. When she still didn't speak, he put his large, strong hand on her bare shoulder, moving it in small, sensuous circles that made every nerve ending in her body spring to life.

"I don't think this is going to work." She swallowed hard. "I still don't even understand why you married me. I'm not exactly the type that drives men crazy,'' she added, aiming for an ironic note that didn't sound self-pitying.

''No, you're definitely not,'' he agreed, his tone so deep, and definite, it made her heart sink. ''But maybe I didn't want a woman who would drive me crazy. Maybe I've already done that.''

''You know what I mean, Doug. You didn't need to settle for me. You could have had anyone.''

She was totally and absolutely serious, voicing doubts she'd had from the start. Yet she heard Doug reply with a low, sexy laugh, as he moved to stand behind her, his other hand coming to rest on her empty shoulder.

''But I picked you.'' His head dipped down low, so that his mouth was right next to her ear before he spoke again. ''Now you're stuck with me. Is that what's really worrying you, Maura?''

''No...not at all. Don't be silly,'' she said softly.

''Good, then.'' His words, spoken so deep and low, penetrated her very bones.

She felt an impulse to reply, but then the words were stolen from her lips as she felt his heavy warm hands brush back her long hair.

''Don't think so much, Maura. Don't doubt,'' he softly urged her. ''I know this will work. Just give it some time.''

The truth was at that moment she couldn't think. She could barely breathe as his touch glided over her smooth, bare skin. Maura felt her senses tingle with awareness, her ragged nerves instantly soothed yet charged with an energy that was totally electric.

''How's that?'' Doug asked quietly.

"That's…good," she finally managed. "Very… good."

She hadn't even been aware of the hard knots in her neck and shoulders until Doug's strong fingers found them and slowly dissolved them with a touch that was pure magic.

"Your hair is so beautiful. You should wear it down like this more often."

Her eyes were closed, and his deep voice seemed to reach her from far away.

"It's not very practical that way for work," she finally replied.

"At home. With me, I mean." Doug's lips were close to her cheek, and she could feel his warm breath on her skin.

"Yes, with you," she replied softly, feeling as if she were talking in a dream.

She felt him kiss her nape, his mouth wet and hot. A bolt of molten heat flashed through her body. She knew that at that moment she would probably agree to anything he asked. A liquid languor flowed into her limbs, warming every inch of her body.

"Maura," he said softly. "I've missed you. I've missed talking with you like this."

She felt her heartbeat quicken. She'd missed him, too. And during those brief hours they'd spent alone here together, she'd felt such a disturbing tension, as if every movement, every breath, wound the sexual tension between them even higher.

"I…I missed you, too," she admitted softly, without even opening her eyes. His touch felt so good, almost hypnotic. Her senses were focused entirely on the feelings he had so easily aroused. His hands slid down from her shoulders to her arms, his fingertips just grazing the sides of her breasts. Her nipples tingled with awareness, instantly taut.

Her eyes were still closed and her head was tilted slightly to one side when she felt Doug's warm lips on the curve of her supple neck. His palms glided down the length of her arms, then up again as his soft, enticing kisses slowly followed the line of her shoulder. Maura felt her body shudder with excitement, every nerve ending tingling. She was shocked by her response, the warm pulse at her center, aching for Doug's touch. What had come over her? Her body had never been awakened so quickly by any man before.

When she felt Doug's hands reach around and cup her aching breasts, she heard herself release a long, deep sigh. She instinctively reached up and covered his hands with her own, urging him to explore her even further. She heard him sigh, exciting her even more as he stroked the hardened nipples, then slipped down the thin straps of nightgown. Maura felt herself sinking into a whirlpool of sensations and she sighed with satisfaction at his pleasuring caress.

Then suddenly he had moved around the chair and was crouched down next to her. She opened her eyes and they were face-to-face. He moved forward and kissed her deeply, their lips twining in an age-old passionate rhythm, her bare breasts pressed against the crisp hair on his chest. Maura returned Doug's feverish kisses with a passion completely new to her. This was it, she suddenly thought in some distant part of her mind. This is what it's meant to be like between a man and a woman. Every romance she'd had before—even believing herself truly in love with Scott Walker—seemed a pale, watered-down imitation.

She realized that from the very start of her relationship with Doug this was what she had always wanted. To be held in his strong arms, to feel his powerful body against hers, to revel in his intimate touch. To allow herself to open up to him, like a flower opening to the heat of the sun. To feel her very soul laid bare to him.

Then his mouth moved from her lips to her neck and lower, exploring the soft curve of her breasts until she thought she'd cry out with pleasure as he covered first one taut nipple then the other. Maura's eyes squeezed closed, her body thrilled with exquisite satisfaction. Her hands gripped his muscular shoulders, gliding over the firm muscle and warm skin.

Finally he stopped, his head pressed into the hollow of her breasts. She felt him breathe deeply, struggling for control.

''God, you're so beautiful, Maura. How could you ever think I'd feel shortchanged? I want you so much.'' His voice sounded raw with desire.

Maura couldn't reply. Did he really think she was beautiful? Her? A total plain Jane if there ever was one? But she didn't think he was lying to her, just saying what he thought she wanted to hear. She truly felt beautiful in his arms, beautiful and desirable. It was unbelievable but true. That was the effect he had on her.

She buried her face in his thick hair and wrapped her arms around his strong back. She felt his hands on her thighs, slipping under the edge of her thin nightgown, the pressure of his touch unnerving and totally tantalizing.

Then he lifted his head and stared straight into her eyes. With his hands on her hips, he pulled her closer, so that she sat at the edge of the chair, her legs slipping around his waist, her warm feminine core pressed against his lower body in a way that left no doubt as to his urgent desire. When he moved his hips, Maura moved against him. He sighed and kissed her deeply, and she felt his body shudder in her arms.

"Maura, if you don't want this to happen, it's okay," he whispered against her lips. "Tell me now, so we can stop."

Maura's head dropped against his shoulder, her body throbbing with longing, the feelings so powerful she could hardly think, no less answer him.

Was there any point in turning him away tonight? From the first time he'd kissed her, she'd secretly felt that sooner or later they would make love. No matter how many times she'd denied it to herself. Not to mention that they were now husband and wife.

Still, she'd never expected his merest touch would send her up in flames. But here she was, totally on fire for him. All she wanted to do right now was show him how he made her feel and how much she wanted him, too. Maybe it wasn't the right thing to do. Maybe she would end up regretting surrendering herself to those feelings. But right now she just couldn't resist.

He tightened his hold on her, silently urging her reply. Maura lifted her head very slightly, her lips just grazing his ear. "Come to my room. The bed is much bigger,'' she whispered. Her seductive tone was totally unfamiliar to her, but it definitely felt good.

''So I've noticed,'' he admitted with a low, sexy laugh.

She met his gaze and felt herself blush at his grin and then blush more when he pressed a hot kiss into the valley between her breasts and lifted the straps of her nightgown back up to her shoulders. Seconds later she was lost in another deep, devouring kiss as Doug stood up and pulled her up off her seat with him.

In her bedroom they kissed again and with Doug's mouth pressed against hers, Maura felt herself falling in his embrace down to her bed, where they landed, their bodies a tangle of arms and legs.

While his mouth worked tender magic on the taut peaks of her breasts, his hands magically smoothed away her nightgown and lacy underpants. Maura's fingers worked on the clasp and zipper of his jeans, and Doug moaned with a mixture of pleasure and frustration at her tantalizing touch. He pulled away for just an instant to shuck off his pants and throw them to the floor. Then he moved back toward her, covering her body with his, and she luxuriated in the feel of him pressing down on her, his bare, hair-roughened skin covering every inch of her, his muscular thigh pressed between her legs. No man had ever made her feel so sensual, so desired. She wanted to taste and touch every inch of him, and as her hands caressed his powerful shoulders and back, her lips pressed warm kisses to his chest. She found one flat male nipple and twirled her tongue around the hardened bud.

Doug groaned his satisfaction and pulled her close,

his hardened manhood pressing against her thigh. "Doug," she sighed, shifting her hips to let him know she was ready for him to make them one.

"Not yet," he murmured. "I spent some long lonely nights in that spare room of yours, Maura. Too long to rush now."

Then his body backed up his words. His mouth laved her breasts and his hand smoothed down the length of her body in a slow, sensuous exploration of each curve. As his questing fingers moved even lower, to the source of her heat, Maura couldn't speak, she couldn't even think. Swept away on a sea of pure sensation, she felt her body rise and dip as Doug's loving touch brought her to the keenest edge of pleasure.

Finally her arms urged him closer and he moved over her, ready to satisfy her completely. She circled his lean hips with her long legs and felt his beating heart close to hers as he moved inside her. His body seemed to fit hers perfectly, and his passionate power overwhelmed her. As she matched and met his rhythm she felt them merge in a deep, mystical way. Something incredible and beyond description.

Her eyes squeezed shut as she reached her peak, her mind exploding with heat and light, her body trembling in his arms. She felt him move against her one last time and then explode with a cry of satisfaction as he called her name.

She held him close against her, feeling as if they were both tumbling out of the sky, and she knew that after tonight she would never be the same. She had let him into her heart and her body. Now he was part of her, in her very breath, her blood and her soul.

* * *

As they drove to the Connelly mansion in Doug's tiny sports car, Maura stared straight ahead, her hands clasped in her lap. She suddenly hated the navy-blue linen suit she had on. The outfit had always been one of her favorites, but now she realized just how long it had been hanging in her closet. She felt so dull and hopelessly out of style.

The Connellys would think Doug had married a dowdy little nurse. And once they found out she was pregnant, they'd think she'd trapped him. They weren't going to like her. Not at all. She could feel it in her bones...

Should she ask Doug to turn back to the house so she could change? But what would she change into? She hated clothes shopping and her closet looked it. So far Doug hadn't seem to notice her wardrobe—or lack of it. Ever since the other night, when he'd surprised her in the kitchen, they had spent every spare minute together making love. The only thing he'd seen her in lately was a bed sheet.

She glanced over at his rugged profile, his eyes intent on the road, his strong hands gripping the wheel. No, she couldn't ask him to turn around. It was too silly. But her hair—that was wrong too. She took a brush out of her purse and started working on it, intent on pulling it back with a clip in her usual style.

"Your hair looks fine, Maura." Doug glanced over at her and then back at the road. "You're going to wear out that brush if you change it one more time."

"I'll feel better with it back. Not so messy," she insisted as she fastened the clip.

"You look great," he assured her for at least the tenth time since they'd started out. "It's just brunch with my family. Not an audience with the queen of England."

"I'm sorry...I'm just nervous. And your stepmother might not be a queen but she is a princess," she pointed out.

He glanced her way again, his expression sympathetic. "I know you feel a bit shy sometimes, Maura. But believe me, there's no reason to feel intimidated. They're just regular people."

"Right, just regular folks. If you forget about the mansion, the yacht, the private jet, their world-famous name and their millions," Maura said dryly. "Sure, they're just like everyone else I know."

Doug laughed. "Okay, I get your point. But you act as if I'm sending you out to a firing squad." He took her hand and held it tight. "You're not going in there all alone. You're with me, remember?"

She met his glance and finally smiled. He was right. Doug would be with her every second. She was letting her natural shyness get the best of her. Wasn't it time she outgrew that problem? Feeling Doug's firm grasp, she resolved that today would be the day.

They'd left the highway and were driving through an area of expensive houses and estates, she noticed. The road was narrow and lined with tall trees. Only the roadside mailboxes and large gates indicated that a home existed somewhere behind the woodsy landscape. It wouldn't be long now before Doug turned up one of the private estate roads. She felt her stomach knot with nerves.

Now she would meet his family, and they'd play

the part of the happy newlyweds. Just as they did at the hospital, where everyone accepted the news of their sudden marriage with far less shock and comment than she'd ever expected.

She stole another secret glance at Doug. He wore a black linen sports jacket with a black knit shirt and gunmetal gray trousers made of some expensive-looking fabric. He looked very sophisticated…and much too handsome. It was easy to pretend to be in love with him. Maybe she wasn't just pretending anymore, Maura realized. For better or worse, whether this marriage worked out or it didn't, she was quickly and steadily falling in love with her husband.

They finally drove up to the Connellys' red brick Georgian mansion, and with the house in full view, Maura seriously considered making a run for it. But of course she couldn't escape now. Besides, Doug had pocketed the car keys much too quickly for her to manage a quick getaway.

A servant opened the door and greeted Doug by name. Then Emma and Grant Connelly immediately appeared. As they stood in the huge entryway making small talk, she wasn't sure how she got through the introductions. As much as she tried to focus on Grant and Emma's conversation, her mind was spinning from the sheer luxury and vastness of her surroundings. Outside of the movies, Maura had never seen a home like this one before. Astounding, distracting sights came into view everywhere she turned—original paintings, sculpture, antique oriental rugs. Even the architectural detail of doorway columns, mantels and the marble flooring and carved moldings was distracting.

But once they settled in the living room for cocktails, Maura was able to relax and focus on the conversation. Doug had been right. His stepmother, Emma, and his father, Grant, were a warm, down-to-earth couple.

Despite his wealth and influence, Grant Connelly had no pretensions or snobbery. He was handsome and distinguished, even more so than his photographs. But his gaze and manner were far warmer and personable than his reputation as a corporate mogul suggested.

Emma was beautiful, so poised and gracious, Maura thought. Regal down to her elegant fingertips. Her engaging manner quickly put Maura at ease. Like most people with excellent social skills, she didn't talk about herself at all but asked Maura questions about herself, how she had met Doug and about her specialty in pediatrics.

Just as Doug had predicted, Emma and Grant soon mentioned that they wanted to throw a party to celebrate their son's marriage. Maura tried to look pleased, but she knew the flash of worry on her face had not escaped Emma's notice.

"Don't worry, dear. It will just be the family and some close friends," she promised her. "Everybody's so eager to meet you."

"We thought a barbecue at the lake house would be fun," Grant added. "We can just relax and visit and do as we please."

"Sounds good to me," Doug said, glancing at Maura. "We'll be there." He squeezed Maura's hand, and she smiled her agreement. But she secretly won-

dered if she was up to a repeat of today's performance, in front of an even larger audience.

When the meal was over, Emma invited Maura for
a walk through the grounds. Doug would have some
time visiting with his father alone.

The gardens were beautiful and arranged in a formal style. Emma showed her the maze formed out of
boxwood shrubs where her many children used to
play.

"I'm looking forward to chasing some grandchil-
dren through there someday," she added with smile.

Maura felt herself blush, but made no reply. Had
Emma guessed that she was expecting? No, that
seemed impossible. Everyone says that sort of thing
to newlyweds, Maura reminded herself.

"We just added this rose garden last spring,"
Emma noted as they passed a beautiful garden laid
out in a circular design with graveled paths and a
stone fountain at the center. "I'd love to get some
really huge blooms this year. Last year it was so rainy
the flowers practically drowned," Emma noted with
a laugh.

"My mother used to feed the roses eggshells,"
Maura recalled. "She said they liked calcium." Then
she suddenly felt silly passing along the household
hint to a woman like Emma, who of course would
have the best gardener money could buy tending her
roses.

"Yes, I've heard that before. I think I'll try it this
year," Emma replied thoughtfully. "You sound as if
you know something about flowers. Do you garden,
Maura?"

She shook her head. "Doug and I are in an apartment now. With my work hours there's really no time for it, anyway.''

''There'll be plenty of time. Before you know it, you and Doug will be starting a family and buying a house and so on and so on,'' she predicted with a laugh. ''One thing just leads to another.''

''We've only been at my place about a week,'' Maura replied with a small smile. ''Doug hasn't even unpacked all his things yet.''

''Yes, I'm sure you're both just getting used to each other. Marriage isn't easy,'' she added with a small knowing smile. ''But you look very happy together. I haven't known Doug for very long, but I've never seen him happier,'' she said with sincerity. ''He really can't take his eyes off you, dear. Enjoy it,'' Emma added in a playful whisper.

Maura felt herself blush again, now even more than before. She didn't know what to say. She had felt Doug glowing with attention and praise for her all afternoon, but she had to keep reminding herself that it was all just a performance for his family. On his part, at least.

As they headed back to the house, Emma reached out and took Maura's arm in an affectionate way. Maura felt surprised at first, then warmed by the gesture. This was what it was like to be with family, she realized. This feeling of warmth and acceptance. It had been so long since she'd experienced it.

Finally it was time to go. Grant and Emma each hugged her in turn, and then Grant put his arm around Maura again. He turned to Doug and said, ''When you called last week and told us you'd eloped, well...we were surprised, to say the least. But now

that we've met Maura, we can see what all the rush
was about. You wouldn't want to let a girl like this
get away.''

Maura thought she saw her husband's cheek flush
under his bronze complexion. But he quickly dis-
guised any embarrassment with a deep laugh. There
were more goodbyes and finally, they were alone in
Doug's car, driving back to their apartment.

After a long silence Doug said, ''Now, that wasn't
so bad, was it?''

''They're great. Just the way you described them,''
she said brightly. ''Still, it was a bit stressful meeting
the real live Connellys,'' she admitted.

''Maybe you need a massage when we get home,''
he offered in an innocent tone. He reached over and
lightly touched her nape with his fingertips. The contact was enough to send shock waves reverberating
through her body. Along with the searing memory of
his last massage…and what happened afterward.

Maura felt her body temperature rise at the mere
memory.

''Hmm…'' She leaned her head back on the seat
and closed her eyes. ''Maybe it's my turn to give you
one,'' she suggested softly. ''Nurses are very good at
that sort of thing, you know.''

''Yes, I've heard that,'' Doug murmured. Maura
felt the car instantly accelerate. Doug sat up straight
in his seat, his attention suddenly focused on the road.

She sat up, too, and glanced at him. ''Something
the matter?''

''Not at all,'' he assured her. ''Check your seat
belt. I think I just remembered a shortcut home.''

* * *

Grant and Emma didn't take long to agree that Doug had chosen a wonderful young woman to be his wife. "It was sudden," Grant said thoughtfully, "but they look perfect together."

"Yes, they do, don't they? She's lovely," Emma said, "and she seems devoted to him."

"As he does to her," Grant noted. He knew that his son Doug had been through so much pain and loss in the past few years, with the betrayal of his wife and the loss of his mother. It was hard for him to trust and reveal his feelings, even to those closest to him. But Grant felt certain that Doug was truly in love with Maura. He hoped that love would go a long way toward ensuring his son's happiness.

"What more could a man ask for?" Emma offered. "She's beautiful, intelligent, sensitive—"

"She sounds great. When can I meet her?" a familiar voice asked with a deep, sexy laugh.

"Seth, what a nice surprise." Emma smiled at her stepson as he leaned to kiss her on the cheek. "Grant, you didn't tell me Seth was stopping by today."

"I didn't know," Grant said honestly. "Too bad you didn't come sooner. You just missed Doug and his new bride."

"Too bad. I wanted to congratulate him," Seth said. "Were you just exchanging notes about his wife when I came in? She sounds terrific."

"She is," Emma replied. "Maybe when you meet her you'll decide marriage isn't such a bad idea after all."

Seth laughed. "I never said marriage was a bad idea. I only said I wasn't ready and don't think I will be for a time."

"Spoken like a true attorney," Emma shot back with a grin.

"Spoken like a true mother," Seth teased in return. "Here, Dad. Here's the paperwork you wanted." He then mentioned an important deal he'd been working on for the company and handed Grant a thick manila envelope.

"Thanks, I've been waiting to see this," Grant said as he took the package from Seth's hand.

"By the way, I had someone look into the product you told me about."

Seth frowned for a moment, then his expression brightened. "Sure, the lace company in Altaria. Angie's father, Ed, told me about it. Port Royal Textile, I think the name was. He just asked me the other day if we were going to take any action. What do you think?"

"Charlotte did some research on the company," Grant said, mentioning his assistant, Charlotte Masters. "The report was very favorable. They seem like a solid outfit and their product is outstanding. I'm going to pursue it. I'm not sure yet when the actual shipments will start and how fast we can market the product. But the firm seems quite easy to deal with so far. It shouldn't be too long."

"Sounds good. I'll have to thank Ed for the tip," Seth said.

"Do you see Angie often?" Emma asked, curious to hear about Seth's new relationship with his birth mother.

"We've met for dinner or lunch a few times and keep in touch by phone," he explained. "She wanted me to meet her father, Ed. 'Your grandad,' she always

calls him,'' Seth added with a laugh. "It's been good
to get to know her. And difficult at times, too,'' he
admitted, breaking Emma's gaze for a moment.
"We've talked about the past, and Angie seems very
sorry for not being...well, not being the greatest parent in the world.'' Grant was surprised to hear that
Angie had apologized and could see that Emma had
the same reaction. "Just hearing her apology has
meant a lot to me. I really think she's changed a great
deal from those years when she was raising me all
alone. She didn't have it very easy then, either,'' he
added sympathetically.

"No, she didn't,'' Grant agreed.

He'd once felt quite sorry for Angie Donahue and
responsible for her, as well. But for a long time he'd
come to see her as the type of person who created a
lot of her own problems and typically pushed the responsibility off on someone else.

He didn't want to voice any negatives about Angie
to Seth, especially not now. Maybe she'd changed, he
reflected. Who was he to judge her?

"That's good, Seth,'' Emma said, reaching out to
take his hand. "I'm glad that you got in touch with
her and it's going so well. You're very generous to
forgive her,'' she added. "You know what they say,
it's good for the soul.''

Grant glanced over at Emma, a woman who knew
about forgiveness, if ever there was one. He could
only imagine how torn she felt, having this conversation. But as always she rose admirably to the moment, her first concern for her stepson Seth, whom
she loved as dearly as any of her natural-born children.

Seth returned Emma's gaze, easing the moment with his charming smile. "You worry too much," he said kindly.

"Well, until you find a wife to look out for you, looks like you're stuck with me," Emma replied with a wry grin.

"Watch out, son," Grant warned, as he slipped on his reading glasses, "she's on a roll."

Seth's handsome features struggled to suppress a grin. "Wow, look at the time," he said suddenly. "Nice seeing you, folks. Looks like I've got to go."

Maura opened her eyes to find Doug's face on the pillow beside her. The room was dark, and it slowly came back to her, how they'd stumbled into the house after the car ride, leaving a trail of clothes from the front door to the bed. After making love, they had fallen into a deep, contented sleep in each other's arms.

She held very still, studying the lines of his rugged features, his wide, smooth brow, high cheekbones and strong, blunt chin. She had the urge to trace each one with her fingertip but didn't want to wake him.

Her heart ached just to look at him. Almost all afternoon at his parents' home he'd stuck by her side like glue, his amber gaze filled with pride and affection. He'd acted the role of a newlywed groom to perfection, she thought. Time and again she had to remind herself it was only an act.

But for her part it was different. Far different now, Maura knew. How had he become so dear to her so quickly? She couldn't say. Sometimes she wondered if she'd always had deep feelings for him, simmering just below the surface of their friendship. Feelings she never dared to acknowledge.

It was a mystery. But now an undeniable truth. She was falling in love with him.

She was besieged by feelings, feelings that were different from any she'd ever known before. Utterly terrifying and unbearably wonderful at the same time. But it was important to remember that while he eagerly shared her bed and enjoyed her body, in his heart he didn't feel the same about her.

Though he'd done his best the other night to dispel her fears, there was still a good chance their impulsive marriage wouldn't last. Maura didn't like to dwell on that dark possibility. But it couldn't be avoided. All she could do was wait and watch...and hope that someday Doug would truly love her. Could she stay in this marriage, knowing she loved him but he didn't feel the same?

Doug's eyes slowly opened, and he smiled at her. "I thought I felt someone staring at me. See anything you like?"

She laughed at his uncharacteristic vanity.

"Sorry, not at all." She forced a serious expression. "I was just wondering how I got stuck with such an unattractive man."

He laughed and reached out, snagging one of her long curls with his finger. "I talked you into it, remember?"

"Yes, you did make a convincing pitch." She smiled and slid back, sitting up against the pillows, the sheet clinging to her bare breasts.

"Having second thoughts again?" His tone was still teasing, yet she sensed a true note of concern.

"Not at all." She met his gaze and held it. He was the first to look away.

"I know we promised not to talk about it, but do you ever think about Scott anymore? You can be honest with me," he added. "I won't get mad."

"No, never," Maura answered without missing a beat. "If I do, it's probably not the way you mean. I only think about how stupid I was to get taken in by him," she said with an edge of bitterness and anger at herself.

"Maura, I'm sorry," Doug moved closer and put his arm around her shoulder. "I shouldn't have brought it up."

Maura sighed and rested her head against Doug's shoulder. She felt instantly better in his embrace.

"What about you?" she asked after a long moment. "Do you ever think about your first marriage? You've never really told me anything about it. I don't even know her name."

"Her name was Karen." She waited, expecting him to say more. But he didn't.

He shifted slightly, and she could tell that it was hard for him to talk about it. She almost said, hey, it's okay, it can wait until another time. But she was too curious. She needed to know what went wrong. At times she sensed that Doug had been deeply hurt by that relationship, wounded in a way that would make it hard for him to ever love again. She needed to know if she even had a chance of scaling the walls around his heart.

"We met in college," he began slowly. "She was bright, fun and very beautiful. Every guy I knew wanted to go out with her. For some reason she picked me. We were as opposite as two people could be. I was really into the books. I knew I needed more scholarship money to go to medical school and I was determined to do it. Karen's family was very wealthy. She grew up in Lake Forest and she had no real ambition beyond being some rich man's wife. She liked the idea of being married to a doctor,'' he added with a sharp edge to his tone. ''At least, at first she did.

''But it didn't turn out the way she'd planned. She had imagined a guy with a pleasant little suburban practice, treating kids with the usual sore throats and stomach viruses. Coming home at five and then fulfilling her busy social calendar. Dinners out in town or golf at the country club. She didn't like her husband caring for the inner-city poor. She didn't like the fact that my hours were unpredictable and my priorities might cut into some doubles match or ski weekend she'd planned for us.''

He paused, and she felt his entire body grow tense beside her.

''I understand. You don't have to say more.''

''No, you asked. Let me get this over with, once and for all,'' he insisted in a low, grating tone that made her stomach knot with dread. ''There isn't much more to the story, actually. When Karen figured out that she couldn't pressure me into being the kind of husband—and the kind of doctor—she wanted, she traded me in a for a more suitable model. She had an affair with a guy I roomed with in med school, a plastic surgeon.''

''I'm sorry.'' Maura lifted her head and met his gaze. ''That must have been devastating for you.''

''It was at first. I'd been hiding in my work,'' he

admitted, "and I felt blindsided by the news. But I had to face that there wasn't much of a marriage left. If there ever had been anything real between us at all."

He took a deep breath, wondering if he should tell Maura about how he wanted a baby and Karen didn't. That had caused their marriage to fall apart as much as anything, he knew. And he had to tell Maura, sooner or later, the real reason he'd married her. One of the real reasons...

He glanced down at her, feeling the words on the tip of his tongue. But as he stared into her soulful, trusting gaze, he felt his mouth grow dry as chalk. The words just couldn't come. He swallowed hard and looked away.

"It was all for the best," he said finally. "Karen got married again right after the divorce. Bought a big place up in Lake Forest, not far from her parents' home. She's very happy, I hear."

As she'd guessed, his ex-wife had hurt him deeply, and he was still very angry. But was Doug still in love with her, despite the way she'd hurt him? Maura wondered. Karen sounded exactly like the type that drove men crazy. Doug had claimed that wasn't what he wanted. But maybe it really was. Maura knew she could never compete with that type of woman—or even her memory.

"It's hard to talk about these things," Maura said quietly. "Thank you for telling me about it."

He held her, saying nothing for a long time. She felt his hand stroking her hair.

Then he said, "I don't think about Karen at all

anymore, Maura, if that's what you're wondering. We had nothing in common, really, when you get right down to it. We could barely talk to each other. Not like you and me.''

His reply was reassuring. Yet Maura wasn't quite sure what he meant. Did he simply mean that they were good friends? ''Because I understand your work, you mean?'' she asked.

''Well, yes. It's hard to explain exactly...'' His deep voice trailed off. She felt his heartbeat, strong and steady under her hand.

He hadn't said he loved her. Far from it. But he was satisfied with their marriage. Maybe because he *wasn't* in love with her, Maura thought with a twinge of pain. He'd been hurt so deeply by his ex-wife, maybe he would never really recover enough to truly love again. Could she live with that, she wondered? She wasn't sure. She didn't feel sure of anything right now and wondered if it had been a mistake after all to give in to her feelings of attraction and make love to Doug.

She felt his strong hand on her cheek, turning her to face him. ''Don't you think it's working out between us?'' he asked.

''Yes...it works,'' she replied quietly. She knew he meant they got along day to day—and the lovemaking was extraordinary. Meanwhile, she wanted to talk about something far different, but couldn't dare say: I never imagined that night you proposed, that I'd fall in love with you so deeply and so fast. Too bad it looks like you can never love me.

His hand slid into her hair and his smile widened.

"I had a feeling it would work out. And I had my fantasies," he admitted, his voice low and rough.

"Fantasies? About me?" she whispered into the curve of his shoulder. How could anyone have fantasies about her? She shook her head and broke her gaze from his.

He must just be saying that, she told herself. Still, the idea was very flattering, and exciting.

"Yes, definitely," he insisted. "Does that embarrass you?"

"Uh, no. I mean, yes," she confessed. Then, feeling just too curious to let it drop, she said, "Like for instance…?"

His soft, sexy laugh excited her even more, and his body moved restlessly against hers with tantalizing, sensual friction.

"For instance…let me show you…" And before she could even murmur her reply, his mouth covered hers in a deep, hard kiss, and his hands glided possessively over her soft curves.

He pulled her closer under the sheet so that their bodies were pressed together, hip to hip. She felt his long muscular legs tangle with hers and knew he was ready to make love again.

Maura surrendered once again to the sensual magic of Doug's touch and the overpowering passion that ignited so quickly between them. It was easy to forget that he'd never said the words she wanted to hear. That he was thinking only about how good it was for them in bed. Astounding, actually. And all he would admit to feeling for her was a mixture of friendship and sexual chemistry, when she was feeling much more.

His hands caressed her body with a newfound knowledge of her secret pleasure points and an eagerness to discover new ones. Her mouth merged with his in a deep, soulful kiss, and she knew she could never resist him…or resist having him as her own for however long their marriage lasted.

Five

Bright and early on Saturday morning Maura stood outside her apartment waiting for the Connelly limousine to arrive. She couldn't believe she had agreed to go on this outing with Emma Connelly and her daughters. But here she was.

When Emma had called a few nights ago and invited her to meet her daughters, Maura had felt intimidated by the idea. But she'd also thought it would be too rude to refuse. She assumed Emma meant they'd meet for lunch out, or perhaps at the Connelly mansion again. She'd be on her own this time, without Doug. But how hard would it be to make small talk with Emma and her daughters for an hour or so?

But Emma's plans were a bit more involved. She was, after all, a princess, Maura reminded herself. Emma wanted to introduce Maura to Alexandra, Tara and Maggie. She was also going to invite Jennifer Anderson, her social secretary, who had recently become engaged to Doug's brother, Chance. The two couples had spoken over the phone but hadn't met yet since their schedules were both so busy.

The group was booked for an entire day of beauty treatments at the Golden Palm, Chicago's most exclusive spa. "Then after lunch I thought we'd go over to Carrington Plaza for some shopping," Emma added cheerfully.

Carrington Plaza? Maura had read about the fantastic collection of exclusive designer shops in magazines, but had never dared set foot inside. She knew she couldn't afford as much as a belt in one of those places. And she couldn't even pronounce half the exotic names of the designers.

Well, it couldn't hurt to look, she thought. Even if she didn't buy anything.

"And guess what?" Emma continued. "When I mentioned the outing to Grant, he insisted on treating everyone."

"How generous," Maura said. Now she had no excuses left to decline.

"The girls loved the idea. They're really all so excited to meet you."

"I'm eager to meet them, too," Maura said honestly.

So it had been settled. But when Maura had told Doug about it, she hadn't been able to hide her nervousness at meeting his stepsisters. He'd tried not to laugh, but finally couldn't help himself.

"Maura, for goodness sake, you sound as if they

plan to boil you in oil. I really think all Emma has in mind is a manicure and maybe a haircut.''

''I'm just not the day-spa type, in case you hadn't noticed.''

''Thank goodness for that.'' With an indulgent smile Doug took hold of her shoulders and gazed into her eyes. ''You can have a day out and pamper yourself a little. You work so hard. And you'll have even less time after the baby comes for this type of thing.'' He pulled out a credit card and forced it into her hand. ''I want you to come home with a big shopping bag of stuff. A present from me. Anything you like,'' he urged her.

Maura took the card in her hand and stared down at it, as if she'd never seen one before. Suddenly everybody wanted to buy her things. She simply wasn't used to all the attention.

''I guess I could look for something to wear to your parents' party,'' Maura replied, feeling moved by his generosity. ''Do you think a dress would be okay? Or something more casual?''

''You look great in anything,'' he insisted. He kissed her softly and smiled into her eyes. ''You look great in nothing, too—'' His hands wandered down to her hips ''—come to think of it…''

She knew that tone by now and felt her body growing warm all over in response.

''Doug, I have to get over to the hospital,'' she reminded him as his mouth moved down to the sensitive spot just below her ear. Doug didn't seem to hear her. Or if he did, he didn't care if she was late. Very soon even she forgot about getting to work on time, and they had made love with urgent need.

Their work hours had not coincided much this week and Maura felt an aching hunger for his love-making. She'd become addicted to him—his touch, his taste, the scent of his warm skin. It was hard to last even a day without having him near her.

Now here she was, at barely half past seven, about to embark on her first spa adventure, when she'd much rather be back upstairs in bed with Doug.

Just then a long white limo pulled up in front her apartment building, dispelling her erotic daydreams. The driver hopped out and opened the rear passenger door. Maura peeked in, and the first person she saw was Emma Connelly, dressed in a spring-green silk suit.

"Good morning, Maura," Emma greeted her. "You're our last stop. Come in, have a seat." She indicated the place next to her. "These are my daughters, Alexandra, Tara and Maggie," she said once Maura was seated. She introduced three beautiful young women sitting on the opposite side of the car. "Jennifer Anderson will meet us at the spa," Emma noted.

Maura said good morning and settled herself on the long leather seat next to Emma. Emma's daughters had the same warmth and social graces as their mother and immediately helped her feel at ease. Within a few blocks from home Maura felt comfort-able and welcomed by them.

The interior of the car was almost as big as her living room, she noticed, as she stretched out her legs. On a wet bar near Emma, she saw coffee in a silver server, croissants and a crystal dish of huge straw-berries.

Well, you're with the Connellys now, she reminded herself. As Doug had often told her, better get used to it.

"Ready for our day out?" Emma asked brightly.

"As ready as I'll ever be," Maura replied with a smile.

As the long limo carried her home that evening, Maura sank back into the seat, exhausted. She'd had no idea that pampering herself would be such hard work.

Doug's stepsisters had been terrific company and had made her feel as if she were a long-lost relative who had finally returned home. She'd also gotten to know Jennifer Anderson, her future sister-in-law. They'd had some fun, one-on-one, comparing private notes on Chance and Doug.

Despite her natural shyness with strangers, Maura had soon relaxed and opened up and enjoyed a certain kind of camaraderie and fun that could only happen in the company of other women. She almost felt as if she was back in college, hanging out with her dorm pals. Only, in those days their nights of beauty treatments followed homemade recipes from magazines—potions like egg white and oatmeal facials.

At the spa the ingredients were far more exotic and outrageously expensive. She'd been buffed and polished, scrubbed with herbal extracts and soothed with vitamin-enriched lotions. She'd been wrapped in seaweed and then massaged into a state of total, mindless relaxation, inhaling intense scents designed to soothe and invigorate.

And that was just the beautification warm-up.

Maura was surprised to hear that Emma had also scheduled her for a marathon session in the salon. "Just the usual," Emma said casually, when Maura's eyes widened.

She'd had a facial and a manicure, then a pedicure that in fact *had* included a foot soak in hot oils. She'd be sure to tell Doug about that.

Even though Maura hadn't want anything special done to her long hair, somehow Emma and her girls had persuaded her to experiment. She wasn't sure now how she'd been talked into it. But before she knew it, she'd been rinsed with something that brought out the gold and red highlights and then had a haircut.

Her stomach knotted in dread as she saw chunks of her hair hit the floor. But it all happened so fast, and she felt silly protesting right in the middle of it.

But when all was said and done, not nearly as much length was lost as she'd thought. Her natural curls were cut in different lengths so that her thick hair bounced up more, creating a halo effect around her oval face.

After it was blown out and finished, Maura admired the style with surprise. Doug loved her hair down loose and now it looked so much better the new way. But it was still long enough to pull back for work.

Maura had thought she would escape the makeup consultant. She never wore makeup and didn't even have time for it most days, she'd protested. But her new pals had again persuaded her to give it a chance. The salon expert had known she was wary and had used a sensitive approach, and when it was all over, Maura actually thought her "new face" was something she could do on her own, though the subtle touches to her eyes and lips made a dramatic difference in her looks.

Maura had felt pleased but definitely relieved when the group finally left the spa. They'd stopped for lunch at a beautiful restaurant that was filled with flowers. Maura was seated next to Jennifer, giving her a chance to get to know her future sister-in-law a bit. Jennifer was as sweet as she was lovely. She looked far too young to Maura to be a widow, but Jennifer's husband, a police officer, had lost his life in the line of duty two years ago. She'd been pregnant at the time. She'd been raising her little girl, Sarah, on her own. That was, until she'd met Chance.

"Chance was totally shocked when Doug told him he'd eloped," Jennifer had confided. "I thought he was going to faint. He had no idea Doug was even seeing anybody."

"It was just very...sudden. We were really just friends for the longest time," Maura tried to explain. She always hated when she was put in this position, having to lie about her relationship with Doug. But there didn't seem to be any way around it.

"I thought it was really romantic," Jennifer confided. "Even though I had to scratch Doug's name off my list for the bachelor auction."

Emma laughed, but Maura didn't quite understand the joke.

"Jennifer is organizing a bachelor auction for a local charity. She's having trouble rounding up enough handsome, eligible men. Any suggestions, girls?" Emma asked her daughters.

"How about Justin?" Alexandra suggested, offering up her younger brother. "Have you asked him yet?"

"No, I haven't. Do you think he'll do it?" Jennifer asked. "I asked Seth and he claims he'll be out of town. But I could tell he was just looking for some polite excuse."

"Maybe if Mom asks him," Tara said, glancing at her mother.

"Of course he'll do it. It's for a very worthy cause," Emma insisted as she pulled out her cell phone and dialed. "And it will be good for him to get out and have some fun. Ever since he took over Daniel's job, he's been working much too hard. I don't even think he's dating anyone right now. It's just work, work, work. I bet he's at the office as we speak, on a Saturday. See, what did I tell you? He's picking up," she whispered with her hand over the mouthpiece.

Then she turned her attention from the table to the phone and greeted her son. They spoke briefly, and Maura could tell from Emma's side of the conversation that though Justin was reluctant to be auctioned off even for charity, he couldn't refuse his mother's request.

"Thank you, dear," Emma said. "All right, I'll tell Jennifer to call your secretary with the details. I do hope you manage to get out of the office for some part of the weekend, Justin. I'm going to check on you, too," she warned him.

When Emma completed the call, Jennifer was pleased to add Justin's name to her list and thanked Emma repeatedly. She also promised Emma that there would be plenty of beautiful, successful single women at the event and Justin wouldn't stay unattached for long.

But Justin's sisters were full of wry comments about their hardworking brother. They weren't sure what type of woman would catch Justin's eye. "But if she had a calculator implanted somewhere on her body, it wouldn't hurt," Tara joked, which sent the others into a fresh wave of laughter.

After lunch the group had moved on to a shopping spree at Carrington Plaza. Again, Maura had felt like a giddy sorority girl, as she and the Connelly sisters virtually took over the dressing rooms in each exclusive boutique, running in and out of each other's rooms to trade clothes and model outfits. Maura was easily caught up in the fun and, with a little encouragement, found herself buying several new outfits.

None of the women had guessed that she was pregnant, however. Maura was certain of it. Her figure had hardly changed at all yet, and certainly not in any way that a stranger would notice. Her choice in clothing tended toward the loose, baggy look anyway.

She chose a formfitting sheath for the barbecue with a scooped neckline and straps that tied on each shoulder. The style of the dress was deceptively simple, but the unusual fabric made it a knockout. The floral pattern in sea blue and gold seemed painted by some master and went perfectly with Maura's coloring. She almost thought it was too dressy, but Emma and her daughters "oohed" and "ahhed" and had so many compliments when Maura modeled it for them, that she couldn't leave the gorgeous designer dress behind.

Maura had stared at her reflection. She couldn't

help it. She looked completely different from the woman who had left her apartment that very morning—from her new hairdo down to the tips of her polished toes.

"Wow, you look great in that, Maura," Alexandra exclaimed.

"Wait till Doug sees you," Maggie warned.

Would he even recognize her? Maura wondered, checking her view from the side.

"That was made for you, dear," Emma insisted. "Please permit me get it for you. Think of it as a little gift for the bride from me and Grant. You didn't even get a bridal shower, you know," Emma reminded her.

While Maura had protested, Emma wouldn't hear of it. Maura finally accepted the dress graciously, thinking how wonderful it was to be part of a family again. The day of luxury had been something special. But for Maura the most precious part had been feeling a bond with the Connelly women.

It was nearly six o'clock when Maura got home. Doug was out and she wasn't sure when he'd be back. She carried her shopping bags straight to the bedroom. The sun was just starting to set, bathing her room in warm, hazy light.

She hung up a few new articles of clothing, feeling a bit disappointed. She'd been anticipating Doug's reaction to her makeover and now he wasn't even home. She picked up the new dress she'd chosen for the barbecue and held it against herself as she looked in the mirror. Why did this always happen to her? The clothes she bought looked so good in the store, but when she got them home, she couldn't imagine what she'd been thinking.

The dress was beautiful. But was it too much for her. Now, after Emma and her daughters had seen it, she really had to wear it for the party. But what if she looked silly in it? What if Doug was embarrassed?

Full of buyer's remorse, Maura decided to try it on one more time before she put it away. She had to stand on a chair in order to see her full reflection in the mirror over her dresser. She was just checking out the length when she caught sight of Doug standing in the doorway.

She turned to face him, noticing the shocked expression on his face. "Doug…is something wrong?"

"You shouldn't be standing on a chair like that, Maura. You could hurt yourself—and the baby."

"Oh, of course." Maura hadn't even thought of that. She started to get down and he was instantly at her side, reaching out to grip her waist. She placed her hands on his shoulders, and as he lifted her down, her body pressed sensuously along the length of his, sending a current of pure heat arcing through her.

"I…I was just checking out this dress. I'm not sure if I should keep it."

For some reason the way he was looking at her made her nervous. He was staring at her like a total stranger might, as if he'd never seen her before. His unreadable expression gave no clue as to whether or not he liked what he saw.

"Emma sort of insisted," she explained, her voice shaking nervously. "Do you like it?"

He was silent for a long moment. He didn't even look at the dress. Or if he had, she hadn't noticed.

"It's great. Take it off." His tone was low, barely audible. He pushed her hair aside roughly, and his mouth pressed hotly against the soft skin on her shoulder. His touch instantly excited her, and it was hard for Maura to keep her mind clear.

"You don't like it, do you?" she managed to ask him as his mouth moved lower.

"I love it. It's terrific," he repeated quietly. "But in about five seconds I'm going to rip it right off your body, sweetheart. And I'm sure it wasn't cheap."

He lifted his head again and surveyed her, from her new hairstyle to the tips of her polished toes. He didn't have to say a word. No flowery compliment could ever convey the look of masculine approval and raw desire in his eyes. A look that stole her breath away and rocked her down to her soul.

Every doubt and question Maura had about her looks was instantly erased. Now she felt only a deep, sure sense that she was attractive to him. Practically irresistible, it seemed, with a special kind of allure she'd never really known she had before.

It was a strange new feeling for her. But when she once again caught the look of raw desire on Doug's face as he watched her unzip her dress, she had to admit it thrilled her.

With Doug's help, she unfastened the zipper at her back, and his large hands swiftly slid the dress off her body. Before the colorful pool of fabric had even hit the floor, he'd lifted her off her feet and tossed her on the bed. Then he pulled off his shirt and pants before dropping down beside her.

Seconds later her eyes closed as their mouths and bodies met in a deep, soulful kiss. While he had been the passionate aggressor this time, she felt a strange, new power over him.

A power purely feminine.

As Doug kissed and caressed her like a starving man sitting down to a feast, Maura had to admit she liked it.

She liked it a lot.

The next morning Maura woke up to full sunlight streaming through the bedroom windows. She quickly sensed that Doug's side of the bed was empty and she was shocked to see that she had slept until nearly ten. She got up and headed for the bathroom, amazed by her reflection. She'd forgotten all about the new haircut and hardly recognized herself as she brushed her teeth and washed her face.

In the kitchen Maura was greeted by the tantalizing scent of hot coffee and bacon. The table was set for breakfast, and Doug stood at the stove, cooking his signature dish—scrambled eggs.

"Gee, that coffee smells good," Maura said, heading straight for the pot with her empty mug. "I can't believe you let me sleep so late."

"Guess your day at the spa just wore you out," he teased her, glancing over one broad shoulder.

"Something wore me out," she replied with a slow smile over the edge of her mug. "I think it was the night after the spa, actually."

He turned and met her glance, the sexy gleam in his golden eyes unmistakable. She knew they were thinking the same thing, recalling the way they'd made love last night. And that with little encouragement there could be a repeat performance this morning. Maura's body reacted just thinking about it, but she tried not to show it.

"We never did get to that dinner reservation," he noted with a deep laugh, spooning some eggs into her dish and then his own.

"I don't think we ever had dinner," Maura realized. No wonder she was so hungry. "Hmm, this looks good."

She took a bite of eggs and put some jelly on a piece of toast. Doug sat down across from her, picked up a section of the newspaper and scanned the front page. Then after a moment or two he said, "What about taking a ride today? There's a wonderful old inn on a lake that I know of. I thought we could drive up there and hike around or maybe rent a rowboat."

"Sounds great," Maura replied around a mouthful of food. "I'd love to get out of the city. Should we pack a picnic?"

Doug smiled and picked up his coffee. "We can have lunch at the inn. You don't need to lift a finger today, Maura. I just want to see you relax."

He gave her a stern look over the top of his newspaper, and Maura felt a rebellious smile turning up the corners of her mouth.

"Yes, Doctor," she said with mock passivity.

"That's more like it," he teased back, snapping his newspaper as he turned the page.

While Doug scanned the headlines, Maura concentrated on her breakfast. She was pleased that he'd thought of spending the day this way with her. They certainly had a lot of boring things around the house they could do instead, including unpacking the rest of his belongings. This would be much more fun. More like a romantic date—the kind of plans you would make with someone you'd recently met and were happy just to be with them. Despite the passionate, physical intimacy they'd shared, she felt oddly excited, as if they were about to go out on a first date.

She and Doug had skipped all the usual trappings of a courtship, Maura realized, and had gone straight for domesticity, with its real-life pressures and unromantic routines. Maybe if they backtracked a little and spent time together, as they would today, or she surprised him with some candlelight dinners and even sexy lingerie, Doug would see her in a more romantic light—less as a friend he was helping out of a jam and more as a woman he could truly fall in love with.

No matter how many nights he spent making passionate love to her, Maura knew by now that it didn't mean he loved her. But she hoped in her heart that somehow she could make him fall in love with her and maybe this day was the start. It gave her hope.

The weather was perfect, and they drove with the top down. Maura loved the feeling of the warm sun on her skin. They didn't have much conversation as they drove, but it was a relaxing kind of quiet between them.

The inn was a rambling Victorian structure, built in the Queen Anne style, with turrets and gables and a wide shady porch that wrapped completely around. "What a beautiful place," Maura exclaimed as they drove up. "It's really fantastic. I love the colors," she added.

The lavender, purple, deep blue and hot pink that colored the building and intricate trim was a risky choice, she thought, but somehow it worked without looking overdone.

"I thought you would like this place." Doug looked pleased, she noticed, as if congratulating himself for predicting her reaction.

They picked up maps of walking trails and set out on their hike. Maura felt as if she could have walked all day, but Doug was concerned about her getting too tired. He'd brought along plenty of water and had her stop to drink every thirty seconds, it seemed to Maura.

"Doug, for goodness' sake. Pregnant women are supposed to exercise. It's good for the baby," she reminded him. "Please stop fussing over me."

She watched the play of emotions on his rugged features and could see him fighting to push back feelings of concern.

"I know all about your condition. I'm a doctor, remember? You're not used to anyone taking care of you, are you, Maura?"

His question was academic. They both knew the answer. "I've been on my own a long time, I guess," she admitted. She took a long sip of her water and turned her gaze toward the distant landscape.

"You'd better get used to it. I'm going to be around for a while."

Maura laughed and looked up at him, surprised by his strong tone. "Is that a threat or a promise?"

"It's a fact," he replied, meeting her eye.

Maura was the one to finally look away, taking another long drink. She forced herself to appear unfazed by their exchange, yet secretly felt cheered by his vow of commitment.

They came to a place in the trail where the walking was more difficult, the path steeper and covered with loose stones. Doug went ahead and gripped her hand, making sure she didn't lose her footing. Maura was surprised at first by his caution. They weren't exactly scaling the Rocky Mountains. But he was worried about the baby, she realized, and he was the type to get that protective male thing going big-time, she thought. Wasn't that a big part of his reason for marrying her in the first place?

After they'd hiked and rested in the cool shade by the lake, they went inside for lunch. As Maura had expected, the decor was elegant and elaborate and perfectly Victorian. Maura knew a little about antiques and the style of that era and was able to answer a few of Doug's questions.

"I can picture you in an old house someday, Maura. Something rambling and needing repairs," he added. "But with definite showplace potential. I bet you'd like that much better than a brand-new house, right?"

"A house? I hadn't really been thinking about moving, to tell you the truth," Maura admitted.

She felt surprised at his comment. She didn't think he imagined her in any specific kind of house. She'd never suspected he gave much thought to their future at all.

"I mean after the baby comes," he explained. "The apartment will be fine at first. But we'll need more room after a while. I thought we'd probably just move out of the city. It would be best for the baby, I think."

"Uh, yes. It probably would be," she agreed.

"We couldn't move too far out. Not right away, anyway," Doug added, then he named a few suburban areas he thought would work out for them. "I understand there are some great old houses in Norwood, too," he added.

It appeared that he'd been giving some thought to their future, Maura realized. She felt surprised but pleased.

"I've heard that, too," she replied. "And I do like old houses. Though they can be a lot of work. I think you probably have to be willing to do a good part of it yourself." She looked down at her menu. "You don't seem to have much spare time. And I'm not sure you'd like to spend it on a fixer-upper," she added with a small smile.

"Me? Are you kidding?" he insisted. "I could make a fortune doing that type of work if I ever decide to give up medicine," he insisted. "I worked on construction jobs all through college. Learned a lot, too."

"Really?" He'd never mentioned that before, but she could definitely picture him on a construction site, with a hard hat and bare, bronzed chest. The image was quite distracting.

"I'm definitely the handy type, Maura," he said with a sexy grin, "in case you haven't noticed."

Maura felt herself blush and lifted her menu a bit higher to hide her face. "I noticed," she replied blandly. Then she heard him laugh.

The waiter took their order, and they talked about other things. But very soon Doug's mind was back on the future again and willing Maura to go there with him.

"So, do you think you'll still want to work after the baby comes?" he asked.

"I'm not sure," Maura replied honestly. "I haven't thought about it much."

"You have time to think about it," Doug replied. He took a bite of his grilled trout. "You don't have to go back to work if you don't want to, Maura. We can afford to let you take a break from nursing for a while. Those first years pass quickly, they say. You might regret it if you don't stay home with the baby."

He was talking to her like a "real" husband now, Maura thought. It made her so emotional, her food fairly stuck in her throat. She put her fork down and took a sip of water, too moved to speak.

"What about our…agreement?" she finally dared to ask. He looked puzzled. "To see how we felt about the marriage after the baby comes."

"Oh…oh, of course." His expression turned from a warm, open look to something darker and far less revealing. She wondered what he was thinking but couldn't tell. "I'm just assuming that we'll both agree to stay together once the baby comes. But maybe I shouldn't. Maybe you're already having some doubts?"

"Me? No, not really," she said quietly. She looked down at the table, collecting her thoughts. She did have doubts. She didn't know how long she could stay with Doug, carrying on this marriage charade, knowing in her heart he didn't love her. Maybe it was time to tell him that. But when she glanced back up at him, she wondered if she'd been making a huge mistake. She already knew he didn't like being handed ultimatums, and if she tried to be honest with him about her feelings, it might sound as if she was pushing him into some kind of emotional corner. Fall in love with me or else. She certainly didn't think that would get her very far.

She stared at him and sighed. If only she could believe that he felt for her what she felt for him, that they were a couple truly in love, anticipating the birth of this baby. But he didn't. He would have told her by now.

"What is it, Maura? Have I said something to upset you?" he asked finally.

She shook her head. "No, not at all," she lied. "I guess it's just about overwhelming to talk about the future like this when I still have a long way to go with my pregnancy."

"Of course it is. I understand," Doug said. He covered her hand with his. "I didn't mean to… overwhelm you. I guess we'll just have to wait and see how you feel. How we both feel after the baby comes," he added in a cautious tone.

"Yes, I guess we will," she murmured.

Surprising her, Doug reached over and touched her hand. "You're not alone in this, Maura. That's the whole idea. I think that sometimes you forget that."

When he met her gaze, his smile was tender and caring and warmed her heart. It wasn't the confession of love she longed to hear…but it was something.

They ended the day, floating around the calm blue lake in a rowboat. Doug did the heavy work as Maura sat back, trailing her hand in the water like a lady of leisure. Sometimes they talked and sometimes they just enjoyed the tranquil atmosphere together. The sunset was stunning, signaling the end of their day.

They watched it sink behind the lush woods on the lake bank, holding hands but not saying a word.

As they drove back to the city, Maura thought back to the night Doug had proposed to her and remembered how dark the future had looked to her then. Today their talk about the days to come had made her a bit anxious. But maybe their future would work out as Doug had envisioned. That seemed too wonderful for her to even imagine.

Even if he didn't love her, if this day together was any clue, given time he might come to feel much more.

Given time, it seemed to Maura just then, anything was possible.

Six

Doug wasn't the only one who noticed Maura's look. Even co-workers and friends began to comment. "It's just something different about you," her friend Liza pointed out as they met for coffee and caught up on each other's lives. "I know it sounds silly, but it's like you just have this wonderful…glow."

Maura suddenly coughed into her steamed milk drink. A glow? Didn't people always say that about pregnant women?

"Must be the new makeup," Maura replied, hiding her reaction behind the large mug.

"More like the new husband," Liza observed. "Doug is a total babe. Even if he wasn't a Connelly, he'd be hot."

Maura blushed. "Thanks," she said quietly.

"It's so hard to meet anyone who's just plain decent, let alone a guy like Doug. You're so lucky, Maura," Liza added, clearly happy for her friend but envious, as well.

Lucky? It certainly must seem that way from the outside. Especially to Liza, Maura realized, who was so focused on getting married. Liza was her closest friend, and Maura had the sudden urge to confess everything—the secret circumstances of her marriage, her pregnancy...and the agonizing fact that she had fallen in love with Doug but he didn't love her.

But she stopped herself. For one thing, she'd promised Doug that they would keep their arrangement a secret and decide together when to tell everyone about the baby.

And for another, it was just too hard to admit even to her best friend. Maura was sure she'd break down and cry uncontrollably. Every day it got harder and harder to keep from confessing her love to him. In her heart she feared that such honesty would scare him and maybe even drive him away. He'd been hurt by his first marriage, and as Maura saw it, he didn't want to relive those messy, complicated emotions. He didn't want to feel so utterly dependent on someone else for his happiness. He'd made no pretense about it, either, she had to admit. Love was never part of their agreement.

Liza had started talking about her current relationship, and Maura turned her full attention back to her friend's conversation. It was far easier to listen to Liza's romantic dilemmas than think about her own.

Maura enjoyed visiting with Liza, but made sure she was home in plenty of time to cook dinner. It was one of the rare nights when she and Doug would be home together, and she wanted to make the evening special. Their afternoon in the country had convinced her that some courtship rituals might be just the thing she needed. Tonight was the perfect chance to move full speed ahead with her secret plan. She decided to make paella, one of her best dishes. She knew Doug liked it and she looked forward to surprising him.

She'd even bought fresh flowers and candles for the table and had taken out her best china. Maura was just about to shower and change when the phone rang. Thinking it was Doug, she picked it up on the first ring.

"Maura? Hi, it's me, Scott."

Shocked to hear Scott Walker's voice, she couldn't answer for a moment. She said hello and endured his small talk for a few moments before asking point-blank why he had called her.

"Oh, I don't know. Heard you got married. To my old pal, Doug, no less. I just wanted to wish you both good luck."

"You're kidding, right?" Maura was incredulous.

"Now, Maura, don't be like that," he urged in a tone that long ago had always soothed her. "I was just curious to find out how it was working out for you two. That's all."

"Your interest is touching, Scott," Maura replied with undisguised bitterness.

"I'm just concerned for you, honestly," he persisted. "I thought it all sounded pretty sudden. Especially considering your…special circumstances."

He knew that was his polite way of referring to her pregnancy. *Her* special circumstances. As if she managed to get pregnant all by herself.

"I knew you two were friends. Maybe I didn't realize how friendly," Scott added.

"Meaning what?" Maura challenged him.

"Meaning...well, you know what I mean. Maybe I'm not even the father of your baby, Maura. Maybe Doug Connelly is. Why else would he jump in and marry you like that? I think I have the right to know the truth," he added in an indignant tone, casting himself as the injured party.

Maura was so angry she couldn't see straight. She took a few deep, calming breaths, remembering that she had to think of the baby.

"The truth is, how was I so gullible to ever get involved with a man like you?" she returned in a ragged voice. "How dare you call me up and make such accusations. I never want to hear from you again in my life, Scott. Do you understand?"

"Now, Maura. You don't have to—"

But Scott's voice was cut off as Maura slammed down the phone.

When Doug walked in moments later, Maura was still sitting at the kitchen table trembling with anger and trying to compose herself.

"Maura, are you all right?" Doug rested a hand on her shoulder, gazing down at her with concern.

"I'm fine. I just had a phone call from Scott is all," she related.

"Walker? What was he calling you for?" Doug asked with an angry edge to his voice.

"He'd heard we'd gotten married and he wanted to wish us luck," Maura relayed with a bitter edge.

"Is that so?" Doug gazed at her quizzically. "That's all he had to say?"

"He did think it was sudden," she added. That was the truth, in part. Still she hesitated to relate the uglier details of the conversation.

Doug was silent for a moment, studying her. "How did you feel talking to him again?"

She shrugged. *Enraged* was a word that came to mind. But if she admitted that, the rest of the story was bound to come tumbling out.

"Mostly shocked that he called, I guess."

Doug crossed his arms over his chest. His face was a dark, unreadable mask. "Did he say something to upset you?"

Maura looked up at him, then away. She hated to lie to him, but the truth was too ugly to relate. She didn't want this to escalate and have Doug react by calling Scott back. She never wanted to have anything to do with Scott again.

"Like what?" she asked finally.

"Like…he had regrets about the way he'd treated you. Or he missed you and he wanted you back," Doug suggested, his tone low and objective, like a prosecuting attorney moving in on the witness.

Maura's eyes widened. She stood up and went over to the sink to pour herself a glass of water. "No, it was nothing like that. Nothing like that at all."

His gaze remained fixed on her. He didn't look convinced. His reaction puzzled her. What was he upset about? If she didn't know better, she'd think he was jealous.

Don't be silly, she told herself. A certain possessive streak had kicked in, perhaps. Combined with his deep disdain for Scott. But jealous? Not likely, Maura decided.

"Do you think you'll hear from him again?" Doug asked.

"Absolutely not. I told him very clearly not to call here anymore," she replied honestly.

Doug didn't reply, his mouth fixed in a hard straight line, his brows drawn together in a dark look. She wanted to move toward him, to put her arms around him and assure him that she had no feelings for Scott Walker other than anger and disdain. It's you I love, don't you know that by now, she wanted to say. But he seemed so distant, and she didn't have the courage to reach out to him.

Besides, Doug didn't love her, she reminded herself. How could he be insecure or even jealous? It was just her own wishful thinking, Maura realized.

Doug's schedule had changed and he needed to return to the hospital that night. Maura took the news easily, but saw her carefully laid romantic plans suddenly dissolve. They ate quickly and discussed unimportant matters. Though Doug kept complimenting her on the dinner, the atmosphere remained heavy and tense, the shadow of Scott Walker's call hovering over them.

"I'm sorry I have to rush through this great meal and take off again, Maura," Doug said as he prepared to go.

"That's okay, I understand." She did understand and tried not to sound too disappointed.

"Don't bother to wait up for me," he added. "I might be late."

Maura nodded. A lump had lodged in her throat, making it hard to speak. She felt sad and confused, as if something important had suddenly changed between them and she couldn't say why.

The apartment seemed silent and empty the instant she heard the front door close. Maura thought it was funny how before Doug had come along she'd never felt lonely when she'd been at home by herself. But now she wandered from room to room, as if missing some lost part of herself.

She blew out the candles and picked up the vase of flowers. The romantic trimmings seemed silly now, and she felt embarrassed by her hopeful plans. She showered and then got into bed with one of her thick what-every-expectant-mother-needs-to-know books and soon fell asleep.

When Doug returned hours later, Maura roused, aware of him undressing in the dark and then slipping into bed beside her. She waited for him to reach for her, as he always did. But when he rolled over and seemed to fall asleep, she didn't have the courage to reach out to him, even though her arms ached to hold him near.

It was the end of a long hard day, a day of meetings and decisions and many people bringing all kinds of problems to his door. Grant Connelly flipped open a folder of documents that required his signature and reviewed the first on the pile. When his intercom buzzed, he reached over and answered it automatically.

"There's a visitor here for you, Mr. Connelly. Ms. Angie Donahue." His assistant's smooth, professional tone could not hide the hint of question. Charlotte Masters knew his daily schedule better than he did, and it rarely included unexpected visitors, unless it was Emma or one of the children.

But Angie Donahue, of all people.

Grant pulled off his reading glasses and tossed them on the desktop. What was she doing here? Maybe it was something to do with Seth, he thought with sudden concern.

But why not call? Why just pop in on him unannounced?

But that was Angie. Always assuming the world revolved around her and would indeed stop if she so much as snapped her fingers.

Grant reached over and pressed the intercom button to reply.

"Send her in," he said briskly. Might as well see what she had to say for herself after all these years. He had to admit, he was curious.

He smoothed back his hair with a careless gesture, straightened his tie and slipped his suit jacket on, just in time to hear a soft knock on the office door. "Come in, please," he called out.

Angie opened the door slowly and entered. He stood up and walked around his large desk to greet her.

"Hello, Grant. Aren't I terrible, popping in on you like this?" she asked with a girlish laugh as she offered her hand. "It's good of you to see me. I know you're always so horribly busy."

He took her hand lightly and shook it in both his own. "What a surprise. Goodness, it's been so long. You look great," he said. "You haven't changed a bit."

In many ways the easy compliment was true. Her

style had changed little since years ago, he noticed. She had never been shy about drawing attention to herself. Her platinum-blond hair and gold jewelry made a striking contrast with a formfitting red suit. She was still slender, and her sexy black heels added to her height so that her amber eyes were nearly staring directly into his own.

"Thank you, Grant. That's nice of you to say," Angie replied graciously. "You look wonderful, too." She lifted her eyes to meet his gaze with a look of pure feminine adoration that had once been so effective at melting his willpower.

Angie was one of those women who fought nobly to preserve their appearance. But the shine on her beauty-queen looks had diminished not without the help of plastic surgery and over the years, he noticed.

Angie settled herself gracefully on a long leather couch, and Grant sat nearby on an upholstered armchair.

"Believe it or not, I was having lunch with a friend at a restaurant just a block or two away and as I passed by the building on my way downtown again, I just stopped and said, hey, why not go up and see Grant?" she explained brightly. "Seth talks about you all the time, you know. And it's made me think of you. About the past, I mean," she added in a softer tone.

Grant forced a smile. He was hardly in the mood to go strolling down memory lane with Angie Donahue, and sincerely hoped that wasn't her agenda.

"Well, we can't go back in time, you know. We can only go forward," he said firmly. "I think it's good that you and Seth are back in touch."

"Oh, yes, it's been wonderful. You and Emma have done such a wonderful job raising him. He's so intelligent and successful. I was just…so proud. How can I ever thank you? I can't really, I know…"

She suddenly looked moved to tears, and Grant averted his gaze for a moment, not knowing what to say. But she'd always had that mercurial quality, he recalled, happy one moment, emotional the next. At first it had seemed so fascinating to him, so exciting. Until he realized that Angie was really quite calculating and theatrical, an actress in search of a stage.

"Yes, we're very proud of him," he said simply. "I know it's meant a lot to him to get to know you. It was good of you to get in touch. It couldn't have been easy," he added, giving her some credit for initiating the relationship.

"Thank you, Grant. That's kind of you to say…all things considered," Angie glanced up at him with wide amber eyes. Still casting those innocent, little-girl glances, even at her age, he noticed. "But I've had a lot of time to think about the past…the mistakes I've made. I could have been a better mother. I can see that now," she said very seriously. "I'm just grateful that he wants to have some relationship with me now, and I'm trying my best to make it up to him any way that I can." Angie met his gaze directly. "You know, I am sorry about the past. The way I treated Seth…and you, too, Grant. I know I can't go back and change any of it now, but I can tell you that I do have regrets."

Grant took a breath and sat back in his chair. This admission was so unlike the woman he'd always known, it was a moment before he could take it all in. Maybe she had changed. Maybe he'd been too cynical, too harsh on her.

"I don't really think about those days," he replied. "We both made our mistakes and I hold no bitterness toward you, believe me," he added honestly. "As for Seth, he appreciates your efforts toward making amends with him," Grant assured her. "We all do."

Angie looked thoughtful for a moment, then her perfectly drawn mouth formed a tentative smile. "Well, enough about me. How have you been?" she asked, suddenly changing the subject. "How's business?"

He replied in a pleasant, general manner, as he might to any stranger. Angie Donahue had once been his assistant, confidante, mistress and everything in between. Privy to his business dealings down to the last detail. How strange it seemed now to realize that they were once on such intimate terms, Grant reflected. Today he'd hardly feel comfortable disclosing even information that was public knowledge. She had long ago lost his trust, and it would take more than a few words of apology to regain it.

The intercom sounded and Grant excused himself to answer it. "I'm leaving now, Mr. Connelly," Charlotte informed him. "Is there anything you need before I go?"

"No, Charlotte. Thank you. Have a good evening," he replied.

"Thanks. Good night," Charlotte replied.

When Grant returned to Angie, she glanced at her watch and abruptly stood up.

"Oh, dear. Look at the time. I didn't mean to keep

you so long. You must need to be off, as well," she apologized.

"I have a nice pile of work to get through first," Grant said, glancing over at the thick report on his desk. "And some calls to make. So I'll be here awhile yet."

"Well, some things never change, I guess," she said with a smile. She picked up her purse and tucked it under her arm.

"Maybe," Grant agreed. "It was good to see you, Angie," he said, holding out his hand. "Glad you stopped by."

She took his hand in both of hers and held it gently. "I think you really mean that. So I'm glad I followed my hunch and surprised you." She opened the door and let herself out. "See you sometime soon, okay? Let's not let another twenty years go by."

"Yes, of course." He smiled, relieved to see her go. "So long, Angie."

The door closed and she was gone. Grant returned to his desk but felt too distracted to get back to work. What was that all about? he wondered. After twenty years and probably passing this building hundreds of times in her travels around the city, she suddenly had the impulse to stop and say hello?

He shook his head and put his reading glasses on again. Maybe it was inspired by seeing Seth and thinking about the past. Since Seth had a relationship with her again, they'd be bound to run into each other at some point, Grant speculated, so maybe it was better to break the ice this way, in private.

Still, he had the niggling feeling that she'd been

after more. That there was some other purpose to her coming here. Though what it was he couldn't say.

He would have to tell Emma about this. She was always very savvy about unraveling a person's motives. He was sure she'd have some interesting insight into Angie's hidden agenda.

In the outer office, Angie was delighted to find herself completely alone. She noticed an extension light illuminated on Charlotte's phone. Grant was busy with his phone calls. She waited just a beat, then smoothly moved behind Charlotte's desk and turned on the computer. In some distant part of her mind she wondered what she would tell Grant if he suddenly came out and caught her here. But he wouldn't, she coached herself as she opened her purse and removed a computer diskette. She would be done with her nasty little deed in a matter of seconds.

She inserted the diskette into the computer and swiftly struck the appropriate keys, then watched the message as the files from her disk transferred onto the hard drive of Charlotte's computer. In a matter of sinister seconds her handiwork was done.

Angie removed her diskette and shut down the computer. Then she removed a small white business card from her purse and left it squarely in the center of Charlotte's neat desk.

Angie snapped her purse closed and swiftly left Charlotte's office. The rest of the floor seemed empty, as well, with the lights off in every office door as she passed by. Her stiletto heels clicking noisily in the empty corridor as she headed for the elevators, Angie felt elated with the success of her visit.

She hadn't been back in here in over twenty years, but her little surprise visit had certainly been a productive one. When Charlotte turned on her computer tomorrow morning, before you could say Connelly Corporation, the virus on the hard drive would spread through the network of computers in the entire company in a matter of seconds. It would contaminate everything, effecting a gigantic crash of the entire system.

Angie stepped into the elevator and felt a gleeful thrill as she punched the button for the lobby. Charlotte would at first be baffled. Then she would remember the anonymous call she'd received last week, informing her that sometime soon the system would crash and she'd find a business card on her desk, with the name of some outside computer technicians. All she had to do to correct the problem was call in the outside experts. She had been told that everything would be easily fixed if she hired the right people to do the job.

But if she didn't cooperate, Grant Connelly and everyone else in the company would soon learn about her brother, Brad, who was currently serving time in Deer Lodge Prison for drug possession and trafficking. Not only would that be embarrassing for Charlotte, who'd gone to great lengths to hide her truth, but it might even cost her her job.

Angie had only met the young woman briefly, but she had a feeling Charlotte would comply. What choice did she have? Angie sighed and slipped on her sunglasses as she strolled through the lobby.

What choice do any of us have, when you get right down to it? she wondered. Sometimes she felt as if her life had been scripted down to each precious minute and she had no choice at all in the paths she'd followed or the mistakes she'd made. But even if it could be different for her, even at this late date, she knew in her heart she didn't really want to change. She was far too comfortable with things just as they were.

Seven

As the car sped along the highway toward the Connelly country home at Lake Geneva, Maura hoped the change of scenery would help dispel the tension that had come between her and Doug these past few days. She'd even worked up the courage to ask him if something was wrong. But he'd shrugged off her inquiry with some mumbled, vague reply. Then he'd hardly said a word to her or even met her eye as they'd packed and started the trip to his parents' cottage.

Maybe he was just nervous about tonight, Maura speculated. She definitely was. The party to celebrate their marriage would officially start sometime during the late afternoon, but Grant and Emma had urged them to arrive a bit earlier. Emma said they had a surprise waiting, which both Maura and Doug expected to be a wedding gift that her in-laws wanted to give in private. Doug was eager to get to the lake, hoping for a sail on one of Grant's boats. Since Maura had been having a lot of morning sickness lately—and not just in the morning—she thought she'd skip the ride. But a refreshing plunge in the lake might be nice.

At other times like these, Doug had always had a way of making her feel better about her shyness. But he seemed so distracted right now she didn't feel comfortable confiding in him. In fact, over the past few days, she'd hardly felt comfortable talking to him at all. And he seemed to feel the same about her. They hadn't made love or even touched each other.

Maura wasn't sure what had happened exactly. There had been no argument or even a quiet disagreement. But ever since Wednesday night, when her plans for a romantic dinner had not worked out, the atmosphere between them had grown strained. She wondered if Doug was suddenly getting nervous about having married her.

Maybe her scheme to romance him had been too transparent and appeared too desperate. There was nothing that would cool a man's interest sooner. Maybe he was intentionally pulling away from her now, just to make it clear that he wasn't about to change the terms of their deal. He'd had enough romance with his first wife. He wasn't interested in falling in love.

If that wasn't the cause of his distant attitude toward her, what was? It seemed so ironic that here they were about to have a huge party thrown in honor of their marriage and they were barely speaking to each

other. And definitely not in love. At least, Doug was
not in love with her, she corrected. Although the lust
factor was certainly strong enough to rival any newlywed pair.

But Maura now knew better than to mistake a
man's sexual appetite for emotional involvement.
Could she ever resolve herself to it, she wondered.
Loving a man who didn't love her? Living with a man
who didn't love her? She didn't think she could. They
had not even been married for a month, and already
the burden was wearing on her.

She shifted in her seat and sighed aloud without
realizing it. Doug turned to her. "Are you okay?" he
asked quietly. "Would you like me to make a stop?"

She met his gaze, then looked out the window
again. "I'm fine. How much longer is the ride?"

"We should be there in another half hour. Here,
why don't you read these directions to me," he suggested, handing her a scrap of paper.

Maura scanned the sheet of directions. "I can see
why you went into medicine," she said dryly. "Your
handwriting is totally illegible. Is that a five or an *S?*"
she asked, pointing out a scribbled word.

He glanced at the paper for a second, then looked
back at the road. "I think it's a three with the top
part squashed," he offered. "But I'm not totally certain."

She could see he was trying hard not to smile, and
that made her smile, too. She took the paper back and
stared at the indecipherable marks once more. "Well,
no big deal. We have the cell phone. If we can't find
our way, we can call."

He glanced at her, then back at the road. "That

would be an excellent solution. Except that I've forgotten to bring the number, and I doubt that it's listed.''

"Oh…'' Maura sat back in her seat again, staring down at the nearly indecipherable marks Doug was calling directions. "That's not so good.''

Doug seemed amused at her distress. "Trust me, Maura. You may be feeling a little lost right now but we'll find our way.''

Maura held his gaze for a moment, feeling as if he was speaking to her about much more than the route to his parents' vacation house.

"I hope so,'' she replied. "I really do.''

Doug looked back at the road. He reached over and covered her hands with his. The simple gesture held more intimacy and affection than he had shown her in days, and Maura soaked up his touch.

Somehow they did find the house, and without too many wrong turns, Maura noticed. A long gravel road led down to the house, which was close to the lake-shore. The property looked vast to Maura, a large part of it wooded. But as they approached the house, she spotted tennis courts, a pool and, in the distance, the stables and riding ring.

Emma and Grant were outdoors and came to the car to meet them. Emma gave Maura a big hug while simultaneously admiring her outfit, one that Maura had bought on the recent shopping trip.

Doug was eager to take a tour of the grounds with Grant to the lake, but Emma insisted that they both come inside first. "Just for a minute,'' she urged. "I just want to give you your surprise.''

Doug glanced at Maura. How could they refuse?

"Of course," he said graciously, touching Maura lightly at the small of her back as they walked up the path to the lake house.

The "cottage," as Grant and Emma called it, was stunning, and Maura paused for a moment on the path to admire the strong, clean lines of its design. The original cottage had been designed by Frank Lloyd Wright, Grant explained, but over the years they'd needed to expand and had made some changes. Floor to ceiling windows in a wide open great room framed a view of the dark blue lake. The Mission-style furnishings looked casual and relaxed, Maura noticed, yet were no doubt the best money could buy.

While Maura and Doug admired the house and took in the view, Emma disappeared for a moment into an adjoining room. She returned moments later and stood in the doorway. "Maura and Doug, here's your surprise," she announced happily. "Tobias and Miss Lilly. When they heard you eloped I couldn't keep them away. They've come up from Palm Springs for the party."

Maura recognized the names instantly. They were Doug's grandparents, Grant's parents. Doug had only met them once, and briefly at a party to welcome him and Chance into the family. Tobias had a stout but solid build and bore a strong facial resemblance to Grant. Miss Lilly was quite attractive with smooth clear skin that was practically wrinkle free and a soft halo of pure white hair.

"Doug, how nice to see you again," Tobias said as he heartily shook Doug's hand.

"Hello, grandson," Lilly said simply. "Goodness,

I can't get over how handsome you are!'' She got up on tiptoe and pulled Doug close for kiss on the cheek.

Doug looked pleased, Maura thought. Grant and Emma stood aside, looking on at the reunion without interrupting.

"Let me introduce you to my wife," Doug said. "Tobias, Lilly, this is Maura."

He put his arm around Maura and drew her close, and Maura suddenly felt connected to him again, as if they were a real couple.

Suddenly Emma announced that lunch was served on the patio, and everyone moved out through the glass doors. As they took their places around the large round table, Maura realized that she was very grateful for the distraction that Tobias and Lilly provided. Now Doug would be the center of attention for a while and she was let off the hook.

The conversation around the table was lively, with Doug's grandparents peppering their grandson with questions. Maura felt her shyness slip away and found it easier than she expected to talk about herself and join in.

Once lunch was cleared away, the men went off to walk the grounds and see about taking the sailboat out for a quick spin. Emma ran off to see to some last-minute details about the party, and Miss Lilly retired to her room for a nap.

Maura was grateful for the time alone. She changed into her bathing suit and walked down to the lake. The swimming and sun felt wonderful, but soon left her feeling too tired to even walk back to her room. But she did, immediately falling across the bed and going to sleep.

Her dreams were vivid—mostly about Doug. She held a baby in her arms and handed it over to him. The look of pure joy on his face was unmistakable as he lifted the child toward the sky. Then he turned toward Maura and kissed her deeply on the mouth. Maura felt herself kissing him back, cupping his cheek with her hand. She inhaled the scent of his warm skin, his hair. It felt so real—too real—and she opened her eyes to find Doug's face close to hers in the darkened room.

"Oh, it's you. You were kissing me," she said groggily.

"Yes, I did. Couldn't resist," he confessed, stroking her hair with his hand.

"I was having a dream." She sat up and pushed back her hair with her hand.

He sat up, too, moving away from her. "About your husband, I hope," he said lightly. Then added, "Wait. You don't have to answer that."

She watched him as he got up from the bed and pulled his shirt over his head. He had such a magnificent body—a sculpted, muscular chest and wide shoulders and narrow waist—it was hard to keep her mind on anything else. She wished they could make love right now, but knew they didn't have enough time before the party.

"Don't be silly. Of course it was about you," she replied with a nervous laugh.

"You can dream about whoever you like, Maura." He slung a towel around his neck and turned to go into the bathroom. "You don't owe me any explanations."

Maura felt taken aback. She didn't know what he

was driving at and felt unable to answer. He closed the door to the bathroom, and she heard the shower run. Glancing at the clock, she saw that it was quite late. The guests would be arriving soon and she wasn't anywhere near ready.

She would have to ask Doug later what he meant by his cryptic remark. Now it was time to play the happy newlyweds. This time for their biggest audience ever. Maura hoped she was up to the challenge.

Doug gripped her hand as they walked through the house and out to the patio. Most of the guests had already arrived, and everyone turned to greet Doug and meet Maura as they slowly made their way through the crowd.

In between introductions Maura gazed around in amazement at the way the outdoor area behind the cottage had been transformed for the gathering, with small white lights in the trees and glittering candles and flowers everywhere.

As waiters passed around trays of delicious-looking hors d'oeuvres and drinks, soft sounds of jazz from a trio of musicians set the perfect mood. A short distance from the deck, several large barbecues stood end to end, manned by chefs in tall white hats and red aprons. Smoke rose in thick plumes, carrying the appetizing scents of ribs, steaks and chicken. Maura was suddenly starving and plucked a huge shrimp canapé from a passing tray.

"If this is what your folks call a casual barbecue, I'd hate to see a really formal affair," Maura whispered to Doug at a rare free moment.

"Emma is used to doing things on a royal scale,"

he whispered back with a smile. "It's just the way she was raised, you might say."

"Please don't misunderstand," Maura added hastily, "I think it's lovely. I can't believe she went to all this trouble. I feel a little guilty actually, as if I don't quite deserve such treatment."

Doug's expression turned suddenly serious. He met her gaze, a questioning light flashing in his amber eyes. "Nonsense, you're my wife. Of course you do. Why would you say that?"

Maybe because this isn't a real marriage, she wanted to say. Because I love you and you don't feel the same about me.

Instead she shrugged and looked away. "I'm just not used to the deluxe treatment, I guess."

Doug did not reply, his expression brooding and unreadable. She wondered again what she had said or done to cause him to withdraw this way. Or was it really his own doubts and regrets at his impulsive proposal finally kicking in?

"There they are. The guests of honor." A tall handsome man, the image of Doug, stepped up and heartily shook Doug's hand, at the same time slapping him on the shoulder. "Where have you been? We've been looking all over for you."

Maura knew this had to be Doug's twin brother, Chance, who was a Navy SEAL. She had already met the beautiful woman who stood beside him, his fiancée, Jennifer.

Doug looked shocked at first, then his expression quickly changed to pure happiness as he first shook his brother's hand, then gave him a quick hug. "What are you doing here? I thought you were away."

"I got a short leave at the last minute. Thought I'd surprise you, Doc. Looks like it worked," Chance dryly observed before he turned to Maura with a wide smile. "Aren't you going to introduce me to your gorgeous wife?"

Doug made the proper introductions, exchanging a few brotherly barbs with Chance. Maura liked her new brother-in-law instantly and could quickly see that though the two men were physically identical, their personalities were just about opposite. Chance was charming, outgoing, even a bit brash—a distinct contrast to Doug's intense and sometimes brooding personality.

Chance and Doug had a lot to catch up on, and while they drifted off to fetch some drinks, Maura sat at a small table with Jennifer. She was glad to see Jennifer again. Although they'd only met once before, Maura had a feeling they could become close friends—if her marriage to Doug lasted that long.

"The dress looks fantastic. I'm so glad you kept it," Jennifer said, taking another look at the designer creation Maura had chosen during her outing with the Connelly women. "I bet Doug loved it," she added with a sly smile.

"Uh, yes, he did," Maura admitted. She could feel her cheeks growing warm as she recalled Doug's ravenous reaction. Though he'd hardly seemed to notice the outfit tonight, she reflected.

"Chance was so happy to make it here tonight," Jennifer confided. "He idolizes Doug, you know."

"Doug feels the same about Chance. I'm glad to have finally met this mysterious superbrother. He's described him as something between a superhero and James Bond,'' she added.

Jennifer's smile widened. ''He's all that and more,'' she admitted with a smile. ''So how's married life? It seems to be agreeing with you so far.''

''So far,'' Maura replied, feeling a little tug at her conscience for the white lie.

''And how are you feeling?'' Jennifer's tone was casual, but Maura could tell by a certain light in her eyes that she knew about the pregnancy.

''Fine.'' Maura shrugged, pretending not to take the hint. ''A little tired from work, I suppose. It's nice to have a break in a place like this.''

''Well, don't overdo,'' Jennifer advised. ''I mean, in your condition.''

Maura felt angry at Doug for giving away their secret, even if it was to his brother. If Chance and Jennifer knew she was pregnant, how many other people here knew, as well?

''Oh, dear. I'm sorry.'' Jennifer leaned over and touched Maura's arm. ''I wasn't supposed to let you know that I know. I promised Chance a million times over that I wouldn't.'' She shook her head regretfully, looking embarrassed, and Maura had to forgive her.

''It's all right. I guess Doug really wanted to tell his brother the news. It's understandable,'' Maura said.

''Well, they are very close. And he's so happy, Maura. You have no idea. Especially since his first marriage broke up because his ex-wife didn't want children. Chance says that Doug has wanted a baby for so long,'' she added. ''This is really a dream come true for him.''

His wife didn't want children? That was why they'd broken up? If this was really true, then it all made sense. Doug had only married her for the baby. He didn't care for her at all, not in the way that really counted.

He'd never love her the way she loved him. He wanted to be a father, and she was a convenient mother-to-be. It was his dream come true—and her heartbreaking nightmare.

Maura felt stunned. She could barely breathe for a moment, and Jennifer's voice seemed to come from far away. She touched her hand to her forehead, feeling light-headed.

"Maura, are you okay?" Jennifer asked with concern. "You look so pale. Can I get something for you?"

"I'm okay. Really." Maura sat up again and tried to smile. She struggled to gain control of her feelings. She was in the middle of a party in her honor. She couldn't think about this now, couldn't face it.

Just then Doug and Chance appeared. "Maura isn't feeling that well," Jennifer reported. "I was just coming to find you."

Maura looked up to meet Doug's gaze. He was already taking her in with a sweeping look of concern. As Doug sat down beside her, she noticed that Chance and Jennifer politely drifted away, leaving them alone.

"Do you feel dizzy?" he asked. "Maybe your blood sugar dropped and you need something to eat," he suggested in a knowledgeable tone.

"Yes, that must be it," Maura agreed. She took a sip of the cold drink he offered and avoided his gaze.

"You didn't fall or anything did you?" Doug asked suddenly.

At first Maura was touched by his concern, then instantly felt resentful. He didn't really care about her, it was all about the baby. That was what had motivated his every action from the first. Only, she'd been too blinded by love to see the plain truth.

"No, I didn't fall," she replied a bit sharply. She stood up, despite the lingering unsteady feeling. "Let's get something to eat. I'm starved."

Doug placed his hand on her shoulder. "Wait here. I'll get it for you."

She had an impulse to shrug off his protective touch and refuse to be waited on. But she didn't. She acquiesced and sat down with a sigh while Doug disappeared into the crowd.

Her appetite suddenly disappeared as every considerate, caring gesture of his returned to mock her. This man didn't care about her, only the life growing inside of her. As if she were some prize broodmare in the Connelly stable!

The situation was intolerable. Maura thought she was going to burst into tears. But she couldn't embarrass the Connellys that way. They'd gone to so much trouble and expense. She had to keep up a good front, at least until she and Doug were alone and she could confront him. Maybe she was getting upset over nothing. Maybe Jennifer hadn't gotten the story straight. There was always that possibility to consider, Maura realized. The way to discover the truth was to ask Doug straight out. That was what she had to do.

While Maura sat waiting for Doug to return, Chance passed by again and began to chat. He took

a seat to keep her company, and they were soon
joined by Grant. Grant then introduced her to his son,
Rafe, who sat down as well.

When Doug returned with a plate of food in each
hand and found Maura sitting with the three men, he
paused, his mouth twisting into a grin.

"Well, if isn't Scarlett O'Hara at the Twelve Oaks
barbecue," he observed dryly. "I've brought you
your dinner, Miss Scarlett. That at least rates a seat,
don't you think?"

Everyone turned to look at him. Chance laughed
out loud.

"Your wife is very charming," Rafe said, congratulating his stepbrother. "You're a lucky man,"
he added with a distinctly male grin.

"Thank you. I think so," Doug said quite definitely. He cast a quick glance in Maura's direction,
but she avoided his gaze.

While Maura ate her dinner, Grant told Rafe about
a major computer crash at Connelly Corporation.
Rafe, it seemed, was a systems analyst and computer
security expert in great demand, traveling around the
country and the world to his top-level clients.

Maura thought she'd seldom seen anyone who
looked less like a computer nerd in her life. With his
easy smile, tanned skin and toned body, he looked
more like an athlete than a desk jockey.

When his father finished talking, Rafe frowned. "I
wish I could help. My schedule—"

Grant waved the apology aside. "I know, I know.
You're booked solid. Phoenix, right?"

Rafe nodded, still frowning. "I'll be there at least

three months, maybe longer. Have your techs been able to get the system back up?''

''We called in some outside people—Broderton's Computing. Charlotte recommended them, and they seemed to be very good. We may want to use them again. They had things up and running again by the end of the day.''

''Broderton...'' Rafe shook his head. ''I'm not familiar with the company. What did they think caused the crash?''

''Some kind of virus. They said it probably arrived through e-mail.'' Grant frowned and added thoughtfully, ''I'm no computer expert, but the whole episode seemed very odd. Our employees know better than to open e-mail attachments from outside the company. We send out reminders quite often. And we've got antivirus software.''

Rafe grinned. ''It doesn't matter how often you tell some people not to open attachments—they do it, anyway. And I've been telling you for two years that your entire system needs to be updated.''

''I suppose.'' Grant took a sip of his drink and swirled the ice in his glass. ''When you get back from Phoenix, we'll talk about you working Connelly Corporation into your schedule.''

''That's what you always say.''

''No, this time I mean it. That episode put a real scare in me.''

''If you're serious, you'd better have Charlotte call my secretarial service in the morning to get you scheduled. I'm booked pretty solid but I think I could work you in after Christmas.''

''Maybe I should just go with Broderton,'' Grant

said dryly. "They seem eager enough for my business that they wouldn't consider a trip to Cozumel more important than getting my system updated. You do still plan to spend a couple of weeks there, I heard."

Rafe grinned. "You know what they say about all work and no play. After Phoenix I'm going to deserve some play time. If you're in a hurry, though, let me check out this Broderton outfit— Wait, there's just the person we need to talk to." He raised his voice. "Hey, Charlie, come here a minute."

An attractive young woman with sleek, strawberry-blond hair was passing by. She stopped, frowned, then came over to their table. "You bellowed?" she said politely.

Rafe chuckled. Grant introduced the young woman to Maura—she was his assistant, Charlotte Masters. She had an interesting face, Maura thought. A little too strong for conventional prettiness, but very attractive.

Rafe seemed to think so, too, from the way he was looking at her. "What do you know about this outfit you called to fix the computers, Charlie? Could Broderton handle a system upgrade, or should my father wait until he gets the best?" He grinned. "Meaning me, of course."

"Broderton?" Her glance darted between Rafe and his father. "I don't know much about them, actually. They were recommended, but—but I don't think I'd use them for something that major." She let out a quick breath, as if she'd crossed some hurdle. "No, I wouldn't recommend them."

Rafe's smile faded and he studied her intently. "What's wrong?"

"What do you mean?"

"You didn't make any attempt to squash my ego just now, and you didn't complain when I called you Charlie. Something must be wrong."

"Oh." Her smile came and went too quickly. "As a matter of fact, I'm not feeling well. I was just going to find Emma and apologize for leaving early."

Grant was immediately concerned. He wouldn't hear of Charlotte driving herself home if she was ill. Rafe, Maura noticed, was quick to volunteer for that chore. Charlotte protested, but when two Connelly males decided to protect a woman, she got protected whether she liked it or not.

The rest of the party passed quickly. Maura was distracted from her worries by the constant conversation and socializing. After dinner Chance got up and made a warm, humorous and touching toast to his brother. Emma and Grant spoke, as well, welcoming Maura into the family with simple, sincere words that made tears come to her eyes. Ever since she'd lost her parents, and her home had been torn apart, Maura had longed to feel part of a family again. Now, after so long, she truly felt welcomed, even loved by these marvelous Connellys.

If only this could last forever, Maura wished. But as she glanced at Doug's strong profile beside her, she felt a dark note of dread in her heart. It wouldn't last. Not now. Not after the bitter truth she'd learned tonight.

When the party ended much later that night, she went up to bed, while Doug lingered, talking to his brother and other stepsiblings. Maura didn't want to seem rude, but she was thoroughly wiped out and fell asleep the moment her head hit the pillow.

The next morning she was awakened by the shrill ring of Doug's cell phone. He picked it up and groggily answered it, his head barely lifted from the pillow. Maura didn't have to ask to figure out the situation. He was needed at the hospital and had to leave right away.

"Shall I come with you? I just need five minutes," Maura promised as she started to get out of bed.

"No, you stay," Doug replied firmly. "Get some more sleep." He pulled on his pants and a clean shirt, then sat near her on the bed as he put on his shoes. "Grant and Emma will give you a ride back to the city. Or maybe Rafe. I think he stayed over last night, too."

"Don't worry. I'll get back all right. Don't bother to pack your things now. I'll take them with me," she offered.

He glanced at her and rested his hand on her hip. "Thanks." He paused and gazed deeply into her eyes. She sensed him leaning toward her and opened her mouth slightly, anticipating his kiss. But then he took a deep breath and turned away.

"Okay, then, I'd better get going." He stood up and grabbed his phone, wallet and keys off the night table. "See you back at home," he added as he headed for the door.

"Yes, see you later," Maura echoed dully.

She felt tears spring to her eyes, but wasn't sure why. She was suddenly grateful that it was barely dawn and the room was so dimly lit he couldn't see her parting reaction.

Eight

Over the next few days Maura tried many times to confront Doug but their schedules were not in synch. She could never quite find the right moment. Or just as she'd summon up her courage to speak to him, they would be interrupted by a call from the hospital or his office.

The tension she'd noticed before the party was now even more intense, since it wasn't just coming from Doug but from her corner, as well. Maura felt totally distracted and worn-out. She wasn't sleeping well and was hardly able to eat. She had to force herself to concentrate at work, and often asked other nurses to double-check her work. She knew she couldn't go on much longer this way, and by Friday morning she had resolved to finally have it out with him.

As Maura stood at the medication counter counting

out pills on Friday afternoon, she was so distracted by her worries she knocked over a full cart of medication. Pills went flying in all directions. Maura looked down at the mess in dismay, feeling so overwhelmed she thought she might burst into tears. She was so emotional lately. She knew it was only her hormones, but it was hard to handle the ups and downs.

Just as Maura bent over and started cleaning up the mess, her supervisor walked past and found her. "Lord, what's happened here?" Gloria exclaimed.

"Just a little clumsy today," Maura replied, coming to her feet.

Gloria looked long and hard into her eyes. "You haven't been yourself for weeks now, Maura. I know it isn't just honeymooning," she said. "I say you're pregnant. Tell the truth now."

"How did you know?" Maura asked in shock.

"I have four kids, remember? Besides, I can just see it in those pretty green eyes."

Maura had to smile at that unscientific pronouncement. "No, you can't. But that's besides the point."

"The point is you look beat and your shift is over in less than an hour so I want you out of here. I don't need any clumsy pregnant ladies messing the place up," Gloria insisted as she gently pushed Maura out to the corridor. "Now you go home and have that handsome husband give you a foot rub or something."

Little did Gloria realize she was sending Maura home to face more problems, not saving her from them. But Maura took her orders without argument, packed up her things and headed home.

She quickly changed out of her uniform and took a shower. As she stood in the bedroom, putting on her clothes, she heard Doug's key in the lock.

He swung open the door and called out to her. "Maura? Where are you?"

"Back here," she replied, wondering at the note of alarm in his voice. He walked back to the bedroom and stared at her. "Are you all right? I came up to your floor, and somebody told me Gloria sent you home early."

Maura took a deep breath. Once again his concern for her well-being struck a raw nerve. She swallowed hard, fighting back harsh words. "I knocked over some meds, and Gloria guessed that I'm pregnant. Nothing to worry about," she said evenly.

He walked closer to her and cupped her cheek in his hand. "Maybe you should rest."

Maura relished his touch for an instant, then abruptly pulled away. Suddenly it struck her how this conversation was almost an exact replay of the night he'd surprised her here and ended up proposing marriage.

If only she'd known then what she knew now, Maura thought.

"What is it?" Doug touched her shoulder, urging her to turn around again and face him.

"You worry about me too much," she said sharply, with her back still turned toward him. "Or maybe it's not me really...it's just the baby."

When she turned to face him, his expression was shocked, his eyes narrowed as he stared at her with a questioning look.

"Of course I'm worried about the baby. You're not

even through the first trimester yet. You're still at high risk for a miscarriage," he reminded her, sounding very much like a physician, she thought.

"And what then, Doug?" she challenged him. "Would the deal be off?"

"The deal? What are you talking about, Maura? What deal?" He stood with his hands on his hips, his brow knitted in a frown, his fine mouth a grim, hard line.

"The deal we made when we agreed to get married. You marry me, give my child a name, I in turn produce one baby. That's really the only reason you married me, isn't it? So you could have a baby." Her voice was thick with emotion, and she hated the sound of her own accusatory tone.

She saw him flinch, his face turning ashen at the sound of her words. She felt awful striking out at him like this, but she had to know the truth.

"I'd never deny that I like the idea of having a family. But I married you so that I could help you. Because you didn't deserve to be treated the way Scott treated you...even though you're probably still in love with him," he added in a burst of anger.

"In love with Scott? Don't be ridiculous," she scoffed. "Now you're just trying to change the subject. I know why your first marriage broke up, Doug. Because you wanted to have a child and your wife refused. Isn't that the real truth?"

"Who told you that?" His rough, low voice was barely above a whisper. He moved closer, his dark expression frightening to behold.

Maura instinctively took a step back, suddenly regretting she'd ever started this confrontation. But they had to get to the end of it, however painful the journey.

"It doesn't matter who," she replied, rallying her nerve. "It's true, isn't it?" she persisted, looking directly into his eyes. "You want a baby and there I was, ready to provide one for you, no questions asked."

Doug looked about to speak, then paused. She saw him take a deep breath, as if consciously trying to calm himself. Finally he said, "Look, I won't deny that I love children and have always wanted to be a father. I want this baby—and more children, too, if possible. But that's not the only reason I married you, Maura. And now that we've been together, I realize that there were other reasons I came to you that night when I proposed." He came closer and took her hands in his shoulders. "Listen," he began, "let's not ruin everything over some gossip, some misunderstanding…"

His words trailed off and he stared into her eyes, looking overwhelmed with feeling. Was he about to say that he loved her? Maura wished with all her heart that he would. It seemed the only way to save things between them now.

Finally, gripping her shoulders a bit tighter, he said, "It's not just the baby, Maura. I know this is right between us. I know it's good."

Maura felt the tears well up in her eyes. He hadn't said the words. He didn't love her. Feelings of heartbreaking disappointment mingled with her deep love for him. A love that would never be returned.

Unable to hold back her tears any longer, Maura pulled away, though his touch urged her to come into his arms. She turned from him, not wanting him to see the crushing disappointment in her eyes. She didn't want him to see how much she loved him.

"You may be perfectly satisfied by the arrangement, Doug. But I'm sorry," she said finally, "it's just not enough for me."

Doug looked stunned at her words. "What do you mean? What are you saying?"

She took a deep breath and whisked away her tears with her fingertips. "Our marriage...it isn't working out for me."

"But we've barely been together a month," he replied. "I thought we'd give this a chance at least until the baby was born."

The baby again. Maura thought she was about to scream.

"I know that's what I said," she replied, willing her voice to be slow and calm, "but I was wrong. I can't stay with you that long. I—" She started to say more, then stopped herself.

I didn't realize how hard it would be to live with you, knowing you only married me for the baby. Knowing that I love you so much and you can't seem to fall in love with me.

The unspoken words echoed in her mind as she stared at Doug's stunned expression.

"You can't do this," he said suddenly, coming toward her again. "I won't let you leave," he insisted with dark intensity.

Maura didn't know what to say. His reaction was some proof of his feelings for her, she supposed. But they were only feelings of possession or propriety.

Maybe he dreaded the embarrassment if she left him now.

Then, just as she was about to reply, the shrill sound of his cell phone cut through the silence.

"Blast!" Doug cursed as he pulled out the phone and answered the call. His words were curt and harsh to the caller. A few seconds later he snapped the phone closed and looked up at her, his expression grim.

"They just brought Jill Dixon back," he reported, mentioning a five-year-old patient who'd just had angioplasty during the week and had gone home yesterday. "The artery collapsed. They're prepping her for surgery."

Maura felt icy chills along her spine. She sent up a silent prayer that the child would survive and recover. Her own problems suddenly seemed small potatoes in comparison.

"Go," she told Doug. "You've got to get over there."

He nodded but didn't move. He stared at her, looking totally torn.

"Just promise me you won't do anything until I get back," he urged. "We can work this out. I know we can."

Maura didn't reply for a long moment.

"All right, I promise. Just go," she said finally. She knew in her heart that she was lying to him. But it was critical that he left for the hospital and worked on Jill Dixon with his mind as clear as possible.

After pausing to take her in with one long, sweeping look, Doug turned and stalked out of the room. She heard the door close and exhaled a long, pent up sigh. Then she sat down on the bed and dropped her head in her hands. She felt like crying her heart out, but knew she couldn't spare the time.

With effort, she rose and pulled an overnight bag out of her closet, then automatically packed some clothes and other essentials. She'd return for the rest later.

When she got outside to the street, the light rain of the early evening was falling heavier. She hardly noticed as she walked to her car, tossed in her suitcase and slipped behind the wheel.

It seemed a bit extreme and dramatic, even under the circumstances, to leave her own apartment, Maura thought as she drove away. But it was the only way. She'd have a hard time persuading Doug to move out. She had to be the one to go. She'd find a hotel for the weekend, she speculated, then maybe arrange for some time off to visit with her sister.

She needed to put some distance between herself and Doug, or else this would never work. She knew that if she gave Doug half a chance and five more minutes of her time, he'd persuade her to put her doubts aside and give their marriage another try.

She switched the windshield wipers to a higher setting, the steady rhythm marking time in her wandering thoughts. There was so much good in their relationship—their connection, their rapport, the respect and understanding they felt for each other. Not to mention the fantastic lovemaking.

She would never deny that there was a solid foundation of feeling here. But if he didn't love her it just wasn't good enough. If he loved her he would have told her by now. Clearly, he didn't want her to go and he knew those were the only words she wanted to hear.

But he'd never said them. He'd never said anything close. So she had no choice now, Maura decided, but to go.

She would miss Doug's passionate touch. She would never know love like that with any other man. She'd never let anyone that close to her again. The cost was far too great, the loss too painful. Doug was her one love, her true love. She'd never want anyone that way again.

She looked ahead to a solitary life, a life devoted to her child. That Doug wouldn't be there with her was too painful an idea to dwell on, and Maura pushed the thought aside. She felt her eyes well up again with tears and reached for some tissues she'd stuck in her purse on the seat beside her. At the intersection ahead, the traffic light turned from yellow to red and she hit the brake, coasting to a stop.

Suddenly she heard the sound of screeching brakes coming from behind. Headlights flooded her rearview mirror with a blinding glare and the driver desperately pressed on the horn.

"Dear God!" Maura uttered. There was no time for any more reaction. She stared straight ahead, squeezed her eyes shut and folded her arms over her abdomen, instinctively protecting her baby from the impact about to come.

Then she heard the sickening crunch of metal hitting metal and felt her car being propelled forward. She heard herself scream and felt a sharp pain in her midsection as her car slammed into a station wagon crossing the intersection and swerved to a stop. Maura saw the hood of her car crumple like a sheet of paper right before the air bag exploded, filling her field of vision.

Then her head dropped forward and she blacked out.

Maura woke up slowly. She immediately knew she was in the hospital. The familiar sounds and smells had penetrated her subconscious. Feeling groggy and confused, she began to sit up, thinking at first that she was at work and needed to be doing her job, not lying around in a bed.

Then she felt a soft hand on her shoulder. An emergency room nurse, named Mae Li, whom she knew by sight, smiled down at her.

"It's all right, Maura. Please lie back and relax. How are you feeling?"

"I'm not sure," she said honestly. It was hard to talk, her mouth felt dry as cotton. "I have a beastly headache."

"I'll page Dr. Tyler," the nurse replied, mentioning Maura's obstetrician. "She's been waiting to speak with you."

Maura nodded and watched the nurse slip through the green curtains that were closed around her bed.

She knew she'd been in a car accident, but it was all so hazy and muddled in her mind. Then in a rush it came back to her—the glaring lights, the screeching brakes, the sound of metal crunching into metal. Then some flashing images of the police and ambulance drivers arriving at the scene, loading her into the ambulance. The memories were scattered pieces in her mind. She must have lost consciousness a few times. Or else it was just the shock.

She felt a sudden pang of worry. The baby! Was the baby all right? She wanted to ask somebody, but the nurse was gone. She turned and pressed the bedside call button, her hands moving down to cover her lower stomach as she waited. She didn't feel any pain there, she thought, trying to calm herself. Still, the impact could have hurt the baby...

No, it was too awful. She didn't want to think about it.

Tears spilled out of the corners of her eyes and dripped down to the pillow. She felt so empty and alone. Had she lost everything at once—Doug and the baby?

She heard the curtain move aside and expected it to be a nurse answering her call or the emergency room doctor coming to examine her. She couldn't open her eyes for a second, scared to ask the question about her baby.

Then suddenly she felt someone very close to her, holding her, kissing her hair and cheeks. "Maura, thank God you're all right."

She opened her eyes to find Doug leaning over her, his face close to hers, his expression grim. His amber eyes looked so bright as he stared down at her. Yet she still couldn't believe he was moved to tears to find her like this.

When she reached up and gently touched his cheek, he turned her hand to his mouth and kissed her palm. "I'm afraid, Doug...I'm afraid I lost the baby," she admitted on a choking sob. "I'm so sorry..."

He pulled her close, surrounding her with his warmth and strength. "Maura, please, as long you're all right. That's what matters most right now. I saw your doctor for a minute before I came in,'' he added. ''She says it looks good. At least you were aware enough at the accident scene to tell the EMS worker that you're pregnant. You had a sonogram when you came in, but you weren't awake. Your doctor wants to examine you again and give you another test. Then we'll know for sure,'' he admitted with a sigh.

Maura took in his words. She tried not to start crying again but couldn't help it. ''But what if—'' She started to voice her worst fear, but couldn't.

''I know it's hard, Maura. But we'll get through this,'' Doug promised in a comforting whisper as he continued to hold her close. ''We'll try again. My God, when I think of how I could have lost you tonight…''

His words trailed off as he buried his face in her hair and held her even closer. ''I love you so much,'' he murmured in a deep voice.

He pulled back just enough so he could see her face, and he lifted her chin with his fingertips. ''I do love you, Maura,'' he insisted, ''with all my heart and soul. I'm sorry it took me so long to say it. I've just been too scared to tell you. Too scared to love someone so much…and maybe lose you. I think I've loved you for a long time. Since the day I met you. I realize now I just couldn't face it.''

His admission was stunning, and Maura had no words to describe her feelings. He looked down a moment, then back up at her. ''You were leaving me tonight, weren't you?''

''Yes,'' she said, nodding. ''I couldn't stay. I thought you didn't love me. And I couldn't keep living with you that way, thinking you only married me for the baby.''

He gazed at her for a long time, his expression unreadable. Then finally he said, ''Maura…the truth is that when I proposed, the baby was part of the reason. A big part,'' he admitted in a grave tone. ''I wanted to tell you. I really tried, so many times. After that first time we made love, I thought, well, I have to tell her now. But somehow I just couldn't. I guess I already knew how you would react. And even though I could admit to myself how much I loved you, I knew I couldn't stand losing you. So I wasn't honest with you.''

''No, you weren't.'' Though Maura felt a spark of anger at his admission, it was squelched by the joy of hearing that he loved her. She could barely believe it.

''But now you know that isn't true. Can you forgive me?'' he asked quietly.

She met his gaze and quickly nodded, unable to speak.

The look of relief and sheer joy on his face made her heart swell. ''No matter what happens tonight, Maura, I'll always love you. Always and forever,'' he repeated in a heartfelt tone as he pulled her close. ''I'll always want to be with you,'' he promised, his voice full of passion. ''Even if it turns out that we can never have children together. I don't care if we adopt or even remain without a family. All I know now is I couldn't stand being without you. I don't know how I could go on.''

Maura's heart was so full she could hardly speak.

This wonderful, extraordinary man truly loved her. She could barely believe it.

But each time she met his adoring gaze, she knew it was true.

"I love you so much, Doug...I can't begin to say," she whispered. "You must know that by now, don't you?"

"No, I didn't," he admitted, his warm hands caressing her back. "I really thought you still had feelings for Scott. Especially after he called that night and you acted so odd and secretive about the conversation."

She pulled back, shocked to hear how drastically he'd misread her. "No, it wasn't that at all."

But now she could understand why he had become tense and distant around her—while she had thought he'd been having regrets about their marriage.

But instead of saying anything more, she leaned forward and kissed him, relishing the tender pressure of his mouth on hers. Their kiss deepened as Maura opened her mouth under his. She felt the antiseptic atmosphere melt away and felt herself transported to that perfect place where only Doug could take her.

Then the sound of someone clearing her throat made Maura and Doug move apart. Maura looked up and was relieved to see her own doctor. Although Doug had moved away from Maura a bit, he still kept one arm around her shoulder.

"Any news about the baby, Dr. Tyler?" Doug asked.

"The blood tests and sonogram look good," Dr. Tyler replied in an even tone. "You've had some bleeding, Maura, but the baby looks fine. We're going to give you another sonogram now and take a second look. Are you ready?''

Maura looked into Doug's steady gaze and found all the strength and love she needed. She turned to the doctor and nodded. "Yes, we're ready," she said.

Minutes later Maura was wheeled into a small testing room. Doug stood beside her, holding her hand as Dr. Tyler prepared her. The doctor took her time and didn't say a word as she conducted the test. Maura could hardly breathe, she felt so anxious. She looked up at Doug, and he gave her hand a reassuring squeeze. Yet in his expression she could also see distress. Even though he was a doctor, right now he was just an anxious parent.

"There's the baby," Dr. Tyler said suddenly, with a sharp note of excitement.

She pointed to a tiny, blurry image on the screen, and Maura strained her neck to catch a glimpse. She met Doug's gaze and they shared a special thrill that only new parents know.

"He looks beautiful," Doug said in awe.

"Or *she* does," Maura said with an indulgent laugh.

"Sorry, folks, it's too soon to settle that debate. But boy or girl, your baby looks fine. I don't see any problems at all," the doctor said with a finality that was very reassuring.

"You're a lucky woman, Maura," Dr. Tyler added as she removed the imaging equipment from Maura's stomach and pulled off her gloves.

"Yes, I know," Maura had to agree. She felt the tender pressure of Doug's kiss on her forehead and knew now that she was luckier than she'd ever dreamed possible.

"I think you can go now," Dr. Tyler said. "As long as you take it really slow for the next few days. And I wouldn't rush to get back to work, either."

"Absolutely," Doug promised in a stern voice. Maura glanced up at him and saw his most serious expression. She knew she didn't have a chance.

After Dr. Tyler left them, Doug helped her sit up. He put his arms around her and held her close. "The baby's okay," he said simply.

"Yes, thank God," Maura replied quietly.

"But no matter what, we'll always have each other." With his arms still circling her in a strong embrace, he leaned back and met her gaze. "Ready to go home now?"

Maura nodded. "And you don't have to worry," she promised. "I'll do just as the doctor said."

"You better believe it," Doug replied with a short, deep laugh. "Because you're going to have this doctor watching your every move, babe."

His tone was a mixture of protectiveness and passion, and Maura felt a secret thrill. "I would hope so," she replied, her green eyes shimmering with longing for him.

Their lips met in a deep, soul-satisfying kiss, and Maura suddenly realized that this moment, this kiss, marked the true start of their marriage. No matter what the years would bring, she would make a real home with the man she truly loved and would always cherish their life together.

*   *   *   *   *

And the Winner Gets...Married!

METSY HINGLE

METSY HINGLE

is an award-winning, bestselling author of romance who resides across the lake from her native New Orleans. Married for more than twenty years to her own hero, she is the busy mother of four children. She recently traded in her business suits and a fast-paced life in the hotel and public-relations arena to pursue writing full-time. Metsy has a strong belief in the power of love and romance. She also believes in happy endings, which she continues to demonstrate with each new story she writes. She loves hearing from readers. For a free doorknob hanger or bookmark, write to Metsy at PO Box 3224, Covington, LA 70433, USA.

For Missy & Molly Brown,
My four-legged babies
who provide continuous joy.

One

"**W**here is he?"

Kimberly Lindgren jerked her gaze up from the computer screen as Tara Connelly Paige stormed into the office suite. "Mrs. Paige," she said, quickly coming to her feet to intercept the other woman, who, given the high color in her cheeks and the snap in her voice, was obviously furious. "I don't think your brother is expecting you."

"Oh, I'm sure he's not. But he *is* going to see me."

After working as an executive assistant for more than two years at Connelly Corporation, Kim had become a master at smoothing ruffled Connelly feathers. Yet something about the fire in this particular Connelly's violet eyes told her this was not going to be one of those times. Still, she had to at least try. "I believe Justin is on the phone at the moment," she said, positioning herself in front of her boss's office door. "If you'll have a seat, I'll let him know that you're here."

"Thanks. But I'll just tell him myself."

Kim didn't move. "That might not be a good idea, Mrs. Paige. Your brother's had a rather difficult morning." Which was an understatement if there ever was one, Kim admitted silently. The day had turned into a disaster—one for which she felt partly responsible since it had been she who had discovered the cost overruns in the firm's new advertising campaign that was set to kick off next month.

"If that's your way of telling me that Justin's in a rotten mood," Tara went on, "I appreciate the warning. Really, I do. But it just so happens that I'm in a rather foul mood myself, and Justin is the reason. I *am* going to see him, Kim. Now the only question is whether you're going to move away from that door and let me pass or am I going to have to go through you?"

Stunned, Kim remained speechless. For several long seconds she simply stared at the petite dark-haired woman dressed in the chic red suit, dashing hat and gloves and killer high heels. At five foot seven, Kim estimated she had at least five inches and twenty pounds on Tara Paige. Yet Kim didn't doubt for a moment that the other woman meant every word she'd said.

"It's your call, Kim. What's it going to be?"

"Why don't we go in together?" she suggested, seeing no alternative. Since Justin really was on the telephone, she tapped on his door and entered without waiting for a response. The sight of Justin at his desk with the magnificent view of the Chicago skyline behind him was something that never failed to make her heart race. But the scowl on his handsome face now made her tense. Glancing past him, Kim noted the storm clouds threatening outside the windows. While she didn't like to think of herself as superstitious, she got a sudden sinking sensation in her stomach.

Of course, having an obviously upset Tara on her heels didn't help.

"Listen, Marsh, I don't care how busy you are with the wedding plans. I want the revised budget and copies of all your correspondence with Schaeffer on my desk by the end of the day. Is that clear?"

Kim nearly winced at the edge in Justin's voice, but it was the way he was rubbing the back of his neck that concerned her. He'd been working too hard again, she thought. Since taking over as vice president of marketing six months ago when his brother Daniel had assumed the throne of Altaria, he'd handled the work of two men. He'd also had to deal with more than his share of problems—beginning with the attempted assassination of his brother, followed by the corporation's computer crash a few weeks ago, and now this latest fiasco with the firm's advertising campaign. The fact that the error started with Robert Marsh, who was about to become Justin's brother-in-law, surely added to Justin's stress.

"I mean it, Marsh. I want everything before the close of business today or you can clear out your desk," he said, and slammed down the phone. Only then did he look up at her. "Kim, I—" He looked past her, and upon spying his sister, his scowl deepened. "I said I didn't want to be disturbed."

"I know, and I'm sorry for the interruption," Kim began, knowing all too well that Tara couldn't have come at a worse time. "But your sister needed to speak with you, and I thought maybe you could see her for a moment before you leave for your next appointment."

"Mother was right about you, Kim. You really are a diplomat," Tara said as she breezed past Kim and placed herself directly in front of Justin's desk. Despite Tara's refined demeanor and tone, Kim sensed the anger still simmering just beneath the surface. "The truth is that, short of tackling me, Kim did everything possible to keep me out of here."

"And naturally you refused to take no for an answer," Justin replied.

"Naturally. And considering it's a skill I learned from you, big brother, I can assure you that I have no intention of taking no for an answer now."

Kim held her breath as Justin and his sister squared off. While she'd always found the size of the Connelly family mind-boggling, it was the dynamics between the siblings that continued to fascinate her. Probably because her own family had consisted of just her and her mother—and now, only her. Suddenly feeling like an intruder, Kim said, "I'll leave you two alone."

"You might as well stay," Justin replied before she'd taken a step toward the door. "This shouldn't take long and there are several things you and I need to go over before I leave." He glanced at his watch. "All right, Tara. I've got all of five minutes to spare. So why don't you tell me what's got you so fired up?"

"I'm fired up, brother dear, because you think you've weaseled your way out of being in the bachelor auction fund-raiser this weekend like you promised."

Justin sighed. "It's not a question of my weaseling out of anything. I simply can't do it."

"Why not? And don't hand me that lame excuse that you gave Jennifer about some unexpected business problem that you need to take care of, because I'm not buying it."

Kim held her breath as temper flashed in Justin's hazel eyes.

"It's not an excuse. It's the truth," Justin countered. "Whether you believe it or not is up to you."

"Well, I don't believe it," Tara returned.

"Suit yourself," Justin told her, and picked up a report from his desk. "Now, if you'll excuse me, I've got work to do."

"I will not excuse you, Justin Connelly," Tara said. She slapped the gloves clutched in her fist against her opposite palm like a whip. "And don't you dare pull that 'I'm too busy' number on me. Have you forgotten how important this fund-raiser is? That the money is going to be used to help the families of slain police officers?"

Tara didn't have to add "families like Jennifer's," Kim thought, because they all knew that until Jennifer's recent marriage to Chance Connelly, the former social secretary and her young daughter had been one of those families. That Justin remembered, too, was evident from his somber expression.

"No, I haven't forgotten," Justin said firmly. "I've already apologized to Jennifer for pulling out at the last minute. But I have an important meeting in New York that afternoon, and it would be nearly impossible to get back in time."

"Then change the meeting or go a day earlier or next week."

"Don't you think I would if I could?" He raked a hand through his hair. "I had a difficult enough time getting this meeting on Friday and it's something that can't wait. If you're worried about the money my pulling out will cost, I've already assured Jennifer that I'll be sending a generous contribution to make up for canceling."

"And just how do you propose we make up for the money that we'll lose in ticket sales when word gets out that Justin Connelly, voted one of Chicago's most eligible bachelors and the key draw for the blasted event, has pulled out of the auction? Of course, that doesn't even begin to take into account the amount of money that we might have been able to raise if your tush were on the auction block.''

Justin frowned at his sister. ''You make me sound like a side of beef.''

Tara sat down on the corner of Justin's desk. ''In a manner of speaking, you are.''

''Thanks a lot.''

Tara shrugged. ''Can I help it if there are women out there willing to pay big bucks for the chance to spend an evening with you? Face it, pal, you're a hot commodity. Not only are you the brother of a king, but you're also an heir to the Connelly fortune. You wouldn't believe the number of women who actually think you've got a pretty face and sexy body. And judging by the comments I've heard, they'd all like nothing better than the chance to get you between the sheets.''

''For Pete's sake, Tara! Will you knock it off?'' Justin snapped, his face heating. Pushing away from his desk, he rose and walked over to the windows to stare out at the rain that had begun to fall.

''Well, if this isn't a first. I do believe I've embarrassed you.''

He whirled around, shot her a withering glance. ''Of course you've embarrassed me. And Kim, too,'' he added. ''Since when do you and your friends sit around discussing men as though they were...were...''

''Sex objects?'' Tara offered.

Justin glared at her.

Tara laughed. ''Oh, come on, Justin. Did you really think that was a privilege reserved only for men?''

''You're my little sister!''

''I'm twenty-five years old, a widow and a mother,'' Tara said, her voice suddenly serious. ''Believe it or not, I do know a thing or two about sex.''

Justin groaned. "I don't want to hear this," he told her, and, returning to his desk, he snatched up the report in front of him. "I've got work to do. I'm truly sorry about the fund-raiser, but I promise I'll send a sizable check."

"What about the auction?"

He sighed again, put down the file. "Tara, I've already explained, there's just no way I can make it," Justin said, and there was no mistaking the regret in his voice at having to deny his sister's request. "I'll admit, I've never been wild about the idea of being in this auction. I only agreed to do it because Jennifer and Mother asked me to and I know it's for a good cause. But as much as I hate letting them or you down, there is simply no way I can be in two places at once."

Kim hadn't been any keener on the idea of Justin spending a romantic evening with some beautiful socialite than he seemed to be, she admitted. And she had been relieved when he'd canceled. But now, witnessing Tara's disappointment and Justin's distress at being the cause of it, she couldn't help but feel guilty. Before she could change her mind, Kim blurted out, "Actually, there is a way you can do both."

Both sets of Connelly eyes turned to her. "How?" Tara asked.

Kim swallowed. "A couple of things would have to be worked out first, but it is possible."

"What do you need?" Tara countered.

"First you and Jennifer would have to arrange it so that Justin would be the last bachelor to be bid on at the auction."

"That's not a problem," Tara assured her. "What else?"

"Justin's meeting scheduled here Friday morning with the marketing department would have to be postponed until next week."

"That shouldn't be a problem, should it?" Tara asked her brother.

"I guess not." He eyed Kim warily. "What about Schaeffer?"

"Your New York meeting with him could be moved up a few hours. Say a meeting over lunch instead of one that spilled over into the dinner hour."

"What makes you think Schaeffer will agree to that?" Justin asked. "I had a devil of a time getting that meeting in the first place."

"I've gotten to be sort of friendly on the phone with Mr. Schaeffer's secretary," Kim said. "She works closely with him. I think I can get her to convince him that it would be...beneficial to have an early meeting and leave his evening free."

"I see," Justin said.

Kim felt her own face heat at the knowing look in his hazel eyes. "That way even if your meeting with Mr. Schaeffer runs over, as long as you made it to the airport by five o'clock or five-thirty, I can get you on a shuttle that would put you back in Chicago in three hours. Allowing thirty minutes travel time to get you from O'Hare to the hotel, you could be there for nine o'clock."

"And I can have a driver waiting at the airport to pick you up and take you to the hotel," Tara concluded. She clasped her hands together and smiled. "Please, Justin, say you'll do it."

"Seeing how my assistant has conspired with you, I don't seem to have much choice."

Tara turned to her and beamed. "Bless you, Kimberly Lindgren. I owe you one."

"Not at all. I was glad to help."

"You did a great deal more than help," Tara insisted before turning back to Justin. "The woman's not only a diplomat, she's a genius, Justin. I wonder if you realize how lucky you are.''

''I'm beginning to.''

Something in Justin's voice and the way he was looking at her caused Kim's pulse to race. Mortified that he might realize how she felt about him, she averted her gaze. ''I'd better go see about making those calls,'' Kim told them.

''And I've got to go or I'll never make it to that meeting on time,'' Justin replied and began shoving papers into his briefcase.

''But we have to discuss your date package,'' Tara informed him even as he snapped the briefcase shut and reached for his suit jacket. She followed him to the door. ''We need to come up with something really special.''

''Get with Kim,'' he told her. ''She'll know what to do.''

''I think dinner and tickets to the theater would be nice,'' Kim suggested a few minutes later.

''Nice, but not special,'' Tara informed her. ''If a woman is going to bid top dollar for a date with Justin, we need to offer her something exciting.''

Just being on a date with Justin would be exciting enough for her, Kim mused silently. But then she was in love with him and had been for months now. Not that Justin had any clue about her feelings for him. He didn't. And for that she was eternally grateful. After all, what could be more cliché than to have a secretary fall in love with her boss—a boss who didn't even know she existed?

''Any ideas?''

Kim gave herself a mental shake and reminded herself to deal in reality. ''How about one of those dinner cruises?''

''Hmm. That would be romantic. But I was hoping for something different,'' Tara replied. She crossed her legs and began to tap one manicured nail against her chin. Suddenly her finger stilled, and, tilting her head to the side, she stared at Kim. "If *you* were the one going on a date with Justin, where would *you* want to go?"

Kim stiffened. Had Tara somehow picked up on her feelings for Justin, she wondered. "Me?"

"Yes, you."

"Really, Mrs. Paige, I don't think—"

"Please," Tara said, wincing. "Do you think you could manage to call me Tara? I'm guessing that we're about the same age, but every time you call me Mrs. Paige I feel like someone's grandmother."

Kim's lips twitched. "You don't look like anyone's grandmother."

"I certainly hope not," Tara told her with a laugh.

The woman was beautiful, glamorous, sophisticated. Everything that she wasn't, Kim thought. And even though at twenty-four she was only a year younger than the other woman, Tara had already been married, widowed and had a child. Kim couldn't help but think that life was passing her by quickly.

"So what would you consider a fun and exciting date?" Tara asked.

"I doubt that my idea of fun and excitement would appeal to the women who'll be bidding at the auction."

"Why not?"

"Because I'm not like them," Kim answered honestly.

"You're a woman, aren't you?"

"I...yes."

"Then whatever appeals to you should appeal to other women."

"But—"

"No buts," Tara told her and stood. She gathered up her

purse and gloves. "I've got to run. But why don't you put a date package together that would appeal to *you*."

"Like what?"

Tara shrugged. "I don't know. Something that *you* would like to do if you were the woman going out on a date with Justin. Make it as simple or elaborate as you want."

"But what if I choose something that's all wrong?"

"You won't," Tara assured her. "Trust your instincts, Kim. Whatever you choose, I'm sure it's going to be perfect."

"Let's hope you're right," Kim told her and wished she had as much confidence in herself as Tara seemed to have in her.

"I am," Tara said with a smile and started toward the door. She paused, turned back. "Oh, I almost forgot. Are you doing anything Friday night?"

"No," Kim replied cautiously.

"Great. I've purchased a couple of tables for the fund-raiser, so I have some extra tickets. Would you do me a favor and attend as my guest?"

"But Mrs.— Tara," she corrected when the other woman gave her a reproving look. "That's very kind of you, but I couldn't possibly go."

"Why not? You said you were free."

"I am, but—"

"No buts. You deserve to enjoy yourself after all your hard work, and you'd be doing me a favor by going. Will you need a ticket for an escort?"

"Uh, no. That won't be necessary." It had been months since she'd been out on a date—and couldn't even fathom whom she would ask to accompany her to something like this.

Tara beamed at her. "Great. Then I'll see that a ticket is messengered over to you in the morning."

Before Kim could argue further and tell Tara that she really didn't belong at such an affair, the other woman was gone.

"Damn it!" Justin pitched the report he'd been reading onto the others on his desk. How he would dearly love to wring Robert Marsh's neck. Unfortunately, he couldn't because the man had covered his tracks well. Frustrated, Justin shoved away from his desk and wandered over to the windows that filled one wall of his office. Normally looking out at the skyline soothed him, helped him to organize his thoughts. Yet watching the shifting colors as the sun began its descent seemed to make him even more restless. Probably something to do with the gloomy weather that had played havoc with the city most of the day, he told himself.

Of course, this mess with Schaeffer hadn't helped. It was going to take a miracle to launch the marketing campaign on time without blowing an even larger chunk of the budget. But somehow he had to find a way, Justin reminded himself. He simply had to. His family was counting on him. Sighing, he returned to his desk and dug in, determined to find that miracle.

More than two hours later, when he lifted his head, Justin gave a grunt of satisfaction. By shifting and scaling back expenses, he'd managed to make some progress and he'd done so without losing the integrity of the plan. Now, if he could bring the rest of the costs into line, he just might be able to pull it off. Rummaging through the papers on his desk, he searched for the file folder containing the billing costs on the marketing campaign to date. Unable to find it, he stopped and tried to recall when he'd had it last. He'd given it to Kim to check out the accuracy of some of the figures, he remembered. Maybe it was still on her desk.

Intent on finding the folder, Justin started out of his office only to stop cold at the sight of Kim. For once she wasn't sitting at her desk, the picture of efficiency in her sensible heels and sedate business suit, hard at work. Instead she stood in her stocking feet with her blouse opened at the neck and her eyes closed while she stretched. And as he watched her extend and stretch her body, all thoughts of the missing folder and business went right out of Justin's head.

In the six months that he'd worked with Kim, she had been the perfect assistant. Not only had she made the difficult task of taking over after his brother's departure for Altaria a smooth one, but her people skills had proven invaluable to him. In all that time she had been poised, efficient, businesslike.

She didn't look the least bit businesslike now. Not with her eyes closed, her head tipped back and a serene expression on her face. Slowly, as though performing a dance, she began to bend her body. And if his life depended on it, Justin couldn't have looked away. Transfixed, he watched her move with the grace of a prima ballerina. When she folded her body in two, her skirt climbed up, and Justin swallowed hard at the view of her legs. Funny, he thought, as Kim brought her head down to press against first one ankle and then the other, but he'd never noticed before just how long and shapely Kim's legs were. And how in the devil had he failed to notice what a small waist she had? Or the enticing lines of her hips?

Justin's blood heated as she unfolded her torso and reached over her head once more, pulling the silky white blouse she wore taut against her breasts. He must have been blind, he decided, not to have realized how lushly curved

Kim was. He noticed now—a fact that was all too evident by the desire stirring in his gut.

Don't be a jerk, Connelly. Say something. Let the woman know she isn't alone.

Justin opened his mouth, intent on announcing his presence, when Kim removed the clip from her hair. He nearly swallowed his tongue as yards and yards of long, honey-blond hair came tumbling down around her shoulders and face.

Sweet heaven, had all that gorgeous, sexy hair been tucked into that no-nonsense twist?

Damn! He scrubbed a hand down his face. He'd always been a sucker for a woman with long hair, beginning with Miss Malone, his kindergarten teacher. Biting back a groan, Justin admitted that next to Kim, Miss Malone wouldn't even stand a chance.

He was absolutely out of his mind, Justin assured himself. He squeezed his eyes shut and tried to block out this new image of Kim. Didn't he have enough on his plate to deal with without this? They'd yet to find out who had tried to assassinate his brother, and he was none too thrilled about his sister Alexandra's upcoming marriage to Marsh. Add to that the problems at work and the headaches resulting from that most-eligible-bachelor status. The last thing he needed was to complicate his life even more with a woman—especially a woman he worked with on a daily basis.

The smart thing to do was to go back to his office and forget he'd ever seen this side of Kim. Which was just what he intended to do, Justin decided as he opened his eyes. Allowing himself one final glimpse of the sensual creature before him, he started to retreat into his office when Kim opened her eyes and stared straight at him.

"Justin," she said his name in a breathless whisper that

did nothing to cool the erotic thoughts that had been running rampant through his head only moments before.

"I'm sorry," he managed to get out. "I didn't mean to disturb you."

"You didn't. Disturb me, I mean," she added while she slipped back into her shoes. "I was...I was just doing a few stretching exercises to try to work out some of the kinks in my shoulders and neck."

Although she told him something about the importance of stretching, the words barely registered because he was far too mesmerized by her attempts to tame all that honey-gold hair into a neat twist. As far as he was concerned, she'd failed big-time, since several thick strands managed to escape the clip and now tumbled carelessly down her nape and the sides of her face. With her cheeks flushed and her hair mussed, Justin could all too easily imagine the way Kim would look after a night spent making love.

Kim took a breath. "Anyway, I guess I got kind of stiff sitting at the computer and— And here I am babbling on. Did you want me for something?"

Justin nearly groaned at the innocent remark as totally inappropriate thoughts came to mind. "No, I was just..." Damn, he couldn't even remember what it was he'd come out here to look for in the first place.

"Justin, are you all right?"

No, he most definitely wasn't all right. Not when he couldn't shake the punch of arousal he'd experienced upon seeing Kim stretching a few moments ago.

"Is something wrong?"

Justin gave himself a mental slap, forced himself to focus on the present. "No. Nothing's wrong." He let out a breath. "It's been a long day. And speaking of long days, what are you still doing here?"

"I had some work that I wanted to finish up."

"Whatever it is, it can wait until tomorrow. You should have left hours ago," he said, more gruffly than he'd intended.

"You're still here."

"My family owns the place," he pointed out.

"Yes, of course. I never meant to imply...I'll leave now and get out of your way," she murmured, then quickly turned away.

But not before Justin caught a glimpse of hurt in those big blue-green eyes. Damned if he didn't feel as though he'd just kicked a puppy. "Kim," he said, moving beside her. He turned her around to face him and tipped up her chin. "I'm sorry. I didn't mean that the way it sounded. Just because I'm in a lousy mood is no reason to take it out on you."

"It's okay."

"No, it's not." He captured the fist she held stiffly at her side and lifted it between them. "If it'll make you feel better, go ahead and sock me one," he said, jutting out his chin. "I deserve it for acting like a jerk."

"You're not a jerk."

"Sure, I am. Or at least I gave a good impression of one a minute ago. I hurt your feelings, and for that I'm sorry."

"But you didn't—"

Justin silenced her with a look. "You may be a terrific assistant, Ms. Lindgren, but you're a lousy liar."

"Thank you. I think."

He grinned at her. "Hey, I'm the one who should be thanking you. The truth is I'm not sure what I'd do without you."

"Oh, I'm sure you'd manage just fine," she said, and reclaimed her fingers. Though she stepped back, she came up against the desk, which prevented her from putting the distance between them that Justin suspected she'd intended.

"Hopefully, I won't have to find out. But seriously, what I should have said, and botched totally, is that as much as I appreciate all your hard work, there's no reason for you to put in such long hours."

"I don't mind," she told him. "I like my job. I like working with you."

"Darned if I understand why," he countered, and smiled at her again. "But how about calling it a day? I bet if you try, you might still be able to book yourself a massage at the health club."

"I probably could if I belonged to a health club. But since I don't, there's really no reason for me to hurry," she said, smiling up at him.

The smile intrigued him almost as much as she did. There was something both innocent and seductive about her smile. And it did nothing to ease his arousal. Taking a step back, Justin tried to shake off this new awareness of Kim as a desirable female.

"You're scowling at me again," she accused.

"Not at you. At myself," he corrected, feeling like an idiot. Of course she didn't belong to a health club. The fact that his family and most of his friends worked out regularly at a club certainly didn't mean that Kim did the same. Chances were she couldn't afford that kind of luxury. Because a luxury is what it was. It was the reason he refused to join the fancy clubs and worked out at a hole-in-the-wall gym. He stared at her and suddenly realized that other than the fact that Kim was single and had no family—facts his brother had told him when he'd taken over the position of vice president of marketing—he knew very little about Kim's personal life despite the fact that they worked so closely together. It was hard to imagine her all alone when he had such a large family himself. "I guess this is my night for apologies. That sounded terribly arrogant of me.

I shouldn't have assumed that you belonged to a health club."

"Don't be silly. It was a logical assumption."

"No, it wasn't. And I'm sorry if I embarrassed you."

"You didn't," she insisted. "Please. There's nothing to be sorry about. Connelly Corporation is very generous to its employees, and most of the clerical staff belongs to health clubs or spas. I could, too, if I wanted."

"But you don't want to?"

She shrugged. "I just don't know when I'd get the chance to use it."

"Which is my fault."

She tipped her head, studied him. "And how do you figure that?"

"Look what time it is and you're still here. I work you too hard."

"No, you don't. Besides, I don't work nearly as hard as you do," she countered.

Justin snorted. "I don't have a choice. My family is depending on me. You, on the other hand, don't have any excuse. I mean it, Kim. No more late nights like this for you."

"But I told you, I like my job. I like working with you."

"Even when I'm a royal pain in the neck?" he teased.

"Even then," she said. "Now, unless you need me for something, I'd really like to finish transcribing these notes," she told him, and reclaimed her seat in front of her computer screen.

"The notes can wait until tomorrow."

"They could, but there's no reason why they have to."

"Correct me if I'm wrong, but which one of us is the boss here?"

Kim laughed. "You are. But all I need is ten minutes to

finish, and then I promise I'll head for home and a long, hot soak in the tub.''

An image of Kim naked in a bathtub covered only in bubbles had Justin gritting his teeth. ''Scouts' honor?''

''Scouts' honor,'' she said and held up three fingers.

''All right. You've got ten minutes and then I want you out of here.''

''You got it,'' she promised and went back to work.

When Justin exited his office fifteen minutes later, Kim was still at her desk, staring at her computer screen and rubbing the back of her neck with one hand.

Even though his brain told him it was a mistake, he started toward her. ''Here, let me do that,'' he said, and pushed her hand away and replaced it with his own.

''You don't have to do this,'' she argued.

Justin ignored the comment. ''No wonder you're hurting. Talk about tense. Relax,'' he commanded, and began to massage her shoulders. Determined to prove to himself that his earlier reaction to Kim had been a fluke, a momentary aberration caused by spending too much time at work and neglecting his social life, he went to work on those stiff muscles. Satisfied that, by analyzing the situation, he now had any earlier sexual attraction he'd experienced toward Kim firmly under his command, Justin skillfully tackled the mass of knots along her spine. Using his thumbs, he applied pressure to a particularly tight spot between her shoulder-blades and began to knead it.

''This really isn't necess— Oh...''

His control slipped a notch at the sounds coming from Kim. Steeling himself, Justin reminded himself this was Kim Lindgren. Kim his assistant. Kim his right hand. Kim, whom he had no right to think of as a woman. But when she moaned again, his body reacted. Desire fisted in his gut, sent heat firing through his veins.

So much for being a master of control, Justin decided. Calling himself ten kinds of fool, he tortured himself further by inching closer and breathing in her scent. Roses, he thought as he dragged in another whiff. Since when had the scent of roses become a turn-on?

But he forgot all about the way she smelled when Kim tipped her head forward, giving him further access to her neck. Although he knew he was playing with fire, he reached for the strands of hair trailing her nape. They slid across his fingers like wisps of silk and did nothing to cool his blood.

The sight of that pale strip of skin where the edge of her blouse ended sent another wave of heat rushing through him. Before he could stop himself, he moved his fingertips along her bare neck. Soft and warm was all he could think. And before he could shut off the voice in his head, he heard the question. *Would she be this soft and warm all over?*

"You have magical hands," Kim murmured.

The husky timbre of her voice stripped off another layer of his control. "Kim, I—"

The sound of the elevator bell in the hall outside the suite sent sanity rushing back. Saved by the bell, Justin thought, and dropped his hands to his sides. Taking a step back, he dragged in a steadying breath just as the building's chief of security entered the suite.

"Evening, Mr. Connelly. Ms. Lindgren," Tom Jenkins said.

"Good evening, Tom," Justin told the other man.

"Hi, Tom," Kim said softly.

"I'm just making my rounds. You folks going to be here awhile longer?"

"I'll be here for another hour or so, but Ms. Lindgren is

leaving now. As a matter of fact, I'd appreciate if you'd see her to her car."

"Sure thing, Mr. Connelly."

"But, Justin, my notes—"

"Can wait until tomorrow," he said briskly. "You've put in enough hours for one day. Go home, Kim. I'll see you in the morning."

Kim's expression fell, and he could have sworn it was disappointment he read in those blue-green eyes. But before he could change his mind, he turned on his heels and retreated to his office, where he sat down at his desk and dropped his head into his hands.

Talk about close calls. He was lucky, Justin assured himself. He'd come dangerously close to crossing the line with Kim just now, and tomorrow he would be grateful he hadn't done so. Because if he'd kissed her as he'd wanted to do, he had no doubt he would have made a major mistake on both a personal and a business front. Silently patting himself on the back, he told himself he'd done the right thing. He'd done the noble thing. He'd walked away when every instinct in him had wanted to pull her close, taste her mouth.

Yes, he was lucky, he reiterated. They both were. Lifting his head, Justin stared unseeingly at the work spread out across his desk. And as the memory of Kim's scent, the feel of her skin came back to haunt him, Justin grimaced and decided that sometimes doing the honorable thing really sucked.

TWO

Justin was just being kind. Don't read anything into it.

Kim repeated the words like a litany—just as she had been doing since she'd left the office hours earlier. Not that it seemed to be doing her much good, she admitted. Because, try as she might, she hadn't been able to stop thinking about the way Justin had been looking at her just before Tom's arrival. Not as a boss would, but the way a man looks at a woman. A woman he wants. And she'd felt the heat of those oh-so-serious hazel eyes trained on her like a caress.

Even now, just remembering that look in his eyes made her shiver with excitement, with longing. Despite her limited experience with men, she knew desire when she saw it. And it had been desire she'd read in Justin's eyes. Desire for her.

Her. Plain, polite and boring Kimberly Lindgren.

A ripple of pleasure raced over Kim even as that nagging

voice inside her reared its head and warned her not to be foolish, not to delude herself by believing that Justin would ever see her as anything more than his assistant.

Be realistic, she told herself. The man was a Connelly. A member of one of Chicago's most prestigious families. Wasn't he just voted one of the city's most eligible bachelors? The man dated models, socialites, gorgeous women—not nobody secretaries with less than sterling pedigrees.

But, lying in the darkness of her bedroom with morning still hours away and her thoughts so filled with Justin, she ignored the warning voices. For once she didn't want to be the sensible and level-headed Kim Lindgren. Instead she wanted to relish the memories of how Justin had looked at her, touched her. Snuggling beneath the covers, she squeezed her eyes shut and allowed herself to relive those magical moments at the office with him. The feel of his hands—so strong, yet gentle. The warmth of his breath tickling her neck as he stood behind her. The hot, hungry look in his eyes when she'd turned around and met his gaze.

Kim clasped her hands to her throat as the image of his face swam before her closed lids. He'd been standing so close to her, close enough that she could see the faint trace of stubble darkening his chin. Close enough for her to smell the woodsy and spicy scent that he always wore. Close enough for her to feel the warmth of his body just inches from her own.

Her heart raced. That ache she got low in her belly whenever she dreamed of how it would be to have Justin hold her in his arms, to have him tell her that he loved her as she loved him, started anew. "And the chances of that ever happening are about as likely as Chicago getting snow in July," she muttered as sanity returned at last.

Grabbing her pillow, she flopped over onto her stomach and ordered herself to go to sleep. And in sleep she allowed herself to play out the fantasy as she never dared do when she was awake. In the safety of slumber she imagined the feel of his mouth—hot and hungry on hers—tasting her, filling her, and then the sound of his voice as he whispered words of love and called out over and over, "Kim...Kim..."

"Kim? Kim, did you hear me?"

The impatient note in Justin's voice startled Kim from her musings. Embarrassed to be caught daydreaming, she looked up and found a somber Justin standing in front of her desk. "Sorry. What was that?"

"I asked if you had a chance to draft that memo of understanding for my meeting with Schaeffer on Friday."

The all-business note in his voice lashed at her like a whip. "It's on your desk in your in basket," Kim answered, doing her best to match his cool tone.

"Good," he grumbled, and started toward his office only to pause and look back at her. "Are you feeling all right? You seemed...distracted."

Kim flushed. "I'm fine. I've just had my mind on putting together that date package for the bachelor auction so I can messenger it over to your sister today," she told him, opting for the half-truth. She had been working on the package, but it hadn't been the real source of her distraction. Justin had—or rather she'd been busy daydreaming that she was the lucky woman who would get to share the date with him.

He groaned. "Don't remind me. I still can't believe I let Tara convince me to go through with that thing instead of just sending a check."

"Your sister's very persuasive."

"Pushy is more like it."

Deciding not to comment on what seemed to be a family trait, she pointed out, "It *is* for a good cause."

"Which is the only reason I agreed to do it in the first place," he informed her, and mumbled something about needing to have his head examined because he'd probably be changing clothes in the limo to get to the thing on time.

Given Justin's reluctance to participate in the auction, Kim suddenly questioned her decision to follow Tara's advice and make the date one that she herself would find appealing. "Do you want to take a look at what I put together as your date package?" she asked, and picked up the envelope that contained a certificate that detailed a romantic sailing date on Lake Geneva.

"I'm sure it's fine," he told her, and started again toward his office.

"It'll only take a minute to look it over, and I'd—"

"I said it's fine," Justin snapped.

Kim clamped her lips together and remained silent.

Justin sighed, rammed a hand through his hair. "Listen, I'm sorry. I didn't mean to bite your head off. It's just that…I have a lot on my mind at the moment."

"I understand," Kim replied, still stinging from his sharp tone. She did understand that Justin worked much too hard, that he demanded too much of himself. In the six months that she'd worked with the man, she had seen him in a number of stressful situations. But never once during that time had he ever raised his voice to her or spoken to her as he had a moment ago. Even worse, she hadn't realized until now just how vulnerable she was to him or how much he could hurt her.

Was it because of last night? she asked herself. Had he somehow picked up on her feelings for him and was now uncomfortable with her?

Mortified at the thought that Justin might know she was in love with him, Kim wished she could simply disappear.

"Kim, I really am sorry," he told her again, his expression softening. "The last thing I would ever want to do is hurt you."

Kim nodded and averted her gaze, afraid she would see pity in his eyes, afraid of what he would see in hers.

He stood there a moment longer, then said, "I'll be in my office the rest of the afternoon. Please hold my calls."

"But what about the lunch with your father?"

"I canceled it so I could work on this Schaeffer deal. I'll need to schedule some time with him when I get back from New York."

"I'll take care of it," she advised him, pleased that her voice could sound so professional and detached when inside she still felt raw, exposed.

"Thanks," he said, and disappeared inside his office.

But the instant the door closed behind him, Kim lost some of the starch in her spine. So much for any notions that something had happened between them last night, she thought. Hoping that Justin might finally have begun to see her as more than just his assistant was obviously nothing more than a fantasy on her part. A fantasy that bore a painful resemblance to her mother's string of hopeless romances. She'd adored her mother, missed her still. But as much as she had loved her, she had hated the constant highs and lows caused by her mother's endless quest to find Mr. Right.

Evidently she had more of Amanda Lindgren's penchant for impossible dreams than she'd thought, Kim decided. Thank heavens she also possessed enough common sense and pride to choke a mule. Whatever change she'd thought she'd detected in Justin's attitude toward her last night, it obviously wasn't romantic in nature. There hadn't been anything remotely romantic about the way he'd looked at her today. If anything, he'd seemed cool and unapproachable—not at all the warm, caring man she'd grown accustomed to working with these past months.

Taking a cue from Justin, she promised herself that no matter how she felt about him, he would never know. She picked up the envelope containing the certificate for the bachelor auction. After enclosing it in a transmittal envelope, she started to attach a cover note to Tara declining the offer of the ticket. Then she hesitated. Maybe she would think about it some more. She tackled the pile of letters and messages on her desk, determined to bury herself in work and forget about those magical moments with Justin last night.

"What else?"

"I need you to sign off on these letters and the checks that go with them," Kim informed Justin two afternoons later.

Quickly he scanned the letters in question, noted the sums of the accompanying checks and scrawled his signature across the documents where indicated. As he did so, he steeled himself against her scent—a whiff of roses and something exotic—that filled his head each time he was near her. "Is that everything?"

"Except for the final draft on the Schaeffer document. I've put in the additional changes you wanted, but you'll probably want to go over it one more time to be sure everything's covered."

She handed him the lengthy document he'd worked and reworked several times already, and as she did so, his fingers brushed hers. Kim snatched her hand away—but not before he'd felt that stab of awareness again. "I'll take a look at it now, then maybe you can get out of here at a decent time, for a change."

"I'll be at my desk."

After she'd exited his office and he was alone again, Justin swore. Something had to give—and soon. Ever since the other night, Kim had been acting differently toward him. Oh, she still was doing a great job as his assistant. He couldn't have asked for anyone more knowledgeable, efficient or reliable. But he sensed a distance now, a wall, that hadn't been there before. While he...he had been going slowly insane with very nonbusinesslike thoughts about her. Despite the fact that he'd driven himself relentlessly at the office during the day, then pounded on the bags at the gym until he was exhausted in the evenings, he'd lain awake for the past two nights thinking about Kim, wanting her. Try as he might, he hadn't been able to forget the image of her the other night. Sighing, he sat back in his chair and closed his eyes.

And there she was again with her hair tumbling down her back and shoulders. He curled his hands into fists, remembered how silky that hair had felt, how soft and warm her skin had been. He dragged in a breath and could have sworn he could smell her—that sweetness of roses and sunshine and secrets.

Get a grip, Connelly.

Justin snapped open his eyes. He had to stop thinking of Kim that way, he reminded himself. Maybe the trip to New York would help. Surely spending all day Friday, plus the weekend away from Kim would help him get his head and hormones straight. And who knows, maybe that bachelor auction would turn out to be a blessing in disguise. With a little luck he just might meet someone interesting. Maybe another female would make him forget all these wild thoughts he'd been having about Kim, Justin decided. And with that plan of action firmly in mind, he picked up a pen and went to work on the agreement.

"That should do it," Justin muttered some time later. He tossed down his pen and leaned back in his chair. Finally, after incorporating several suggestions from his father and fine-tuning the document once more, he was satisfied. Now he just needed to sell it to Schaeffer. Stretching to ease the stiffness in his shoulders, he cupped his hands behind his head and spun his chair around to face the windows.

"Aw, hell," he grumbled at the sight of the star-filled skyline. A quick glance at his watch told him he'd been at it for hours, which meant that Kim had been forced to stay late again. Shoving out of his seat, he tore out of his office.

"What's wrong?" Kim asked, jerking her gaze up from the computer screen.

"It's late, and I promised that you'd get out of here at a decent hour for a change."

"It's only half past eight," she informed him, and averted her gaze.

"Only? You're supposed to be able to leave at five." He could probably count the times on one hand that she'd left at quitting time. He claimed a seat on the corner of her desk. "And thanks to me, you've had to work late again."

"I didn't mind. I had some things I needed to catch up on. So did you finish?"

"Yes," he told her, but made no attempt to give her the agreement.

Finally she shifted her gaze back to his for a moment. "If you intend for me to put in those changes, you're going to have to give that to me," she said, and held out her hand for the document.

"I'll plug in the changes. Just pull up the original agreement on the screen and then you can get out of here."

"Don't be silly. I'll do it," she argued.

"No. Go on home. You've stayed late enough."

Kim hesitated a moment. "Justin, is there something in that agreement that you'd prefer I not know about?"

"Of course not."

"Then since it is part of my job, I'll make the changes," she informed him. "Besides, as you'll recall, the last time you used my computer, you, um, had some difficulties."

"That wasn't my fault," he said, recalling that the system had ended up crashing when the terminal had insisted he'd performed an illegal operation.

"I'm sure it was just a coincidence. All the same I'll feel better if you let me make the changes."

Reluctantly Justin handed over the pages.

She scanned the edited sections a moment. "It'll probably take me about twenty minutes to do these and print up a fresh copy. If you want to go home, I can drop the revised set by your apartment on my way home."

He found the idea of Kim visiting his apartment appealing. Which was why he said, "I'll wait."

When his stomach grumbled a few seconds later, Kim looked up. "Maybe you should go down the street and have dinner while I take care of this. By the time you get back, it'll be finished."

"What about you? You haven't eaten yet, either. And don't tell me you're not starved because I wouldn't believe you."

"I'm all right," she said as she continued to scroll down on the screen and make changes. "I'll pick myself up something on the way home."

"Do you like pizza?"

"Yes," she said, pausing, her voice cautious, as were her eyes.

"Everything on it?"

"Justin, this isn't necessary."

He ignored her and reached for the phone. After dialing information, he had the number connected. "Everything on it?"

She frowned at him. "No anchovies."

Justin grinned at that. "You're a girl after my own heart, Kim Lindgren," he told her, and placed an order for a super-size pizza extravaganza with everything except anchovies.

"You shouldn't have done that," she admonished. "I'll never be able to eat even a third of that pizza."

"Good. That means there's more for me."

"But I thought…"

"You thought?" Justin prompted.

"I thought you would prefer to sit down to a real meal, something from a nice restaurant."

"By a 'real meal' I take it you mean a thick steak or some expensive entrée with a fancy sauce served on china?" Justin countered.

"Yes."

Justin grinned at that. "You obviously don't know many teenagers, do you?"

She gave him a puzzled look, which caused her brow to wrinkle in the most adorable way. "No."

"Well if you did, you'd know that pizza isn't only considered a real meal. It's the best meal possible."

Justin had been right. The pizza was a fabulous meal, especially when it was accompanied by an enormous Italian salad, bread sticks and a glass of wine from the bar in his office. Kim couldn't remember when she'd enjoyed a meal half as much.

Maybe it was the wine, she thought, as she breathed in the merlot and watched Justin over the rim of her glass. He seemed more relaxed, warmer toward her than he'd been in days. And she…she was enjoying herself, enjoying him. Sitting back in her chair at the conference table in Justin's office, Kim allowed herself the pleasure of watching him.

"How's the wine?" he asked.

"Wonderful," she replied, and took another sip to prove it. Remembering what she'd read about wine, she allowed the flavor to rest on her palate to fully enjoy its taste before swallowing.

"Don't tell me you're full," Justin teased.

"Hardly." She took a third slice of the pizza. "Tell me more about the teenagers you work with at the youth center."

"They're a challenge," he began, and told her about how bright some of the troubled teens he'd been working with really were. "They keep me on my toes, that's for sure. You should think about coming down. There's a lot they could learn from you."

"I doubt that. You're the marketing whiz."

"But there's more to business than marketing. You're smart, organized and you have a way of putting people at ease. Those are rare qualities, Kim. You instill even a fraction of them in those kids and it'll go a long way toward shaping their future."

"Thank you," she murmured, touched by the sincerity of his words.

"Nothing to thank me for. It's the truth. And I hope you'll at least think about coming down to the center."

"I will," she promised, and nearly choked when he smiled at her. God, but he was beautiful, she thought as she watched him tackle another slice of pizza. With that hint of red in his brown hair, the hazel eyes filled with laughter, the strong cheekbones and stubborn chin. For him to be so nice and honorable, too, just made him that much more attractive. Who could blame her for falling in love with him?

"You going to eat that?" he asked, pointing to the last slice of pizza on her plate.

"No. You go ahead and finish it," she told him.

"Tell you what. Why don't we split it," he suggested, and proceeded to divide the slice in two.

Justin polished off his half in a matter of seconds, but it took her a while longer. "Full?" he asked as he refilled both of their glasses.

"Stuffed is more like it," she confessed, dropping her napkin on the paper plate.

"Hang on a second. You've got a little tomato sauce on your face."

"Where?" she asked, and reached for a napkin to blot at her chin.

"Here, let me do that," he said, and, taking the napkin from her, he caught her chin in his hand and gently dabbed at a corner of her mouth.

He was so close Kim could see the stubble on his chin, smell the woodsy scent he wore. And when his fingers stilled and he looked into her eyes, she could scarcely breathe.

"You have the most incredible-colored eyes," he told her.

"They're blue."

"No. Not blue. Not green. But a combination. They're the color of water in the Caribbean where I sailed my boat last summer."

He stroked her cheek with his thumb, brought his face a fraction closer. "Kim, I…"

Kim's heart beat wildly in her chest. The breath stalled in her lungs. Instinctively she tipped up her head, closed her eyes and waited for the touch of his mouth.

"I-it's getting late. We probably should call it a night," Justin said, and dropped his hand from her face.

The words hit Kim like a blast of cold water. Her eyes snapped open and she scrambled to her feet, horrified of what Justin must think of her. Unable to meet his gaze for fear he would realize she'd wanted him to kiss her, she began to frantically snatch up the empty plates and napkins. "You can go on home. I'll clear away this stuff and lock up," she told him as she piled the paper goods atop the now-empty pizza box.

"Here, let me get that," Justin offered when her unsteady fingers began dropping the soiled napkins.

"I've got it," she argued.

But Justin ignored her. "You've worked hard enough today. Go ahead and close up shop at your desk while I handle the cleanup."

Eager to escape, Kim didn't argue. She simply fled Justin's office, praying she could get out of there before he saw the tears prickling at the backs of her eyes. Quickly she grabbed her purse from inside the drawer of her desk where she kept it and snatched up her car keys. "Good night, Justin," she called out, and started for the door. "Thanks again for dinner."

"What? Wait a minute," he said, sticking his head out the door of his office. "Let me get rid of this," he told her, indicating the wineglasses and wine bottle he held in his hands. "It'll only take me a second and then I'll walk you to your car."

"That's really not necessary. Tom or one of the other security guards will see that I get there safely."

"But—"

"I've got to go. Have a safe trip and good luck with Schaeffer tomorrow," she said, and exited the office suite quickly before the first tears began to fall.

Three

"Kim, wait!"

The door swooshed closed behind her. But not before Justin had a chance to see her face. Had those been tears in her eyes? he wondered. Were they because of him? Had Kim realized what he'd been thinking of doing a few moments ago? What he *still* wanted to do?

Damn!

Staring at the door through which Kim had just exited, Justin checked the urge to go after her. He scrubbed a hand down his face. To do so would be a mistake, he reasoned. He'd come dangerously close to kissing her a few minutes ago. Were he to follow her now, he wasn't at all sure that he wouldn't give in to the desire that had been nagging at him for days.

Definitely not a good idea, Connelly.

Not only would he risk losing the best assistant he'd ever worked with, but Kim would have every right to slap him and the company with a sexual harassment suit. Still, for a moment there, he'd almost believed that Kim had *wanted* him to kiss her.

Right! More like wishful thinking on his part, Justin conceded as he headed back into his office. Kim probably hadn't given him a second thought. She'd certainly never indicated that she had any romantic interest in him. Why should she? Despite that most-eligible-bachelor tag he'd been labeled with, the truth was he was a dull guy who spent most of his time working and little time on fun. If women were drawn to him, it probably had more to do with the fact that he'd been lucky enough to be born of a gene pool that provided him with decent looks. Being a part of the Connelly dynasty that had amassed a fortune and having ties to royalty didn't hurt, either. Kim, on the other hand, was a bright and attractive young woman. No doubt any number of guys were interested in her. And while he knew little about her personal life, it stood to reason that there would be a man in her life.

Justin frowned at the notion of Kim in the arms of another man. Disturbed by how much the idea bothered him, he told himself it was because he was protective of Kim. After all, they worked closely together. He'd become fond of her, valued her as his assistant and depended upon her. It was only normal that he should feel some concern about her, he reasoned.

He was going to drive himself crazy if he didn't stop thinking about Kim and whom she might or might not be involved with. Determined to wipe Kim and thoughts of her love life from his mind, Justin focused all his attention on making sure he had everything he would need while he was in New York.

For the next ten minutes the impending business meetings drove all other thoughts from his mind. After adding two other file folders he would need for his meetings in New York, as well as the redrafted contracts for the Schaeffer deal, he surveyed the contents of his briefcase.

"I'm forgetting something," he muttered. But what?

Don't forget your Palm Pilot.

Justin jerked his head up as he remembered Kim's earlier instructions. Striding out of his office, he marched over to Kim's desk. There was his Palm Pilot resting in the caddy where Kim had placed it when she'd taken the hand-held computer gadget in order to synchronize it with the updated data on his computer's main network. He picked up the palm-size marvel that contained not only his schedule for the entire year, but also the addresses and phone numbers of his family, friends and business associates. As he turned to leave, he spied the single white rose on Kim's desk that she'd bought from a street vendor the previous day.

And quick as a wink she was back in his head again.

Only this time she wasn't at Connelly headquarters. She was on the beach with her faced tipped up to the sun and her lips turned up in a smile. She'd exchanged the neat, ladylike blue suit she'd worn that day for a pair of shorts and a T-shirt that made the most of those curves he'd caught a glimpse of the other evening. And instead of that prim, sleek twist, her hair was loose and flowing like silk in the wind. But it was Kim's eyes—those serious blue-green eyes that had been haunting him for nearly a week—that he saw most clearly. Those eyes were bright with laughter and expectation and desire.

Justin's mouth went dry. He sucked in a breath. "Oh, man." He definitely needed to get a grip, he told himself, and strode back into his office. He tossed the Palm Pilot into the briefcase, then snapped it closed and forced himself to shut off the enticing images of Kim in his head.

He was going to be in serious trouble if he didn't get a

handle on these crazy thoughts he'd been having about his assistant, Justin reminded himself. He snatched up his brief-case, retrieved his suit coat and headed toward the exit.

So, he would get a handle on it, he assured himself, as he stepped into the elevator. All he had to do was treat this new attraction he was experiencing toward Kim as he would a business or marketing problem. These next few days away from Kim—tomorrow in New York and then the weekend—would provide him with the perfect oppor-tunity to do just that. Squaring his shoulders, Justin stepped off the elevator and, after signing out with the guard on duty, he headed for the garage.

A few days away from Kim was just what he needed to put things back into their proper perspective. He and Kim made a good working team. No way did he plan to mess that up by giving in to some crazy urges he'd had to kiss her. He'd already figured out it was his own lack of a social life that had triggered this new attraction he'd felt toward Kim. He'd simply force himself to reclaim some time for a social life. Already feeling better, he breathed a sigh of relief as he slid behind the wheel of his Mercedes. With any luck Kim would never find out just how close he'd come to crossing the line, and their relationship would go back to being business as usual.

It was business as usual when he called Kim from New York the next day. Seated in the back seat of the taxi en route to his meeting, Justin listened on his cell phone as Kim relayed his messages.

"Ashley Powers called. She said that you owe her a dinner and she'd like to collect soon."

Justin thought of the striking brunette stockbroker he'd taken out a few times this spring. The woman was beauti-ful, intelligent and had been sending him signals that she was more than ready to take their relationship to the next level. He'd been prepared to take her up on her offer for more than a month now, but their busy schedules kept getting in the way. Maybe Ashley was just what he needed to firmly shut off any lingering attraction he felt for Kim. "What's on my calendar for next Friday night?" Justin paused, and when Kim didn't answer, he asked, "Kim, you still there?"

"Yes. I was just pulling up your calendar on my screen. Right now you're open."

"See if Ashley's free for the evening. If she is, make us dinner reservations. Try that new place mentioned in that food critic's column last week."

"All right," Kim replied.

"What else have you got for me?"

"Robert Marsh said he needs to speak with you."

"What does he want?" Justin asked, agitated that Marsh was the reason he was in New York. Had the other man paid closer attention to the details, he wouldn't be scrambling to clean up a mess now.

"He wouldn't tell me. He said it was personal and had to do with family business."

Justin frowned, disliking the way Marsh had taken to identifying himself as a member of the Connelly family. Perhaps Justin had become jaded, but every instinct in him said Marsh was far more in love with the idea of marrying into the Connellys than he was in love with Alexandra. "Inform Marsh that he can either tell you what it is he wants or he can wait until I get back in the office on Monday."

"I'll tell him."

"Is that it?"

"Not quite. You have two more phone messages. One is from Patrice Barlow, who said to tell you that she and her daughter Bethany will be at the bachelor auction tonight and that Bethany will be making a substantial bid on you.''

Justin groaned aloud. ''Let's hope that her bid's not too substantial. I'm not sure I could handle spending an entire evening with Bethany the debutante.''

''She's not that bad,'' Kim told him.

''Easy for you to say. You've never been trapped at a dinner party with her and forced to listen to her ramble on and on about sororities in that squeaky voice of hers.''

''She's very pretty,'' Kim offered.

''How can you tell under all that makeup? The last time I saw her she was wearing so much gloss on her mouth that I thought the wineglass was going to slip across her lips and she'd end up with wine in her ear.''

''You're making that up!''

''All right, maybe I am exaggerating a little,'' he said. ''But you have to admit, the woman does overdo the makeup.''

''Maybe a little,'' Kim conceded.

He didn't have to see Kim's face to hear the smile in her voice, to imagine the grin curving her lips—lips with just a touch of rose color, and far more inviting than Bethany Barlow's could ever be. Realizing where his thoughts were headed, Justin sobered at once. ''You said I had another message.'' he prompted, reverting to business.

''Yes, from your sister Tara. She just wanted to wish you luck today and to say thanks in advance for agreeing to participate in the auction tonight.''

''In other words, she called to remind me that I'd better show up tonight or I'm toast,'' Justin countered.

''I wouldn't put it that way exactly. She's just a little nervous and wants to make sure there are no glitches.''

''Nice try, Kim. But I know my little sister. She had you double-check the flight arrangements, didn't she?''

Kim hesitated. "I *offered* to check."

Uh-huh, Justin thought. No doubt his sister had made an ally of Kim. Not that he was surprised. People seemed to gravitate toward Kim, and heaven knew that Tara could use a friend after the rough time she'd had these past years. "Tell Tara not to worry. A promise is a promise. I'll be there."

"I'll tell her," Kim replied. After a moment's pause, she said, "That's everything for the moment."

"Good," he said, but found himself reluctant to cut the connection.

"Was there anything else you needed me to do?" Kim asked.

"No. No, you've covered everything as usual."

"Just doing my job," she informed him. "Speaking of which, I better start making those calls."

"Kim, wait."

"Yes?"

"Promise me that you'll get out of there on time for a change. I don't like the idea of you working late alone."

"Justin, I'm perfectly safe. The security—"

"Promise me," he insisted.

"All right. I promise to leave on time. I was going to leave at five today, anyway."

"Big plans for the evening?" The question slipped out before he could stop himself.

"Kind of. I'm going to the fund-raiser tonight at the hotel. Your sister bought extra seats and insisted on giving me a ticket to attend. That is if my being there doesn't make you uncomfortable. If it does, I can tell Tara I can't make it."

"Why would your presence make me uncomfortable?"

"I...don't know. It's just that you've seemed a little

edgy the past few days. I thought that maybe it was me, that I'd done something to make you uncomfortable."

"I'm just uptight about the Schaeffer meeting," Justin lied. "By all means go to the fund-raiser. It'll be nice to see a friendly face there."

"If you're sure..."

"Positive. Come. Bring your boyfriend, and the two of you can have a great time." Before she could reply, he ended the call by saying, "Got to run. I'm at Schaeffer's now. I'll see you tonight."

Kim stared at her reflection in the mirror, unable to believe that the elegant creature who looked back was actually her. She smoothed her hands down the skirt of the strapless black evening gown. And when her gloved fingers whispered along the moiré silk fabric, she fell in love with the dress all over again. Dismissing the last pangs of guilt over splurging on the outfit, Kim smiled. Both the dress and the matching eighteen-button doeskin gloves had been worth every penny, she decided, as she turned to admire the way the skirt swished about her ankles.

The store clerk had been right. It was the type of gown that made a woman feel like a princess. And Kim couldn't help feeling a bit like Cinderella on her way to the ball. Lifting her skirt, she studied the high-heeled shoes with their delicate straps. "Not exactly glass slippers," she murmured.

But every bit as impractical, she thought, and laughed aloud at her own foolish purchase. She'd probably never wear the shoes again. And the likelihood that she'd ever have an occasion to wear the gown and gloves again were just as slim, she admitted. Yet for now, for tonight, it didn't matter. Tonight she could pretend she was a princess attending her first ball.

"Good evening, My Lord," she mimicked. Enjoying the game, she executed a curtsy and giggled when she wobbled on the skyscraper heels. Definitely not walking shoes, she reminded herself, and made a mental note to take small, slow steps tonight. Otherwise, she'd be tumbling in the middle of the ballroom floor in front of all those important people. The idea of disgracing herself that way sent a shudder through Kim. She hugged her arms to herself. She could just imagine what Justin's reaction would be to the sight of her sprawled on the floor.

Justin.

She pressed a palm to her belly to quell the flurry of butterflies set off by thoughts of seeing him tonight. Studying her reflection in the mirror, she couldn't help wonder what he would think when he saw her. Would he think she looked pretty or...?

What on earth was she doing?

Furious with herself for indulging in foolish fantasies, Kim reminded herself that fancy clothes couldn't change who or what she was. It certainly wouldn't alter the way Justin thought of her. She was his dependable, boring assistant, and nothing more. Any notions that Justin might see her in any other light had surely been dispelled that last evening they were alone at the office together, hadn't it?

Shame heated her cheeks as she recalled how she'd gotten the insane idea in her head that Justin was going to kiss her that night. Well, he hadn't, she recalled and felt another sharp jolt of embarrassment. Irritated that the memory of Justin's rejection could still rattle her so, she gave herself a mental shake. Instead of feeling sorry for herself, she should be grateful that Justin hadn't known what she'd been thinking, what she'd been wanting him to do. Another shudder went through her at the idea. It was bad enough that she'd allowed herself to fall in love with Justin Connelly. The only thing worse would be her humiliation if he had discovered that fact. Had he done so, she would never have been able to face him again. Which meant she would have no choice but to resign her position at Connelly Corporation.

Drawing in a calming breath, Kim told herself it was better this way. It was past time that she put to rest the ridiculous idea of a relationship between her and Justin. To do otherwise would surely lead to disaster. She needed only to look at all the heartache her own mother had endured by clinging to such foolish romantic notions. As always was the case when she thought of her mother, Kim felt the pang of loss anew. Despite the fact that she'd often felt their roles had been reversed and that she had assumed the parental responsibility, she still missed her mother terribly. She could only pray that at long last Amanda Lindgren had found the fairy-tale ending that had eluded her in life.

Thank heavens she had been born with a healthy dose of pragmatism, Kim told herself. This was the real world—not some fairy tale. Handsome, multimillionaires like Justin Connelly simply didn't fall in love with their assistants. They fell in love with beautiful models or wealthy debutantes or chic businesswomen who belonged to country clubs and moved in the same social circles. No, when a man like Justin fell in love, it would be with a woman who could trace her ancestors back to the *Mayflower* or who had a royal bloodline like his. Not with the illegitimate daughter of a pretty but flighty file clerk who'd become pregnant before discovering the man who'd professed his love was already married to someone else.

Kim had long since come to terms with who she was, and would be forever thankful that she'd had a mother who'd truly loved and wanted her. While her mother's romantic disasters might have been despairing to watch, it had grounded her and made her all the more determined not to delude herself. She was quiet, reliable Kim Lindgren—not at all the type of woman who would appeal to the likes of Justin Connelly.

Yet as she stared at her reflection in the mirror, Kim found it difficult to reconcile the woman she saw there with the shy woman inside her. The woman in the elegant evening gown didn't resemble mousy Kim at all. She looked as if she actually belonged in Justin's world.

Realizing what she was doing, Kim put a halt to her ridiculous musings and blamed her errant thoughts on the dress. But as she subjected herself to another critical once-over, she frowned. It wasn't just the dress. It was the hair, Kim determined as she eyed the sweep of blond tresses that fell down around her shoulders. Wearing her hair down to cover her bare shoulders had seemed like a good idea at the time. But now she wondered if it had been a mistake. It made her look…sensual, almost sexy.

Which just went to show how deceiving appearances could be, Kim mused. She was practical and level-headed Kim Lindgren, not some sexy femme fatale. And there was no point in sending out false signals. Walking over to the vanity table, she dug out her hairpins and reached for the brush, intent on redoing her hair in its customary twist. But before she'd had time to do more than gather the hair into her fist, the doorbell sounded.

The driver Tara had insisted on sending for her, Kim surmised. The last thing she wanted to do was keep the man or Tara waiting for her. Sighing, she released the rope of blond hair from her fist, and it tumbled back down about her shoulders. The hair would just have to do as it was, she decided. Snatching up her evening bag, she headed for the door.

"Good evening, Miss Lindgren. My name is James."

"Good evening, James."

She allowed the driver to escort her from her apartment building to the sleek, black limousine parked out front. After opening the car door, he took her arm gently and assisted her inside.

"Thank you," she murmured, and slipped inside the vehicle. Despite the fact that she'd worked for the Connellys for two years, she still found herself in awe of the amenities their wealth provided. The dark leather seats looked butter soft. Unable to resist, she swept her gloved fingers along the smooth surface as her gaze flitted over the plush carpeting and tinted windows. There was enough room inside for at least ten people, Kim thought. Amused and delighted, she settled against the cushiony backrest and reached for her seat belt.

Having already resumed his position behind the wheel, James turned to address her. "We should arrive at the hotel in approximately twenty minutes, Miss Lindgren. Mrs. Paige instructed me to tell you to sit back, relax and enjoy the ride. Should you care for a cocktail or something to drink while we're en route to the hotel, you'll find a fully stocked bar to your left."

"Thank you. But I'm fine," Kim told him as she noted the built-in bar he had indicated.

"Very well, ma'am. I'll be closing the privacy window, but if you should need me for anything or have any questions, just press the call button next to your seat."

"Thank you. I'll do that, if I need anything."

James nodded. Within seconds the glass partition separating them slid shut, and moments later the car slipped out into the Friday evening traffic.

From the back of the limousine Kim stared out at the familiar streets and landmarks. But as she watched the city of Chicago transform beneath the shimmer of stars and the glow of the streetlights, Kim could feel the anticipation dancing in her own veins. And if she didn't chill out, she was going to burn out like a shooting star before she ever got to the hotel.

Taking a deep breath she pressed a hand to her midsection in an effort to quell the nerves that were playing havoc with her stomach. It didn't help. Nothing did, she admitted. She simply found it impossible to relax.

But then, who could blame her? Here she was, sitting in the back of a limousine, dressed to the nines and on her way to a black-tie fund-raiser as Tara Connelly Paige's guest.

She might as well enjoy it while she could, Kim decided, since this would probably be her first and last ride in a limo. Oddly enough, that realization and the decision to enjoy herself seemed to settle her nerves somewhat. She was just beginning to relax when the phone rang and she tensed up all over again.

"It's for you, miss," James informed her seconds later as he lowered the privacy panel. His eyes met hers briefly in the rearview mirror. "There's a receiver in the panel directly in front of you."

"Thank you," Kim murmured and reached for the phone. "Hello?"

"Kim, it's Tara. What a relief. I had visions of you changing your mind and canceling on me tonight."

"Well, I did think about it," Kim admitted. In fact, she'd considered begging off several times during the past few days. But then she'd spied the evening gown in a store window yesterday, and when she'd gone inside the boutique and discovered it was her size and on sale to boot, she'd taken it as a sign.

"I'm certainly glad you didn't," Tara told her, and proceeded to recount for Kim the maddening day she'd had.

"As if the problems with the centerpiece weren't enough to deal with, one of our bachelors managed to break his leg while skydiving and wanted to bow out of the auction. Fortunately, Jennifer and I were able to convince him that parading around in a cast would drive up his bidding price."

"And I take it he believed you?"

"Of course," Tara told her with the assurance of a woman who had never accepted the word no from anyone.

"Sounds like you've had quite a day."

"I have. That's why the thought of you canceling on me tonight would have been one problem I simply couldn't have handled."

Surprised, Kim said, "Thanks. But I hardly think one empty seat at a table would make a big difference."

"Actually, it would, since you'll be doing a bit more than just filling a seat."

Kim drew her brows together. "What do you mean?"

"Oh, it's nothing much really," Tara said breezily. "I just need you to do me a little favor, to sort of help out with the auction."

"Help out how?" Kim asked, suddenly uneasy.

"Like I said, it's just a little favor, and it'll keep Justin from wringing my neck. But it's nothing for you to worry about. I'll explain it all to you when you get here."

Warning bells went off. "Tara, about this favor—"

"Don't worry. I'll explain it all to you later."

"But—"

"Oops, got to run," Tara said. "See you in a little bit."

"Tara, wait—"

But it was too late. The dial tone was already buzzing in her ear. And as she hung up the phone, Kim realized her nervous excitement had been replaced by a new emotion—worry.

Four

"**Y**our tuxedo and shoes are in the back seat, Mr. Connelly."

"Thanks, Hal," Justin told the stoic-looking driver who'd met him at O'Hare Airport moments earlier. He reached inside and grabbed the garment bag, intent on changing in the airport men's room.

Hal cleared his throat. "If you'll pardon me, sir. Miss Tara suggested that it might save time if you were to change clothes in the limo while we're en route to the hotel."

"In other words, my sister told you to make sure I don't leave your sight until you deliver me to her cattle auction."

"Not at all, sir," Hal said formally, standing beside the sleek black limo. "Miss Tara merely said I should make the suggestion."

"If you say so," Justin replied, and climbed into the back of the limo. Even as he stripped off his tie and ditched his suit coat, the car pulled away from the curb. Knowing his sister as he did, Justin had no doubt that Tara had batted her violet eyes at the long-time driver and told the man that she was depending on him to get Justin to the fund-raiser on time.

Justin grimaced as he thought of the bachelor auction and wished, yet again, that he hadn't agreed to participate. He still believed a generous check to the charity would have sufficed. But then, he'd always found it difficult to say no to his sister. And then there had been Kim, calmly pointing out how simple it would be for him to keep his promise to attend the event.

Kim.

As happy as he was about salvaging the Schaeffer deal, he was even more pleased that he had been able to put this new attraction to Kim into perspective. Until this thing with Schaeffer had gotten settled, he hadn't realized how consumed he'd been with business during these past few months. Since Kim had been the woman he'd spent most of his time with, it was only natural that he had been drawn to her. That was all it was, he assured himself. Now that he had himself in hand, he could only be grateful that he hadn't given in to the urge that night to kiss her.

Pleased with his assessment of the situation and confident that he had everything under control again, Justin smiled as he reached for the cummerbund. Kim said she would be at the fund-raiser tonight. The fact that he was looking forward to seeing her had nothing to do with his growing attraction to her, he reasoned. It was simply that he knew she'd be as excited as he was about the way the Schaeffer deal had turned out. Slipping the tie around his neck, Justin sat back and thought of the evening ahead.

As much as he disliked the idea of being auctioned off, it really was for a good cause. The fact that it would make

Tara and Jennifer happy made it somewhat more palatable. And, of course, not having to wait until Monday to see Kim's face when he told her about the outcome of the Schaeffer meeting made the evening ahead actually appealing.

Who knew, Justin mused as he gave up on getting the tie right. Maybe tonight wouldn't be so bad after all.

"I feel like a prize steer at a cattle auction," Justin complained thirty minutes later as he waited backstage for the bachelor auction to begin.

"Oh, for heaven's sake, quit bellyaching," Tara countered as she looked him over with a critical eye and zeroed in on the tie he'd managed to mangle. "This is going to be fun."

"Easy for you to say. You're not the one who has to parade around on that stage out there in front of a man-hungry audience."

"And since when do you dislike being the center of attention in a roomful of females?" she asked as she proceeded to redo his tie.

"Since Eve Novak cornered me on my way backstage."

Tara paused. She lifted her gaze to his and arched her brow. "Oh? And what did Evie say to put you into such a foul mood?"

Ignoring the foul-mood accusation, he said, "It's not so much what she said, it's the way she looked at me when she said it."

"And just how did she look at you, big brother?" Tara teased.

"Like a hungry cat that had just cornered its next meal," Justin grumbled. "Now I know what women mean when they complain about a guy undressing them with his eyes.

For a minute there I half expected her to pinch my a—my, uh, butt.''

"I'm sure she thought about it," Tara informed him as she went back to adjusting his tie. "Word at the country club is that Eve's in the market for a new husband."

"I thought she just got married again last year."

"She did. But apparently marriage to a cowboy wasn't what Eve expected. As of last week, she's single again."

"I'll probably kick myself for asking," Justin began, "but what happened?"

"It seems that Mr. Tall, Dark and Texan was under the mistaken impression that Evie was going to ride off into the sunset with him. The poor guy actually thought the two of them were going to have little cowboys and cowgirls of their own and live happily ever after on his ranch."

Poor guy was right, Justin thought. How anyone would believe the self-indulgent, spoiled Eve Novak would even agree to have a child, let alone actually raise one was beyond him. "The guy must have had a little too much cactus juice if he believed that. Eve has never struck me as the maternal type."

"Me, neither," Tara replied. "But then, I suspect it wasn't her maternal instincts that Tex was drawn to in the first place."

His sister was right. Eve Novak was a beautiful and glamorous woman—the kind who always drew a man's eye. But he had never been even slightly interested in her, Justin admitted. Probably because there was something almost predatory about the woman that turned him off. Which was why he'd never even been tempted to follow through on any of the invitations, blatant or otherwise, that she'd cast his way over the years. And he didn't intend to start tonight, either.

"But you shouldn't have anything to worry about where

Eve is concerned,'' Tara told him, and stepped back to survey her handiwork.

Justin narrowed his eyes. ''What do you mean?''

''I mean that I doubt Eve has any intention of treating you like a son if she wins you in the auction tonight.''

Justin's blood ran cold at his sister's gibe. ''You'd better be joking, brat. Because if I thought for one minute that there was a chance I'd get stuck on a date with Eve Novak, I'd be out of here so fast it would make your head spin.''

When Tara bit her bottom lip and remained silent, Justin broke out in a sweat. ''Tara, tell me that there's no way Eve Novak has any chance of winning me in this auction.''

''And just how am I supposed to do that?'' she demanded. ''It's an auction, Justin. I don't have any control over who bids what. Considering her trust fund and the settlements from her last three divorces, Eve might very well be in a position to outbid everyone else here tonight.''

Justin swore.

''Justin,'' Tara admonished.

''Sorry,'' he muttered. And he was sorry. Sorry that he'd ever let himself be talked into this stunt—even if it was for charity. His mind raced for a way out of this mess without going back on his word to his sister and to Jennifer.

''Justin, you really aren't going to leave us in the lurch, are you?''

''No,'' he told her. ''But there's no way I'm going to get stuck with that man-eater, either. Give me a minute. I need to figure this out.''

''You may want to think fast, big brother. The auction's going to start in about fifteen minutes.''

Justin raked a hand through his hair, resisted the urge to loosen his tie as he paced. ''I've got it,'' he told Tara. ''*You* bid on me.''

''I can't do that. I'm your sister.''

"So?"

"So, how would it look for your own sister to win a date with you?"

Desperate, he suggested, "Then have Jennifer do it."

"She's married to Chance," Tara reminded him. "Somehow I doubt that Chance would appreciate having his wife win a date with his brother."

She was right, Justin admitted. He thought of suggesting Kim since she'd said she would be attending. But he immediately rejected the idea. He'd just got his head straight where she was concerned. Having Kim bid on his date package would be asking for trouble. "I'm not getting saddled for an evening with Eve Novak—not even if it is for a good cause."

Tara patted his jaw. "Relax, big brother. You don't know for sure that Eve will bid on you. After all, you're the last bachelor to go on the block. Eve's never been the patient type. She just might decide to go after one of our other bachelor babes."

He certainly hoped so, Justin thought.

"Besides, I have it on good authority that Ashley Powers plans to bid on you tonight. And who knows, maybe Bethany Barlow's mother will decide to buy you for her daughter."

Justin glared at his sister. "You're enjoying this, aren't you?"

Tara laughed. "Of course I am. Consider it payback for all the times you were mean to me when we were kids."

"I was never mean to you."

"What about the time you refused to let me go sailing with you and Mindy Hastings?"

"Mindy and I were on a date," he returned. "No guy in his right mind lets his kid sister tag along on a date."

"See, I told you. You were mean."

"Tara," Justin said, a warning edge to his voice. He took a step toward his sister.

"Oops. Got to run. It's almost time for the auction to start," she said, and after giving him a quick kiss on the cheek, she dashed off.

"And to think I thought tonight wouldn't be so bad," Justin muttered.

"You say something, Connelly?" Brad Parker, one of the other bachelors on the block, asked.

"Yeah. Be grateful you don't have any sisters."

Kim moved about the ballroom and did her best not to gawk. The room resembled something out of a fairy tale, she thought, as she took in the splendor that surrounded her. While she had been mesmerized by the sight of the room itself—from the sweep of windows that looked out over the Chicago night sky to the breathtaking crystal centerpieces bursting with lilies, white roses and sprigs of freesia on each table—it was the people in attendance who fascinated her. They were gorgeous. Both the men and the women. And she couldn't recall ever seeing so many beautiful people in one room at the same time.

All right, where the men were concerned it probably was the tuxedos, Kim conceded. After all, what fellow didn't look good in a tux? But as far as the women went, it was a different story. The outfits ran the gamut from fabulous to outrageous. Each one looked more stunning than the next. Surely every yard of silk and lace, not to mention every sequin and bead, in Chicago had gone into the gowns being worn. And despite the large number of people in attendance, she'd yet to see any two dresses alike.

Kim tightened her gloved fingers around her evening bag and couldn't help but be glad that she had splurged on her own outfit. She was also glad she'd taken time with her appearance. As she began making her way back to her table, she spied Ashley Powers, the stockbroker that Justin had taken out on several occasions. Kim couldn't quite help feeling a slight stab of envy as she looked at the statuesque brunette. The woman was breathtaking. When the other woman tipped her head back in laughter, Kim caught the flash of sapphires and diamonds at her neck and ears. Automatically her hand went to her own bare throat and she became keenly aware of the tiny diamond chips in her ears. That old adage about not being able to turn a sow's ear into a silk purse flashed into her mind. And it sent her stomach plummeting—along with her self-confidence.

She didn't belong here.

It had been ludicrous to think that she would. She shouldn't have come, Kim told herself, feeling suddenly foolish. How on earth had she ever convinced herself that a fancy dress and high heels would make any difference? She was Kim Lindgren, not some society darling. And she needed to get out of here before Justin or anyone else saw her and she made an even bigger fool of herself. Her mind made up, she turned toward the exit intent on escape.

"Kim! Kim, wait!"

Kim wanted to ignore the familiar voice but couldn't. Stopping, she turned around and spied Tara hurrying toward her. Mentally she began to prepare a speech about having a headache.

"Thank goodness I found you. I've been trying to get over to your table for the past thirty minutes," she said as she reached her. "And I— Why Kim, you look absolutely stunning."

Caught off guard by the compliment, Kim faltered. "I, um, thank you," she murmured. "It's the dress. I found it on sale." No sooner were the words out of her mouth than

Kim wanted to snatch them back because they sounded so lame.

Tara smiled. "That makes it even better, then. But trust me, it's not the dress. It's you. Why I had no idea you had such beautiful hair."

Kim felt the color race up her cheeks. "Yes, well, I thought I'd wear it down for a change," she told her, and nearly groaned. Could she possibly sound any more inane?

"And I'm sure every man here—including my brother Justin—will be glad that you did. It looks perfect, Kim. If I didn't like you so much, I'd be pea-green with envy that you were born with such gorgeous hair and I got stuck with this mop."

Kim blinked. "But your hair is beautiful. And it always looks so…so chic."

Tara laughed. She ran a hand through her short, dark tresses. "I'm not sure I'd call this chic as much as convenient."

"It's chic. And it suits you," Kim told her. And it did. Tara Connelly Paige had always reminded her of a young Audrey Hepburn with her dark hair and elegant features, and those violet eyes made her think of Elizabeth Taylor in her youth.

"You're very kind," Tara said, her eyes twinkling with humor. "And I'm going to take shameless advantage of that kindness by asking you to do me that little favor I mentioned earlier."

"Tara, I—"

"Well, if it isn't my future sister-in-law Tara, and looking absolutely gorgeous as usual."

"Hello, Robert," Tara said coolly. "What can I do for you?"

"I just wanted to say hello," he said smoothly, his lips

curving into a smile. "Aren't you going to introduce me to your pretty friend?"

Kim sucked in a breath as she realized Marsh didn't recognize her, and she couldn't help wishing that she had been able to make her escape before running into him.

"You mean you don't recognize Kim?" Tara countered.

Marsh whipped his gaze from her bare shoulders up to her face. "Kim Lindgren?"

"Hello, Robert," Kim managed.

"Good Lord, who'd have thought that underneath those prim suits—"

Tara's eyes narrowed. "Don't stop now, Robert. Who'd have thought under those prim suits what?" she prompted.

"Who'd have thought that our little Kim could look so grown-up. You look lovely," he told her, and took her hand in a courtly gesture that didn't match the covetous look in his eyes.

"Thank you," she said, and tugged her hand free, grateful that the gloves she'd worn had protected her from his touch. There had always been something about Robert Marsh that set her on edge. Tonight even more so.

"Where's Alexandra?" Tara asked.

"She's in the ladies' room," Robert replied, but his eyes remained fixed on Kim, which only made her feel more uncomfortable.

"Since Kim and I were just heading there ourselves, I'll let her know where she can find you." And without waiting for Marsh to respond, Tara linked her arm with Kim's and headed across the room.

"Um, Tara, the ladies' room is in the opposite direction," Kim advised when the other woman continued to march them down the hotel corridor away from the ballroom.

"I know. I didn't really have to go to the ladies' room.

I just wanted to get away from Marsh. I know I should at least try to be nice to the man since he's going to marry my sister. But I swear, every time I'm around the guy and he starts laying on the charm, it's as though a neon sign starts flashing the word *phony* in my head and I can't wait to get away from him.''

Kim could certainly understand, because from the first day she'd met Robert Marsh, he had rubbed her the wrong way. He seemed to have a way of watching her that made her skin crawl.

Tara paused next to a column that was far enough away that they could observe the comings and goings in the main ballroom but were somewhat removed from the din. She met Kim's gaze. "What do you think of Marsh?"

"I..." Kim fumbled for an answer, unwilling to tell Tara the truth. "He's obviously a good businessman or he wouldn't be working at Connelly."

Tara grinned. "I keep forgetting what a diplomat you are. I know I'm putting you on the spot, but I'd really like you to be honest with me."

"Well, I can't say that I'm particularly fond of him, but I think the only opinion that really matters is your sister Alexandra's. If she loves him enough to marry him, she obviously sees something in him that you and I don't."

Tara frowned and seemed to consider that. "I guess you're right. I just can't help worrying that she's making a mistake."

"Maybe. But it's her mistake to make." And none of the well-meaning lectures or pleas would be able to prevent Alexandra from making that mistake, Kim concluded. Heaven knows, they'd never worked any of the times she'd tried to dissuade her mother from leaping into a romance that had heartache written all over it.

"How did you get so wise?" Tara asked, her voice teasing.

Kim shrugged. "Probably because I didn't have any sisters or brothers to worry about me."

"Oh, my heavens, speaking of brothers, I nearly forgot. I need you to do me a teensy little favor so that I can get out of the doghouse with Justin."

"What's the favor?" she asked warily.

"I need you to buy Justin in the auction."

"What!"

"You've got to do this for me, Kim. For Justin. He was freaking out backstage when he heard that Eve Novak was here and looking for husband number four. She sort of insinuated to Justin that she intended to bid on him. And now he's threatening to pull out of the auction because he's afraid Eve the man-eater will outbid everyone else and he'll get stuck spending an evening with the woman."

Kim knew who Eve Novak was. And man-eater was an accurate description if even half of the stories she'd heard about the woman were true. But as much as she disliked the idea of Justin with Eve Novak, or anyone else for that matter, there was little she could do about it. "I'm sorry, Tara. But I don't see how I can possibly help you. Maybe you should talk to Ashley Powers or Bethany Barlow. I know they both intend to bid on Justin."

Tara shook her head. "Neither one of them is going to be willing to come up with the kind of bid that will make Eve back off."

And Tara thought that she could? She didn't live in the same world that Tara Connelly Paige did. For that matter, she didn't live in the same world that most of the people attending tonight's gala did. Deciding she needed to be blunt, Kim said, "Even if I wanted to, I couldn't bid on

Justin. I know what kind of money these auctions raise. And I...I simply can't afford it. I'm sorry.''

"Oh, Kim, sweetie, I could just kick myself," Tara told her and there was genuine regret in the other woman's eyes. "I never meant that I wanted you to use your own money to bid on Justin. I want you to use mine."

"Yours? But then why—"

"Because how would it look for me to buy a date with my own brother?"

While Kim was still digesting that tidbit, Tara caught her hand and pressed a check into her palm. "That's a cashier's check made out to the Police Association's Fund for Widows and Orphans. Use it to buy Justin in the auction."

"Tara, I don't think—"

"Please," she pleaded when Kim attempted to refuse the check. "Do this as a favor to me. And to Justin."

Still unsure what to do, Kim looked at the check that Tara had closed into her palm. "It's for fifteen thousand dollars."

"I know," Tara said, a mischievous gleam in her violet eyes. "That should help you give Eve a run for her money, don't you think?"

Kim nodded.

"But what happens if I win?"

Tara grinned. "Why, you enjoy your date with Justin, of course. Because something tells me he's certainly going to enjoy his date with you."

"You're wrong," Kim insisted, but looked away for fear Tara would see the truth in her eyes. "Justin's my boss. He and I— It's not that way between us."

"Are you sure? I thought I picked up on something the other day."

"You're mistaken," Kim told her.

"I'm sorry, Kim. But you really don't lie worth beans."

Giving up, Kim asked, "Am I that obvious?"

"Only to someone who remembers what it's like to be in love with someone who doesn't exactly belong to the same social register as you do."

"But you and your family are rich," Kim blurted out.

"But Michael wasn't. I might have been the one with money but that doesn't mean it was easier."

"I guess I never thought of it that way," Kim murmured, knowing that the other woman was referring to her brief marriage to Michael Paige. She thought of how Tara had been declared a widow when her husband's body had failed to turn up following a train derailment two years earlier. "I'm sorry," Kim said, and touched the other woman's arm. "I can't imagine what it's been like for you these past two years."

Tara shrugged. "At least I have my son."

"Yes," Kim replied, recalling the little boy she'd seen with Tara on occasion.

The sound of drum rolls from the ballroom spilled out into the corridor. "Sounds like the auction's about to start. We'd better get inside."

Suddenly nervous again, Kim said, "Tara, about the auction. I'll make the bid, but as for the date, I'd rather you'd let Justin give the package to one of his lady friends."

"But why?"

"Because it would be awkward. We work together and he...doesn't see me that way."

"How do you know, when you're so busy trying to make sure he never sees the real you?"

Five

"**A**ll right, ladies, I have thirty-eight hundred dollars for Mr. David Brighton and his gourmet dinner for two, followed by an evening of dancing. Do I hear thirty-nine hundred dollars?" the auctioneer prompted from her position behind the dais on the stage where the bachelors had been marched out like prize cattle for the past forty-five minutes.

"Thirty-eight fifty," a redhead with fawn-colored eyes called out, and waved her numbered paddle enthusiastically.

"I have thirty-eight hundred and fifty dollars. Do I hear thirty-nine hundred?" When no one responded, the auctioneer, milking the crowd for more, said, "Come on, ladies. Remember this is for charity. And Mr. Brighton here is offering a five-course gourmet meal and an evening of dancing at one of Chicago's hot new nightspots for the lucky lady with the winning bid."

"All right, thirty-nine hundred dollars," a sulky-mouthed

brunette declared and immediately shot a menacing glance to the redhead at the next table who had started to raise her paddle. "And don't you dare top my bid, Sarah Hartley."

"I wasn't going to," Sarah replied, and tipped her nose up.

The auctioneer, evidently realizing the bidding war was over said, "Going once. Going twice. Going three times. Sold," she pronounced with a bang of her gavel. "To Ms. Candace Larson for thirty-nine hundred dollars."

From his position backstage, Justin watched Brighton strut offstage to be claimed. Turning away, he tuned out the next bachelor being put on the block and resigned himself to the fact that he was next. He reminded himself that it was for a good cause and tried not to think that he would much rather have gone to the office and tackled some paperwork.

Thinking of the office made him think of Kim again. He hadn't seen her as yet—at least, she hadn't been seated at Tara's table. Nor had he spotted her when he'd scanned the crowd. Had she changed her mind about coming? he wondered. Surprised at how disappointed that idea made him, Justin assured himself he was simply anxious to tell Kim about the Schaeffer meeting. After all, he reasoned, she'd worked as hard as he had to put it back together.

Lost in thought, he didn't even realize the emcee had given the signal for him to come out onstage until the hotel liaison assigned backstage for the event cleared his throat and said, "Mr. Connelly, sir, that's your cue."

Justin jerked his gaze to the young man. "Um, thanks," he said, and bracing himself, he walked out on stage.

"Our final bachelor up for bid tonight is Mr. Justin Connelly."

Justin walked out onto the stage and managed what he

hoped would pass as a happy-to-be-there smile while cameras flashed, party-goers clapped and one or two unladylike whistles rang out. Between the stage lights and camera flashes, it took Justin a moment to adjust his eyes. Once he did, he began to scan the sea of faces as he moved down the length of the stage.

"The vice president of marketing for the Connelly Corporation, Justin is a member of one of Chicago's finest families and the brother of the recently crowned king of Altaria. A familiar face on the business, civic and social scene, he was recently voted one of the most eligible bachelors in Chicago."

Ignoring the catcalls that followed that little tidbit, Justin shoved his hand into his pocket and started back toward the center of the stage. As he did so, he couldn't help feeling a whole new level of respect for the women who participated in beauty pageants. He knew many of them did so for scholarship money or a break in show biz. And all he could think now was how on earth did they handle this sort of thing?

"Now, let's see what special date Justin is offering our bidders." Smiling, the emcee untied the ribbon around the envelope that held a certificate describing his date package. After adjusting her spectacles, the woman practically beamed when she said, "Ladies, all I can say is get out your checkbooks."

Evidently Kim had managed to secure tickets for some hot new show, Justin thought as he approached his mark at the center of the stage. And he couldn't help but wish it were Kim he'd be taking to dinner and the theater. But even as the thought formed, he quashed it.

"You'd also better get out your suntan lotion and bathing suits because some lucky lady is going to spend the day sailing Lake Geneva with Justin aboard his boat *Calypso*.

Then you'll be treated to a catered lunch followed by cock-tails at sunset. Now, who's going to get the ball rolling with an opening bid of one thousand dollars?''

Stunned to discover just what Kim had put together as a date package for him, Justin silently vowed to wring his assistant's pretty neck. As much as he loved sailing, he hadn't been on his boat in months because of work. He certainly hadn't realized that Kim even knew about his passion for sailing. One thing was for sure. He positively didn't want to spend an entire day on his boat with some debutante or, even worse, Eve Novak by his side. The idea that he might have to had acid churning in his gut. What in the devil had caused Kim to do such a thing? he wondered. Just as quickly, he admitted it was his own fault. He should have looked at the certificate when Kim had offered. Lost in thought and trying to figure out how he was going to get out of this mess, Justin didn't even realize the bidding was moving fast and furiously until he heard someone say eight thousand.

Eight thousand? Justin yanked his attention to the emcee at the podium.

''I have eight thousand dollars from Ms. Eve Novak. Do I hear eighty-five hundred?'' the woman asked.

''Eighty-five hundred.''

Justin jerked his gaze back to the audience, and to his left he noted Ashley Powers. He tried to manage a smile of gratitude to the stockbroker, whom he had convinced himself to pursue romantically only a few days earlier,.

''I have eighty-five hundred. Do I hear nine thousand?'' The auctioneer asked hopefully. ''Ah, I have nine from the lovely young lady in the back.''

Justin shifted his gaze toward the rear of the room, tried to see the face of the woman holding paddle number twenty-three. But between the paddle and the persons seated at the front of her table, all he could make out was that she was a blonde.

"Ten thousand," Eve Novak said, drawing his attention back to the front of the room.

"I have ten thousand dollars from Ms. Novak. Do I have—"

"Eleven thousand," Ashley Powers offered from the opposite end of the stage.

"Twelve thousand," Eve countered.

"The bid is at twelve thousand. Do I hear—"

"Fifteen thousand," the blonde in the back called out.

Justin narrowed his eyes and stared at the back of the room. He knew that voice. He was sure of it. And there was something familiar about her. But try as he might, he couldn't quite place the voice or the woman. The brief glimpse he'd gotten of slender shoulders bared by the strapless black dress also drew a blank. No way would he forget a woman with a figure like that. Yet...

"I have fifteen thousand dollars. Do I hear more?" the auctioneer asked, and looked directly at Eve.

"Hey, Justin, you offering more than a boat ride and a sunset?" one of his male friends teased.

"Just my company, Mick."

When the laughter settled down, the auctioneer repeated, "Do I hear more?"

Eve Novak shook her head. Lifting her flute of champagne in a toast, she looked directly at him. "Sorry, Justin honey, but no sailboat ride is worth that kind of money."

"Evidently not everyone agrees," a female voice called out that sounded suspiciously like his sister Tara's, and the room broke out into laughter again.

"All right. Going once. Going twice. Gone." The emcee slammed the gavel down and said, "Sold for fifteen thousand dollars to the owner of paddle number twenty-three.

That concludes our bachelor auction. Thank you, ladies and gentlemen, for your generosity. Enjoy the rest of the evening.''

Relieved to be off the auction block, Justin exited the stage, intent on finding out who the mystery blonde was who'd just paid an extraordinary sum for a date with him. But he'd barely taken two steps when Eve Novak blocked his path.

"Justin." She all but purred his name. "You can't imagine how disappointed I am. I was so counting on having the winning bid for your little sailing date. But even for charity, fifteen thousand dollars seemed awfully high."

"Yeah, it was a surprise to me, too," Justin said, and tried to look past Eve to where the blonde had been seated. Much to his disappointment she was already gone.

"Is she a special friend of yours?"

"Who?" Justin replied, and only then became aware of how close Eve was standing to him.

"The skinny blonde who just bought the date with you," she replied sweetly. But there was no mistaking the hard look in her eyes.

From what little he'd been able to see, his mystery lady might have been on the slender side, but the body in that black number hadn't fit his definition of skinny. "Actually, I'm not sure."

"Really? How interesting," Eve replied, and Justin felt a prickle of unease snake down his spine at the smile she gave him. She traced one red-tipped nail along his jaw. "Then perhaps I can convince you to take me out for a spin on your boat even if I didn't win the auction."

"Now, Eve, how would it look if my brother were to turn around and offer to take all the losing bidders out on his sailboat when someone just paid all that money for the privilege?"

Justin could have kissed Tara for coming to his rescue. Judging from the way her violet eyes sparkled, she knew it, too.

"Hello, Tara," Eve said and there was no mistaking her displeasure at the interruption. "What a surprise seeing you here."

"I don't see why, since both my mother and my brother Chance's wife, Jennifer, are on the fund-raising committee."

"I know. One of the main reasons I came tonight was to support them. And, of course, because your handsome brother here was one of the bachelors being auctioned off." Eve gave Justin a look that smoldered before turning her focus back to Tara. "It's just that when I called this week asking for you to redecorate my apartment, I had the impression you were backlogged. At least, I assumed that's the reason you referred me to an associate."

His sister didn't so much as blink an eye at the underlying accusation in Eve's tone. She simply said, "Business has certainly kept me hopping lately. So has my son. But this fund-raiser is important to my family. Naturally, I made time for it."

"Perhaps you could make time for me as well," Eve suggested.

"Not unless you're willing to wait a few months, until I'm free."

"A few months?" Eve repeated.

"Afraid so. Apparently, my services are in demand at the moment," Tara said smoothly.

Half listening, Justin scoped out the ballroom and spied his mystery blonde walking toward the area designated for tickets and pledges. "Speaking of being in demand," Justin said to Eve and flashed her his most charming smile. "I'm afraid you'll have to excuse me. I just saw my father, and there's something I need to discuss with him.''

Before Eve Novak could object, Justin stepped back and made an immediate bee-line in the direction he'd seen the blonde heading.

''That certainly was an exciting finish for the bachelor auction,'' the woman who'd introduced herself as Linda told Kim as they stood in line with the other winning bidders to settle up their accounts.

''It was exciting for me, too,'' Kim told her. Which was true. It had been exciting and terrifying at the same time. She still couldn't believe she had just shouted out that final bid of $15,000.00. But she'd been so nervous. Then when that sexy blonde in the red dress kept topping the bids for Justin and the people began looking from the blonde to her, she'd only become more nervous. She hadn't been sure she could handle any more rounds of volleying bids and scrutiny, so she'd simply thrown out her top bid, hoping to be done with it.

And she'd won.

''Personally,'' Linda told her, lowering her voice and leaning slightly closer, ''I'm glad you beat that snooty Eve Novak.''

Kim paused, suddenly realizing why the woman seemed familiar. She'd seen her in the society section of the local newspaper and remembered her calling the office for Justin. ''Why?'' Kim asked, curious as to the woman's reason for the comment.

''Because the woman's a real gold digger. She dated the brother of a friend of mine who's an investment banker, but when she found out his own portfolio was modest, she dumped him. Rumor is that she runs D&B checks on all the men she goes out with, and I believe it. Especially considering that all her ex-husbands are millionaires.''

"All?''

"She just got divorced from husband number three,'' Linda explained. "And since she's here, one can only assume she's on the hunt again. I'm sure she would have just loved the chance to get her hooks into someone with Justin Connelly's money and connections.''

Not sure what to say and feeling guilty for listening to the gossip, Kim remained silent.

"Anyway, congratulations again.''

"Thanks,'' Kim murmured. She was grateful when the line began to move, distracting Linda from discussing Eve Novak or Justin further.

By the time she'd handed over the cashier's check that Tara had given her and was awaiting her receipt, Kim was enjoying herself.

"Here's your receipt and the certificate,'' the woman manning the table told her. "Enjoy your date.''

"Thank you,'' Kim replied. She turned to leave, only to run into Robert Marsh.

"My, my, you certainly are full of surprises tonight,'' Marsh told her. All the enjoyment of the evening suddenly faded beneath his blatant once-over.

"Excuse me,'' she said, but Marsh blocked her path.

"I just wanted to add my congratulations. That was quite a show you put on during the auction. Justin must be paying you very well if you can afford to spend fifteen grand for a date with him. Or maybe you consider it an investment.''

Kim narrowed her eyes. "What's that supposed to mean?''

He shrugged and flashed her a smile that did nothing to reassure her. "Just that I hadn't figured you for someone with designs on snaring her boss.''

"I'm not," Kim informed him, bristling at the implication.

"I certainly hope not because, to be honest, you're not Justin's type. He's into blue-blooded beauties, if you know what I mean."

She did know what he meant, but refused to give him the satisfaction of seeing that his arrow had hit home. "Is there a point to this conversation, Marsh?"

He smiled again. "Just trying to be a friend and offering you the benefit of my experience with the Connellys. I mean, they're a breed unto themselves. Whereas you and I..."

Kim backed away before he could finish his sentence. "Thanks, but I'm afraid you've got the wrong idea. My bidding on Justin tonight was a favor to a friend. Nothing more. Now if you'll excuse me, I just spotted someone that I need to speak with."

Before Marsh could object, Kim dashed past him. She was so intent on getting away that she was scarcely aware the lights had been dimmed and music was now playing. Or that a great many people were making their way to the dance floor. She spied Tara being escorted to the dance floor by an older gentleman, and though she knew she shouldn't intrude, she rushed over to her. "Excuse me, please," she told the man who obviously was surprised by her interruption. Ignoring his arched eyebrow, she shifted her attention to Tara. "I just wanted to thank you again for inviting me tonight."

"I'm the one who should be thanking you," Tara replied, but it was obvious from her expression she didn't understand why Kim was so distressed. "I'm glad that you decided to come."

"Well, it was fun, but I'm going home now and I wanted to say good-night."

"But the evening's just getting started, and—"

"I know. But I'm afraid I do have to go," Kim told her.

"But you can't possibly leave now," a male voice said from behind her, causing Kim's heart to stutter as she recognized the voice. "Not when I've finally tracked down the mystery lady who bought me."

Seeing no way out, Kim dragged in a breath and turned to face him. "I hate to disappoint you but I'm no mystery lady."

"Kim!"

"Afraid so." Her heart sank at the shock she read in Justin's eyes. "I'm sorry. I thought you'd recognized me." Or she had hoped he had, since he'd been looking directly at her when she'd made that final bid.

"I thought…I mean, I knew you seemed familiar, but with the lighting and your hair like that, I didn't realize it was you."

Self-conscious, Kim caught a lock of hair that fell across her shoulder. "I probably should have worn it up."

"No," he said emphatically, surprising Kim. "I like it. You look wonderful."

"I hate to interrupt such an interesting conversation," Tara began, and by her expression, it was clear she wasn't sorry at all. "But in case you haven't noticed, the two of you are standing in the middle of the dance floor. A dance floor that I might add is getting a little crowded."

"Watch out," Justin advised and pulled Kim out of harm's way as an enthusiastic pair nearly collided with her.

"Thanks," Kim murmured, and steadied herself on the sky-high heels, but not before she caught the "I told you so" look from Tara.

"Tara?" the older gentleman who had been standing beside Tara touched her arm. "Shall we?"

"By all means," she replied. Turning her attention back

to the two of them for a moment, she looked straight at her brother and said, "If you can manage to talk and dance at the same time, I suggest you ask Kim to dance."

"Brat," Justin responded, but there was only affection in his eyes as he looked at his sister.

Tara gave him a cheeky smile. "Oh, and no need to thank me now, big brother. You can tell me later how wonderful I am."

"Thank her for what?" Justin asked Kim as Tara danced away.

"For having me buy your date package."

"Tara was responsible?"

Kim nodded. "Maybe we'd better go find someplace where we can talk."

By the time Justin had gotten them each a glass of wine and they had retreated to a relatively quiet corner, Kim had explained how Tara had asked her to attend and bid on him in the bachelor auction. "Anyway, Tara thought you'd prefer to choose your own date and not get stuck with someone because of the auction. So I agreed to bid on you at her request."

"Remind me to send my sister flowers on Monday," Justin told her.

"Then you're not upset?"

"Hardly. I will admit that at first I was ready to strangle you when I discovered that instead of dinner and theater tickets, you'd locked me into an all-day sailing date. Especially when I thought I might have to spend it trapped on the boat with Eve Novak."

"And now?"

"Now I'm looking forward to it," he told her. "But I am curious about something."

"What?"

"How did you know I had a passion for sailing?"

"Oh, that was easy," Kim explained. "You keep a picture in your office of you and some friends on a sailboat. And I remember when your mother was in the office a month or so ago, complaining that you were working too hard. She mentioned something about you not even taking your sailboat out anymore."

"And naturally, you remembered," he said, and the smile he gave made her insides melt.

"Yes." What would he say if he knew that there was little about him that she didn't remember? The way his hair had a tendency to curl at his nape. The way he absently fingered his pen and paced when he was trying to figure out a problem. The way he always removed the pickles from his sandwiches and ate them separately as though they were a treat.

"Then I guess it's a good thing for Connelly Corporation that you're not an industrial spy, because you'd know all our secrets."

"I don't think you have to worry about that. I love my job." And you, she added silently.

"The corporation is lucky to have you. So am I," he told her, and smiled at her once more. "Thanks again for coming to my rescue tonight."

"You're welcome." Setting down her wineglass, Kim retrieved the envelope that contained the certificate that entitled the bearer to a sailing date with Justin and offered it to him. "Here you go. I hope you have a wonderful time."

Justin glanced at the envelope she held out to him, but made no attempt to take it. The look he gave her was filled with confusion and what Kim wanted to believe was disappointment. "Don't *you* want to go with me?"

Kim's heartbeat quickened. She looked away, stared down at her hands, afraid what Justin might read in her eyes. "Well, I just assumed...that is, I thought you would want to ask someone else, maybe Ashley Powers,'' she offered, recalling that he had had her book a dinner reservation for the two of them. ''You know, somebody whose company you enjoyed.''

Justin tipped her chin up, and her pulse leaped at the warmth in his hazel eyes. ''I enjoy your company, Kim Lindgren, and I can't think of anyone I'd rather take sailing than you. But if you'd rather not go—''

''No. I'd love to go,'' Kim said, the words tumbling out before she could stop them. ''I mean, I've never been sailing before, but I love the water.''

''Then it's settled. The two of us have a date to go sailing.''

''Well, if you're sure…''

''In the time we've worked together, have you ever known me to be unsure of what I want?''

''No,'' she conceded. It was one of the things she admired about Justin. He didn't flinch or waver from making decisions.

''In fact, suddenly I can't wait to get out on the water. What do you say we go tomorrow?''

''Tomorrow?''

Justin grimaced. ''Already have plans, huh? I should have realized that. All right, we'll just pick another day.''

''I don't have plans,'' she told him. ''It's just that I thought…I assumed since you've been out of town, you'd be going to the office tomorrow.''

''The office will still be there on Monday, won't it?''

''Well, yes, but—''

''Then, it's settled. Tomorrow you and I are going sailing. All right?''

''All right,'' she told him, more pleased than he could imagine.

''But seeing how the night's still young, what do you

say we take advantage of the music?'' He stood and held out his hands to her. ''Dance with me?''

''I'm afraid I'm not a very good dancer,'' she told him as the band segued into a cha-cha. She noted the couples on the floor beginning to move in unison. Suddenly she wished she had gone to one of those tony schools that taught young ladies how to ballroom dance.

''I find that hard to believe,'' Justin told her as he drew her to her feet and led her to the dance floor. ''I've yet to discover anything that you don't do well. Besides, I distinctly remember watching you doing those stretching movements not very long ago. The way you moved, I could have sworn you heard music in your head.''

''I did. Well sort of,'' she said, in explanation. ''I exercise to a CD at home, so whenever I do stretches, the music plays in my head. I guess it's a reflex action,'' she continued, only to think what an idiot she must sound like rambling on this way.

But then she couldn't think at all as Justin pulled her into his arms. They were so close she could feel the heat of his body, the warmth of his hand at her back, the way his other palm engulfed her own. She could smell that woods and outdoor scent that she always associated with him. And she could see the flecks of gold in his eyes as he looked down at her.

''Relax and listen to the music,'' he told her.

But as he began to move them about the floor, she couldn't relax. She could barely hear anything, either, save for the frantic beat of her own heart that echoed in her ears.

As though sensing her feelings, Justin pressed her hand against his chest and asked, ''Feel that? Thump-thump, thump-thump, thump-thump.''

''Yes,'' she whispered.

"The music has the same beat. Just like my heart. Thump-thump. Thump-thump. Thump-thump."

And suddenly she felt it. That same thump-thump sound. Or maybe it was Justin's heartbeat she felt, heard in her head. She wasn't sure. All she knew was that when he slid his hand to her hip and began to lead her into the dance, her body moved in tandem with his. His eyes never left hers, nor did her eyes leave his. Even when the tempo increased, when thigh brushed against thigh, when his hand tightened on her hip, when he spun her around. Each time, she stayed with him, followed his lead, felt the beat of the music, the beat of Justin's heart.

By the time the song finally ended and Justin pulled her against him, her own heart was beating in tune with his. It was as if there was no one else in the world but the two of them.

His eyes flashed with heat, and anticipation shot through her like a rocket as his head began to lower. "Kim." He whispered her name.

"Justin, my man, I've been looking for you."

Kim jolted at the sound of Robert Marsh's voice. Instinctively she took a step back and crossed her arms.

"Marsh." Justin acknowledged the other man with a curt greeting.

"I was wondering how your meeting with Schaeffer went?"

"My meeting went fine."

"Great, did he—"

"We'll discuss it on Monday," Justin said, his voice and expression hard. "Now if you'll excuse us, I want to tell Jennifer what a great job she did on the fund-raiser."

"I'm glad things went well in New York. I meant to ask you about it," Kim told him. "But with the excitement of the auction I guess I forgot."

He smiled at her, and Kim's stomach quivered. "You're not the only one. I was just as eager to tell you how well the meeting went, but I'm afraid business has been the last thing on my mind tonight."

Kim tried not to read anything into what he said, but she was finding it more and more difficult not to do so. "Yes, well. I'll look forward to hearing all about it on Monday."

The music started up again, this time a slow, haunting love song. "Shall we?"

Kim hesitated. "I really should go."

"Don't," he said, stroking her cheek with the back of his hand. "Stay."

She stayed.

And by the time Justin had insisted on accompanying her home, Kim had to pinch herself to be sure she wasn't dreaming. Suddenly the back of the limo that had seemed so large en route to the gala seemed small with Justin seated beside her. In the dim interior, there was something so intimate in the sight of his leg next to hers, of his shoulder just grazing hers, of his arm draped along the back of the seat. Lost in thought, she didn't even realize the car had stopped until the driver was opening her door.

"I'll only be a few minutes," Justin informed the chauffeur as he led Kim to her apartment building.

"Justin, you don't have to walk me up. I'll be fine."

He leveled a reproachful look at her. "And risk my mother's wrath for not seeing a young lady to her door? Never."

"Your mother would never know unless you told her," Kim informed him even as they started up the stairs.

"I'd know."

"This is it," she said, standing outside her apartment.

Justin took the key from her, unlocked the door. "I had a great time tonight," he told her.

"So did I," she murmured, and wished the night didn't have to end. Feeling awkward, unsure what to do, she pasted a bright smile on her face. "Well, I guess I'll see you in the morning. Good night."

"Kim, aren't you forgetting something?"

Confused, Kim squinched her brows together, looked at Justin's face, then down at her apartment key in his out-stretched hand. "Oh," she said, feeling like an idiot and reached for the key.

Justin closed his fingers around her hand and pulled her toward him. "I wasn't talking about the key. I was talking about this," he told her just before his mouth touched hers.

His lips moved over hers tentatively at first, as though he were testing, tasting, coaxing. His gentleness disarmed her. And when his tongue traced the seam of her mouth, Kim's lips parted instinctively. He made some sound deep in his throat, part groan, part moan that sent a trill of excitement skating up her spine.

He still held her hand between them, but with his free arm he pulled her against him, and the feel of his arousal pressed against her unleashed a wave of longing inside her. His tongue thrust into her mouth, parried with her tongue, engaged in a mating dance as old as time. Heat arrowed through her belly, between her thighs. And when Kim was sure that she would die if he didn't make love to her in the next five minutes, Justin pulled back.

It took her a moment to register his hot and thunderous expression. "Justin?"

"I'll see you in the morning. Nine o'clock okay?"

"Yes," she replied.

"Great."

He bolted and was halfway down the stairs before she'd had a chance to ask him what was wrong.

Six

So they'd both had a little too much wine to drink last night and had kissed. It was no big deal, Justin reassured himself the next morning as he exited the Loop and headed for Kim's apartment. Given the circumstances and the tenor of the evening, kissing her good-night had been the natural thing to do.

And if the feel of Kim in his arms, the taste of her mouth beneath his own, had shaken him with the force of an earthquake and kept him awake half the night, then it was to be expected. After all, he was a healthy, red-blooded male whose lack of a social life of late had resulted in a long bout of celibacy. Besides, the sight of Kim in that strapless number with those skinny high heels and all that blond hair tumbling down her back would have tempted even a saint.

He'd never claimed to be a saint.

But he did consider himself honorable. Which was why he'd hightailed it out of there last night before he'd followed through on his instinct to make wild, passionate love to her. Kim was his assistant and his friend, Justin reminded himself as he wheeled his Jeep onto Kim's street. He'd use the sailing outing today to reestablish those boundaries of friendship and squash any lingering lustful thoughts he'd been harboring about his assistant.

Feeling better, he pulled his Jeep up to the curb in front of Kim's building, then hopped out and climbed the stairs to her apartment. He rapped on her door and she answered almost at once.

"Good morning," she said.

The smile she gave him hit him square in the solar plexus, and all he could do was stand there and stare.

She glanced down at her clothes, then back up at him. "Am I dressed wrong?" she asked, her smile dimming.

"No. You look perfect." She looked better than perfect. She looked downright delectable, he admitted. The navy-and-white-striped T-shirt emphasized the curves that he'd glimpsed last night and had tried his best to forget. The white shorts revealed a pair of long, slender legs that her sedate suits and slacks had only hinted at, and triggered his most erotic fantasies. So much for his notion of seeing Kim as only his assistant and friend. It simply wasn't going to happen. The only question was what did Kim want? Had he read more into Kim's response to his kiss last night than had been there?

"Is everything okay?"

"Everything's fine," he assured her. "You all set for your first sailing lesson?"

"All set," she said with a grin, and reached for the tote bag sitting next to the door.

"I'll take that." His hand brushed hers as they both reached for the bag. There was no mistaking the spark that shot through him at the innocent touch. And judging by the way those blue-green eyes of hers had widened, he wasn't the only one who'd felt it.

"I wasn't quite sure what I should bring," she informed him as she locked the door.

"Sunscreen?" he asked, lifting the tote bag.

"Yes. Plus a visor, towel and swimsuit."

"Then we're in business," he told her, and followed her down the stairs and out to the street. "All set?" he asked after he'd stowed her tote bag and they'd both buckled their seat belts.

"All set."

He started the Jeep's engine. "Then sit back, relax and enjoy the ride."

They both enjoyed the ride, Justin admitted ninety minutes later as he and Kim set off from the docks of the yacht harbor and headed for the open waters of Lake Geneva. The conversation during the drive had been spirited and fun, with an edge of excitement that he could only attribute to the sexual tension that hummed between them. With an eagerness that he dared not examine too closely, he'd wasted no time loading Kim's tote bag and the picnic-basket lunch he'd picked up at a gourmet deli en route to the lake.

"Are you sure there's nothing I can do to help?" Kim asked him from her position at the bow.

"Don't worry, I intend to make you work for your lunch, sailor. But not until we get past the bend in the harbor and away from the docks."

"All right," she told him, a smile spreading across her lips before she turned away and looked out to the open water.

Mindful to keep his attention on the operation of the sailboat and not Kim's long legs, Justin maneuvered the thirty-five-foot beauty around the final bend and into the mouth of the lake. "Okay, sailor," he said as he cut the engine. "Ready for your first lesson?"

"Aye, aye, captain," she said, and gave him a sassy salute. "What do you want me to do?"

"Now, that's a loaded question if I ever heard one," he teased.

She gave him a reproachful look. "I meant what do you want me to do to help with the boat."

"How about coming over here and manning the wheel while I hoist the sails?"

"You want me to drive the boat?"

"Actually, I want you to keep her steady while I run up the jib and mainsail." After a brief explanation, during which time he did his best not to notice just how silky her skin felt or how her hair smelled of apples and sunshine, he asked, "Got it?"

"I think so," she told him. "But promise you'll teach me how to work the sails, too?"

"I promise," he told her.

More than two hours later, when they anchored the boat in a relatively quiet spot on the lake, he taught her the difference between the mainsail and the jib, explained the workings of the boom and masthead, the keel and rudder while they feasted on lunch.

Justin shaved off a chunk of pepper-jack cheese with his knife, and as he ate it he studied Kim. Stretched out on the foredeck, with the breeze from the lake fingering the hair that she'd pulled up into a ponytail, Kim looked even more tempting now than she had last night in that knockout black dress. If she'd been wearing any makeup other than lip gloss and sunscreen, he hadn't been able to tell it. The few hours they'd spent in the sun had put a healthy shot of color in her cheeks. He grinned as he noted a tiny sprinkling of freckles across her nose. She bit into a grape, and Justin's mouth watered as she licked the juice from her lips. He couldn't help remembering how sweet those lips had tasted last night when he'd kissed her.

"How old were you when you first started sailing?" Kim asked, breaking into his none-too-appropriate thoughts.

"Probably right around the time I got potty trained," Justin admitted. "At least that's when my dad started taking me out with him. When I was growing up, my family spent a lot of time at the lake cottage, especially during the summers. Anyway, my dad used to like to go out on the sailboat in the mornings just when the sun was coming up. I've always been an early riser, so he'd let me tag along."

"I'll bet he enjoyed your company."

"Maybe some of the time," Justin conceded, even though he had always considered those mornings a special bonding time between him and his father. "My dad claimed the lake was a good place for a man to go when he needed to think or when life seemed to be too much. He said being on the lake helped a body to remember that there are more important things in life than making money or building empires."

"I can see why your father is so successful. He's a very wise man."

"Yes, he is." Reminiscing about those quiet mornings he'd spent with his father, Justin realized just how wise a man Grant Connelly had been—even back then. He himself, on the other hand, had not been nearly as wise, Justin decided, as he thought of how consumed with work he'd been these past six months.

"Why the name *Calypso?*" Kim asked, referring to the sailboat's name.

Justin smiled and shook off his deep thoughts. "It's after the sea nymph."

"The one who detained Odysseus on the island of Ogygia for seven years?"

"One and the same," Justin said, impressed that she remembered the tale. "The minute I saw her, I fell under her spell and knew I had to have her. I didn't even haggle about the price. I just wrote out the check."

"Somehow I don't think you have any regrets."

"I don't," he admitted. "At least not about buying the boat. I do, however, regret that it took my very wise assistant putting together a date package for a bachelor auction to get me to come out on her again."

She shrugged and the smile she gave him was filled with sass. "We very wise assistants do what we have to, to keep our bosses from working themselves to death."

"Have I really been that bad?"

"Worse," she told him, and burst into laughter.

"You should do that more often," Justin said.

"What? Book sailing dates with you to be auctioned off for charity?"

"Funny," he said, and pitched a grape at her, which she caught and promptly popped into her mouth. "I meant you should laugh more often. You have a beautiful laugh, Kim."

"Thanks," she murmured and lowered her eyes. She began to toy with the bunch of grapes.

Justin reached over, tipped up her chin. "I didn't mean to embarrass you."

"You didn't," she said, then sighed. "I guess I'm just not used to all this."

"What? Eating lunch?"

She made a face at him. "You know that's not what I meant."

"No? Then you must be talking about sailing. Wait, now

I remember. You did mention something about being a land lover, didn't you?'' he teased.

''I said that I loved the water, and this is the first time I've ever been sailing.''

''Then what is it you're not used to, Kimberly Lindgren? You can't make me believe that before now you haven't had men telling you how beautiful you are.''

''I haven't,'' she whispered so softly that Justin wasn't sure if he heard the words or read the movement of her lips.

''Then the men in Chicago must be blind or mute or both, because you are beautiful, Kim. Incredibly beautiful,'' he told her. Unable to resist, he pressed his mouth against hers.

He took his time. First he kissed the corner of her mouth, slowly savoring the feel of her lips. He lost his fingers in her hair, held her head in his hands while he tested, shaped, explored her mouth. All the while desire burned inside him, spreading like fire, making him hard, making him ache to lose himself in her softness.

Kim's fingers dug into his shoulders, and the sharp bite of her nails served only to feed the fierce hunger churning inside him. But he held himself in check, determined to let Kim set the pace. ''Justin,'' she sighed against his lips.

When she opened her mouth to him, his control slipped a notch. He wanted to drink her in and because he did, he forced himself to slow down. She tasted of grapes and lemonade. Of sunshine and sweetness. Of innocence and seduction. She tasted of everything he'd ever wanted and needed in this world, Justin thought. Suddenly he forgot all about the fact that they were anchored in Lake Geneva. That it was the middle of the day and the sun was still shining in the sky. That they were out in the open where anyone and everyone could see them. He forgot about everything but the taste and the feel of the woman in his arms.

Slowly she pulled back, stared up at him out of blue-green eyes shimmering with desire and Justin lost the last of his control. He no longer cared where they were or who saw them. He no longer cared that he'd told himself just last night that this wasn't a good idea. All that mattered now was Kim and the way she was looking at him—as if she wanted him and needed him as much as he wanted and needed her.

Angling his head, he took her mouth again. This time he gave in to the desire that had been driving him mad for weeks. This time he kissed her deeply, thoroughly, with all the hunger inside him that he'd fought to deny. And she kissed him back. Never before had anything felt so right, Justin thought. Never before had he wanted a woman so much. As though sensing his thoughts, she made some mewling sound and pressed herself closer to him.

Justin took the kiss even deeper. He drank in her gasps, mated with her tongue, showed her with his mouth what he wanted to do to her with his body. What he wanted her to do to him with hers. He slid his hands down her back, around her waist, then cupped her breasts.

She tore her mouth free and arched her back, giving him access. While he kissed her neck, he kneaded her breasts. He moved his mouth lower, tasting her collarbone. Then he closed his mouth over one breast, suckled her through her T-shirt and bra. When he closed his teeth on her nipple, she gasped.

"Justin, I—"

The blare from a boat horn drowned out her words as Justin blocked her from view with his body. He glared at the waving passengers on the pleasure craft as they sped by, causing *Calypso* to rock in its wake.

When he looked at Kim again, her cheeks were pink and her eyes were wide with what he suspected was shock. "You okay?" he asked, more gruffly than he'd intended. He still couldn't believe he'd subjected her to the speculation of the idiots in the other boats.

"I'm fine," she told him.

Noting her blouse was still damp from his mouth, he frowned. Evidently she caught the direction of his gaze and crossed her arms over her chest. "I'm sorry," he told her.

"Nothing to be sorry about," she said brightly.

Too brightly, Justin thought, as she stood up and began clearing away the remains of their lunch. "Here, let me give you a hand with that," he offered.

"No need," she informed him, looking everywhere but at him. "You mentioned something earlier about taking a swim. Why don't you go ahead while I take care of this?"

Justin hesitated a moment. He could see that she was upset. What he didn't know was if she was upset because of what had almost happened between them or because he'd subjected her to the jeers of the idiots in the passing boat. Unsure what to do or say, Justin decided that maybe taking a swim wasn't such a bad idea after all.

The swim had been every bit as effective as a cold shower, Kim decided more than an hour later after she'd changed back into her shorts and top and rejoined Justin on deck. Each time she thought of how close she'd come to pleading with Justin to make love to her, she was torn between wanting to curse or thanking the boatload of revelers who'd interrupted them. There was no longer any question in her mind that Justin had wanted her. Still wanted her if she could believe that smoldering look in his eyes when she'd changed into her suit and joined him in the water.

But the scowl on his face following the other boaters' departure had confused her. So had his gruff inquiry of her. And while Justin may have kissed her like he wanted to swallow her whole a short time ago, the swim seemed to have taken the edge off his desire for her. In fact, given his relaxed appearance behind the wheel of the boat now, she could almost believe that she'd imagined those passionate kisses.

"The wind's starting to kick up a bit," Justin said. "What do you say we run up the sails and I show you what it's like to race with the wind?"

"That was absolutely incredible," Kim told him several hours later while she helped him secure the mainsail. "I felt like I was flying."

"You were," Justin informed her as he expertly knotted the ropes. "You were just doing it on top of the water."

The awkwardness following their earlier kisses had vanished sometime during those hours they'd spent zipping along the crystal-blue waters of Lake Geneva. With a patience that astonished her, Justin had kept his promise and taught her how to hoist the sails. They'd both laughed when he'd saved her from being knocked over by the boom. He'd stood beside her in the cockpit when she'd taken a turn at the wheel. And he hadn't even flinched when she'd come dangerously close to sending them onto the shore of Big Foot Beach.

"I can understand now why you love this," she told him. "What I don't know is how you could have stayed away so long."

"Right now I'm asking myself that same question," he said, his smile slipping a notch as he stared up at the sky.

She followed the direction of his gaze, noted that the sun

was already beginning to set. A wave of disappointment rolled over her as she realized the day was nearly over.

"Looks like a storm's headed this way. A big one."

Kim yanked her attention back to the weather. "That's not a problem, is it? I mean, we're already heading back to the harbor, and those dark clouds look pretty far off."

"They're just moving faster than I'd like. Can you take the wheel a minute? I'm going to drop the jib, then motor us in. The last thing I want is for your first sailing experience to end with you caught in a storm."

Kim took the wheel and kept *Calypso* steady while Justin dispatched the jib. But even with the sails down, the increased wind whistled loudly across the deck.

Justin joined her in the cockpit and started up the engine. And when Kim would have moved away to give him more room, he put his arm around her shoulders and kept her close. "What do you say we try to outrun that storm?"

Kim glanced back at the swiftly darkening sky and noted that the ugly black clouds were now much closer than they had been a few minutes ago. "You think we can beat it?"

"There's only one way to find out." He opened the engine's throttle, and *Calypso* shot forward, sending them racing toward the harbor with the wind and thunder at their backs.

Fifteen minutes later when Justin guided *Calypso* into the boat slip, fat raindrops had begun to fall. Darkness had come quickly, and the harbor, abuzz with activity and people when they'd arrived earlier that morning, now resembled a deserted graveyard of boats.

After securing the boat's lines and double-checking the cleats, Justin helped Kim from the boat. "Here, I'll take that," he told her and took her tote bag, along with the picnic basket. "Ready to make a run for the Jeep?"

"Ready," she called out to make herself heard above the shriek of the wind.

"Okay, let's go," he said. Holding hands they ran from the dock to the parking lot where Justin's Jeep now sat alone.

By the time they reached the Jeep, Kim was soaked to the skin. So was Justin. "You all right?" he asked as he started up the vehicle.

"A little wet," she said, and laughed at the understatement.

"I don't suppose you're interested in a slightly wet towel, are you?" he asked, referring to the fact that he had dropped her tote bag in a puddle while crossing the parking lot.

"Thanks. But I think I'll pass."

"We've got an hour-and-a-half drive back to Chicago. Do you want me to stop by my place at the lake and see about getting you some dry clothes? My sisters are always leaving things at my place or the main cottage. I'm sure Tara or Alexandra wouldn't mind if you borrowed something of theirs."

Kim was tempted. Not because she minded the wet clothes, but because she hated to see this day end. Still, even though earlier on the boat Justin had kissed her like a man possessed and had watched her hungrily throughout the rest of the day, he'd made no move to kiss her again. "That's okay. I'm sure I'll dry out in no time."

"All right," he said, and Kim allowed herself to believe that the disappointment she heard in his voice was because he didn't want the day to end, either.

Lost in thought, Kim didn't realize that something was wrong for several minutes, until Justin pulled the car off the road. "I need to check the wipers," he told her, and stepped out into the now driving rain.

Kim watched him through the windshield as he lifted, fiddled with and reset the wiper blades. When he got back inside the car, his face was pulled into a frown, and rain streamed down his hair and neck. "What's wrong?"

"The windshield wipers are shot." As if to show her, he flipped on the switch, and Kim noted the sluggish movement of the blade on the driver's side of the car while the blade on the passenger's side sat unmoving in the middle of the windshield. He looked at her then, his expression solemn. "I can't drive in this downpour with the wipers like this. It wouldn't be safe."

"No, it wouldn't." She bit her lower lip. "What are we going to do?"

"We can sit out the storm here in the Jeep until the worst of it is over, then I can try to find a service station and see if they can fix it."

"Is that what you think we should do?" Kim asked, and then nearly jumped out of her skin as a bolt of lightning flashed, illuminating the interior of the car. Thunder crashed a second later, causing her to jump again.

Justin said nothing for a moment, simply stared out into the night before shifting his gaze to her. His eyes met hers, held. "No. I think it would be dangerous to stay here."

"Then what do you recommend?"

"That we go to my place on the lake and wait out the storm."

Kim's heart raced as she looked into his eyes. The sexual tension that had been like a living thing between them all day seemed to snap and sizzle as he watched her and waited. "Then let's go to your place."

Justin's place was only a few minutes away. A small cottage, it was located on the large stretch of Connelly land that boasted a horse stable, several apartments and the family's lake cottage, an architectural gem designed by Frank Lloyd Wright. Kim had seen pictures of the Connellys' lake cottage featured in several architectural journals. Even in the rain the cottage looked wonderful. So did Justin's smaller version, she thought as he pulled up in front of the place and shut off the engine.

They dashed from the Jeep to the front door of the cottage, which Justin unlocked before ushering her inside.

"Damn," he muttered as he flipped the light switches and the room remained in darkness. He went to the window and looked out across the neighboring grounds that showed no signs of life or light. "It looks like the storm took out a power line." He came back to where she stood just inside the front door and looked down at her. "Will you be okay while I go see about lighting some candles?"

"I'll be fine," she told him.

"Good. Don't move. I'll be right back."

She didn't move. Instead she stood at the windows and took advantage of the floor-to-ceiling glass to watch the fireworks display being conducted by the lightning storm over the lake. Rain battered against the windowpanes, and Kim pressed her fingers against the glass. There was a savage beauty to the storm, she thought, transfixed by the power of the jagged bolts of light that sliced through the dark sky like a sword. There was something elemental and inevitable about the storm that struck some chord inside her.

"You're shivering," Justin said from behind her.

As she turned to face him, only then did Kim realize that she was indeed shivering. He draped a towel around her, pulled the ends together under her chin. "Better?" he asked.

She looked up into his hazel eyes. "Yes," she murmured. But her shaking off the chill had less to do with the dry towel and more to do with the way Justin was looking at her.

"Kim, don't look at me like that."

"Like what?"

"Like you want me."

"And if I told you that I do?" she asked, surprising herself as much as him by her boldness.

This time it was Justin who shivered. He squeezed his eyes shut, and for a moment she feared he was going to reject her. But when he opened his eyes again, the desire she saw reflected in them stole her breath. Gripping the edges of the towel, he brought her closer until her mouth was only a breath from his own.

Impatient, afraid he might change his mind yet again, Kim lifted up onto her toes and pressed her lips against his. The touch of her mouth seemed to unleash something inside him, because suddenly Justin was kissing her. Deeply. Passionately. Hungrily. When he tore his mouth free, his eyes were wild, almost savage. He didn't speak. He simply picked her up and began to carry her deeper into the house.

Thunder sounded outside, echoing the wild pounding of her heart as Justin brought her into the great room. She was vaguely aware of candles flickering about the room—on a table in front of a couch, atop the fireplace mantel, on a countertop. Flames glinted off glass vases and picture frames scattered about the room, reflected off the polished wooden floor. More flames licked from inside the fireplace where a row of candles in various shapes and sizes burned and gave the illusion of firelight.

Justin lowered her to the rug in front of the fireplace, then he knelt beside her. He removed the towel from around her shoulders and smoothed her hair. "You have the most beautiful hair," he told her as he combed his fingers into her damp tresses. "Ever since last night— No, ever since that night at the office when I saw you stretching, I've been dreaming of doing this.''

''But that night at the office, and today on the boat after we'd kissed...I thought you were angry.''

''I was angry,'' he explained. ''With myself.''

''I don't understand.''

''I was angry because I wanted you, Kim. That night. Last night. Today. Now.''

Pleasure shot through her at his admission. ''And is wanting me so wrong?''

''Maybe not wrong, but I didn't think it was fair to you. We work together. I'm your boss. You're my assistant.''

''I'm also a woman,'' she reminded him.

He grinned at that. ''I'm well aware of that fact. I have been for some time. The number of cold showers I've taken lately are certainly proof of that. Not that it seems to have done me much good,'' he said as he sieved his fingers through her hair. ''Because I still want you.''

Emboldened by his confession, Kim asked, ''Does that mean you're going to take another cold shower?''

''Hardly. I doubt it would do any good.''

''I'm glad,'' she whispered. She touched his jaw, aware of the coarse stubble against her palm. She met his eyes. ''Because I want you to make love to me, Justin. I have for a long time.'' Because I've loved you for a long time, she added in silence, as she slid her arms around his neck and kissed him.

She kissed him as deeply as he had kissed her. This time she pierced the seam of his lips and mated her tongue with his, trying to tell him with her mouth of the love she'd held in her heart for him all these months. She pulled at his shirt, eager to feel his skin. Justin ripped the shirt over his head and tossed it aside. Then she was kissing his neck, his mouth, tracing his nipple with her tongue while her hands roamed his chest, his back, memorized the feel of him.

"Kim," he gasped as he caught her questing fingers.

Still dazed and driven by this burning inside her for more of him, she needed a minute to focus. When she did, her courage faltered at his fierce expression. "Did I do something wrong?"

Justin groaned, squeezed his eyes shut a moment and dragged in a breath. "Sweetheart, the only one who's done anything wrong is me. I'm about to go up in flames and we've hardly started."

She eyed him warily, not sure how to respond.

His expression softened. "We're going to make love, Kim. Make no mistake about that. I'm just slowing things down a bit and giving you a chance to catch up with me."

And before she could tell him that she didn't need to catch up, that she already wanted him, he began to kiss her again. Slowly. Tenderly. Lovingly. He kissed her eyes, her mouth, her jaw. He kissed a spot just below her ear that made her shiver. Then, taking his time, he went on to her throat and planted kisses on the slope of her shoulder where her T-shirt started.

The blood sluiced through her veins, heated with each kiss until she was churning inside again and feeling as restless as the storm outside. She sought his mouth, tried to convey to him with her kiss that she didn't want to go slow. When he pulled his mouth free, Kim tried to take satisfaction in the fact that his breathing was far from steady.

He reached for the hem of her T-shirt, removed it. Excited and anxious, she was suddenly grateful for the storm and the shadowed light. As though sensing her nervousness, Justin resumed the slow kisses, pressing his moist, hot mouth to her collarbone, to the swells of her breasts. He released the catch at the front of her bra, peeled away the silky fabric, exposing her. His eyes darkened, and Kim trembled beneath the heat of his gaze, felt it like a caress.

"So beautiful. So perfect," he whispered as he filled his palms with her breasts.

Kim gasped as he stroked her nipples with his thumbs. Instinctively she arched her back. In answer, Justin lowered his head, laving first one nipple, then the next. When his teeth grazed the sensitive tip, Kim cried out, "Justin!"

"It's all right. Let me love you," he soothed, and gentled her with another kiss as he eased her down to the pillows scattered on the rug.

Kim was sure she was on fire when Justin resumed trailing kisses down her stomach, to the waistband of her shorts. With a familiarity that would have disturbed her had she not been so awash in sensations, he removed her shorts and stripped away her panties. Then his mouth was on her again, his tongue tracing her navel, his teeth nipping her hip, the inside of her thigh.

When his fingers brushed the mouth of her sex, Kim writhed in embarrassment as she felt herself grow even more damp. "Justin, I—"

He opened her then, began to stroke the sensitive flesh at her center with his finger. Kim could no longer think, let alone speak. Curling her fists into the towel that had fallen discarded on the rug beneath her, she could scarcely breathe as need began to spiral through her. And when Justin replaced his fingers with his mouth and stroked her with his tongue, everything inside her shattered.

Seven

Justin nearly lost it as Kim came apart beneath him, her body trembling in the throes of her climax. She was so sweet and responsive it had made holding back his own pleasure even more difficult. Witnessing her stunned look of satisfaction now as she opened her eyes and attempted to focus made him all the more glad that he had held back.

"Justin, I…you…"

He smiled, enchanted by her expressive face. He didn't need her to tell him that she was a stranger to oral sex. And he couldn't help feeling glad that he was the one to initiate her. While he knew it wasn't fair, the idea of another man touching Kim, sharing intimacies with her, struck some primal chord within him.

She touched his face. "What just happened…it was…incredible."

He kissed the palm at his jaw. "*You* were incredible," he told her, and meant it.

She smiled at him then, that woman's smile. Much like the smile he imagined the nymph Calypso had used on Odysseus. And like Odysseus, he found her impossible to resist.

She kissed him deeply, hungrily. Sitting up, she kissed his shoulder, nipped the skin, then laved it with her tongue. All the while her hands were on him, stroking, exploring. He filled his palms with her breasts, felt his manhood throb as the nipples hardened beneath his touch.

Her tongue circled his nipples, and Justin groaned when she closed her teeth around them and suckled. "Kim, you're driving me crazy."

"Good," she replied, and began a trail of kisses down his chest to his belly. After unbuckling his belt, she loosened the snap of his cutoffs. But when she fumbled with the zipper, the innocent brush of her fingers nearly sent him over the edge. Quickly, Justin dispensed with the cutoffs and briefs and returned to Kim.

"You're beautiful," she whispered, and ran her fingers down his male length.

The sensation was erotic and as arousing as hell. Like being stroked by velvet, Justin thought. When she closed her fist around him, his vision blurred. "Kim, sweetheart," he cautioned, and captured her wrist. Sucking in a breath, he grappled for control. He'd been teetering on the edge since she'd kissed him and told him she wanted him. He didn't want to ruin it for both of them by exploding now.

Trying to slow things down again, he pressed her back into the pillows and kissed her softly.

It didn't work. How could it? he reasoned when she was nipping his mouth with her teeth? When she was guiding him to her moist center? When she was looking up at him out of those incredible blue-green eyes that mirrored his own desire? With a Herculean effort, Justin held himself back and forced himself to ask, "Are you sure this is what you want? It'll probably kill me to stop now, but I will if you're not sure."

"I'm sure," she told him, and pulled his mouth down to hers. "I want this. I want *you*."

The kiss was hot, explosive, carnal. Justin wasn't sure where his mouth ended and where Kim's began. He only knew that he couldn't get close enough to her. She moved against him, brushing her lower body against his sex. He went weak with need as she guided him to her warm, moist center.

"Wait," he told her, feeling the last vestiges of his sanity and control slip. He scanned the shadows, searching the floor for his pants, intent on getting protection.

"Please, Justin. Now!"

And before he could stop her, Kim was lifting her hips.

Justin swore. Unable to stop himself, he caught her hips and drove himself home. He felt the brief resistance, heard Kim's soft cry and froze as he realized the reason behind it. He tried to remain perfectly still, terrified that he would hurt her even more.

"Justin?"

"Sweetheart, try not to move," he told her when she stirred beneath him. Sweat broke out across his brow with the effort it took him not to finish what they'd begun. "I don't want to hurt you any more than I already have."

She caught his face between her palms and forced him to look at her. "You didn't hurt me. But you will if you tell me that my being a virgin makes a difference and you no longer want me."

"Oh, I want you." He wanted her as he'd never wanted anyone or anything before in his life.

"Then show me."

"Kim—"

She tightened her feminine muscles, and Justin groaned at the sensation.

Lightning flashed outside, illuminating the room with streaks of light. Thunder struck nearby. But the storm outside was no match for the storm inside him as Kim began to move beneath him. Then all he could see was Kim. All he wanted was Kim.

Driven by desire and the need to make this special for her, to make her his, Justin eased his hand between them and began to stroke that sensitive spot with his finger even as he moved himself inside her. He brought her up, took her to the brink.

Her eyes were glazed as she looked at him and gasped, "Justin, I can't. I—"

"You can," he assured her, urging her to take. When she shuddered, cried out in wonder, Justin's own need spiked. Drinking in her cries of pleasure, he strained to hold himself back as she pulsed around him and brought him closer and closer to the edge.

Sweat trickled down his back with the effort it took not to follow her over the crest into those storm-tossed waves. Still, he waited. And when her spasms subsided, he took her up again and again, and watched her come apart in his arms. While he liked to believe he was a generous lover, never before had he felt this need to give so much. Never before had he found such pleasure in the giving.

When she pulsed around him and cried out his name, his control broke. He plunged into her one last time and the world around him exploded as he followed Kim into the storm.

Now he knew what it must feel like to be shipwrecked, Justin thought a short time later. He eased himself up onto his elbows and looked down at Kim. Something warm and tender unfurled inside him as he stared at her flushed face. He pressed a kiss to her mouth. "Are you all right?"

Her lashes fluttered, and she opened her eyes. A smile curved her lips. "Am I alive?"

"I think so," he told her, feeling a measure of relief at her response. "You're sure I didn't hurt you?"

"Positive. You're a wonderful lover, Justin Connelly. Just as I knew you would be."

Justin sobered at the reminder of the gift she'd given him. He lay down beside her and held her in the circle of his arms. Kissing the top of her head, he asked, "Will you be all right by yourself for a few minutes? There's something I want to do."

"Yes, but—"

He silenced her with a kiss. "No buts. Wait here. I'll be right back."

Snagging his cutoffs, Justin took one of the candles from the mantel and headed for the bathroom, where he turned on the taps and began to fill the old-fashioned claw-foot tub with water. Once he had the tub filled and had lit the room with the fat, scented candles Tara had insisted he needed the last time she visited, he went to retrieve Kim.

She lay sleeping on the rug in front of the fireplace where he'd left her. With the towel wrapped around her body, her arms and legs were bare. For several moments Justin stood over her and watched the candlelight play over her features. She looked so beautiful and tempting that he wondered how on earth he had managed to work with her for six months and not realize it.

But on some level he had recognized just how beautiful and special Kim was, Justin admitted as he knelt beside her and brushed a strand of hair from her face. He'd simply tried his best to ignore it and his feelings for Kim because deep down inside he'd known that once he did acknowledge them, he and Kim would find themselves right where they were now. As lovers.

When it came to making decisions, he and Kim becoming lovers was probably not the wisest thing to do, Justin conceded. After all, he'd seen firsthand just how his father's involvement with his former secretary Angie Donahue had impacted his parents' marriage. Though his parents had patched up their differences and his mother had raised his half brother, Seth, as her own, it had not been easy for any of them, including Seth. That was why Justin had been determined to avoid just such a situation by ignoring his attraction to Kim.

But then, he and Kim were not his father and Seth's mother, he reasoned. And he was no longer sure he'd really had any choice in the matter. Even now, less than thirty minutes since he'd made love to her, he wanted her again with an intensity that shook him.

Kim stirred, and when she opened her eyes, she asked, "Where did you go?"

"I'll show you," he said, and slid his arms beneath her legs and lifted her. He carried her into the bathroom, where he removed the towel she'd draped over her body and lowered her into the tub. Reaching for the hair clip he'd found stashed in a drawer, he gathered her hair onto her head to keep it from getting wet again.

"Thank you," she murmured, and eased down into the tub of bubbles.

Justin picked up the sponge, dipped it in the water, then began moving it gently along her leg, up the inside of her thigh.

Kim stilled his hand. "You don't have to do that."

"I know I don't have to. I want to." When her fingers remained locked around his wrist, he met her gaze and explained, "You gave me the most incredible gift a little while ago, Kim. Had I known, I would have tried to be more gentle.''

"You were gentle. I told you, you were wonderful.''

"Not gentle enough. I wanted you too badly.''

"But—''

"Please,'' he said. "Let me do this. Let me show you gentleness now.''

He showed her.

Though he never planned for the gentle bathing of her tender flesh as foreplay, there was no denying that he was fully aroused when he lifted her from the tub and wrapped her in the bath sheet. He just hoped that Kim wouldn't notice.

She noticed.

At least, Justin assumed she'd noticed because he caught the hint of a smile on her lips when she reached for the body lotion and brushed her hip up against his zipper. He bit off a groan.

"Sorry,'' she said, but the contrite tone didn't match her expression.

He wanted her. And watching her smooth lotion on her legs wasn't helping. Despite the bath, he knew darned well that she had to be tender from their earlier lovemaking. Only a beast would consider making love to her again now.

"You mentioned something about a bathrobe earlier?''

Justin jerked his gaze from her legs to her face. "Yeah. I think Tara left one in the bedroom closet. I'll go get it for you.''

He returned in time to see her release her hair from the clip and send long, blond waves cascading down her bare shoulders and back. Justin swallowed hard. Deciding the only way he was going to be able to keep his hands off her was to make himself scarce, he said, "Here you go. I don't know about you, but I'm starved. I'm going to go raid the kitchen and see if I can find us something to eat.''

While he was at it, he was going to stand outside and pray that the rain cooled him off.

The rain didn't cool him off. Nor did sharing the remainder of the pâté and French bread from their lunch and washing it down with one of the bottles of wine he'd found in the liquor cabinet. Somehow the simple meal became a sensual minefield. And before he knew it, they were kissing again. One kiss strung into another and another, until he ended up carrying Kim and the opened bottle of wine upstairs to the bedroom.

He made love to her again. This time he loved her slowly. Gently. Completely. And when he lowered her onto his shaft and joined their bodies, she rode him. He filled his palms with her breasts, gloried in the sight of her astride him as she set the pace. She moved slowly, sensuously, her face reflecting her shock and pleasure as sensation rolled through her. When she increased the tempo, Justin clutched her hips and matched her pace. And when she cried out his name, Justin flipped her beneath him and raced to join her as she plunged into the storm.

Kim blinked at the wash of bright sunshine streaming through the window. She glanced around the unfamiliar room and bed, noted the man's arm draped over her, the hand closed possessively over her breast. Then she remembered. Justin. The sailboat. The storm. Memories of the night came rushing back to her. Of Justin telling her he wanted her. Of his hands and mouth on her. Of her own hands and mouth on him. Heat flooded her cheeks as she recalled the intimacies she'd shared with him, of how completely she'd surrendered her body and heart to him.

Making love with Justin had been the most beautiful experience of her life. If this was how her mother had felt, she could understand now why Amanda Lindgren had spent her life searching to find love like this a second time when her relationship with Kim's father hadn't worked out. Kim thought of how loving Justin had been with her. How he had bathed her so gently, the tender way he had looked at her as he'd brought her to his bed. His every touch, his every look had been filled with love. Only, he'd never given her the words, she reminded herself.

Kim bit her lip, remembered how difficult it had been for her to keep the words locked inside. Yet even in those intense moments when Justin had filled her, merged their bodies as one, he'd cried out how much he wanted her, needed her. But never once had he said that he loved her.

And he hadn't said that he loved her because he didn't love her, Kim reasoned.

You knew that going in, Kim. Did you really think that because you slept together Justin would fall in love with you?

Kim frowned at the nagging voice in her head, knew it was true. She was neither naive nor foolish enough to delude herself into believing that last night meant as much to Justin as it had to her. Why should it? He'd been a perfect gentleman, had given her more than one chance to call a halt before things had gone too far. But she hadn't ended it, because she had wanted Justin to make love to her, had practically begged him to do so, she admitted. And if she was going to be honest, she might as well admit that the moment she realized Justin actually desired her, nothing short of death would have made her say no last night.

The problem was, what did she do now? How did one act the morning after spending the night in the boss's bed? Kim fisted her fingers in the sheets and wished she hadn't shied away from those Monday-morning coffee-and-sex chats that went on among a few of her female co-workers. If she had listened, she might have a clue as to just what she was supposed to do this morning. Did she say thank you and tell him what a fantastic lover he was? Or was it considered more savvy to act as though nothing extraordinary had happened? And what about when she went back to work on Monday? Kim bit back a moan as she considered the awkwardness of sitting across a desk from Justin and remembering that he had seen her naked. That she had seen him naked. If only—

"Do you always wake up so tense?"

Kim's heart leaped at the sound of Justin's voice. Unsure what to do, what to say, she simply froze.

Justin reached for her sheet-tangled fingers, and her breath hitched as his arm grazed her breasts. After tugging the fabric free, he coaxed her to turn over so that she faced him. He'd pushed up onto his elbow and was staring down into her face, and all she could think was how handsome he looked, with his hair mussed, whiskers shadowing his jaw and his mouth curved into a wicked grin.

"Good morning," he told her, and brushed his mouth against hers.

"Morning." Kim finally managed to get the words past her lips.

He frowned. "You okay?"

"I'm fine," she lied. She was nervous, confused, unsure. He eyed her closely. "Any regrets about last night?"

"No," she answered honestly. She didn't regret making love with him. How could she regret something so beautiful? So right? But it was obvious from his somber expression that Justin did have regrets. "What about you? Do you regret what happened?"

The smile he gave her was fleeting. "Not making love to you. What you gave me...it was a wonderful and special gift, Kim. But what I do regret was not being more gentle that first time. I'm sorry I hurt you."

"I told you, you didn't hurt me." When he arched his brow in disbelief, she conceded, "Well, it only hurt a little and just for a moment."

"Thank you for that," he said softly.

"It's the truth," she told him, and tried to decipher the reason for the worry line that creased his brow. She'd worked too closely with him during the past six months not to recognize that something was bothering him. "Are you sure you don't regret what happened between us, Justin?"

His expression softened, and he stroked her cheek with the same tenderness he had exhibited when he'd bathed her last night. "I'm sure. I'm just wishing I hadn't been so out of my head with desire for you that I didn't use any protection the first time we made love."

"Oh."

"'Oh' is right," Justin responded. "Even if you're on birth control pills, using protection would have been the smart thing to do."

Especially since she wasn't on the pill, Kim added in silence. Suddenly the repercussions of last night hit her like a dash of cold water in the face. The room spun. Justin's voice echoed through her head. All she could think of was her mother. How Amanda Lindgren had ended up pregnant and alone because her lover hadn't loved her. How the man who had fathered her hadn't even been free to love her mother because he was already married. An image of herself alone and pregnant flitted through Kim's mind. She sat up, hugged the sheet around her breasts.

"Kim?" Justin cupped her shoulders and gave her a tiny shake. "Kim, sweetheart, what is it?"

She met his eyes, registered his concern. "I'm not on the pill."

Justin's gaze shifted from her face to her abdomen, then back to her eyes. "You...if we..." he whooshed out a breath. "If there's a baby because of last night, you have my word that I'll take full responsibility for you and our child."

It had never occurred to her that Justin would be anything less than honorable. But as much as she loved him, the last thing she wanted was a relationship with him based on obligation. Feeling far too vulnerable with only the sheet as protection, Kim reached for the robe lying on the floor beside the bed. She slipped it on and walked over to the window and stared out at the blue sky.

"Kim?" Justin said from behind her. He turned her around to face him. "I meant what I said. I'll take care of you and the baby if there is one. So please don't worry that you'll be alone, because you won't."

"I know that. And I'm not worried. Really I'm not. Last night...well, it was a safe time for me. The chances of my getting pregnant...well, they're slim." She fibbed and prayed it was the truth.

"Slim or not, it's still a possibility," Justin reminded her. "In the future I promise to be more responsible about using protection."

Talk of pregnancy and the future stripped away any illusions she'd harbored, and sobered Kim as nothing else could. She knew in that moment that she could never settle for an affair with Justin, and an affair was all that he was offering. "Actually, I'm not sure continuing this is a good idea."

Justin dropped his hands from her shoulders. "What are you saying? You said you didn't regret last night."

"I don't. Last night was wonderful. But it wasn't smart for either of us. I think the wise thing to do is forget last night ever happened."

Justin's eyes hardened. "I'm afraid that isn't going to be possible. You see, I made love with *you* last night—not just a warm body. And contrary to what you obviously believe, I don't just hop into bed with a woman and forget about it. Considering the fact that you were a virgin until last night, I know damn well it's not something you do on a regular basis, either. So don't insult both of us by insinuating that last night didn't mean anything. Because it did."

"Of course it meant something to me," she retorted. Moving past him, she pressed her lips together tightly and blinked hard to keep back the tears burning behind her eyes. When she had regained control of herself, she turned to face him. "I care about you, Justin. And it's obvious that I'm attracted to you. That we're attracted to each other."

"So what's the problem?"

"The problem is that sooner or later an affair has to end. And when it does, things can get messy." She held up her hand when he started to speak. "I love my job. I love working with you. Having an affair would jeopardize that."

"How?" Justin asked.

"Because when the affair's over, it would be impossible for us to go on working together."

"Who says it has to end?" he argued.

"It would."

He moved closer, tucked a strand of hair behind her ear. "I care about you, Kim."

Kim's heart ached because she knew what he said was true. He did care about her. He just didn't love her. And it was his love that she wanted. "Then don't ask me to risk losing what I value most—your friendship and my job. Because that's what I'd be doing. Can't we just go back to the way things were before last night?"

"Is that really what you want? To forget last night ever happened?"

"That's what I want," she said, even though she knew she would never be able to forget last night or how much it had meant to her.

"All right," Justin said, and there was such desolation in his voice, in his eyes, that for a moment Kim thought she might actually have hurt him. "I'll try to do what you've asked."

"Thank you."

"Don't thank me yet. I said I'd try. That doesn't mean I'll succeed."

"I understand," Kim replied.

"Then you should also understand that if you're pregnant, all bets are off. And there's no way you'll be able to keep me out of your life or our baby's life."

Everything Kim had said made sense, Justin reminded himself as he sat at the dinner table at his parents' Lake Shore home more than a week later. The fact that he and Kim worked together made a romantic involvement between them potentially messy. One of the larger textile importers in the country, Connelly Corporation was like a small city unto itself—which meant people talked—and among their favorite topics was the Connelly family members and their personal lives. So a personal relationship with him would only subject Kim to gossip. He didn't want that.

No, a boss-employee relationship simply wasn't smart, Justin told himself again. For proof of that fact he had only to look to his brother Seth and the slights he had suffered because his mother had been Grant Connelly's secretary. Kim had been right to call a halt to things between them. She'd been right to insist they forget about that night at the cottage and what had happened between them. That was why he had respected her wishes, done what she'd asked and firmly closed that door.

And it wasn't working worth spit.

Disgusted, Justin closed his fist around the stem of his wineglass and admitted the truth. He hadn't been able to forget a minute of that day and night he'd spent with Kim. He couldn't look at her without remembering how beautiful she'd looked by firelight with her hair flowing down about her shoulders like silk, with her head tipped back and her cheeks flushed, with that look of utter wonder on her face as she'd ridden him. Nor could he forget how soft her skin had felt, how she had trembled when he'd touched her, how perfectly her body had fitted with his. And if he lived to be a hundred, he didn't think he would ever be able to forget how sweet her lips had tasted or the way he had felt when she'd climaxed and cried out his name.

Dammit! Justin slammed down his glass on the table. This business of pretending nothing had happened between him and Kim wasn't working.

"Is there a problem with your wine, Justin?"

Justin yanked his gaze to the end of the table at the sound of his father's voice, and only then realized that everyone at the table had gone silent. All eyes were fixed on the glass he held in a death grip. A quick scan revealed he had come dangerously close to spilling wine on his mother's lace tablecloth. "No, sir. The wine is fine," he told his father and to prove it, he took a sip of the merlot. "I'm sorry. My mind was somewhere else."

His father frowned, deepening the creases in his tanned face. "You've seemed distracted quite a lot lately. Is there a problem at the office?"

"Nothing I can't handle, sir."

When his father started to pursue that line of questioning, Emma Connelly placed her hand on her husband's arm.

"Leave the boy alone, Grant. If Justin said it's nothing to worry about, then there's nothing to worry about. We have more pressing problems than Connelly Corporation."

Justin knew at once that his mother was referring to the assassination attempt on his brother Daniel several months ago. Noting the worried expression on his mother's face, Justin felt a rush of guilt that he'd been so wrapped up over his own dilemma concerning Kim that he'd barely given his older brother's situation a thought. So he paid attention now when his mother focused her sad blue eyes on his brother Brett's wife, Elena, who had been the police detective called in to investigate the attempt on Daniel's life.

"Elena, dear, I know this isn't the appropriate time or place, and it probably goes against your regulations as a police detective, but can you tell me if you've been able to turn up anything new in your investigation?"

"I'm afraid not. While we're sure whoever tried to kill Daniel was a pro, so far we haven't been able to come up with any solid leads on who contracted the hit. I'm sorry. I wish I had better news."

Grant tossed down his napkin and leaned forward, a forbidding expression on his face. Despite his sixty-five years, there was no mistaking the determination and presence of power he wore like a mantle. His father still possessed the same air of invincibility that had enabled him to found the Connelly dynasty, Justin thought. "This is taking too long. I want the person or persons responsible for trying to kill my son found," Grant informed his daughter-in-law.

"That's what we all want," Elena told him, and Justin gave her credit for not flinching under Grant's granite gaze. "This case has been given top priority, Grant. We're doing everything we can to find them."

"We know you are, dear," Emma said, taking some of the sting out of her husband's words. "Don't we, Grant?"

His father covered Emma's hand that lay on his sleeve. When he looked up again, his steel-gray eyes had softened. "Yes, we know you're doing everything possible, Elena. I'm sorry if I sounded like I believed otherwise. I just don't like knowing that there's someone out there who's willing to go to such lengths to eliminate one of my children."

"I understand," Elena told him.

"Find out who's responsible and stop them, Elena. Please."

"We will," Elena promised. She slanted a glance to her husband, Brett, who sat beside her, and Justin tried to decipher the look that passed between them. "I was going to wait until tomorrow to tell you this in my official capacity, but I don't see any point in waiting now. Because of my pregnancy and the direction this case is taking, I've decided to turn the investigation over to a colleague of mine named Tom Reynolds and his partner Lucas Starwind."

"Is there anything wrong with the baby?" Emma asked.

"No. But Brett and I don't want to take any chances," Elena explained, and Justin recalled his brother telling him that prior to this pregnancy, Elena had suffered two miscarriages.

"These detectives—Reynolds and Starwind—are they as good as you?" Grant asked.

"Tom's first-rate. He's the one who showed me the ropes when I joined the police force. I'd trust him with my life."

"And Starwind?" Grant prompted.

"Him I don't know much about. But he's Tom's partner, and according to Tom he's good. Real good. And that's a direct quote from Tom, who's known for being flat-out stingy when it comes to handing out praise," Elena explained. "I have every confidence that between the two of them, they'll find out who's behind the attempt on Daniel's life."

"Then we'll trust them to put an end to this nightmare, too," Emma declared. "The important thing for you is to take care of yourself and our future grandchild."

"Don't worry, she will," Brett offered. "I'll see to that."

Justin stared at his younger brother and Elena, saw a look pass between them. He'd seen that same look before between his parents and grandparents—an unspoken communication that signaled they were one. Justin's gaze dropped, and he noted the way Elena's and Brett's joined hands rested on her swollen stomach.

Once more Justin's thoughts turned to Kim, and he recalled his shock upon realizing they had used no form of protection that first time they'd made love. Despite Kim's claims, there was a possibility she could be pregnant with his child.

And if she was?

The idea didn't shake him nearly as much now as it had earlier. All right, he told himself. He'd tried things Kim's way, and it wasn't working, for either of them, if those dark circles he'd seen under Kim's eyes meant anything. So maybe it was time to try things his way.

Eight

"**W**orking late again, Kim?" Dina Dietrich asked as she stood at the elevator with several other members of the clerical staff who were leaving for the day.

"Just for a few minutes," Kim replied, and silently cursed her luck. Another five minutes and she would have missed Dina. While she got along well with most of her co-workers, there were a few females who were much too catty for her taste. And Dina Dietrich was the worst. Ever since she had lost out to Kim on the position as Justin's assistant, she never missed the chance to make some snide remark or try to embarrass her in front of the other employees. "As soon as I finish up these memos for Mr. Connelly, I'll be on my way."

"Oh, I didn't realize that Justin still expected you to call him Mr. Connelly," Dina said, the sly look in her eyes belying her innocent tone.

Kim bit back her temper at the innuendo—one of several

she'd endured since Robert Marsh had "accidentally" mentioned that she had gone sailing with Justin. From what her friends had told her, Marsh's spin on the bachelor auction was that Kim had emptied her savings account to make the winning bid. According to Marsh, the reason Kim seldom dated was because she'd set her sights on marrying rich. And who fit that bill better than a Connelly? The sailing date was supposedly the first step in her grand scheme to land Justin. Despite Marsh's denials when she'd confronted him, Kim didn't doubt for a minute that he was behind the gossip. The tale had made her the center of office scuttlebutt for more than two weeks. And a prime target for Dina. Determined not to take the bait, Kim kept her voice level and said, "No, he doesn't expect me to call him Mr. Connelly. I do so out of respect since he's my boss."

Obviously aware that she was playing to an audience, Dina made a show of scanning the area for eavesdroppers before lowering her voice conspiratorially and asking, "Come on, Kim. You don't really expect me to believe that you spent the weekend with the man and didn't even call him by his first name, do you?"

"The truth is, Dina, I don't really care what you believe," Kim said, gripping the files she held tightly to stop her hands from trembling with anger. She met the sultry brunette's green eyes. "But if I were you, I'd think twice before spreading gossip about Justin Connelly. While you may find it amusing to make insinuations about my reputation and character, I doubt that the Connellys would find it amusing if they were to discover you've been making disparaging innuendos about one of its family members. Someone who not only happens to be a vice president of this company, but who also happens to be your boss."

For once Dina remained speechless. And had the floor

not been carpeted, Kim was sure she would have been able to hear a pin drop. The ding of the elevator, announcing its arrival, echoed loudly in the silence. Choosing that moment to make her exit, Kim said, "Have a good evening." Without waiting for a response, she turned and headed for her office.

Once she was alone, all the fury she'd held in check came rushing to the surface. Kim slapped the folders she'd been holding on top of her desk. It was all Robert Marsh's fault, she fumed. She curled her hands into fists at her sides. For two cents she would gladly wring the man's neck. Feeling as though she was about to explode, she closed her eyes and silently counted to ten in an effort to calm down.

When counting to ten didn't work, she started over and went to twenty. Twice. Seventeen. Eighteen. Nineteen. She ran through the numbers again in her head, but to no avail. It wasn't helping. Frustrated and still angry enough to chew nails, she kicked her chair, pretending it was Robert Marsh's head.

Kim yelped as pain radiated up her leg, and she grabbed her foot.

"You have a disagreement with the chair?"

Kim nearly groaned at the sound of Justin's voice behind her. Feeling like an idiot, she released her aching foot, and turned to face him. "My foot slipped," she offered, unable to come up with any reasonable excuse for pounding on the company's furniture.

While he didn't call her on the fib, he slanted a glance downward to where she was rubbing her aching toe against the back of her calf. "You probably bruised your toe. Why don't I have a look and—"

"No," Kim fired back, and retreated a step. Swallowing past the panic, she said more calmly, "I mean, my foot's fine. Really. If you're looking for those memos on the Ge-

nome Project, I have them right here for your signature.''
Turning away from the questions in his hazel eyes, she
retrieved the file folder containing the transcribed memos
from her desk. Then she handed it to Justin.

He hesitated a moment. There was something sad and
vulnerable in his expression before he took the folder she
offered. ''Thank you,'' he said, and retreated into his office.

For several moments Kim stood there, staring after him.
That couldn't have possibly been hurt in Justin's eyes when
she'd shied away from him, could it? No, she told herself.
More than likely it was disappointment because the great
sex—or at least she thought it had been great—would not
be repeated. And if she felt some disappointment of her
own at the decision, she reminded herself it was best to
end things now. Otherwise she stood a good chance of falling into that hopeless trap of believing that Justin might
actually love her someday the way she loved him. She'd
spent too many years watching her mother spin dreams of
happily-ever-after only to come crashing down when they
didn't happen. She wouldn't put herself through that same
torture. No, it was best to deal in reality. And the reality
of the situation was that she and Justin were not going to
happen. Besides, she had enough on her plate now without
adding impossible dreams to it.

Kim glanced at the open calendar on her desk and felt
that tiny flutter of panic. She was now nearly three weeks
late for her menstrual cycle—and she'd never, ever been
this late before. She worried her bottom lip and recalled
the fib she'd told Justin about it being a safe time for her.
She prayed her words wouldn't come back to haunt her.

''Kim, I have a few more minor changes,'' Justin said
as he came up behind her. ''I'd appreciate it if you'd make
them before you leave.''

''Be glad to.''

"And when you're finished, I'd like to take you to dinner. If you're free this evening."

"Thanks, but I'm afraid I already have plans for this evening." So maybe doing her laundry wasn't exactly what he thought she meant, but she did have to do it.

"What about tomorrow?"

"I'm going to be busy."

"Sunday?" he countered, his mouth going flat.

"Tied up. Now if you'll excuse me, I'd better get these changes done or I'll be late."

"All right," he conceded. "But sooner or later you and I are going to talk. You can't go on avoiding me forever."

Kim did manage to avoid him—or at least avoid talking to him—for most of the next week, thanks in large measure to an unexpected emergency that had taken Justin back to New York. When he returned on Friday, he'd been in a bear of a mood and so busy she'd had little trouble avoiding any personal conversation. She watched the clock on her desk, noted the hands edging just past five o'clock. This had nothing to do with being a coward, Kim assured herself as she gathered up the mail and notes and headed for Justin's office. She would dump his messages and correspondence on his desk while he was still on the phone and get out the door before he even knew she was gone. Bracing herself, she tapped lightly on his door and prayed her luck would hold out a little longer.

She stepped inside his office, and Justin hung up the phone. Kim knew at once that her luck had run out. "I have a few messages for you, the letters you dictated and the financial reports you wanted." Quickly dispensing with the items, she said, "If there's nothing else, I'm going to call it a day."

"Actually, I'd like you to bring me up to speed on several projects. Would you mind staying a few minutes longer?''

Kim hesitated but saw no way around it. ''No problem,'' she said, and took a seat across from him. For the next fifteen minutes Justin went over routine business matters and projects, and Kim began to relax.

''What about that problem we had a while ago with the computer system? That technician Charlotte Masters hired seems to have done a good job. Everything running okay?''

''Yes. Everything seems to be running smoothly now,'' Kim assured him.

Justin nodded. ''Is there anything else we need to cover?''

Kim glanced at her notes, then back up at him. ''No. You should be up to speed on everything in the department now.''

''Good.'' He put down his pen, sat back in his chair and stared at her. ''Now we can talk about us.''

Kim's stomach fluttered. ''Us?''

''Yes, Kim. Us,'' he said, an edge in his voice. He sat forward. ''As in you and me. Or maybe you've done such a good job of pretending nothing happened between us that night in the cottage that you've forgotten we were lovers.''

''Hardly,'' Kim shot back, not bothering to hide the irony of his claim. Since she was now nearly four weeks late, she might have an even more tangible reminder of that night.

Evidently reading something in her expression, Justin's eyes widened. ''Kim, What are you saying? Are you…?'' His gaze dropped to her belly, then shot back to her face. He stood, started around the desk. ''No wonder you haven't been yourself. Sweetheart, you should have told me. I promised you that if you became pregnant, I'd take responsibility. And I will. All you had—''

His words swiped at Kim's heart. She rushed to her feet. "First off, there's no reason for you to panic, because I don't know whether I'm pregnant or not," Kim told him, reasoning it was true since she'd yet to take a pregnancy test. "And second, if I am pregnant, I have a generous employer who provides an excellent salary and benefits, so I'm quite capable of taking care of myself and a baby if it comes to it. And third," she ticked off her finger as temper took hold. "I'm not out to trap you into a relationship you don't want. So there's no need for you to worry on that score."

"Are you finished?" Justin asked her, his voice deadly soft, his expression inscrutable.

Refusing to be intimidated, she jutted out her chin and met his hazel eyes. "Yes."

"Then let me set you straight on a few things. First off, I never panic. Second, I know Connelly's salaries and benefits are generous, since I had a hand in drawing them up. And third," he said menacingly as he caught her by the shoulders and pulled her to within a breath of him, "I'm not the one who needs to be worried about getting trapped into a relationship I don't want. You are."

And before she could even think of a response, Justin kissed her. His mouth was hard, angry, demanding. When his tongue demanded entry, she didn't even try to resist. She opened to him. Someone moaned. Kim didn't know if it was her or Justin. All she knew was that she was drowning in sensation, in the need for more. No longer innocent, her body knew the joys of making love with this man and responded accordingly. She roped her arms around him, took and demanded, even as she gave. When she felt the weight of his arousal pressed against her belly, an answering need throbbed inside her.

He lifted his head and speared his fingers through her

hair, loosening the pins. "Kim, I—" Suddenly, Justin stilled. He dropped his hands to her shoulders.

"Justin, what is it?"

"Shh." He pressed his fingers to her lips and looked past her toward the door.

Kim turned slightly, stared in the direction that had caught his attention, and she noted that the door had been left ajar. But as far as she could tell, they were alone. She shifted her gaze to him and waited for him to explain.

"I thought I saw someone at the door," he said as he released her and walked over to the door to investigate.

Kim thought of the kiss they had just shared, and instinctively, she reached up and smoothed a hand over her hair. She nearly groaned as she imagined Dina Dietrich or one of her cohorts getting an eyeful of her kissing Justin. Considering her conversation with the other woman just a short time ago, she knew the office rumor mill would have a field day.

"I don't see anyone," Justin told her when he returned to her side. "We need to talk, Kim. But I'm supposed to be meeting Marsh in a few minutes."

The mention of Robert Marsh sobered Kim. He was the last person she wanted to have find her alone with Justin, her hair mussed and her lipstick ruined. "I'll get out of your way."

"You're not in my way, and you and I have some unfinished business to discuss," he told her, and gave her a quick, hard kiss. "Personal business," he clarified. "But I could be a while with Marsh. I'll call you later."

He didn't ask if he could call her, simply told her he intended to do so, Kim noted. But before she could call him on it, there was a tap at his door and Robert Marsh was sticking his head inside.

"Am I interrupting?" he asked, flashing them a smile

that Kim thought was as slick and phony as the man himself.

"I was just leaving," Kim replied coolly and started past Marsh toward the door. "Good night, Justin."

"Here, let me get that for you," Marsh said politely, and opened the door for her.

"Thank you," she murmured.

"My pleasure," he told her.

One look at the gleam in his eyes and Kim's stomach knotted like a fist. Marsh had seen her kissing Justin. She knew it in her heart. She could only hope that he hadn't also heard their conversation.

"Hi, this is Kim. I'm not able to come to the phone right now. Leave a message and I'll get back to you."

Justin slammed down the telephone. Shoving his hands through his hair, he paced the length of his apartment. Where in the devil could she be? he asked himself as he stared out the window and watched the sun begin its descent in the sky. He considered driving by her apartment again, but nixed the idea. He'd driven by twice yesterday and once today already. And it was the memory of his last attempt to see her that ate at him now.

He scrubbed a hand down his face as he recalled the scene a few hours ago.

He'd hit the buzzer on the door repeatedly, and when she hadn't answered, he'd rapped on the door. "Come on, Kim. Open the door." Frustrated by the game she was playing, he'd knocked again and told her, "Sweetheart, I saw your car parked outside, so I know you're in there."

"No, she's not."

Justin had spun around to see a pair of faded brown eyes in a weathered face watching him through the crack between the door and the safety chain. Despite the woman's orange-colored hair and rouged cheeks, Justin made her to be seventy if she was a day. Realizing that he was staring, he cleared his throat and said, "I was trying to reach Kim. I'm sorry if I disturbed you."

"You didn't disturb me," she said matter-of-factly. "But, like I told you, Kim's not home. She left early yesterday morning."

Uneasiness coiled in his gut at that news. Since he knew Kim had no family, he couldn't help wondering where Kim had gone that she would have left her car. And why had she gone when she'd known he'd wanted to see her? Because she wanted to get away—from him. Deciding his best hope of finding her was the little old lady sizing him up, he tried turning on the charm. "I'm Justin Connelly," he said. "Kim's my assistant."

"I'm Lucille Brown."

He flashed her a smile. "A pleasure Ms. Brown. I was wondering, do—"

"It's Miss," she informed him. After releasing the safety chain, she opened the door wider to reveal a tiny woman in a bright green running suit. She smiled at him. "I'm still waiting for Mr. Right to come along."

Justin cleared his throat. Given her age, he suspected that Mr. Right had come and gone some time ago. "Um, Miss Brown—"

"You can call me Lucy," she told him, and batted her eyelashes at him.

"Um, Lucy, would you happen to know where Kim went?"

"She said she was going to spend the weekend at the beach with her friend."

"Her friend," Justin repeated, more to himself than to Lucy, as he tried to remember if there was anyone in particular that Kim gravitated to among the office staff. "Did Kim happen to mention the name of this friend?"

"No, but it was the same young man who came by for her a couple of weeks ago."

Justin's blood iced, then ran hot in his veins.

"Whoever he is, he's a good-looking one. Almost as tall as you, with nice, tight buns."

Justin nearly choked. "Thanks, Lucy," he murmured and made his exit.

Several hours later jealousy was like a beast clawing inside him. The idea of Kim with someone else, with another man kissing her, touching her as he had, put blood in his eye. He needed to beat something or someone, Justin decided. Preferably the man who was with Kim. But since he didn't know who the guy was yet, he'd settle for picking a fight with one of his brothers. Every one of the Connellys was good with his fists. He'd never known any of them to shy from a fight, particularly if goaded properly. Since he possessed the same quick temper, it shouldn't be too difficult to get the fists flying, he reasoned. And maybe if he was busy pounding on one of his brothers and being pounded on in return, he wouldn't have time to think about Kim. And whom she was with, or what she was doing with him.

Snatching up his car keys, Justin headed for Brett's house.

"All that baiting wasted," Justin complained as a smiling Brett and Elena waved goodbye. For a moment, there, he'd been sure Brett was going to take a swing at him. Then Elena had come in, showing him some things she'd picked up for the baby, and his tough, take-no-prisoners brother had turned into a marshmallow.

"Disgusting," Justin muttered as he pointed his Jeep to-

ward Seth's. Seth was who he should have gone to in the
first place, Justin decided. Seth was always up for a fight.
Probably because he was sensitive to the fact that his birth
had been the result of his mother's affair with their father.
While Justin might understand some of Seth's feelings of
not quite belonging, he couldn't honestly identify with
them. As far as Justin was concerned, Seth was a Connelly.
It didn't matter who had given birth to him, Emma Connelly considered him her son—and that was good enough
for Justin.

Didn't anyone stay home anymore? Justin wondered as
he put the Jeep into reverse and sped away from Seth's
place. He considered going to his brother Rafe's, then decided against it since he wasn't sure if Rafe was even in
town. Instead he opted for the gym—where he pounded on
the bag until his arms ached and fed his blood lust by
sparring with an up-and-coming professional boxer.

By the time he arrived at Connelly Corporation headquarters the next morning, Justin's mood matched the dark
shiner he sported on his left eye courtesy of yesterday's
sparring match. And it was in keeping with his string of
bad luck that the first person he saw was Brett.

Brett whistled. "That's a real beauty you've got there.
The shade almost matches your suit."

"You're a real comedian," Justin told him with a scowl,
and continued on to his office. He'd slept little the previous
night, imagining Kim with some unknown man. Finally in
the early-morning hours he'd chucked the line he'd been
feeding himself about feeling responsible for her because
he had been the one to awaken her passion. Responsibility
had nothing to do with the feelings churning inside him, he
admitted. He'd been flat-out jealous because he wanted
Kim for himself. A fact he intended to make clear to Kim
the first chance he got.

Only, he never got the chance until late that afternoon—thanks to a bout of flu that had swept through the office and left the clerical staff at half-force. His own pressing workload hadn't helped. Finally, near the end of the workday he got his chance, when Kim came in with a folder of documents requiring his signature.

As he began signing the documents, he was sharply aware of her nearness, her scent. "I tried to reach you this weekend," he told her.

"I know. I got your messages when I got home last night. By then it was too late to return your call."

"Did you and your friend have a nice weekend at the beach?" he asked, not bothering to hide his irritation.

Kim wrinkled her brow. "How did you know I'd gone to the beach?"

"Your neighbor Lucy told me."

"You spoke to Lucy?" Kim asked, her surprise evident.

"Yeah. When you didn't answer the phone, I thought you might be avoiding me. So I went over to your place. Imagine my surprise at learning that you and your boyfriend had gone away to the beach for the weekend."

"My boyfriend?"

"Dammit, Kim. Don't play innocent. Lucy told me he was the same guy who came by for you a couple of weeks ago. What I don't understand is if you were already involved with somebody, then why in the hell did you make love with me?"

Kim opened her mouth, closed it, and Justin watched in fascination as those blue-green eyes of hers turned stormy. She walked away from him, then turned back. "First off, I don't owe you any explanations, Justin Connelly."

"I know that, but—"

"Secondly, I was not and have not been involved with anyone except you."

He narrowed his eyes. "What about the guy with the tight buns?"

"The tight...Lucy," she said.

"That's right," Justin told her. "He made quite an impression on Lucy."

"*Every* man makes an impression on Lucy," Kim countered. "And in this case, the man happened to be the driver for the limo service your sister Tara uses. Evidently she requests a particular driver whenever she engages the service—such as the night of the auction and again this weekend when she invited me to join her at the beach."

"You were with my sister?"

"That's right. I called Tara to thank her again for inviting me to the fund-raiser. When she mentioned that she had some things she needed to handle for Alexandra's wedding and was searching for a sitter, I volunteered. So she insisted that I join them at the beach for the weekend. Since I didn't have any plans, I accepted."

Feeling like an idiot, Justin sank down in his chair. "Kim, I'm sorry. I thought—"

"I know exactly what you thought. Now if you'll excuse me, I have a ton of work to do."

Work proved to be a panacea. Because of the bout of flu that had hit the office, Kim stayed too busy the rest of the week to brood over the mess she'd made of her personal life and her relationship with Justin. She could only be grateful that business had kept Justin away from the office a great deal of the time and she'd managed to avoid any further encounters with him. What she could no longer avoid was the fact that she was seriously late for her menstrual cycle.

Opening the pregnancy-test kit she'd purchased the previous evening, she followed the directions. A short time later she held her breath as she checked the test strip for the results.

Pink.

She was pregnant.

Kim sank to the chair at her kitchen table as myriad emotions rushed through her. Excitement. Fear. Happiness. She was going to be a mother. She thought of Tara's little boy, recalled how good it had felt to hold him in her arms. Imagined how it would feel to hold her and Justin's child.

Justin.

She sobered as she thought of him. How was she going to tell him? What would he say? Maybe she didn't have to tell him. She and the baby could go away, start a new life somewhere else. Just as quickly she dismissed that notion. Justin deserved to know he was going to be a father, and their child deserved to know about him. She'd grown up without a father. No way could she put her own child in that situation.

Her head spinning, Kim took a deep breath. First things first, she decided. She needed to make an appointment with her gynecologist and have the pregnancy confirmed. Then she would decide how to tell Justin. A quick glance at the clock told her she'd have to hustle to make it to the office on time. She'd call and make an appointment the first chance she got.

The first chance she got didn't come until late that afternoon. "Doesn't Dr. Stevens have anything available tomorrow?"

"I'm sorry, Miss Lindgren, but Dr. Stevens doesn't have any openings until next week. If it's an emergency—"

"No. No, it's not an emergency. But would you take my name in case there's a cancellation? I'd really like to see her as soon as possible."

"Of course."

When she hung up the phone, Kim wondered how she was going to be able to wait until next week to find out if she was really pregnant. And how did one go about telling one of Chicago's wealthiest and most eligible bachelors that he was going to be a father? At the buzz of her intercom, Kim tried to quell her rising sense of panic and concentrate on getting through the rest of the day.

"I'll need you to make me five copies of the contracts and the exhibits for my meeting," Justin told her a short time later.

"I'll take care of it," Kim said, and started to leave.

"Kim, are you all right? You seem...distracted. If it's because of the things I said earlier this week, I've already apologized. And if you'd just let me—"

"Justin, I really don't want to get into this now," she told him.

He came around the desk, touched her shoulder. "I've been trying my best not to push you. But dammit, sooner or later we're going to have to deal with what's happening between us. It isn't going to go away."

"I know," she admitted. "But not now. Please."

"All right," he said, and released her.

Kim hurried out of his office, fearful she'd start blubbering and tell him everything if he kept being so nice to her. How could she accept his kindness when she was on the verge of turning his entire life upside down?

She made her way to the copy room on automatic pilot, scarcely aware that the office was nearly empty now. To her relief, so was the copy room. Grateful not to be forced to make small talk with anyone, she went about feeding the documents into the machine. Lost in thought, it took Kim a moment to register that the click she'd heard was the door to the copy room closing. She whipped around and spied

Robert Marsh standing in front of the closed door, a smirk on his face. "If you're waiting for the copier, I'll be finished in a minute," she said.

"Take your time," he said and moved toward her. "You know, Kim, you really ought to ditch those prissy little suits. After seeing your assets displayed so nicely at the charity auction, it seems a shame to hide them."

"When I want your fashion advice, I'll ask for it," Kim told him, and turned away. Eager to leave, she began gathering her documents from the sorter bins.

"I could give you a lot more than fashion advice," he said, his voice suddenly closer. "For instance, I bet I can satisfy a hot little number like you better than Justin Connelly can."

Kim flinched when she felt his hand brush her hair. Hugging the copies against her like a shield, she whirled around and said, "You put your hands on me again and I swear I'll break your fingers. Now get out of my way."

"What's the matter? My name's not Connelly so I'm not good enough for you? Well, I'm about to marry a Connelly, so that should be worth something."

"Get out of my way," Kim ordered again, not liking the angry glint in Marsh's eyes.

"Not until I sample some of what you've been giving to Connelly."

Suddenly realizing how vulnerable she was, Kim started to shove past him. Robert blocked her path. And when she took a step back, she came up against the worktable. The grin on Marsh's lips as he moved in turned Kim's stomach. "Back off," she ordered.

He grabbed at her. The papers she held scattered like confetti as Kim tried to pry his hands away from her face even as she aimed her knee where it hurt a man most. Robert dodged her attempt to cripple him with a well-directed knee. Laughing, he said, "You're feisty. I like that in a woman."

Angry and more than a little frightened, Kim groped the table behind her for a weapon and closed her fingers around the staple gun. When he came at her again, she wielded the weapon like a sword. "Back off, Marsh. Or I swear I'll use this on your head."

"You know, I think you just might," Robert told her, and swift as lightning he clamped his hand around her wrist and sent the stapler crashing to the floor.

Kim nearly whimpered at the pain in her wrist, but fear-induced adrenaline had her go at his face with her free hand. She raked her nails down the side of his face, had the satisfaction of him crying out.

"Why you little bi—"

And then Marsh was being yanked backward, his body slammed against the wall by Justin, who proceeded to smash his fist against Marsh's jaw.

Marsh swung out, grazed Justin near his eye. Justin barely flinched. Within moments Marsh's body grew limp. Justin whipped his gaze to Kim. "Did he hurt you?"

"No," Kim told him. "I'm all right. Let him go."

Finally Justin released him, and a moaning Marsh slumped to the floor. "Do you want to press attempted-rape charges?" he asked her.

"No."

"Consider yourself lucky, Marsh. Now get out of here before I change my mind and give you the beating you deserve," Justin told him.

Robert scrambled to his feet and swiped at his bloody nose. "I didn't try to rape her. She came on to me. She tried—"

Justin grabbed him by his shirtfront, got in his face and

said, "Shut up, Marsh. Shut up before I rip that lying tongue right out of your head and feed it to you."

"But, Justin—"

"I said to get out!" Walking over to the worktable, Justin grabbed the phone and punched the number for security. "This is Justin Connelly. Send someone up here to the copy room to escort Robert Marsh from the building."

"You can't do that," Robert objected when Justin hung up the phone.

"That's where you're wrong, pal. You see, I can do just about anything I damn well please."

Two security officers arrived at the door. "Mr. Marsh, if you'll come with us, please."

Marsh jerked his arms free. "You won't get away with this."

"Watch me. What do you think Alexandra is going to say when I tell her what happened in here tonight?"

Despite the blood oozing from his mouth, there was no mistaking the cockiness in Marsh's smile. "And just who do you think Alexandra is going to believe? The little gold digger who's sleeping with her boss? Or the word of the man she loves and is about to marry?"

Kim caught Justin's arm when he started for Marsh again. "Please, Justin, let him go. He's not worth it."

"Get him out of here," Justin told the officers.

And once they were alone, he closed his arms around Kim and held her.

Nine

"Justin?" Kim murmured against his chest.

"Give me a minute." He continued to hold her close, quelling the violence that had gripped him upon seeing Marsh manhandle her. When he finally had some measure of control over the emotions running rampant through him, he eased his hold on Kim. With a gentleness that belied the fury that he was struggling to hold in check, he cupped her face in his hands. "Are you really okay?"

"Yes," she whispered. "Your hand," she said, pulling them away from her face and looking horrified at his bruised knuckles.

"Forget about my hand," he said, and caught her fingers. "I want to know how long Marsh has been after you."

Kim lowered her gaze. "This is the first time he's ever tried anything physical," she admitted. "Until now, he's been content to spread rumors."

"Rumors?"

"About you and me. How I was out to trap you."

He tipped her chin up so that he could see her eyes. "Why didn't you tell me? I would have handled him. I could have put a stop to it. And you can bet that I'll have a talk with the staff and—"

"No. That would only make matters worse. Please swear you won't say anything."

"All right," he conceded. "But I don't like it. It's not fair to you."

"Maybe not, but ignoring the rumors is the best way to let them die down."

She was probably right, Justin reasoned. But it did nothing to alleviate his own guilt. "I'm sorry. For what Marsh did to you. For putting you in this position in the first place."

"It's not your fault. I made the decision to go on the sailing date with you, and I knew by going that I'd be leaving myself open to speculation."

"You went as a favor to me," he argued.

"I went because I wanted to go. I don't have any regrets, Justin. But maybe…maybe it would be better for everyone if I resigned."

"No," Justin said firmly.

"But what about Robert Marsh? And your sister?"

"I'll handle Marsh. And if my sister Alexandra has any sense, she'll dump the guy when I tell her what he's done."

"But—"

"I don't want you to go. I need you," he told her, panic swiftly replacing some of his earlier fury. "What would I do without you?"

"Justin, you'll have no problem getting another assistant and—"

"I want *you*."

Tears filled Kim's eyes, and she turned away, but not before the first tear slid down her cheek. In all the time he'd worked with Kim, he'd never seen her cry. That he had caused her to cry now made him feel lower than the belly of a snake. "Please, don't cry. Sweetheart, whatever's wrong, I'll fix it," he promised as he turned her to face him.

She shook her head and the tears continued to fall. "Not even you can fix this."

"What is it?" he pleaded, hating to see her in such distress. When she still said nothing, he pressed. "Tell me. I promise there's nothing you can say that will shock me."

"I think I'm pregnant."

She'd shocked him, Justin admitted, and it took him a moment before he could regain command of his tongue. By then he had processed the information. "You said you 'think'. Does that mean you aren't sure?"

She nodded. "I did one of those over-the-counter pregnancy tests and it came back positive. I have an appointment with my doctor next week just to be sure. But I've never been this late before."

"We'll get married."

The words simply popped out, shocking him as much as they obviously had shocked Kim, given her expression.

"You can't be serious."

But he was serious, Justin realized. Suddenly it all made perfect sense to him. He had never been so tied up in knots over a woman the way he had been with Kim. He cared for her—more than he could recall ever caring for another woman. "Why not?" he responded. "It makes perfect sense. We like each other, enjoy each other's company. And we've already proven that we're sexually compatible. The fact that you're carrying my child is just one more reason why we should get married."

"I don't know," she hedged, a sadness in her voice that affected him far more deeply than her tears. "Marriage is a big step."

"So is having a child," he argued. "I don't want to be a part-time father, Kim. I want to be part of my child's life. And after what you told me about your own childhood, growing up without a father, I would think you'd want the same thing for our baby."

"I do," she said.

Even though Justin knew he hadn't been completely fair to use that particular argument, he'd done so because he realized that he honestly did want Kim as his wife. He tipped her chin up and said, "Marry me, Kim."

"I..." She looked away. "Why don't we wait until I see the doctor?"

"But—"

"Please, Justin. We need to wait."

"All right. But as soon as you see the doctor, we start making plans. I'd like us to get married as soon as possible."

Kim didn't respond to that. Instead she stepped back and made a show of looking at the scattered papers on the floor of the copy room. "Look at this mess. I'd better start clearing this up."

"Leave it," Justin ordered.

"But you'll need these for your meeting in the morning."

"I said leave it." Catching her arm, he urged Kim to her feet. "I'm going to take you home."

"That's not necessary."

"It's necessary for me," he informed her, guiding her out of the copy room. After retrieving her purse, he led her to the elevator.

"But what about my car?"

"I'll have it delivered. No more arguments, Miss Lindgren," he said, and silenced her with a quick kiss. "I'm taking you home."

* * *

Justin took her home and insisted on seeing her inside. And once he'd made it through the door of her apartment, he set about taking care of her. He fixed her tea, called and ordered Chinese takeout from a nearby restaurant. While they waited for the food to arrive, Kim suggested, "Let me look at your hand."

"It's fine."

But he allowed her to bathe his bruised fist. "Thank you for coming to my rescue tonight," she said as she swabbed ointment on the scrapes. "No one's ever fought for me before."

"If it hadn't been for me, you wouldn't have been in the situation to begin with. I ignored my instincts about Marsh. I let his relationship with Alexandra cause me to turn a blind eye to what my gut told me about the man."

She applied a bandage over the worst of the damage to his hand. "All done," she said. Glancing up, she found his eyes trained on her. He looked so intense, so fierce, Kim's pulse fluttered. "Does your eye hurt very much?" she asked as she put away the first-aid kit.

"Only when I breathe," he said, making her laugh.

The doorbell sounded, and Kim latched on to the distraction. "That, I believe, is dinner."

"You sit down," Justin told her. "I'll handle this."

He handled everything.

After lighting the candles on her coffee table, he spread out a feast of tempting dishes on the glass-topped table and escorted her to one of the cushions he'd removed from the couch. Sitting beside her, Justin insisted on teaching her to use the chopsticks.

Thirty minutes later she was still laughing at her own inability to master the two wooden sticks sufficiently. "I'll never get the hang of this," she confessed.

"Then I guess I'll just have to feed you," he told her.

Which he did. All the while Kim had the feeling she was

being seduced. There was something erotic and sexual about the way he'd feed her a bite, then take a taste himself. Even as her hunger for food became sated, new hungers sprang to life inside her. Not trusting herself, Kim held up her hand when Justin lifted the chopsticks to her lips with another bite of mandarin chicken. "No more. I'm stuffed," she told him. And her senses were on overload, too, she admitted.

"All right." He put down the chopsticks. "But you still need to have a fortune cookie." He chose one, handed it to her. "Go ahead. Open it."

Kim hesitated. As much as she hated to admit it, she was superstitious, and as a rule she shied away from things like fortune cookies, tarot cards and palm readings. "Why don't I save it for later?"

"You can eat the cookie later, but don't you want to at least read your fortune? Maybe you're going to find out there's this tall, auburn-haired fellow in your future," he teased.

Kim laughed. "You don't really believe these things, do you?"

He smiled and crossed his heart. "Absolutely. Now quit stalling and read it."

Kim broke the cookie in two and removed the slip of paper.

"Come on, read it to me," he said when she simply stared at the fortune.

She swallowed, then read the inscription, "'Great happiness awaits you.'"

"Sounds good to me," Justin said.

"What does yours say?" Kim asked, afraid to give much credence to the fortune but unable to stop herself from doing so.

"Let's see," Justin said, and removed the slip of paper from his cookie. "It says, 'A wise man turns chance into good fortune.' Makes sense to me.'' The teasing glint in his eyes died and was replaced by something darker, more intense. ''It doesn't take a wise man to know that your becoming pregnant and marrying me is going to prove to be my good fortune.''

''It's getting late,'' Kim said. She stood and began clearing away the remains of their dinner.

Justin sighed. ''I guess that's my cue to leave,'' he said, and helped her carry the paper cartons to the kitchen.

Once everything was cleared away, Kim walked him to the door. ''Thank you again for everything.''

''I'll see you in the morning,'' Justin told her, and before she could respond, he took her face in his hands and kissed her. ''Dream of me.''

Kim dreamed of him. That night, and the next. And when she wasn't dreaming of Justin, she was thinking of him.

If anyone questioned Robert Marsh's abrupt departure on out-of-town business so close to his wedding date, she didn't hear about it. Justin had claimed it was for his sister's sake that he'd kept quiet about what had happened that night. He didn't want Alexandra to hear of her fiancé's actions before she'd returned to town and Justin spoke with her personally. But Kim suspected that was only half-true. She suspected he'd also wanted to protect her.

In fact, he'd even used not trusting Marsh to come after her again as an excuse to spend time with her during the next several days. That's why it took her a while to realize that Justin had insinuated himself into her life as completely as he had. He took her to a ball game at Wrigley Field, determined to teach her the art of baseball. He showed up on a rainy evening with an armful of old movies and the makings for fresh popcorn. He cajoled her into flying a kite with him, and she'd dragged him through several museums. He'd wheedled her weakness for chocolate brownies out of her and had surprised her with some from her favorite bakery one morning. She'd discovered firsthand what a difference he'd made after meeting the boys he worked with at the youth center. She'd learned he was enthralled with anything sports-related and a sucker when it came to stray kittens. And the more time she spent with him, the more deeply she fell in love with him.

One day spun into another and yet another still. Being an only child, she had grown up accustomed to being alone, to not sharing her days and nights with someone. Justin had changed that. In the space of little less than a week, he had woven himself into her life until she'd come to expect him there. While he took care not to cross the line at the office, she'd catch him looking at her across a room in such a way that made her body go hot, made her want to forget what her head said and to listen to her heart.

When he kissed her good-night, Kim's body came alive, yearned for his touch. That he didn't attempt to make love to her again when it was obvious that he wanted her confused her as much as it reassured her. The only thing that had kept her from dragging him to bed herself was that Justin had never once said that he'd loved her. Sure he'd asked her to marry him, and he made no secret of the fact that he wanted her. She believed him when he said he respected her. And she didn't doubt his sincerity when he talked about the life they could have together, with their baby. But never once did he offer her what she wanted most—his love.

Kim stared at her desk calendar, noted she only had two more days before her doctor's appointment. Once she knew the pregnancy test had been accurate, she would need to give Justin an answer to his marriage proposal.

Maybe she could love him enough for both of them, she reasoned. He desired her. She didn't doubt that. Could desire turn into love?

The phone buzzed on her desk, jarring Kim from her deep thoughts. "Kim Lindgren," she answered.

"What are you still doing there?"

"Justin," she said, unable to keep the smile from her voice. "You've only had three calls since the last time you phoned me. Mr.—"

"I'm not calling for my messages. I'm calling to tell you to close up shop and get over to my place. Or did you forget I'm fixing you dinner tonight?"

"I didn't forget," she told him.

"Then shake a leg. I'm already missing you."

Justin hung up the phone and smiled to himself as he realized he'd told Kim the truth. Although he'd only been away overnight, the need to see her was like a fever in his blood. He didn't question it. He simply accepted it. Just as he simply accepted that he would be able to convince Kim to marry him.

He never doubted that for a moment, Justin told himself as he lit the candles on the table and turned on the music he'd selected. Once he'd dealt with that scumbag Marsh and waded through the roller coaster of emotions he'd experienced at finding out Kim was pregnant, he'd been able to logically approach the problem of convincing Kim to marry him. She loved him. In hindsight he had realized that fact. Kim was not the sort of woman who slept with a man unless her heart was involved. The way he saw it, her loving him was a point in his favor. The fact that she was pregnant with his child was another. And she wanted him as much as he wanted her.

Not making love to her this past week when he'd wanted to so desperately had been one of the most difficult things he'd ever had to do, Justin admitted. But when he made love to her again, he wanted it understood that they would soon be man and wife. Justin stood back, surveyed the scene. Satisfied, he patted his pants pocket for the ring box. Now all he needed was Kim.

At the sound of the doorbell, he smiled.

Justin was still smiling when they finished dinner, and he led Kim out onto the terrace. "Would you like a sweater?" he asked.

"No, I'm fine." She stood at the railing and looked up at the sky. "It's so beautiful."

"Yes, it is," he said as he joined her.

She slanted a glance at him. "I was talking about the sky."

"I was talking about you."

Kim flushed, then turned to look up at the sky again. "I don't think I've ever seen so many stars at one time before. And the moon. It's what my mother used to call a lover's moon."

The CD player clicked to another tune, this time something even softer, more romantic. Justin touched Kim's arm. "Dance with me."

She went into his arms. Justin didn't even question how right she felt there, how perfectly her steps matched his as he danced her around the terrace beneath the moonlight. When the song ended, it seemed the most natural thing in the world to kiss her. And when he lifted his mouth, looked down at her lovely face, he said, "Make love with me."

"Yes," she whispered.

Justin didn't hesitate. He scooped her up into his arms and carried her into his bedroom, where he lowered her to the bed. And slowly he began to undress her. Unlike the night at the lake cottage, there was no storm darkening their surroundings. He wasn't forced to view her through the shadowed light of candles. Tonight moonlight spilled through the opened window to mingle with the soft glow of the lamp from the bedside table, bathing Kim in an ethereal glow.

Because he knew the thrill that awaited him when he joined his body to Kim's, the desire to take her greedily and lose himself in her was even sharper than it had been that first time. Which made him all the more determined to go slowly now, to awaken Kim to the pleasure he could bring her, to brand her with the feverish need as she had branded him that first night.

So he took his time. He released the catch at the back of the dress she'd worn. Turning her around, he unzipped the floral silk inch by inch, kissing his way down her spine as he bared her flesh. When the dress fell in a puddle at her feet, he slid his arms around her and pulled her against him so that her rear was nestled against his hardness.

"Justin," she whispered, her voice thready, her breathing labored.

Keeping her back to him, he kissed her neck and slid his palms up from her midriff to just below her breasts. He opened the clasp at the front of her bra and, brushing the lace aside, he closed his palms over her breasts. Kim's whimper spiked his need and sent blood throbbing through his veins.

Justin plucked at the nipple of one breast while he smoothed his other palm down her belly. Her muscles quivered beneath his hand as he slid his hand beneath her panties and cupped her. He eased a finger inside to test her, and when he found her warm and moist and ready for him, his control began to fray.

"Justin, I..."

"Don't fight it. Take it," he commanded as he held her against him and stroked her, brought her to the peak, urged her to go over.

Sweat beaded across his brow as he took her up again, listened to her cries of pleasure, felt her convulse around his fingers. She reached behind her, fumbled with his zipper until she freed him. When she closed her fist around him, Justin groaned. Before he could catch his breath, she began to coax him. The feeling of her soft fingers rubbing his hot flesh against the silk of her panties was maddening. And when he didn't think he could wait another moment longer, he stripped away the silk barrier that separated them. Making a place between her legs for himself, he entered her from the rear.

He stilled at her gasp, fearful that he had shocked her. Then she shocked him by beginning to move slowly, encouraging him. Using his finger, he found that sensitive spot at her center again even as he continued to move in and out of her from the rear. He felt her body strain as he increased the tempo, and when she stiffened, then shuddered in release, the last thread of his control snapped and he followed her over the cliff.

Later, when he could think again, Justin looked over at Kim lying beside him in the bed and realized he had never felt this content before. It was as though being with her had filled some emptiness inside him that he'd been unaware had been there. She made him complete somehow. He thought about the baby and imagined the three of them building a life together.

And he realized he hadn't given her the engagement ring.

"Is something wrong?" Kim asked, obviously sensing the change in him.

"I was just thinking this isn't exactly how I planned for things to go this evening."

"No? I had the distinct impression when I arrived tonight and saw the candlelight and heard the soft music that this is exactly what you had planned."

Justin grinned. "Let me rephrase that. I wanted to make

love with you, hoped that we would make love. But I had something else I'd wanted to do first.''

"Something else?"

He laughed at the look in her eyes and gave her a swift kiss on the lips. "Not that. I bought you something today and I wanted to give it to you before we reached this stage in the evening.''

The laughter disappeared from her eyes. "You don't need to buy me gifts.''

"It's not exactly a gift. More like a promise.'' He groped the floor beside the bed for his pants and wrestled the box from the pocket. He held out the black velvet box to her. "Aren't you going to open it?''

Kim opened the box. "Oh, Justin.''

"If you don't like it or would rather a gold band instead of the platinum, we can change it.''

"No. It's beautiful. It's the most beautiful ring in the world.''

He removed the emerald-cut diamond from the bed of velvet. He took her left hand in his and looking into her eyes, he slid the ring onto her finger and said, "Marry me, Kim.''

"I...'' Tears welled up in her eyes. "Justin, I can't take this. At least not yet. We agreed we would wait until I saw the doctor and confirmed the pregnancy.''

"That's just a formality. We already know that you're pregnant with my child, and I'm asking you to be my wife,'' he argued.

"We still need to wait,'' she insisted. "I'm seeing the doctor the day after tomorrow. If he confirms I'm pregnant, then I'll marry you.''

When she started to remove the ring, Justin caught her fingers and closed them. "Keep the ring. Because you are going to marry me.''

Ten

She was dreaming.

Kim knew it was a dream, but smiled anyway as she imagined Justin's lips brush lightly across hers, felt his hand caress her hair. Keeping her eyes closed tightly, she stayed in bed and tried to hold on to the dream a few moments longer.

"I wish I could stay here with you, but I've got to go."

Kim snapped open her eyes and stared up into Justin's face. "You're real," she told him, touching his cheek.

He smiled and kissed her fingertips. "Sure am."

"I thought I was dreaming."

"Hmm. Was it a good one?" he asked, peeling the sheet away and exposing her bare breasts.

"Yes," she gasped as he took her in his mouth.

Lifting his head, Justin sighed, then he covered her. "Damn, I wish I could stay. But I've got over a two-hour drive ahead of me. If I don't leave now, I'll be late for my meeting.''

Kim glanced at the clock and, holding the sheet around her, sat up. As she did so, she felt a slight ache in her stomach and made a face.

"What's wrong?" Justin asked, concern darkening his hazel eyes.

"Just a little indigestion, I think. Must have been your cooking," she teased.

"You weren't complaining last night," he reminded her.

"I was being polite."

"A likely story. But since you're casting aspersions on my cooking talents, you can cook dinner tonight."

"All right," Kim conceded. "It's a date. But right now you need to go, and I need to get moving or I'll be late for work. I have a real slavedriver for a boss."

"Slavedriver, huh? Just for that, Miss Lindgren, be prepared to work a lot of overtime tonight when I get back." He kissed her again, then took her hand and stared at the ring he'd insisted on putting on her finger last night. "It looks good there."

"Yes, it does." It did look good on her finger, Kim thought, her heart swelling with love for him. When she glanced up and saw the glint in his eyes, she laughed. "Go."

"All right. I'm going. I'll call you later," he promised, and then he was gone.

Alone in Justin's apartment, Kim hugged the pillow to herself, breathed in his scent. She envisioned herself waking to Justin like this every day, sharing his bed, his home, his life.

She pressed her hand to her still-flat stomach, thought of the life growing inside her. Would he want more children with her? she wondered. She hoped so. She'd hated being an only child. And she could already imagine a little boy and girl with his auburn hair and her blue-green eyes. Smiling, she pulled back the covers, and the light reflected off the diamond in her ring. Kim stared at the ring on her hand, recalled the way Justin had looked at her when he'd put it on her finger and asked her to marry him.

The only thing that had been missing was him saying that he loved her. For a moment she felt an ache in her chest that he hadn't given her the words. Just as quickly she cut off the negative thoughts, refusing to allow anything to intrude on her happiness. Tossing aside the covers, she headed for the shower.

While she showered, she thought of Justin. So maybe he didn't love her the way she loved him, but he did care for her. She was sure of that. And they did have a baby to consider. Their child. It would be enough. It *was* enough, she amended. She would be a good wife to him, be a good mother to their child, Kim promised herself as she shut off the shower and slipped on Justin's robe and went in search of her clothes.

She found them scattered on the floor of Justin's bedroom. When she found herself reliving how her clothes had ended up on the floor, Kim laughed aloud at herself. Justin wasn't the only one in danger of running late this morning, she thought as she dressed and hurried out the door. Unless she planned to show up at Connelly Corporation wearing last night's dress, she needed to hustle to get to her apartment and change clothes before going to work. Feeling another twinge, Kim pressed her fingers to her middle. Evidently Justin's tomato sauce really hadn't agreed with her, she thought, and made a mental note to remember to grab a few antacid tablets from the medicine cabinet.

Kim headed for the medicine cabinet the moment she got home. She reached for the bottle of antacid tablets and, after reading the label to be sure it was safe to take during pregnancy, she popped a few into her mouth. While she chewed the chalky tablets, she quickly changed into a lightweight persimmon dress. Reaching for her hairpins, she started to put her hair up in its customary twist, then opted to leave it down instead.

Reluctantly she removed the ring from her finger and tucked it inside her purse. Even though the gossip had died down at the office, she knew there was no way the diamond on her finger would go unnoticed. Besides, she intended to accept Justin's proposal, but she had promised herself and him that she wouldn't do so until the pregnancy was official. Once it was, she would need to brace herself for the reactions at the office, she realized. Strangely, the thought of doing so didn't bother her nearly as much now as it had a short time ago. Grabbing her purse and keys, she headed off to work and prayed that by the time she arrived at Connelly headquarters those antacid tablets she'd taken would have begun to do their magic.

But they hadn't. Nor did the tablets she took when she arrived at the office. After an hour into her day, the slight twinges she'd experienced that morning had become a bellyache. Becoming alarmed, Kim made a trip to the ladies room. Her blood ran cold when she discovered she had begun to spot.

No, Kim told herself, as she fought back the panic that threatened to paralyze her. She'd read that pregnant women sometimes experienced some spotting. It didn't mean she was having a miscarriage. But fearful that she might be, she hurried back to her office and, after shutting the door, called the doctor.

"This is Kimberly Lindgren," she said. "I have an appointment to see Dr. Stevens tomorrow afternoon, but I need to see her today. Right away."

"Is this an emergency, Miss Lindgren?"

"Yes. Yes, it is. I'm...I'm pregnant. Or at least, I think I am, and I've begun to spot."

After answering several questions, she hung up the phone. As calmly as she could, she notified the receptionist that she was leaving and started for the doctor's office.

By the time she'd arrived at the medical complex, the spotting had become a warm flow of blood. Sobbing, she sat across the desk from Dr. Stevens following her exam. "You're sure it wasn't a miscarriage?" she asked the woman who had been her gynecologist for the past five years.

"I'm positive, Kim. There was no baby."

"But the pregnancy test I took..."

"They aren't always accurate. While they're right most of the time, occasionally they give a false positive reading. I'm afraid that's what happened in your case."

"But I was so late. And I've never been that late before," Kim explained. While she was glad there had been no miscarriage, she felt as though she had just lost her baby all the same.

"I can't give you a reason why this happened now, Kim. You said you've been under a great deal of stress, perhaps your cycle being late is your body's way of reacting to that stress." Dr. Stevens handed her another tissue.

"Thank you," Kim murmured, trying to get a handle on her emotions.

"From your reaction, I assume that had you been pregnant you would have wanted the child."

"Yes," Kim told her, knowing that the doctor was referring to her unmarried status. "I would have wanted it." Only now did she realize just how much she had wanted the baby, how much she had begun to think of it growing inside her.

"I'm sorry, then."

Kim nodded, wiped at her eyes.

"The good news is that you're a healthy young woman. There's no reason you can't conceive a child in the future."

"Yes, I'm sure you're right," Kim said, and stood. "Thank you for seeing me so quickly, doctor."

"Not a problem. Those samples I gave you should help with the cramping. If it doesn't, let me know and I'll phone in a prescription for you."

"Yes. Thank you again," Kim said. But she didn't think there was anything the good doctor could give her to ease the ache in her heart. As far as she knew, no one had yet discovered any magic pill to wipe away the pain of losing one's dreams.

Kim managed to find her car in the parking lot. Once she was inside, she rested her head against the steering wheel and began to cry.

She was still crying when she drove past Connelly Corporation headquarters and when she arrived at her apartment. She spied the flashing light on her answering machine and ignored it. She didn't want to speak to anyone. Not yet. Not when her pain was still so sharp.

Unable the bear the cheery sunshine spilling through the windows, Kim went from room to room and yanked closed all the drapes in the apartment. Then she retreated to her bedroom, where she turned off the telephone ringer and left her dress on the floor where it fell. She crawled beneath the covers, curled up into a ball and began to sob. She sobbed deeply, her chest shaking with the depth of her grief.

She grieved because there was no baby growing inside her, because there would never be Justin's baby growing inside her. She grieved for what the two of them might have shared and never would. And she grieved because there would be no Justin in her life. Not even from a distance as he had been before, because she couldn't possibly remain at Connelly Corporation now. As she thought of all the dreams that would never come true now, she continued to cry until there were no more tears left. And when the tears finally stopped, she slept.

When Kim awoke, the apartment was in total darkness and there was a pounding inside her head. Sitting up, she felt almost drunk, and it took a few minutes to orient herself. A glance at the bedside clock told her it was past eleven o'clock at night. She'd obviously crashed, Kim reasoned. No wonder since she'd gotten little sleep the previous night at Justin's place.

Justin.

Suddenly the memories came slamming back. Justin giving her the engagement ring, asking her to marry him. Then today, her finding out there was no baby, that she hadn't been pregnant at all. Pain sliced through her like a jagged blade, making her ache all over again.

The pounding started again, and she held her head. Finally she realized the pounding was at her door. Scrambling from the bed, she began flipping on lights and made her way to the front door.

"Kim!" Justin shouted, as he beat against her door.

"You sure you don't want me to call the police? That's what they do on the detective shows," Lucy Brown informed him.

"Lucy, I—"

Kim opened the door. "Justin? What on earth—"

Justin caught her by the shoulders and nearly lifted her off her feet. "Are you all right?"

Taken aback by the wild look in his eyes, it took her a moment to find her voice. "Yes," she finally managed, stunned to see him looking such a wreck. His tie was askew, stubble darkened his cheeks and his hair looked as if it had been styled with a pitchfork.

Before she could ask him what was wrong, he muttered, "Thank God." Then he pulled her into his arms and kissed her. The desperation in his kiss surprised her, because she couldn't imagine anything that would cause him such distress.

"I don't suppose there's any point in calling the police now," Lucy said.

Justin ended the kiss, but his eyes never left Kim's. "No, no point," Justin told the older woman. "Thanks, anyway. I think I've got things under control now."

"Looks like it to me," Lucy commented, then disappeared into her own apartment.

"Are you all right? Were you in some kind of an accident? Did something happen at the office? Is that why you left early?"

He fired the questions at her, and Kim wasn't quite sure where to start to answer. So she said, "I'm all right. And nothing happened at the office. Not the way you mean. I just needed...I needed to come home."

"But I called you here. I left at least half a dozen messages and then the machine stopped picking up. If you were here, why didn't you answer the phone?"

"You'd better come inside, Justin. We need to talk."

The knot that had formed in Justin's stomach when he'd called the office and learned that Kim had left early took on the proportions of a boulder. Now that the worst of his fears—that she'd been injured or in some terrible accident—had been dismissed, he could see that something else was wrong. Seriously wrong. Even without the benefit of growing up under the same roof with three sisters, he'd been in the world long enough to know that when a woman said "We need to talk," whatever it was she was going to tell him, he wasn't going to like.

He followed Kim inside, spied her purse and keys lying on the floor beside her shoes. She was always so neat and orderly, it seemed out of character for her. Just as her leaving the office early without any explanation had been totally out of character for Kim. Justin noted the droop in her shoulders as she walked over to the table and switched on the lamp. And that feeling that something terrible had occurred increased tenfold.

"I know it's late," she said, turning around to face him. "But would you like a drink? Or maybe some coffee?"

Justin strode over to her, tipped her face to the light and swore. Dark smudges lay like bruises beneath her eyes, and her cheeks were streaked from what he suspected were dried tears. "I don't want a drink or any coffee. I want to know what's wrong. What's happened?"

"I went to see my doctor today," she told him in a voice that seemed devoid of life.

His heart, already in a vise, suddenly felt as though someone had reached inside him and squeezed it even tighter. "Are you all right?" he asked, and led her to the couch to sit down, but continued to hold her hand. "Sweetheart, why didn't you tell me you were sick?"

"I'm not sick," she informed him, and tugged her fingers free.

He dropped his gaze to her stomach, noted the way she was hugging her arms around her middle. "The baby?" he asked, his heart in his throat. "Is something wrong with the baby?"

"There is no baby."

Justin felt as though he'd been coldcocked. A dozen different emotions hit him at once, savaged him. "Did you..."

He swallowed, worked through the red haze of fury and tried again. "Did you terminate it?"

Kim's head jerked up, and for the first time since he'd walked into the apartment, there was a spark of life in her eyes. "There was no baby. I was never pregnant."

"But the pregnancy test—"

"Was wrong," she said. "One of those one-in-a-zillion or whatever the figure is that's wrong. I'm not pregnant. I never was."

Stunned, Justin was barely aware of Kim standing and walking over to retrieve her purse from the floor. He continued to sit there on her couch as he tried to digest what she'd told him.

There was no baby. There never was a baby.

So why did he feel this sudden sense of loss?

Because he had begun to think of himself as a father, he realized. He had begun to think of himself as a husband— of him and Kim and their baby as a family.

"I was going to call you tomorrow and give you the good news. And return this."

Justin looked up to where Kim now stood before him, holding out the engagement ring he had put on her finger the previous night. He rose, looked into her eyes. "Is it good news, Kim?"

"Sure," she said. "You offering to marry me when I thought I was pregnant...it was very noble of you, Justin. A lot of men in your position wouldn't have been willing to take responsibility and sacrifice their freedom. It meant a great deal to me that you were willing to. But now," she said, her voice catching, "it's not necessary. So I'm returning the ring."

It was that catch in her voice and the shimmer of fresh tears in Kim's eyes that gave Justin hope. He stood, but made no attempt to take the ring she held out to him. "I thought you liked the ring."

"I did. I do," she amended.

"Then why are you giving it back?"

She squinched her brows together the way she did when she was trying to work out a puzzling problem. "Didn't you hear me? There's no reason for us to get married now."

"Sure there is. When two people love each other, when they want to spend the rest of their lives together, getting married is generally what they do. At least that's what my parents did. And I figure if it's good enough for them, it's good enough for us."

"You love me?"

"Yes," Justin told her, realizing it was true. "And unless I'm mistaken, you love me, too. Don't you?"

Kim nodded.

Taking the ring from her, he took her hand. "So will you marry me, Kim Lindgren? Will you be my family? Make babies with me? Grow old and gray with me?"

"Yes," she told him.

He slid the ring onto her finger, kissed it. "I love you, Kim."

"And I love you," she said, and offered her mouth to him.

Justin kissed her deeply with all the love in his heart. And when he lifted her into his arms and asked her where the bedroom was, she showed him.

Much later as he lay in bed with the woman he loved in his arms, Justin's stomach grumbled. "That reminds me. You still owe me dinner."

Laughing, Kim raised herself up on one elbow. "I seem to recall offering to fix you a snack a few hours ago, and you insisted all you needed was to hold me, that you didn't need food.''

''What can I say? My heart says one thing, but my stomach says another. Right now the stomach is winning the battle, and it's none too happy that I skipped dinner.''

''You never did say what happened that caused you to be so late.''

Justin frowned. ''Alexandra came back to town this evening, and I went by to see her.''

''You told her about Robert.''

''Yes,'' Justin said, his jaw tightening as he thought of the other man.

''She must have been devastated.''

''She was upset. I mean, she has to feel like a fool, seeing how Marsh has been using her.''

''I can't even begin to imagine how she must feel,'' Kim told him. ''She must be terribly hurt.''

''I guess. But I'm not sure if it was her heart that hurt so much as it was her pride.''

''Did she say what she's going to do?''

''I know what she should do,'' Justin informed her. ''She should dump him and be grateful she found out what a low-life he is before she married him.''

''But I take it that's not what Alexandra plans to do.''

Justin sighed. ''She said she wanted to talk to Marsh first before she makes any decision.''

''Well, you'll know soon enough. The wedding is only three days away.''

''Two,'' Justin corrected, and pointed to the window where the sun was beginning its rise. He looked at Kim, thought of the new life they were beginning. ''I'd like you to come with me this morning and tell my parents our news. And as much as I want to shout out to the world that you're going to be my wife, we probably should wait until we see what Alexandra is going to do first.''

"Justin, how do you think your parents are going to feel about this? About us?''

"Sweetheart, they're going to love you as much as I do.''

Justin had been right, Kim realized as Emma and Grant gave her a hug the next evening upon their arrival at the family's Lake Shore home. His parents had seemed thrilled over their engagement when they'd told them the news the previous day. But not wanting to steal any of the limelight from their daughter, they had agreed with Kim and Justin to keep the news quiet until after Alexandra's wedding.

"I can't believe she's still going to marry the guy,'' Justin told Kim as he brought her a glass of wine. "You'd think that after I told her what he tried to do to you she'd have given him the boot. Instead she's going to marry him tomorrow. There's got to be something I can do to make her see it's a mistake.''

"You've done everything you can. It's your sister's decision, Justin. Not yours.''

"Yeah. Well, I'm tempted to have the guy shanghaied and shipped to Daniel in Altaria so she can't marry him.''

Kim placed a hand on his arm. "Your brother Daniel has enough worries.''

"You're right,'' Justin said, and squeezed her fingertips. "Have I told you lately that I love you?''

"Not in the last five minutes.''

Emma came over to them. "I can hardly wait to tell Lilly and Tobias your good news,'' she told them.

"I hope they'll be pleased,'' Kim said, somewhat nervous at the prospect of telling Justin's grandparents about their engagement.

"They'll be thrilled. Just as Grant and I are thrilled," Emma assured her.

"Emma, what on earth is keeping Alexandra?" Lilly demanded as she made her way over to them.

"I'll send Ruby to check on her," Emma offered, and escaped to dispatch the housekeeper to see what was keeping Alexandra.

"Grandmother, let me help you to your chair," Justin offered.

"Quit fussing over me," Lilly told her grandson. "Just because I have to use this cane doesn't mean I'm addle-pated. Why don't you go get me a sherry while I talk to your young lady?"

Lilly turned her deep-blue eyes on Kim. "So, Kimberly, are you in love with my grandson?"

Taken aback by the woman's candor, Kim hesitated a moment. But there was no mistaking the sharp mind behind those eyes. "Yes, I am."

She nodded, apparently satisfied with the answer. "How do you feel about babies?"

Kim nearly choked on her wine. "I like them."

"Good," Lilly said, and smiled.

"Miss Emma." Ruby came rushing down the stairs and headed for Justin's mother.

"Now, I wonder what has her all aflutter," Lilly said.

"Ruby, for heaven's sake. What is it? What's wrong?" Emma's voice held concern.

"It's Miss Alexandra. She's gone."

"Gone?" Emma repeated.

Ruby held out a sheet of paper. "She left a note. She says she's sorry, but there isn't going to be any wedding, and that she's going away for a while."

"My poor baby," Emma said as she took the note from Ruby, read it and passed it on to her husband.

"Hey, what's going on?" Tara asked as she entered the room. "What's all the fuss about?"

"It's Alexandra," Kim explained. "She's gone. She left a note saying that the wedding is off."

"It's my fault," Justin told his family, and relayed his conversation with Alexandra the previous evening.

"I always knew that guy was a louse," Tara said. "Alexandra's better off without him."

"I agree," Justin told them. "I'll admit I wanted her to dump Marsh, but I never meant to hurt her."

"I'm sure your sister knows that," Emma assured her son.

"The truth is, I thought she took it pretty well," Justin advised his family. "I mean, I thought it was more a question of her pride being hurt than her feelings. She didn't act all broken up when I told her what Marsh was up to."

"Of course the girl wasn't broken up," Lilly interjected. "Any fool with eyes in his head could see that the girl wasn't in love with that scoundrel Marsh."

"I think your grandmother's right," Emma replied.

"Of course, I'm right. All a body had to do was see them together to know that they weren't in love with each other," Lilly informed them.

"Tell me, Grandmother," Tara began, a sly look in her eyes. "Just exactly how do two people look when they're in love with each other?"

"The way you and that Paige boy used to look at each other. The same way your brother and his young lady look at each other now." She shifted her gaze to Justin and Kim. "All you have to do is see the way that boy looks at her to know he's in love with her."

"You're right, Grandmother," Justin said laughing. "I am in love with her."

"And I love him," Kim replied, seeing no point in denying it since she'd already told the lady.

"So what do you intend to do about it?" Lilly asked her grandson.

"I'm going to marry her," Justin informed his grandmother.

"Soon, I hope. Your grandfather and I are getting tired of waiting for more great-grandchildren."

"As soon as I can," Justin replied.

"And those great-grandchildren?" Lilly prompted.

"We intend to get to work on them right away."

* * * * *

0107/SH/LC157

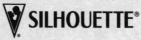

SILHOUETTE®

Desire™

Dynasties:
THE ELLIOTTS
Mixing business with pleasure

January 2007
BILLIONAIRE PROPOSITION *Leanne Banks*
TAKING CARE OF BUSINESS *Brenda Jackson*

March 2007
CAUSE FOR SCANDAL *Anna DePalo*
THE FORBIDDEN TWIN *Susan Crosby*

May 2007
MR AND MISTRESS *Heidi Betts*
HEIRESS BEWARE *Charlene Sands*

July 2007
UNDER DEEPEST COVER *Kara Lennox*
MARRIAGE TERMS *Barbara Dunlop*

September 2007
THE INTERN AFFAIR *Roxanne St Claire*
FORBIDDEN MERGER *Emilie Rose*

November 2007
THE EXPECTANT EXECUTIVE *Kathie DeNosky*
BEYOND THE BOARDROOM *Maureen Child*

prima new beginnings

There's the life you planned and there's what comes next...

A LONG WALK HOME
by Diane Amos

Annie remembers her young niece, Summer, as a sweet girl, and is happy to have her stay. So the wild child with piercings is a bit of a shock. Sullen and scared, Summer turns Annie's life upside down. But Annie is determined to get through to her. For her, the journey to what matters most will be worth every step.

STARTING FROM SCRATCH
by Marie Ferrarella

Elisha Reed loved her job and her life. But when Elisha's world changed over night, it was time for a rethink. With two teenagers to care for, Elisha couldn't disappear in the bliss of a creamy confection...unless she had several forks. She decided to start from scratch...and from here on in, it would be a piece of cake!

Because every life has more than one chapter...

On sale 18th May 2007

Available at WHSmith, Tesco, ASDA, and all good bookshops
www.millsandboon.co.uk

MILLS & BOON

*Three utterly romantic, red-hot
stories of heroines who travel back in
time to meet the one!*

What if you had the night of your life...

60 Years Ago?

80 Years Ago?

200 Years Ago?

"The idea of finding your soulmate in the
past is romantic and all three contributing authors
have done an excellent job providing a little bit of
magic in this anthology."
—*Romantic Times*

Available 20th April 2007

Queens of Romance

Were these sisters destined to be wives?

To Have a Husband
Harriet found enigmatic stranger Quinn McBride incredibly attractive, but she wasn't sure she could believe or trust him. Could she really be falling for the enemy?

To Become a Bride
Right from the beginning Danie crossed swords with Jonas Noble, but the secretive, handsome male was still unwittingly tempting her to imagine herself as his blushing bride!

To Make a Marriage
Her unborn baby had been conceived in a moment of irresistible passionate madness. But how much longer could she keep her secret? How was Adam Munroe going to react to impending fatherhood?

Available 20th April 2007

Collect all 4 superb books in the collection!

Victorian London is brought to vibrant life in this mesmeric new novel!

London, 1876

All her life, Olivia Moreland has denied her clairvoyant abilities, working instead to disprove the mediums that flock to London. But when Stephen, Lord St Leger, requests her help in investigating an alleged psychic, she can't ignore the ominous presence she feels within the walls of his ancient estate. Nor can she ignore the intimate connection she feels to Stephen, as if she has somehow known him before…

Available 20th April 2007

M&B

Three timeless tales of love and marriage from international bestseller Betty Neels

Featuring

Heidelberg Wedding

When surgeon Gerard Grenfell offered her the chance to work with him in Europe, Eugenia Smith went happily, but that was before she realised she was falling in love with a man who already had wedding plans.

Wedding Bells for Beatrice

Beatrice told single father Gijs van der Eekerk to marry again, but she hadn't bargained on him offering her the position! Especially when love didn't appear to be part of the deal...

Making Sure of Sarah

Having fallen in love with Sarah at first sight, Litrik ter Breukel vowed to go slowly because of her youth and innocence. But perhaps he simply needed to propose!

Available 4th May 2007

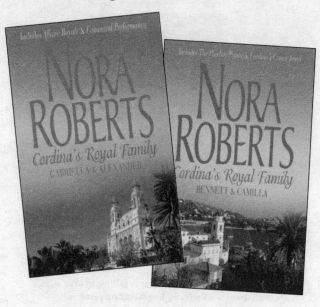

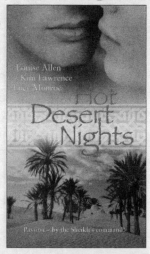

What lurks beneath the surface
of the powerful and prestigious
Chrighton Dynasty?

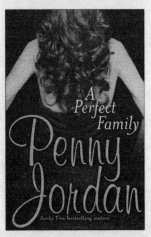

As three generations of the Chrighton family
gather for a special birthday celebration, no one
could possibly have anticipated that their secure
world was about to be rocked by the events of
one fateful weekend.

One dramatic revelation leads to another
– a secret war-time liaison, a carefully concealed
embezzlement scam, the illicit seduction of
somebody else's wife.

And the results are going to be explosive…

Available 1st June 2007

What do you do when the other woman is you?

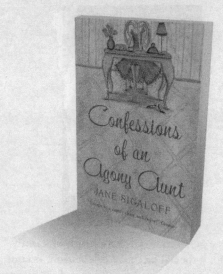

Lizzie Ford is London's most popular agony aunt who's been sitting on the bench for three years waiting to get back in the game. So Lizzie can't believe her good luck when she meets Matt Baker, only there's one problem – Matt's wife may not be happy with this new arrangement.

The strange thing is that even while she's hoping that Matt will get a divorce, she's actively helping a writer to her column save her crumbling marriage – a marriage that bears more than a passing resemblance to Matt's…

Available from 16th March 2007